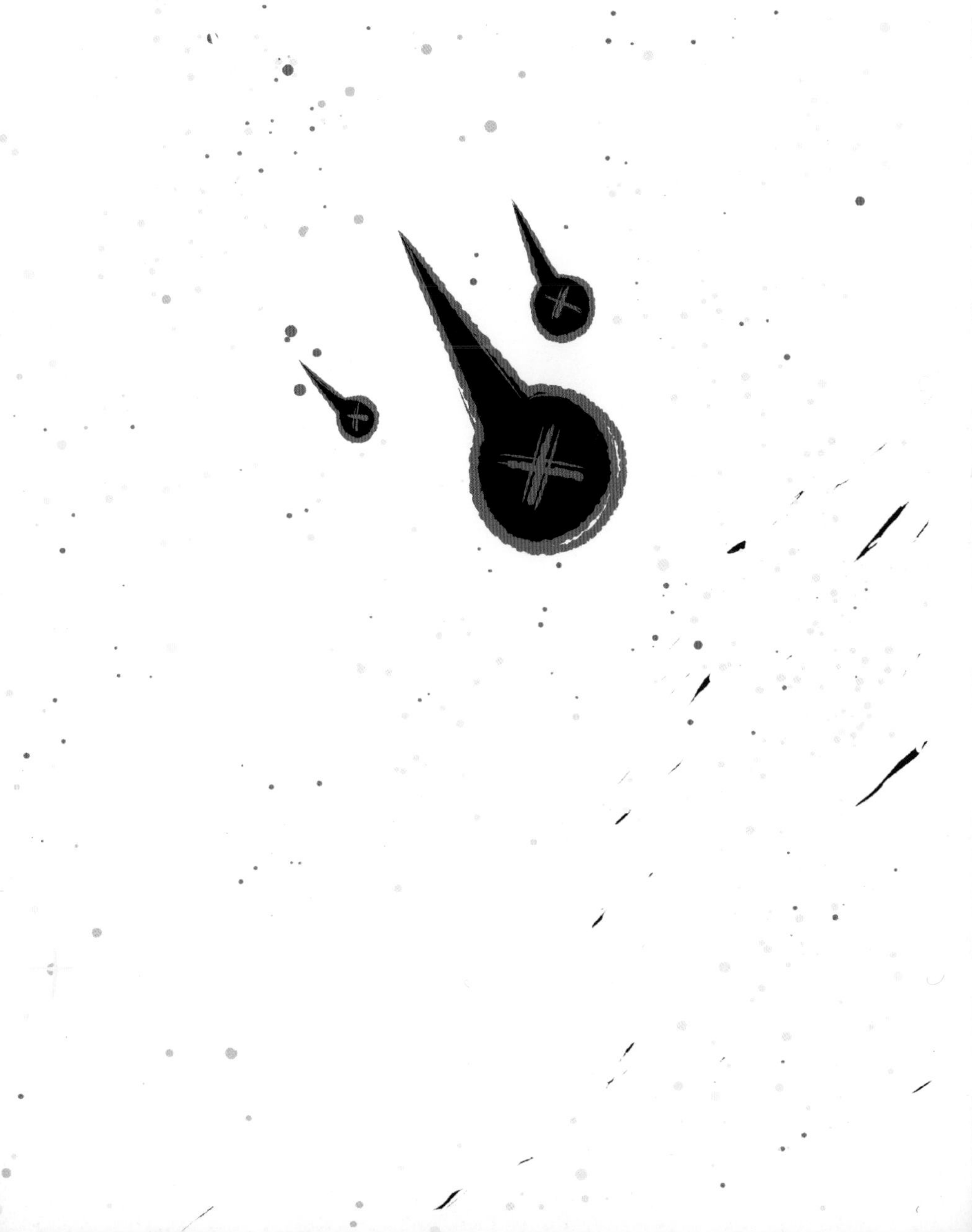

Stephen McCranie's

SPACE

BOY

CLICK
CLICK
CLAK
CLACK

VOLUME 12

Written and illustrated by
STEPHEN McCRANIE

DARK HORSE BOOKS

President and Publisher **Mike Richardson**
Editor **Shantel LaRocque**
Associate Editor **Brett Israel**
Assistant Editor **Sanjay Dharawat**
Designer **Anita Magaña**
Digital Art Technician **Allyson Haller**

STEPHEN MCCRANIE'S SPACE BOY VOLUME 12
Space Boy™ © 2022 Stephen McCranie. All rights reserved. Dark Horse
Books® and the Dark Horse logo are registered trademarks of Dark Horse
Comics LLC. All rights reserved. No portion of this publication may be
reproduced or transmitted, in any form or by any means, without the
express written permission of Dark Horse Comics LLC. Names, characters,
places, and incidents featured in this publication either are the product of
the author's imagination or are used fictitiously. Any resemblance to actual
persons (living or dead), events, institutions, or locales, without satiric intent,
is coincidental.

This book collects *Space Boy* episodes 176–195, previously published
online at WebToons.com.

Published by Dark Horse Books
A division of Dark Horse Comics LLC
10956 SE Main Street | Milwaukie, OR 97222
StephenMcCranie.com | DarkHorse.com

To find a comics shop in your area, visit comicshoplocator.com

First edition: March 2022
ISBN 978-1-50672-577-2
10 9 8 7 6 5 4 3 2 1
Printed in China

Neil Hankerson Executive Vice President • **Tom Weddle** Chief Financial
Officer • **Dale LaFountain** Chief Information Officer • **Tim Wiesch** Vice
President of Licensing • **Matt Parkinson** Vice President of Marketing •
Vanessa Todd-Holmes Vice President of Production and Scheduling •
Mark Bernardi Vice President of Book Trade and Digital Sales • **Randy
Lahrman** Vice President of Product Development • **Ken Lizzi** General
Counsel • **Dave Marshall** Editor in Chief • **Davey Estrada** Editorial
Director • **Chris Warner** Senior Books Editor • **Cary Grazzini** Director of
Specialty Projects • **Lia Ribacchi** Art Director • **Matt Dryer** Director of
Digital Art and Prepress • **Michael Gombos** Senior Director of Licensed
Publications • **Kari Yadro** Director of Custom Programs • **Kari Torson**
Director of International Licensing

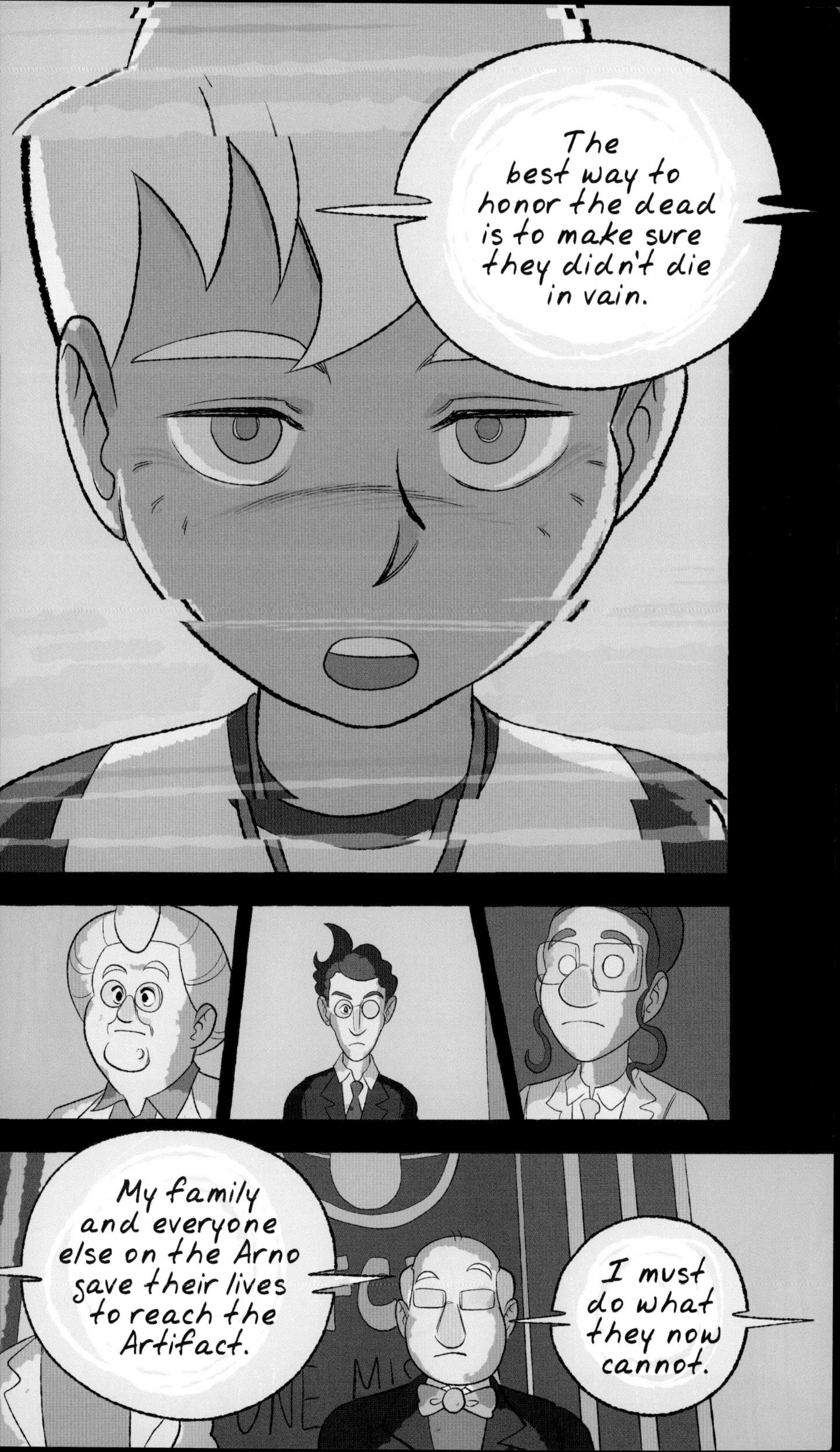
The best way to honor the dead is to make sure they didn't die in vain.
My family and everyone else on the Arno save their lives to reach the Artifact.
I must do what they now cannot.

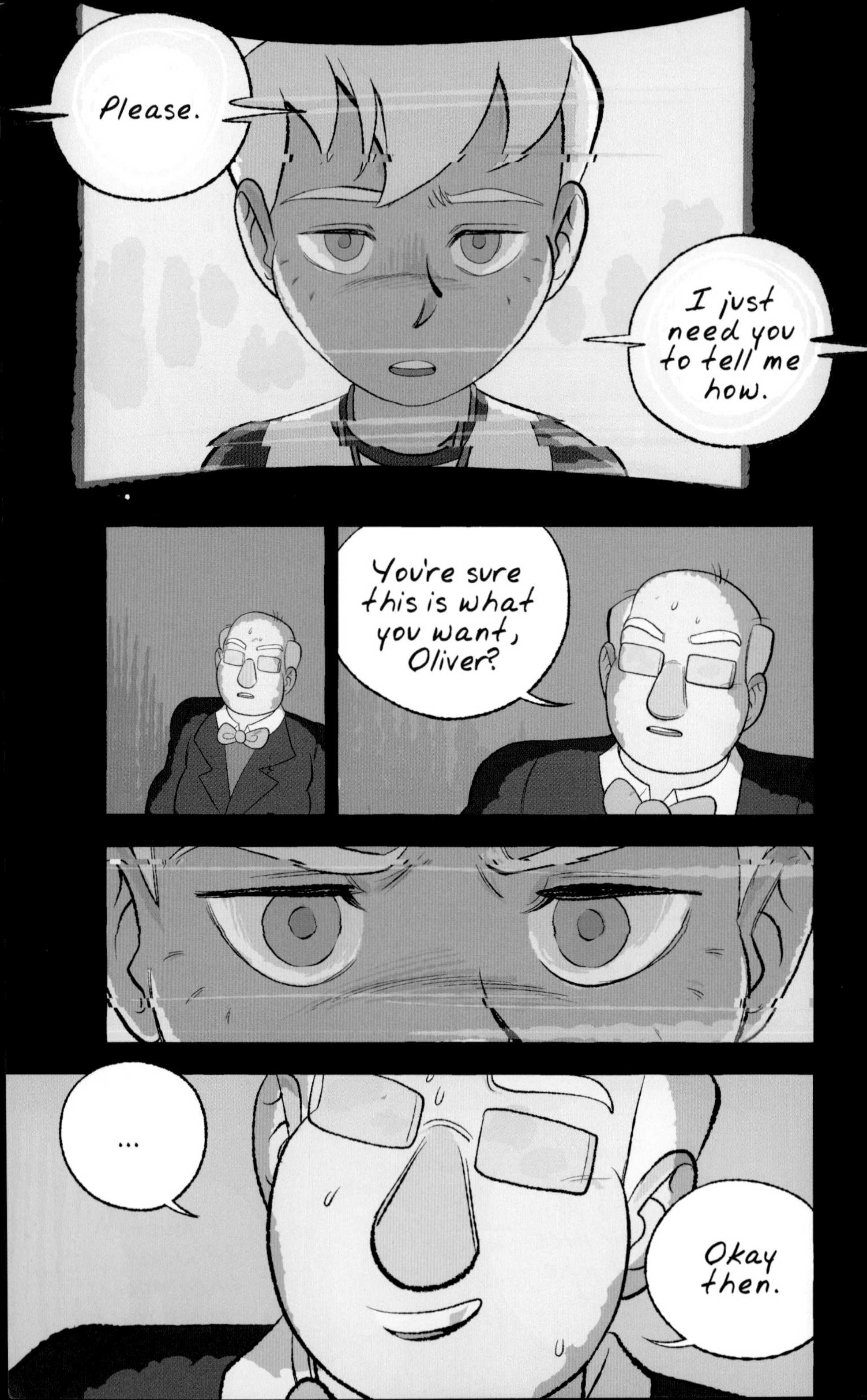
Please.
I just need you to tell me how.
You're sure this is what you want, Oliver?
...
Okay then.

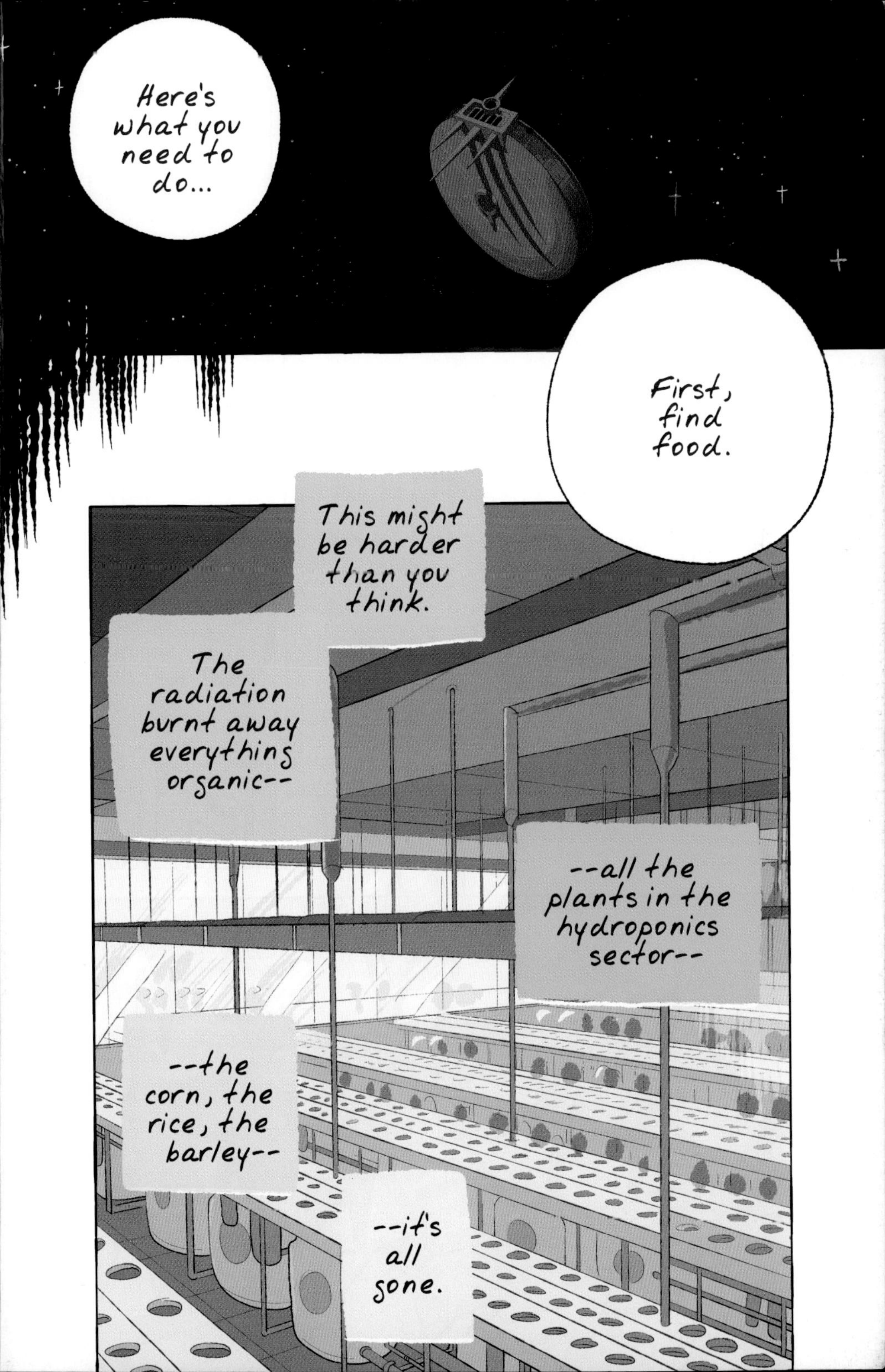
Here's what you need to do...
First, find food.
This might be harder than you think.
The radiation burnt away everything organic--
--all the plants in the hydroponics sector--
--the corn, the rice, the barley--
--it's all gone.

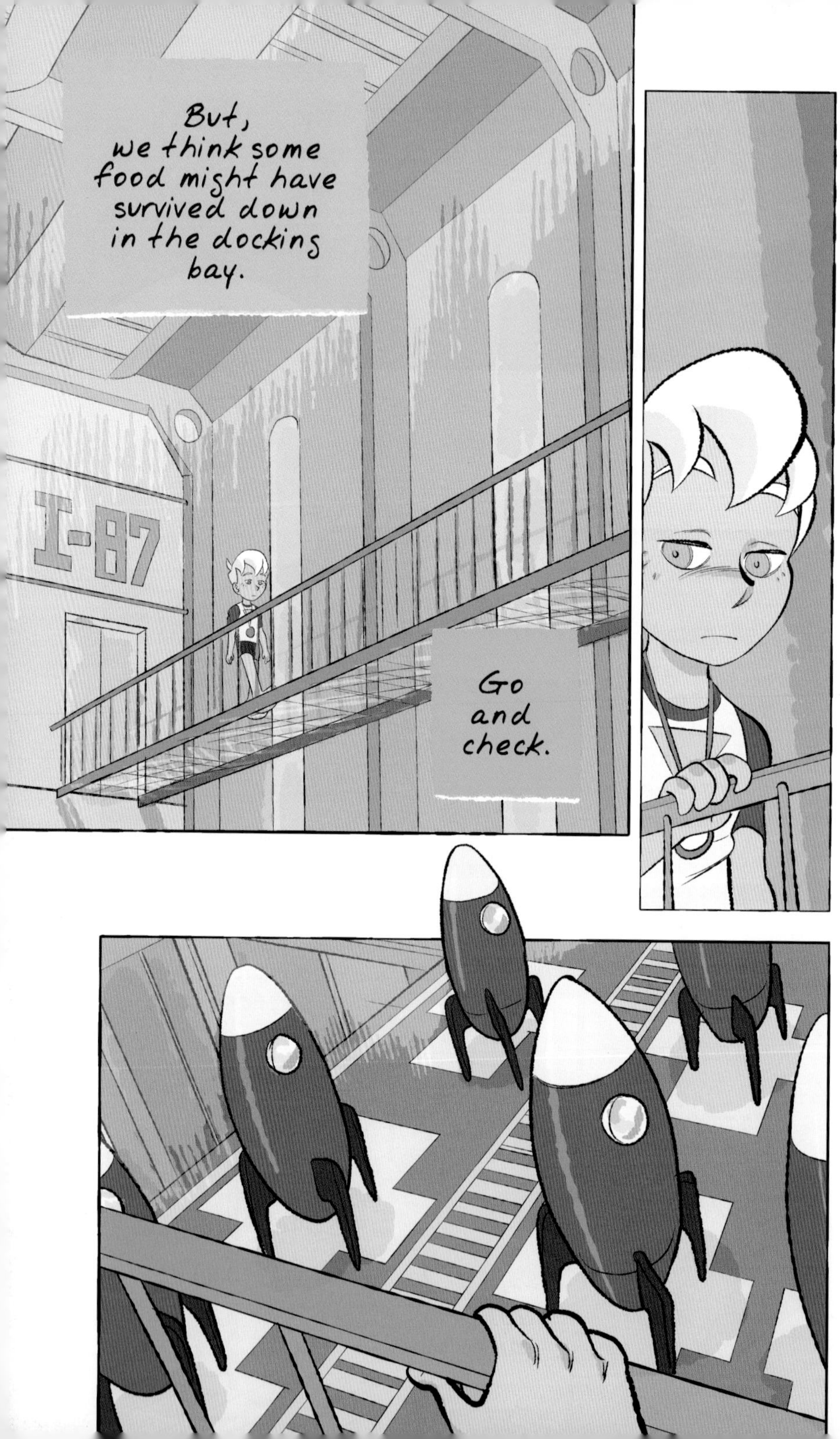
But, we think some food might have survived down in the docking bay.
I-87
Go and check.

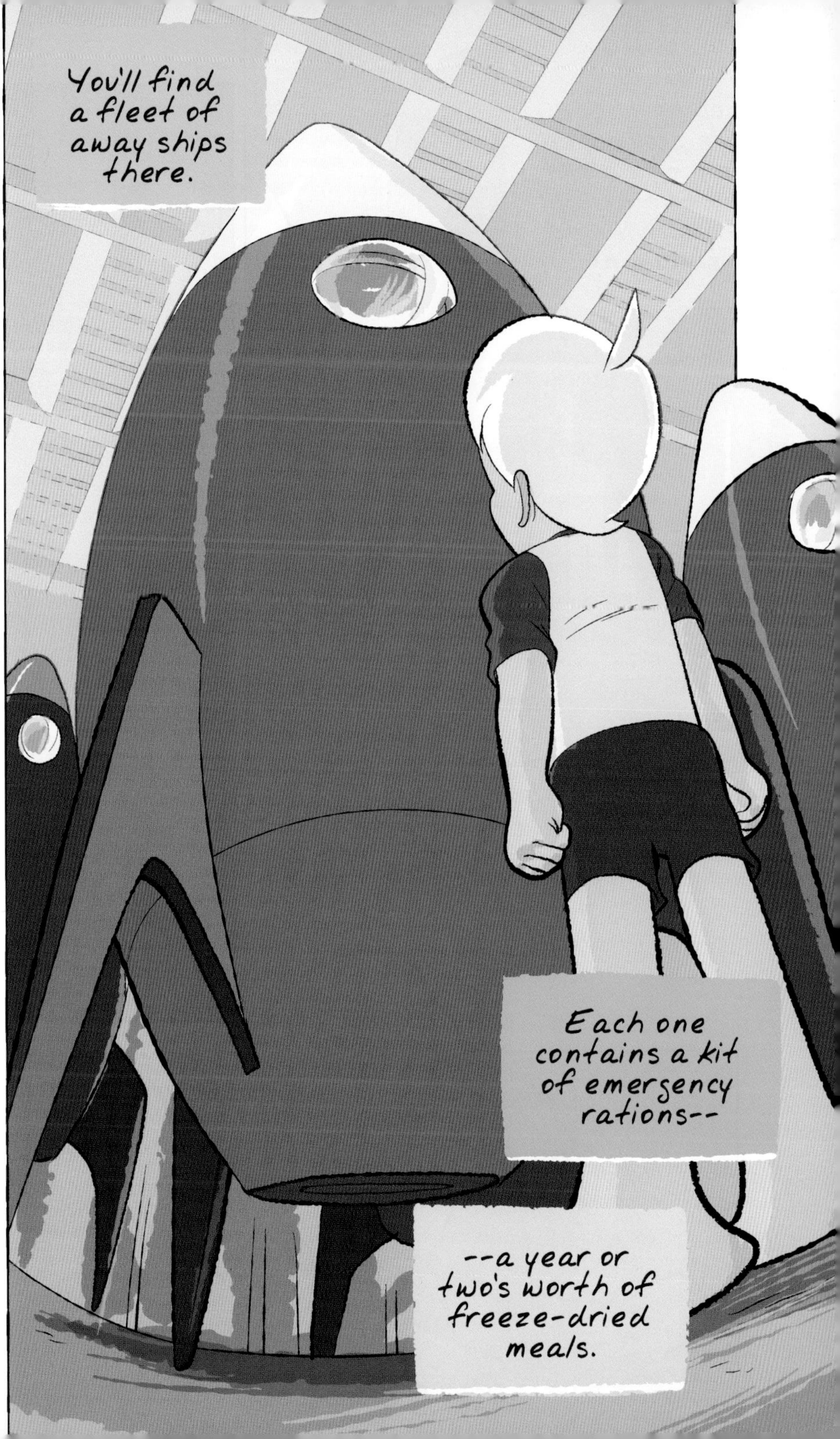
You'll find a fleet of away ships there.
Each one contains a kit of emergency rations--
--a year or two's worth of freeze-dried meals.

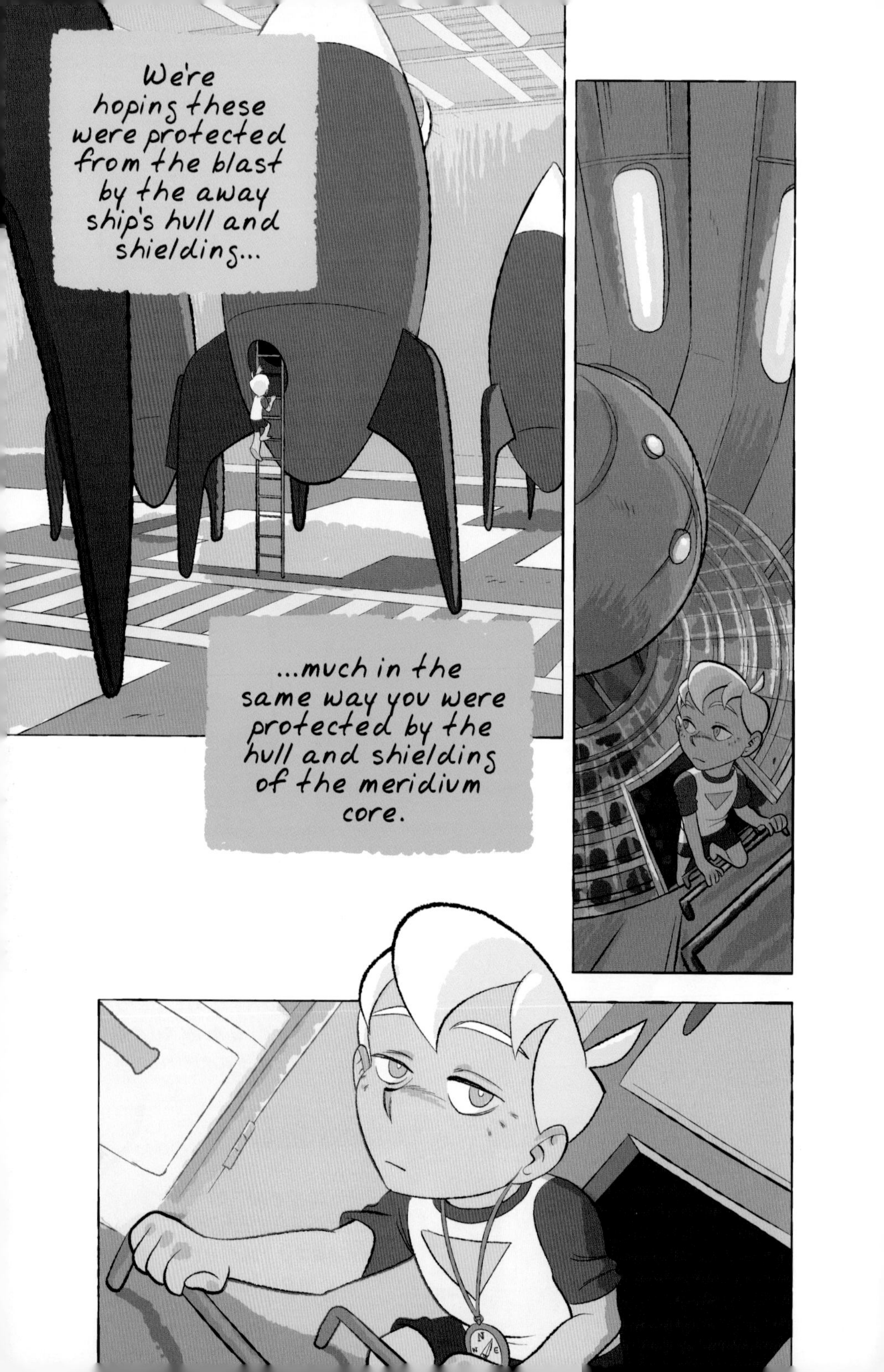
We're hoping these were protected from the blast by the away ship's hull and shieldings...
...much in the same way you were protected by the hull and shieldings of the meridium core.

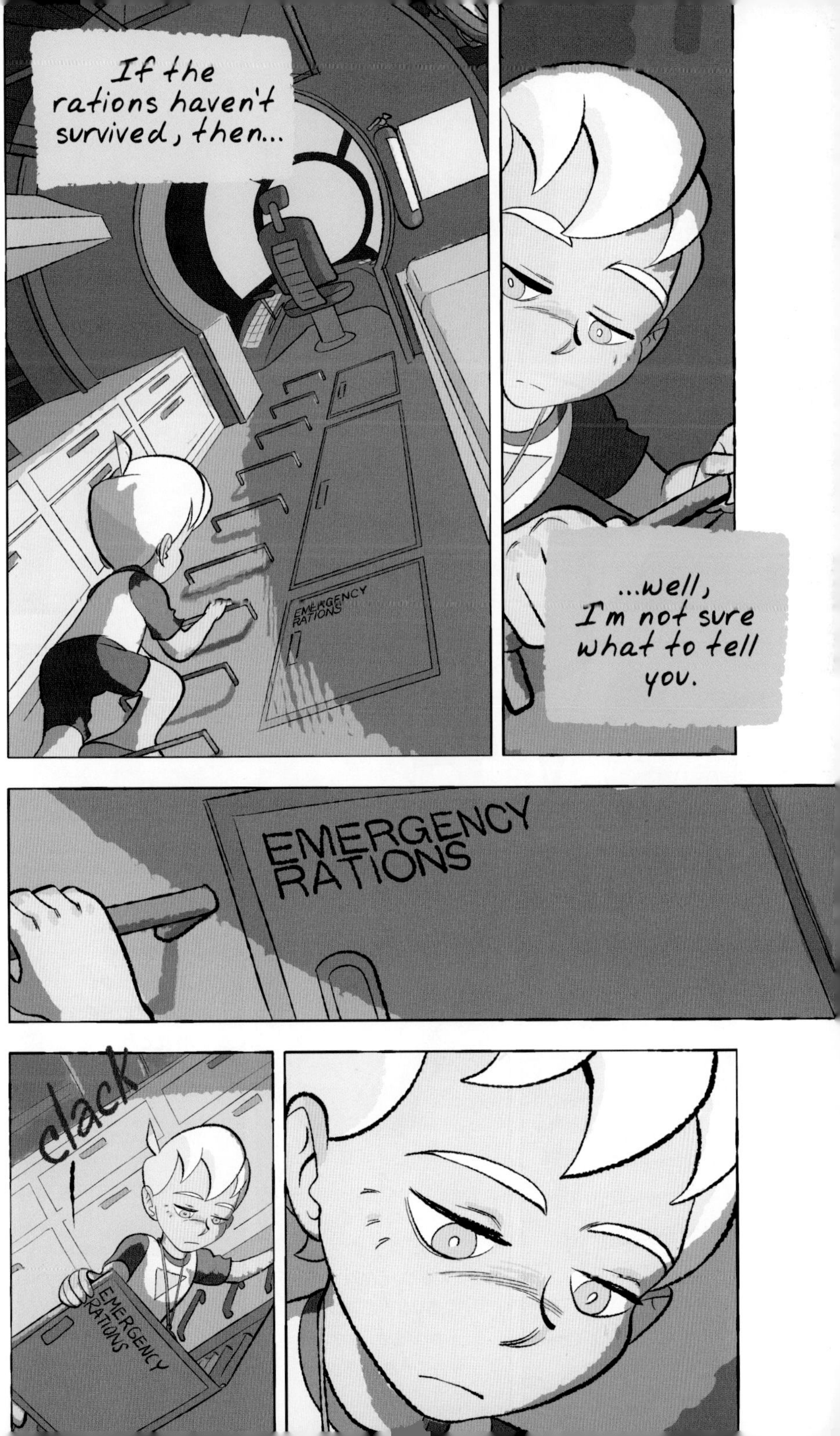
If the rations haven't survived, then...
EMERGENCY RATIONS
...well, I'm not sure what to tell you.
EMERGENCY RATIONS
clack
EMERGENCY RATIONS

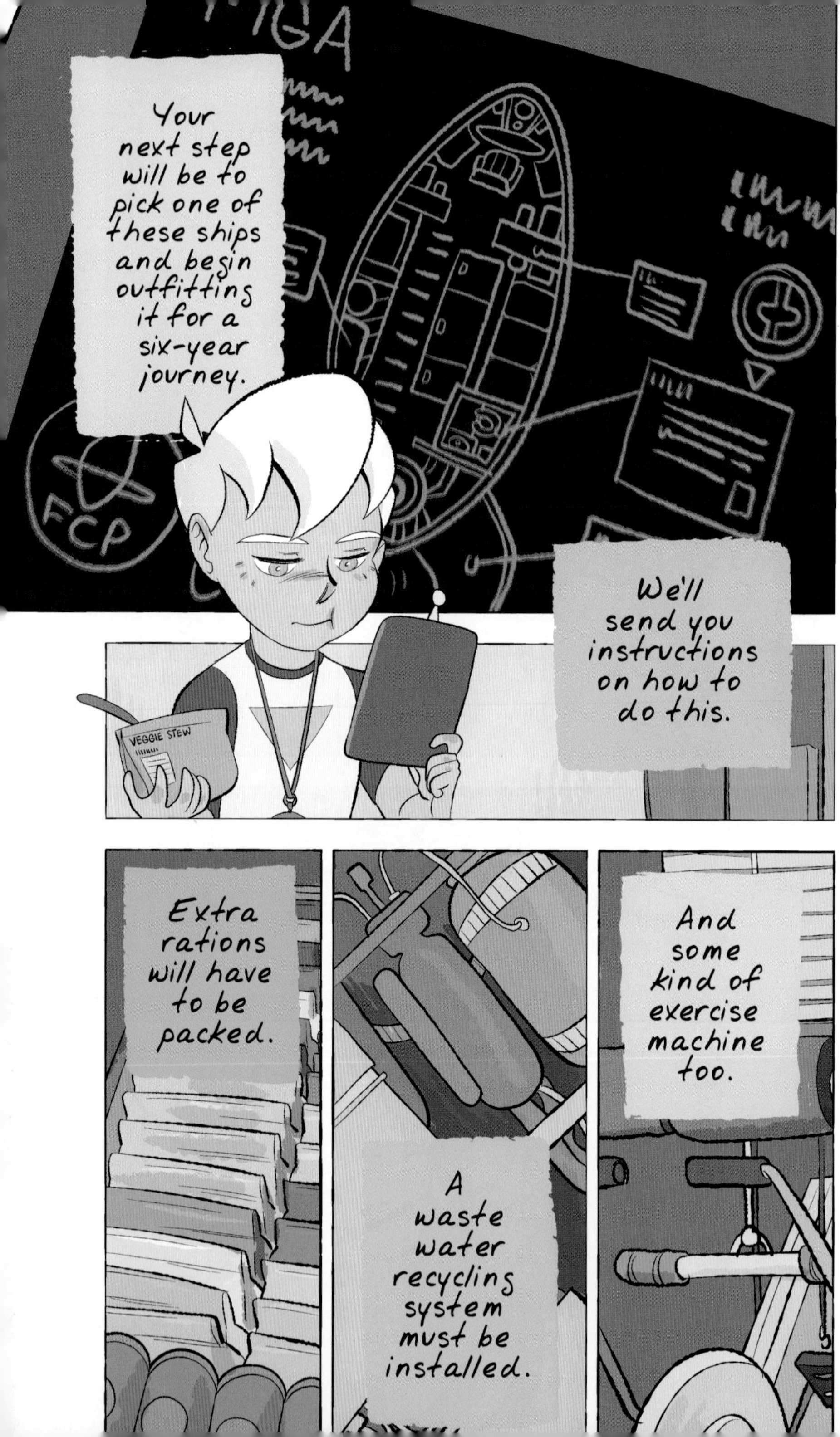
Your next step will be to pick one of these ships and begin outfitting it for a six-year journey.
FCP
We'll send you instructions on how to do this.
VEGGIE STEW
Extra rations will have to be packed.
A waste water recycling system must be installed.
And some kind of exercise machine too.

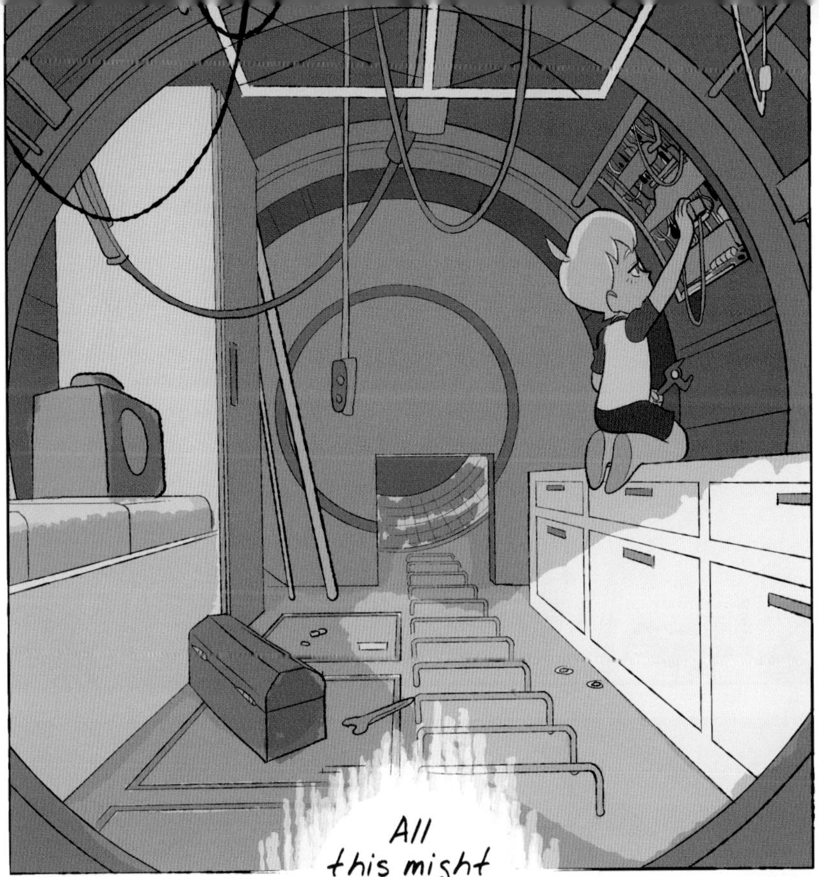

All this might take a while.

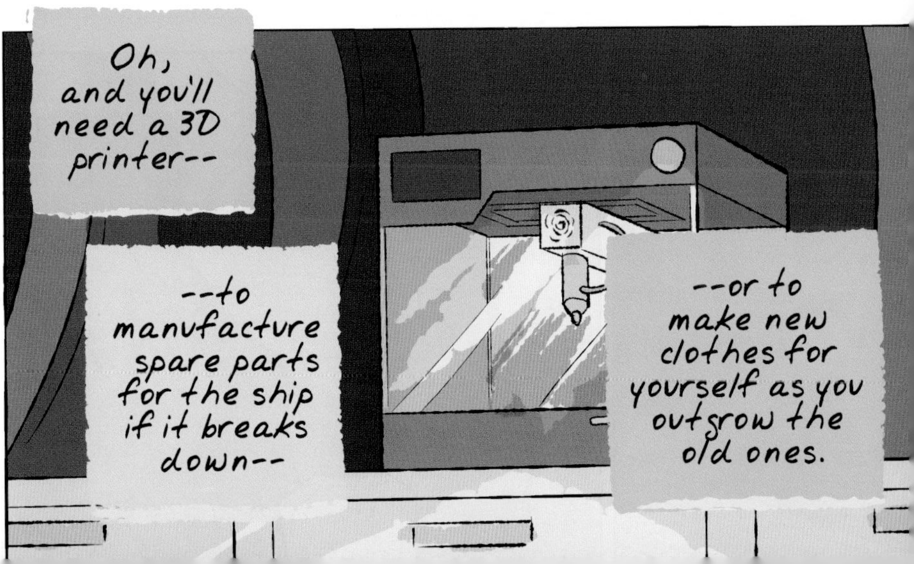
Oh, and you'll need a 3D printer--
--to manufacture spare parts for the ship if it breaks down--
--or to make new clothes for yourself as you outgrow the old ones.

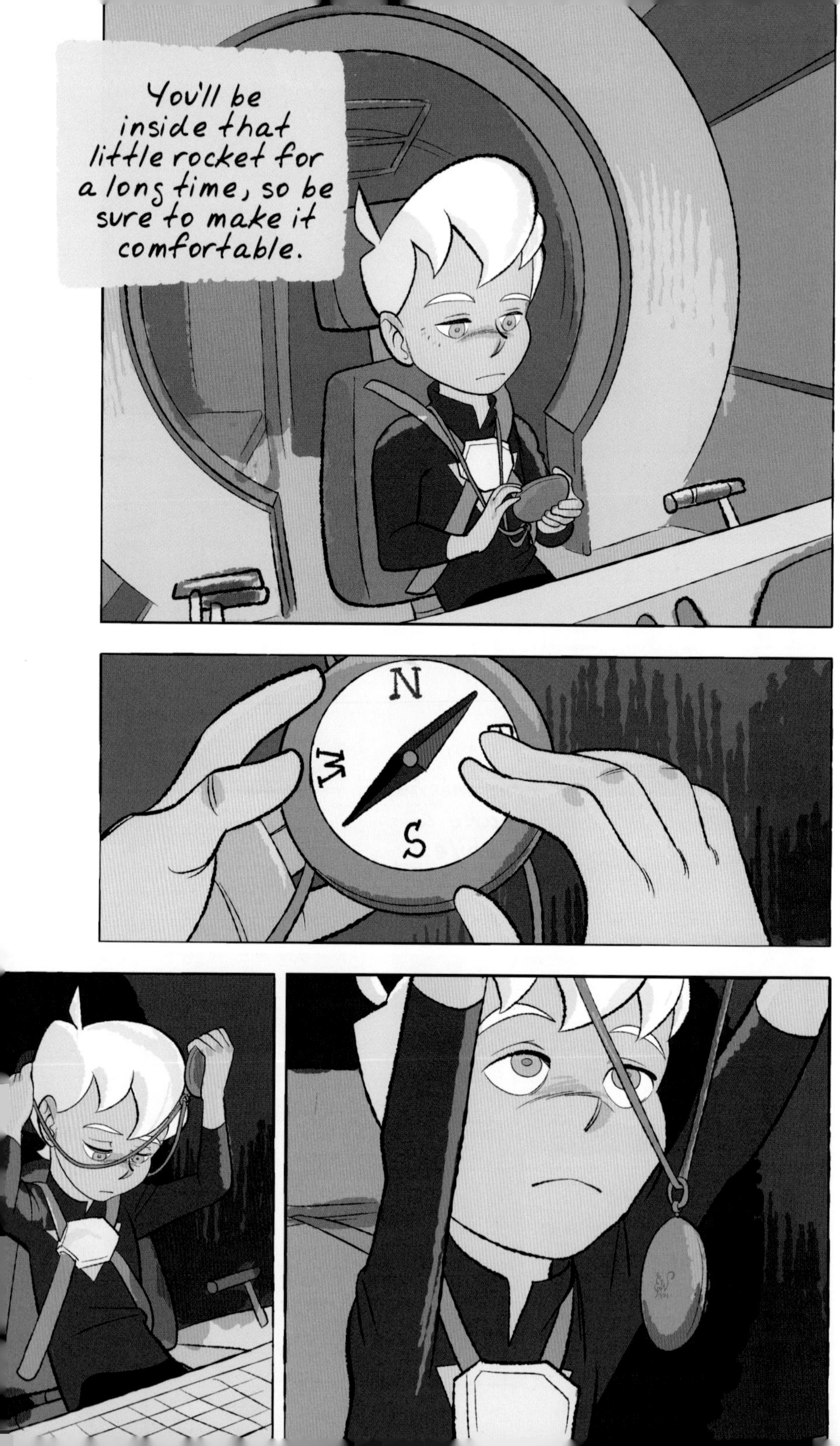
You'll be inside that little rocket for a long time, so be sure to make it comfortable.
N
W
S

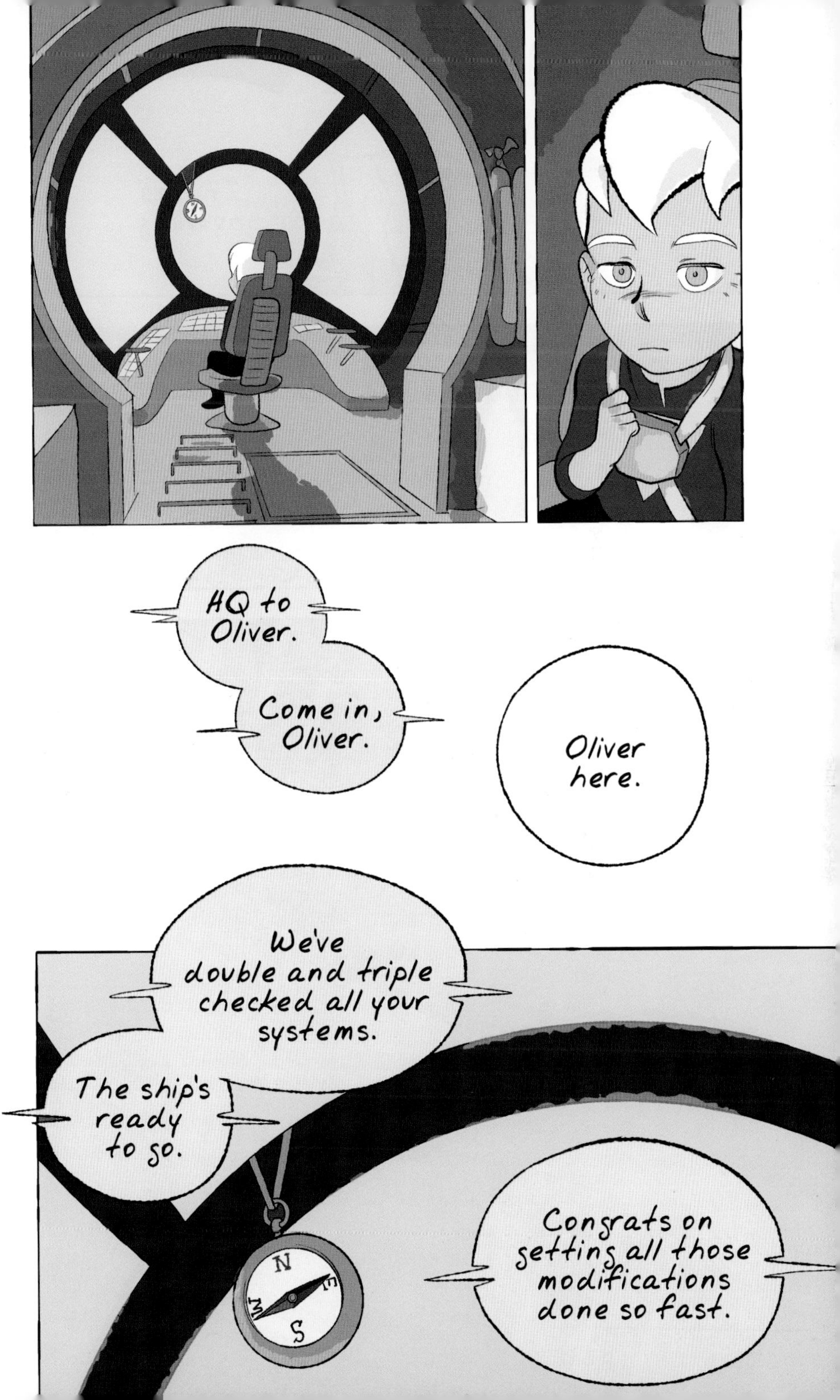
HQ to Oliver.
Come in, Oliver.
Oliver here.
We've double and triple checked all your systems.
The ship's ready to go.
Congrats on getting all those modifications done so fast.

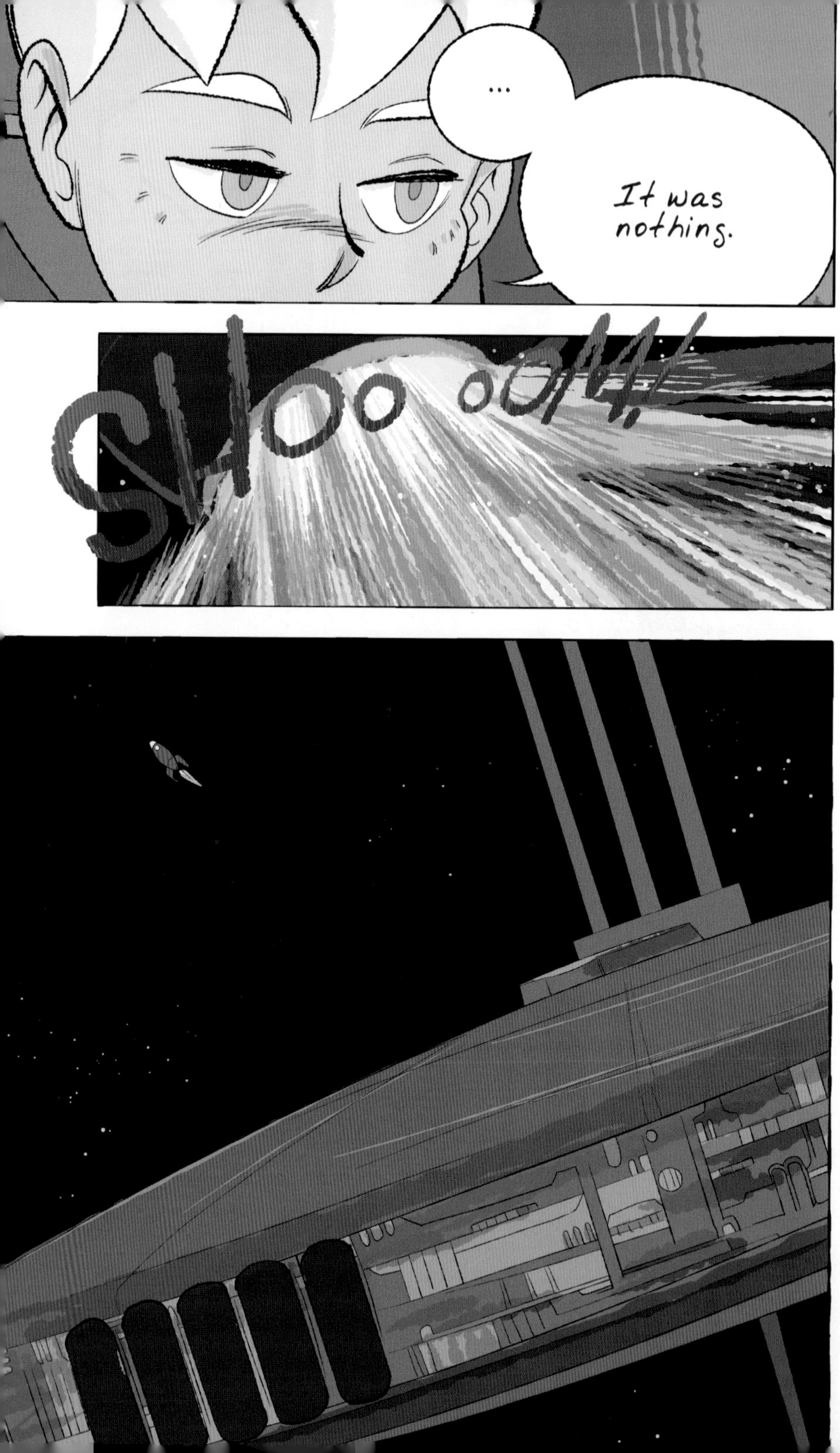
...
It was nothing.
SHOO OOM!!

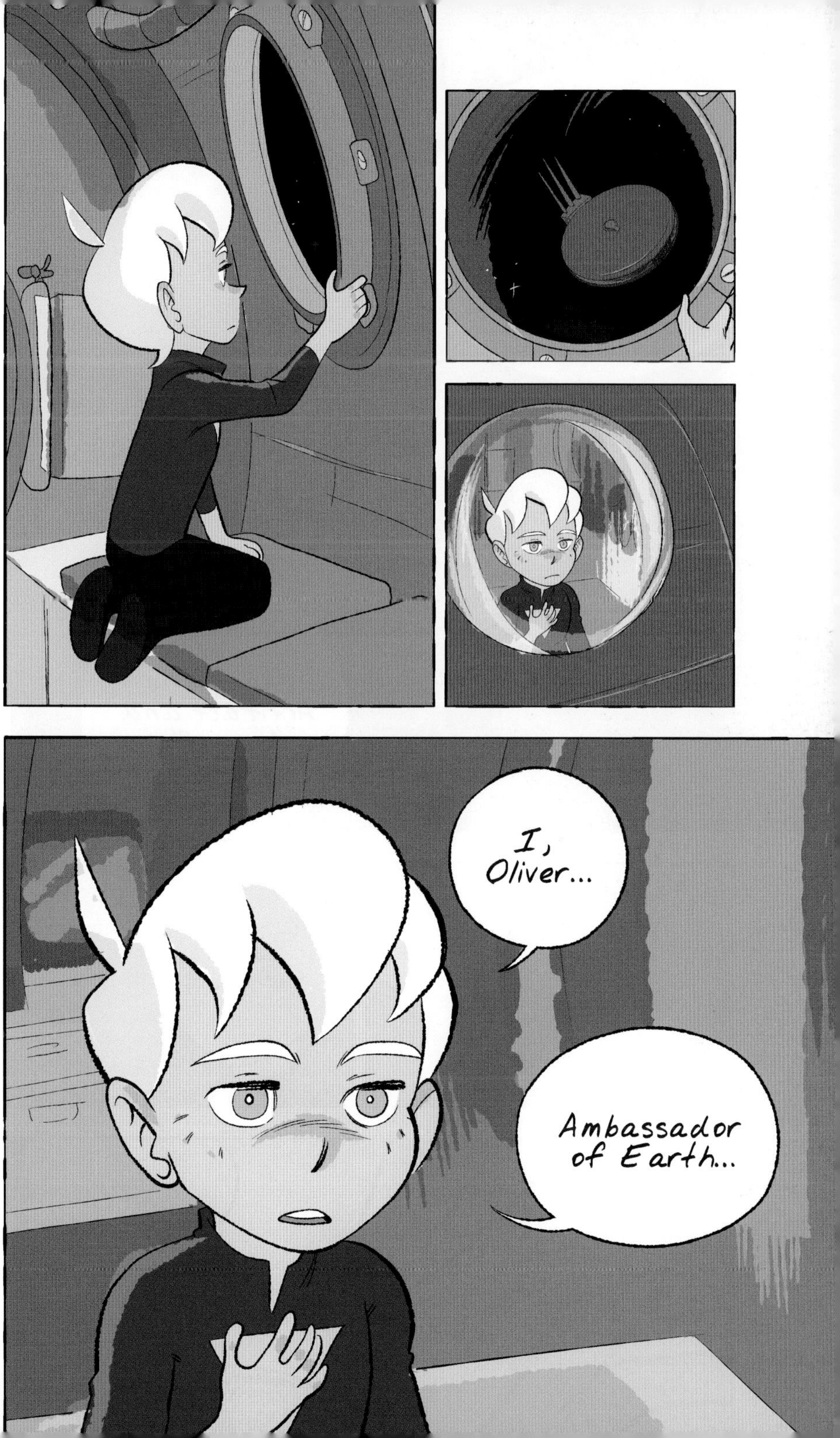
I, Oliver...
Ambassador of Earth...

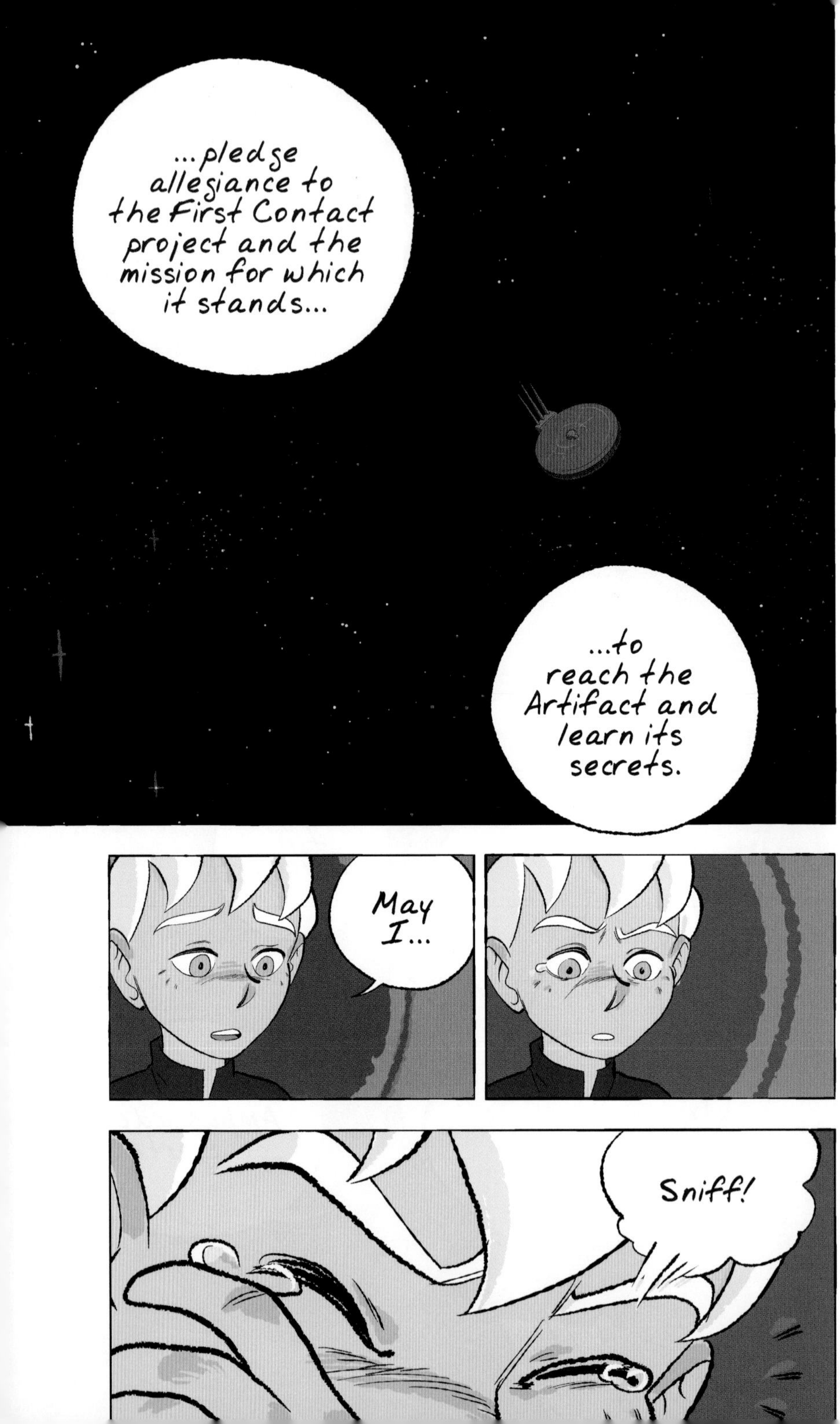
...pledge allegiance to the First Contact project and the mission for which it stands...
...to reach the Artifact and learn its secrets.
May I...
Sniff!

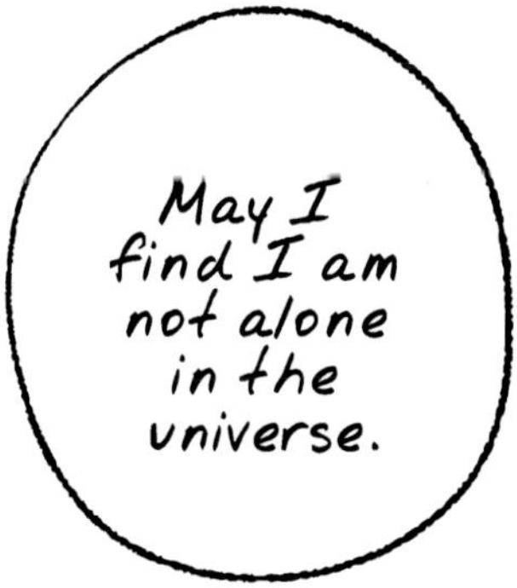
May I find I am not alone in the universe.

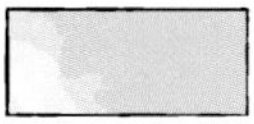

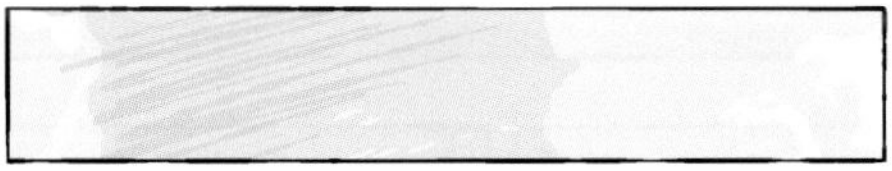

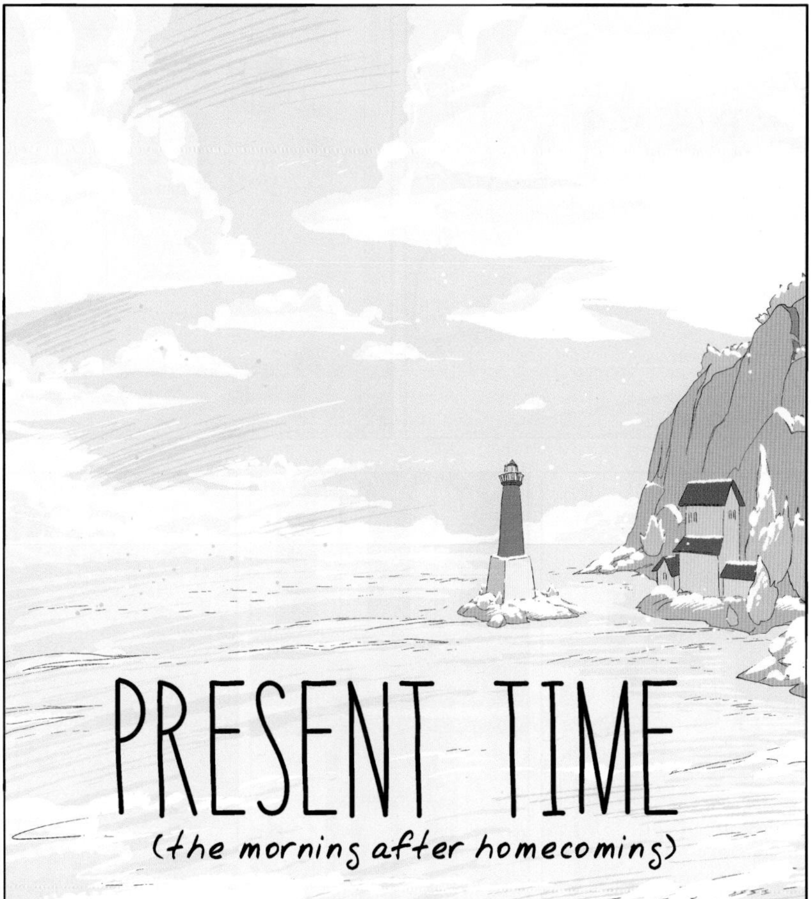
PRESENT TIME
(the morning after homecoming)

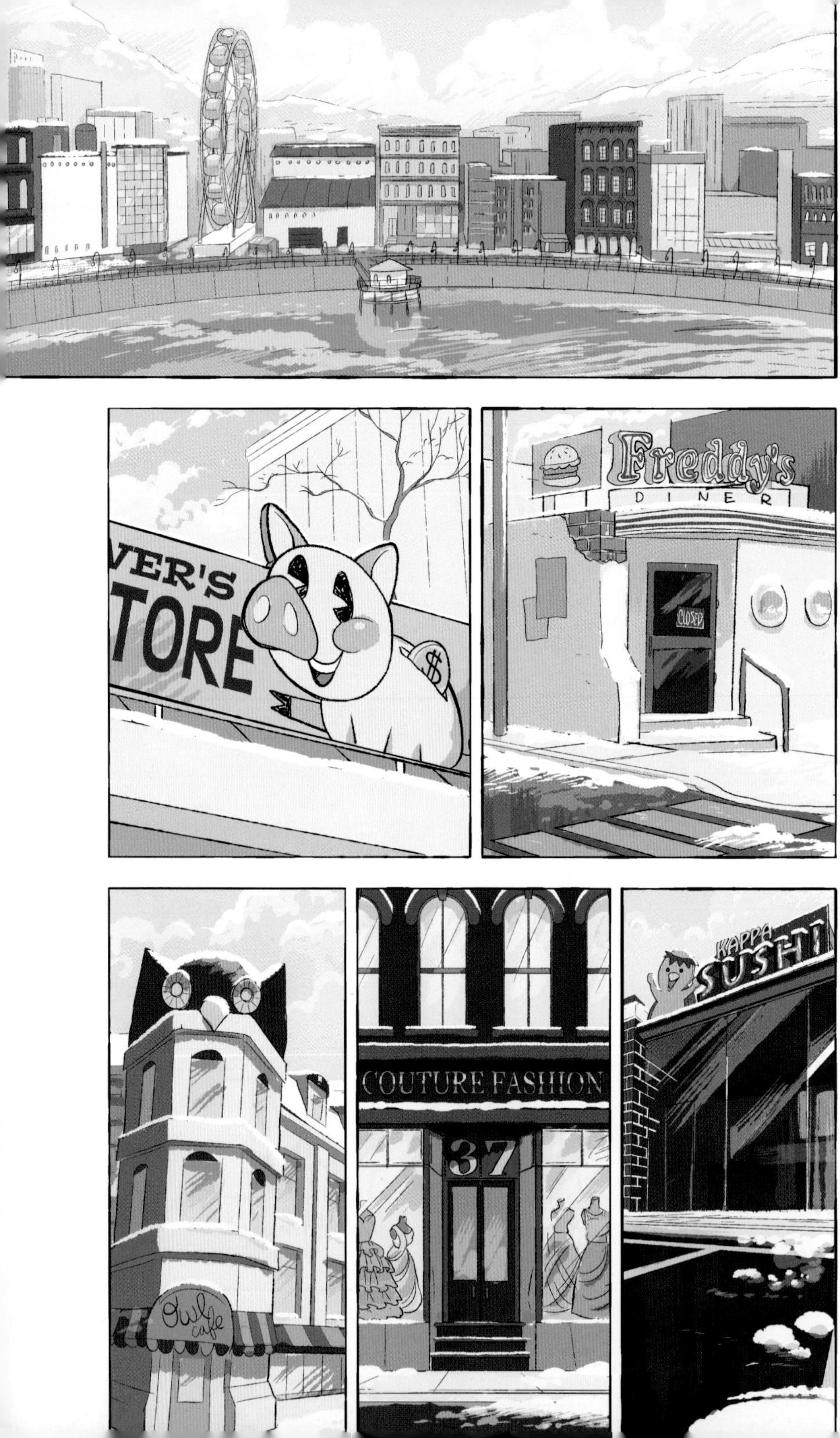
VER'S
TORE
Freddy's
DINER
CLOSED
Owl cafe
COUTURE FASHION
37
KAPPA
SUSHI

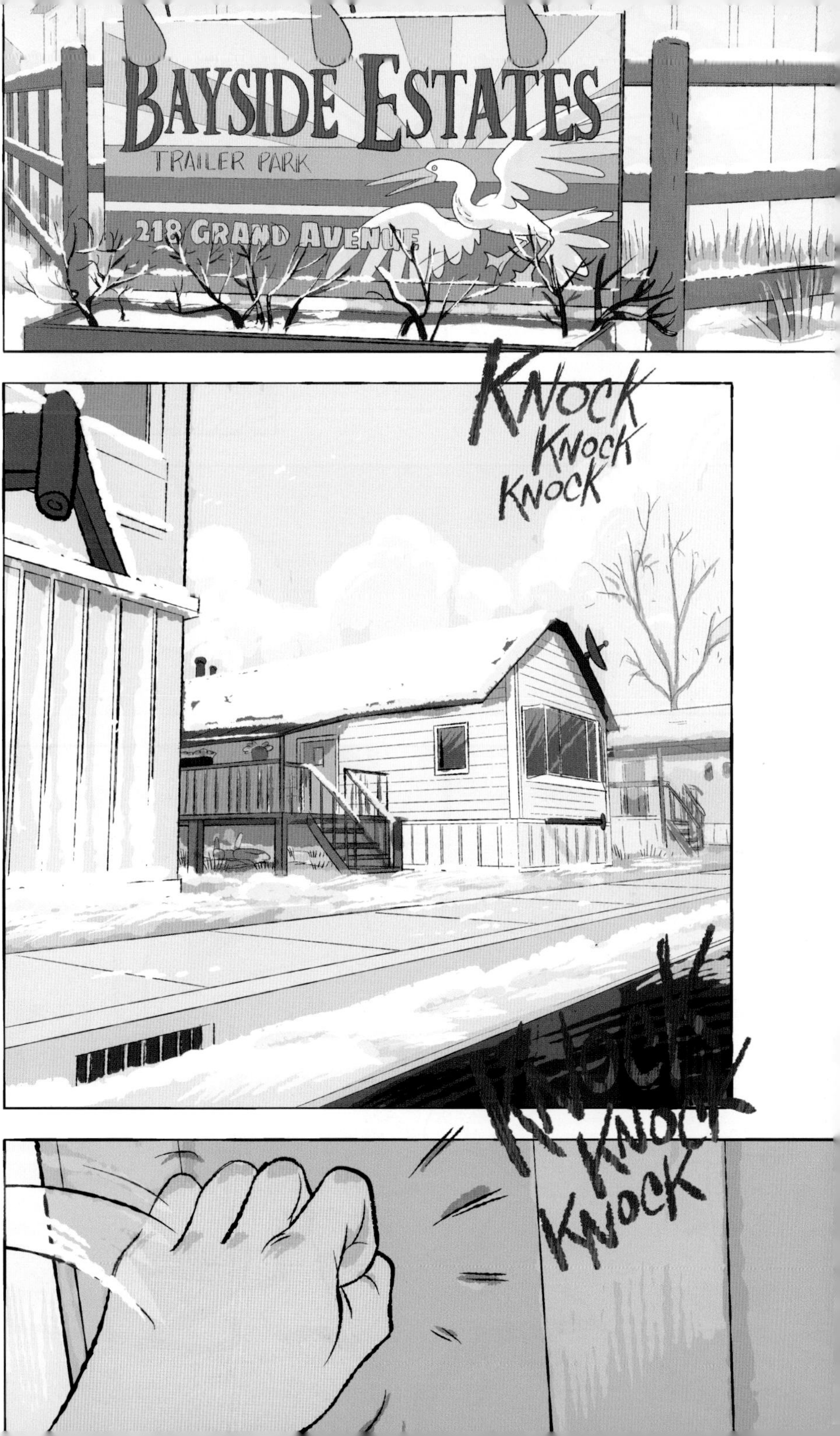
BAYSIDE ESTATES
TRAILER PARK
218 GRAND AVENUE
KNOCK
KNOCK
KNOCK
KNOCK
KNOCK
KNOCK

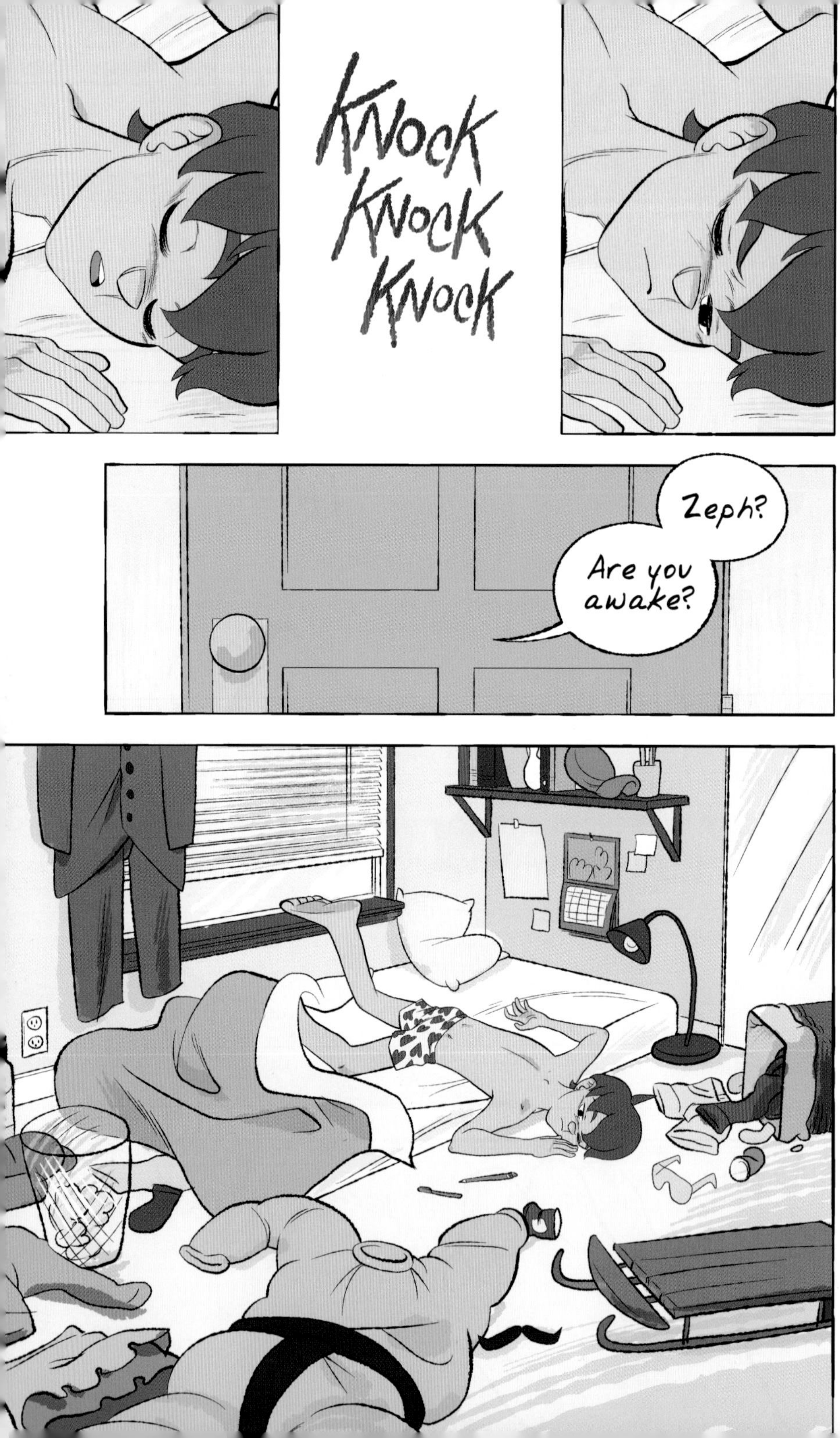
KNOCK
KNOCK
KNOCK
Zeph?
Are you awake?

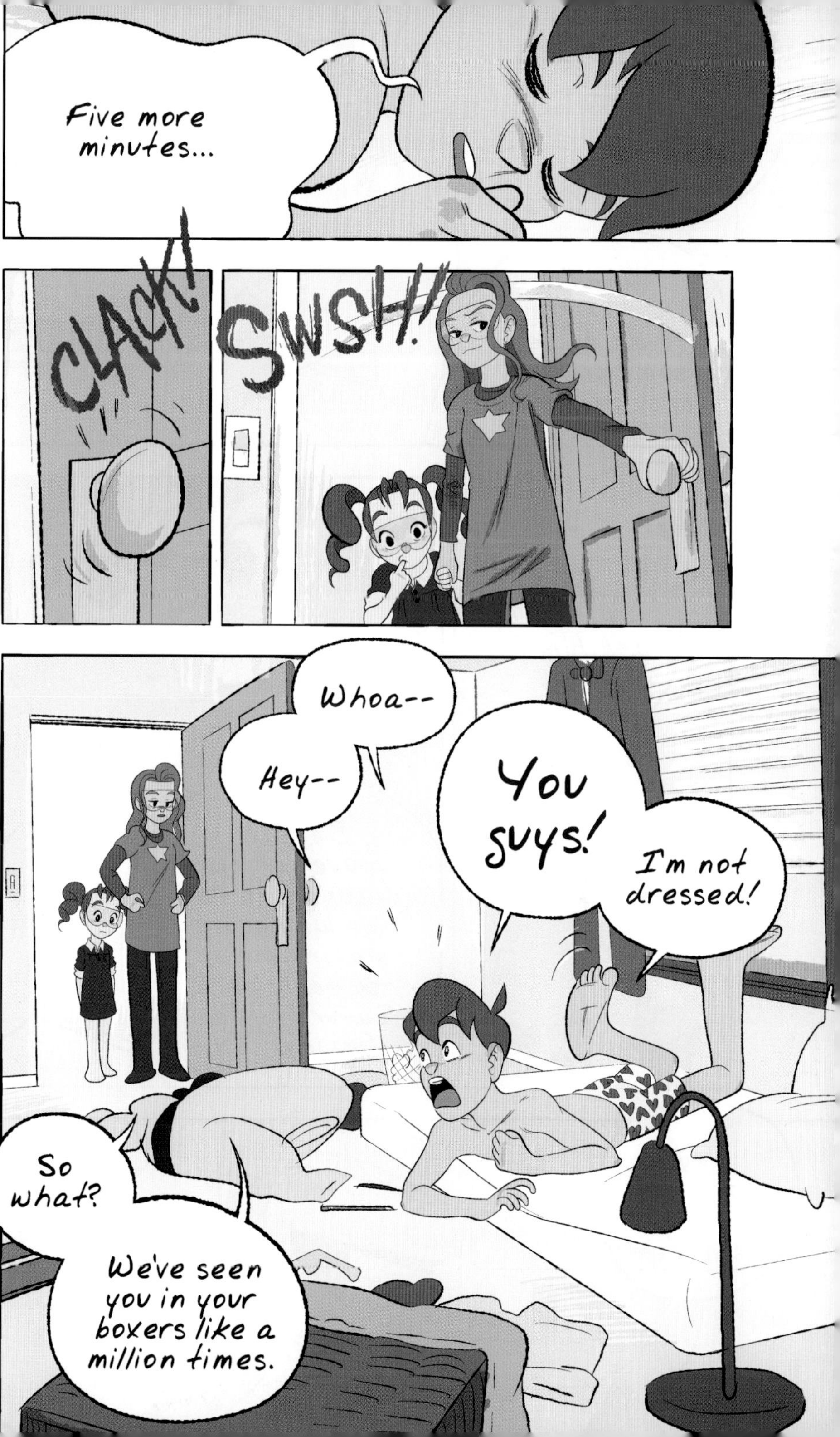
Five more minutes...
CLACK!
SWSH!!
Whoa--
Hey--
You guys!
I'm not dressed!
So what?
We've seen you in your boxers like a million times.

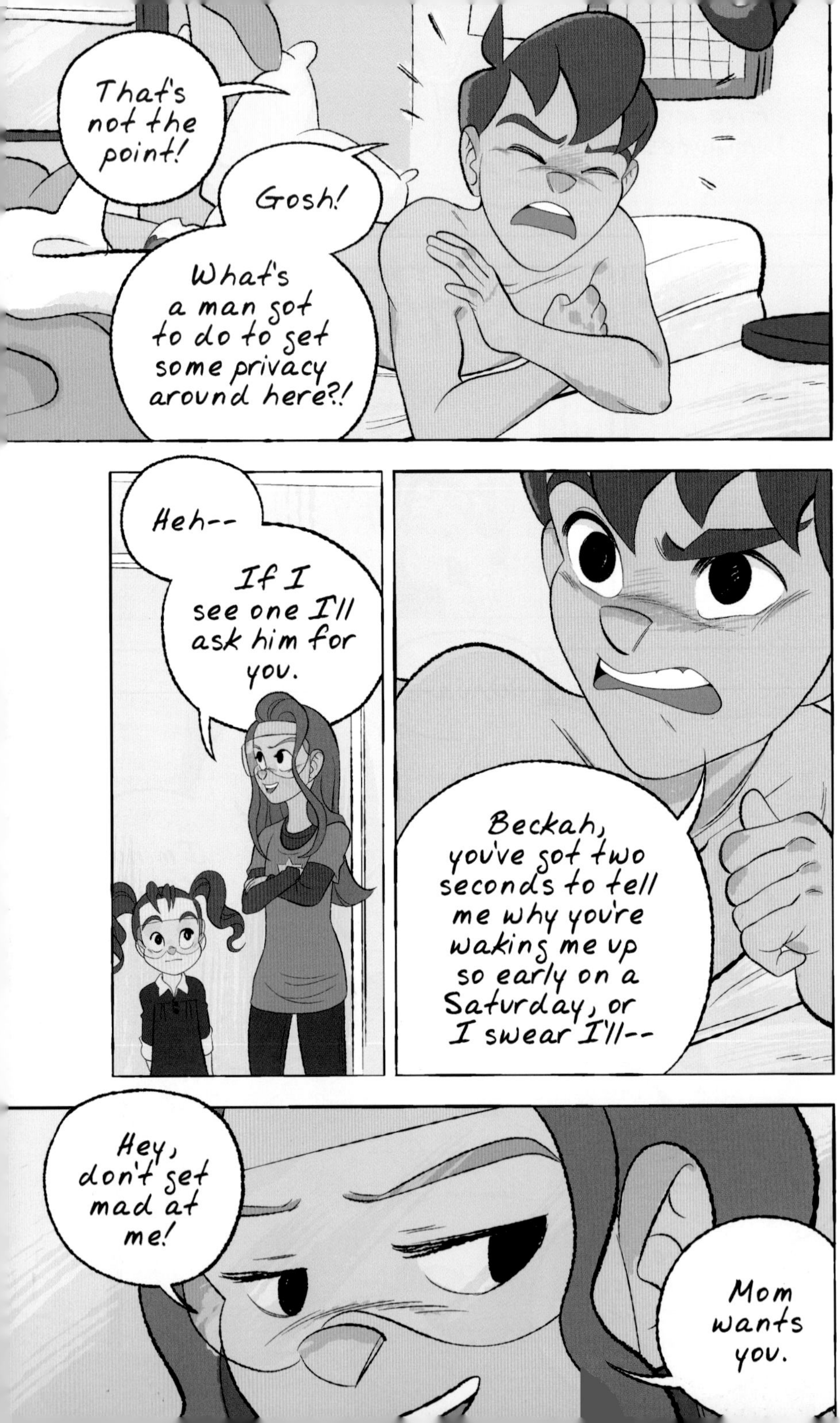
That's not the point!
Gosh!
What's a man got to do to get some privacy around here?!
Heh--
If I see one I'll ask him for you.
Beckah, you've got two seconds to tell me why you're waking me up so early on a Saturday, or I swear I'll--
Hey, don't get mad at me!
Mom wants you.

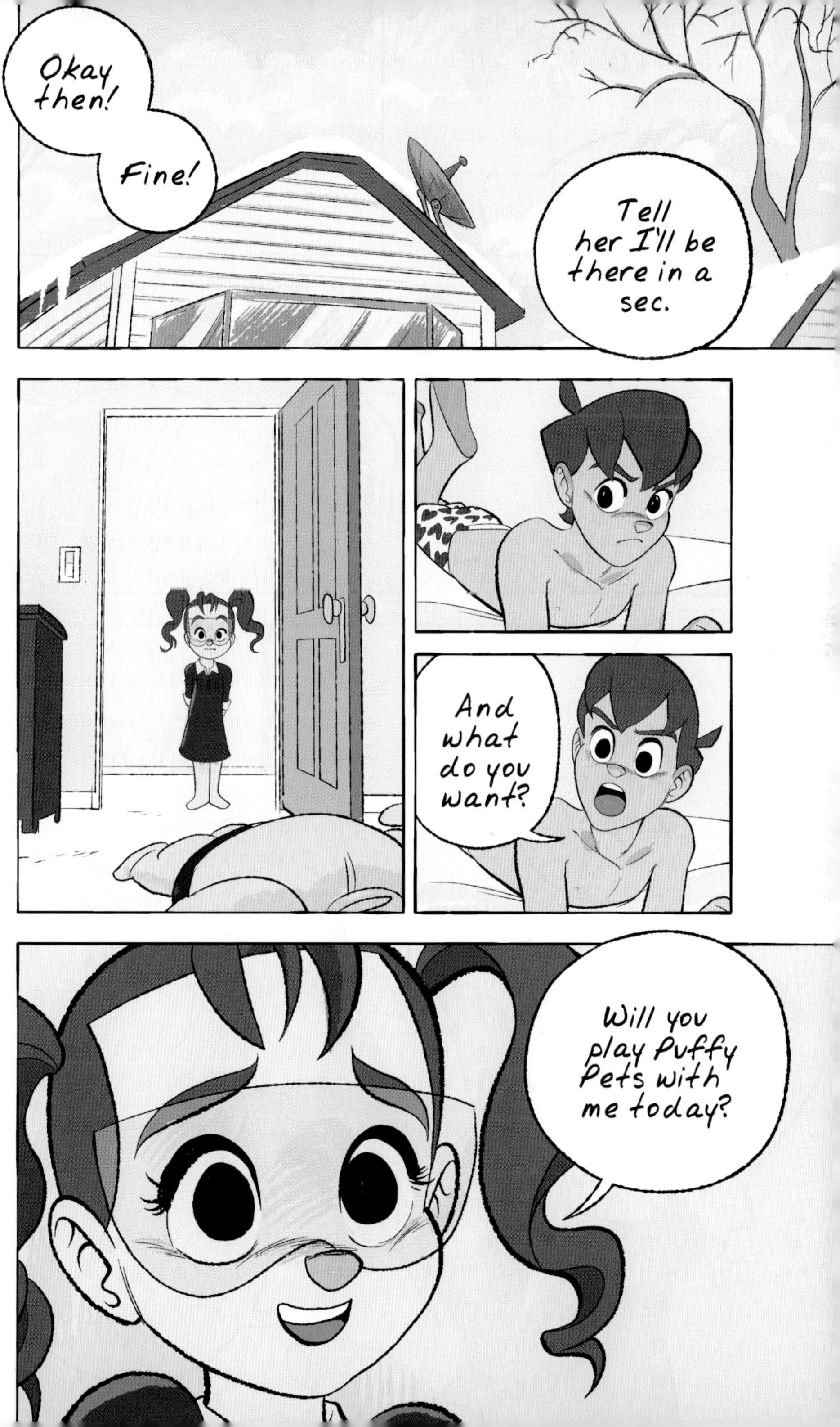
Okay then!
Fine!
Tell her I'll be there in a sec.
And what do you want?
Will you play Puffy Pets with me today?

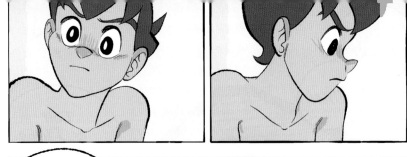

Of course I will!

As long as I get to be the baby aardvark!

YAY!

Thanks, Zeph!

You're the best.

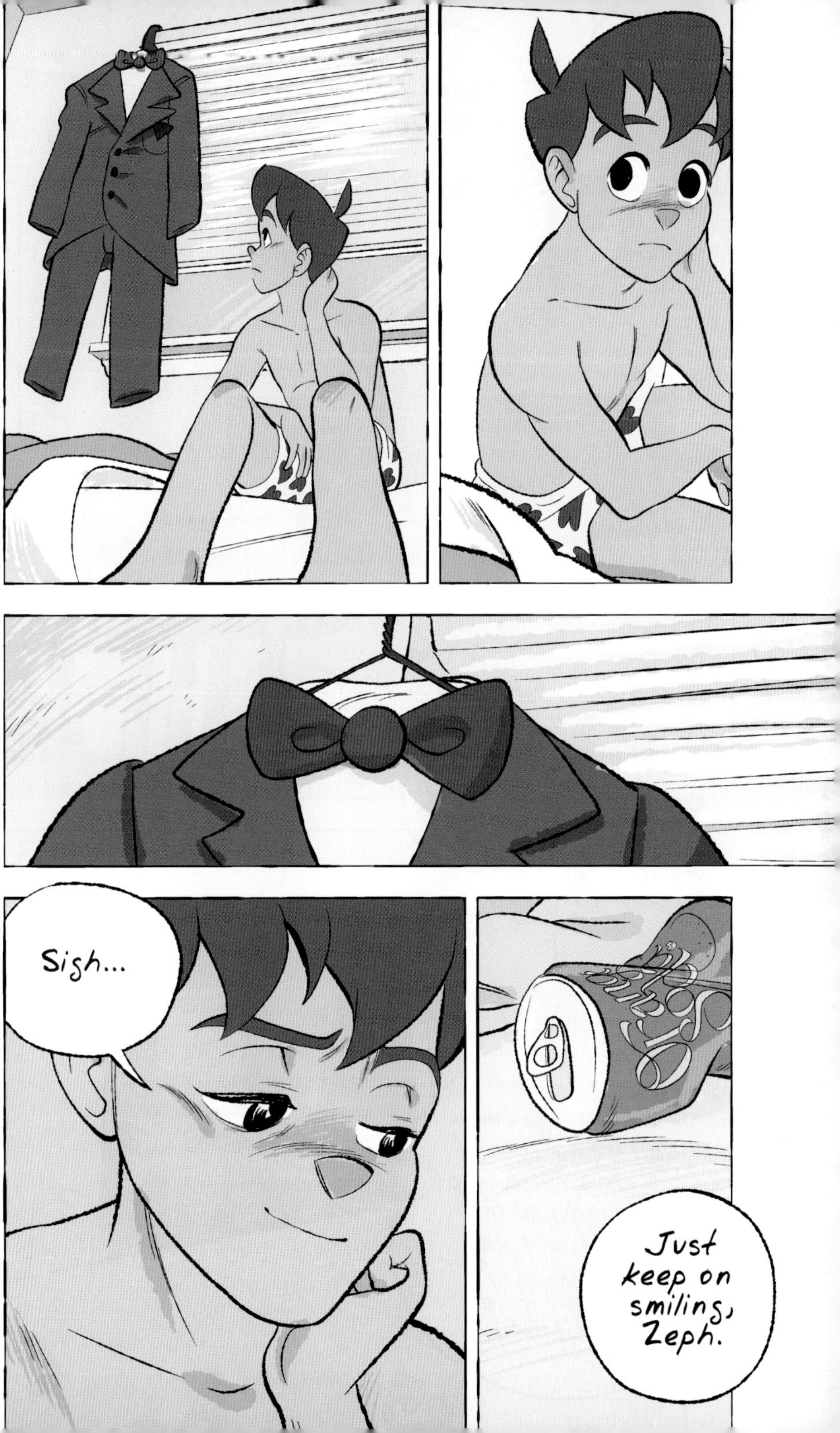
Sigh...
Just keep on smiling, Zeph.

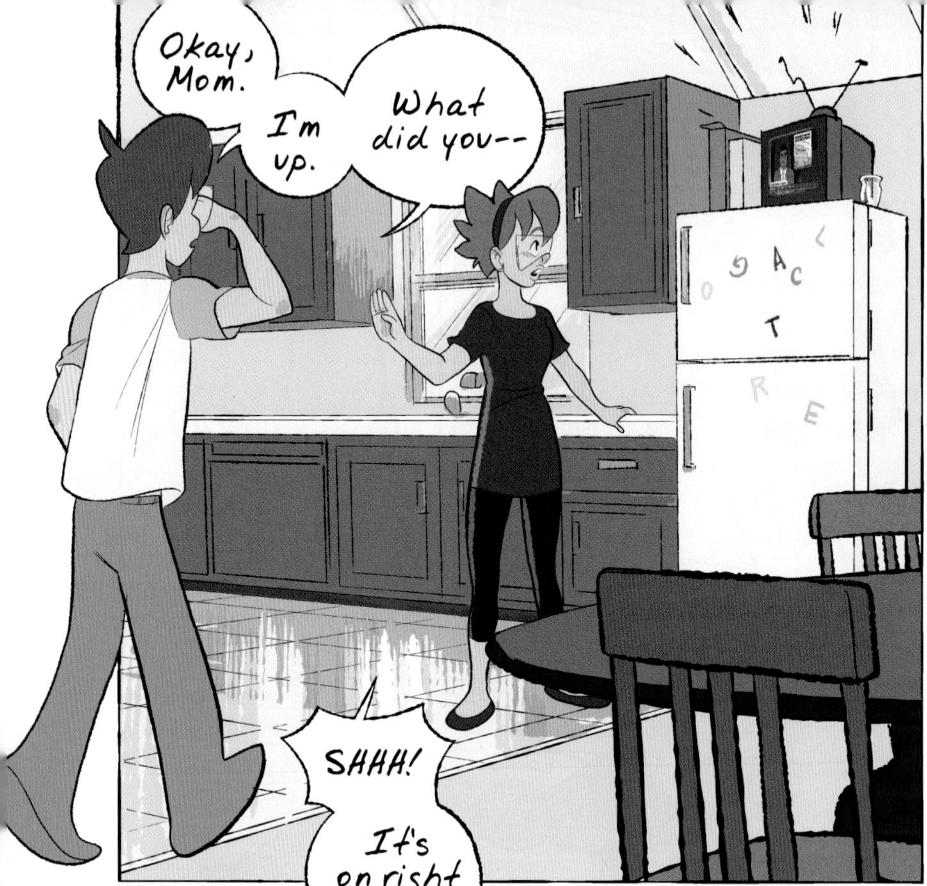
Okay, Mom.
I'm up.
What did you--
SHHH!
It's on right now!

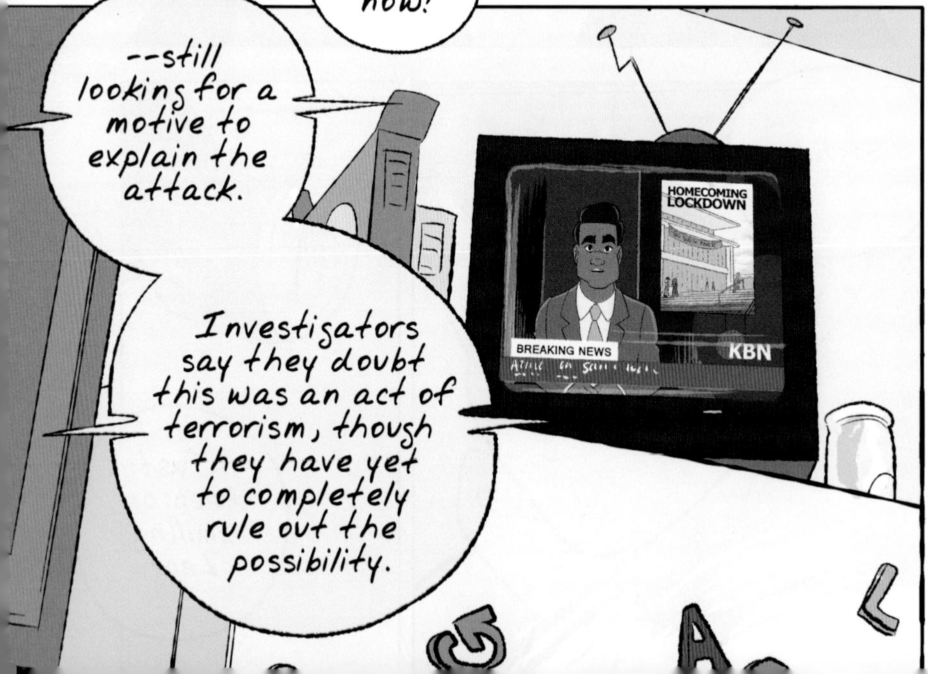
--still looking for a motive to explain the attack.
HOMECOMING LOCKDOWN
BREAKING NEWS
KBN
Investigators say they doubt this was an act of terrorism, though they have yet to completely rule out the possibility.

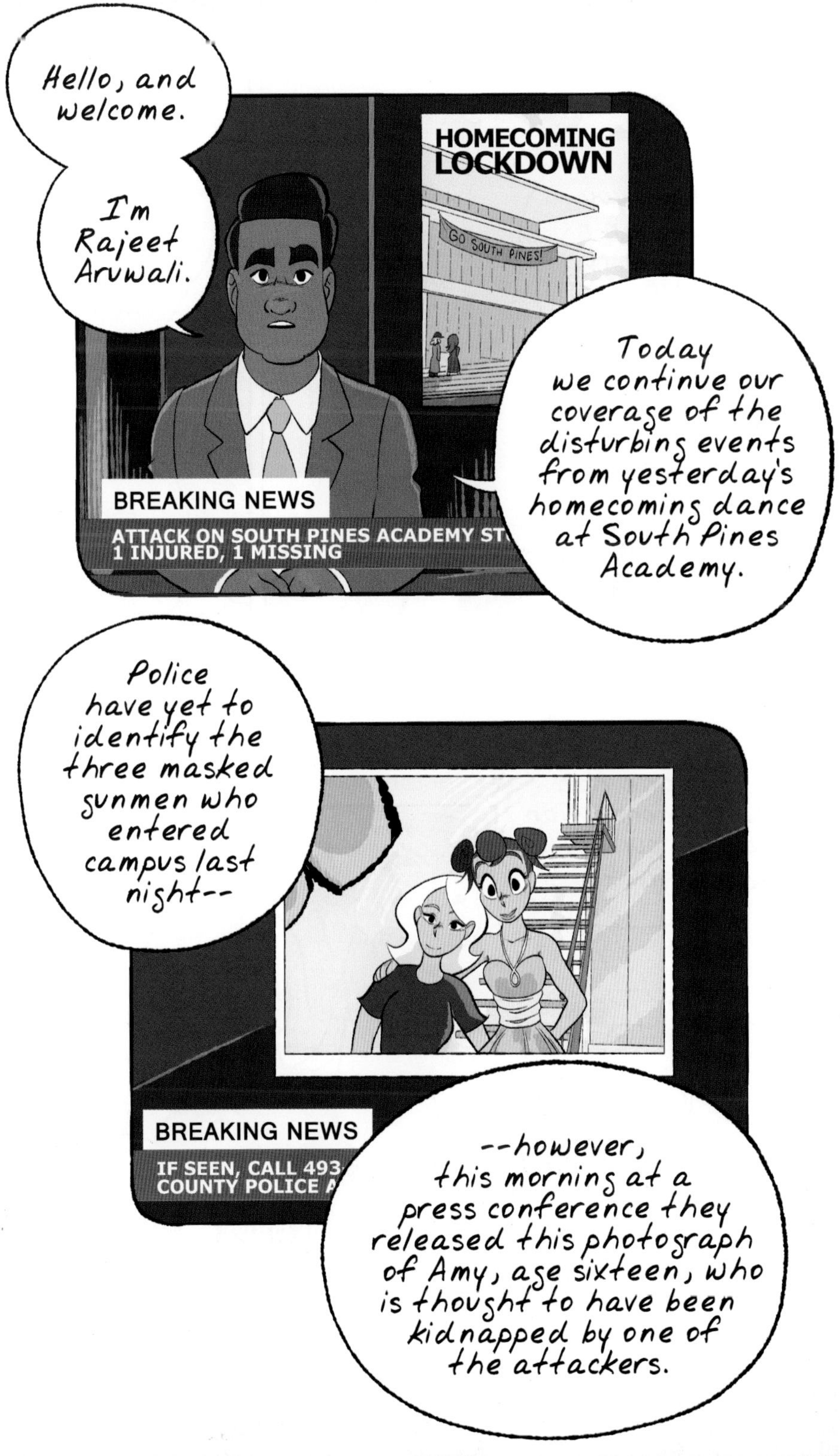
Hello, and welcome.
I'm Rajeet Aruwali.
HOMECOMING LOCKDOWN
GO SOUTH PINES!
BREAKING NEWS
ATTACK ON SOUTH PINES ACADEMY ST
1 INJURED, 1 MISSING
Today we continue our coverage of the disturbing events from yesterday's homecoming dance at South Pines Academy.
Police have yet to identify the three masked gunmen who entered campus last night--
BREAKING NEWS
IF SEEN, CALL 493-
COUNTY POLICE A
--however, this morning at a press conference they released this photograph of Amy, age sixteen, who is thought to have been kidnapped by one of the attackers.

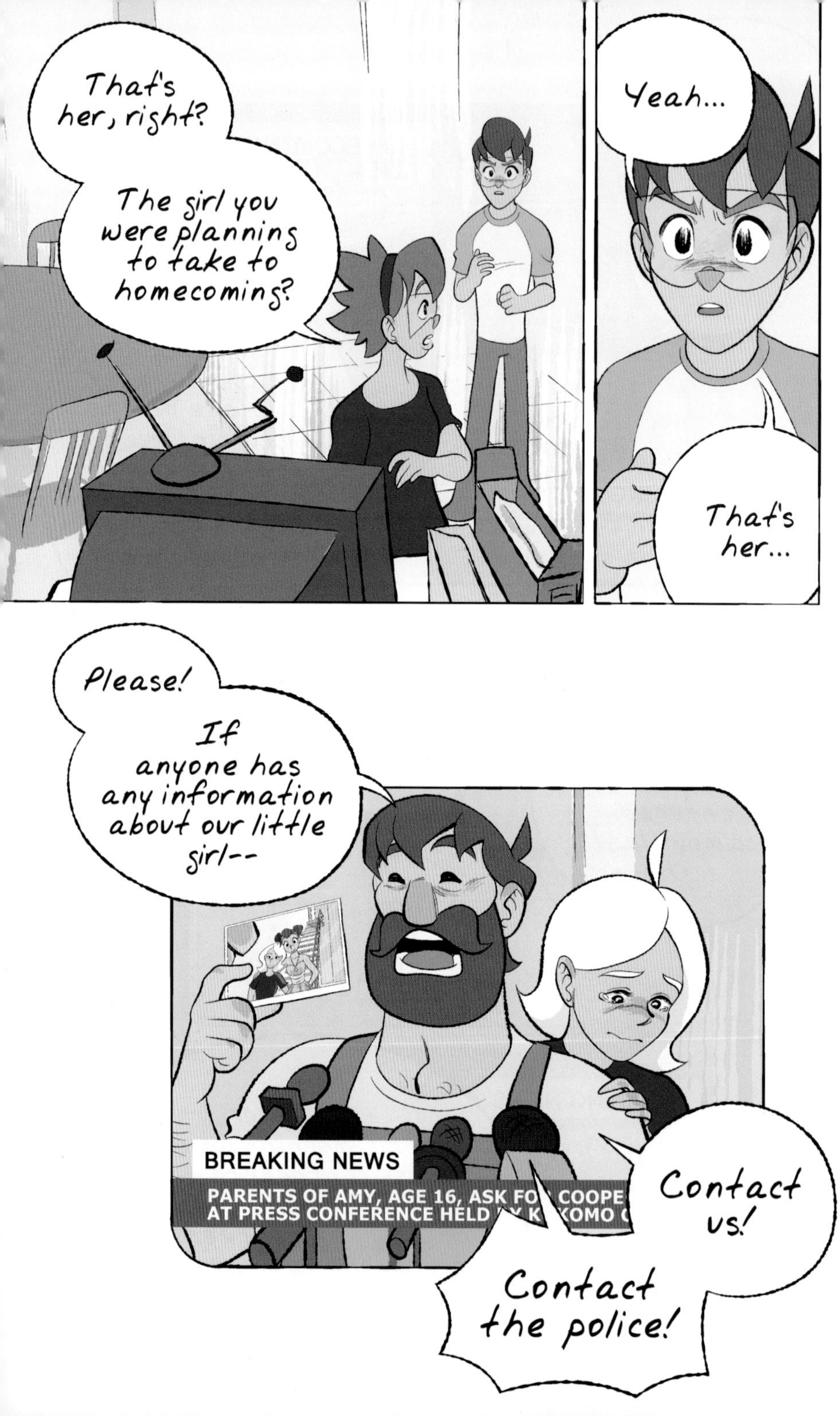

That's her, right?
The girl you were planning to take to homecoming?
Yeah...
That's her...
Please!
If anyone has any information about our little girl--
BREAKING NEWS
PARENTS OF AMY, AGE 16, ASK FO COOPE
AT PRESS CONFERENCE HELD
Contact us!
Contact the police!

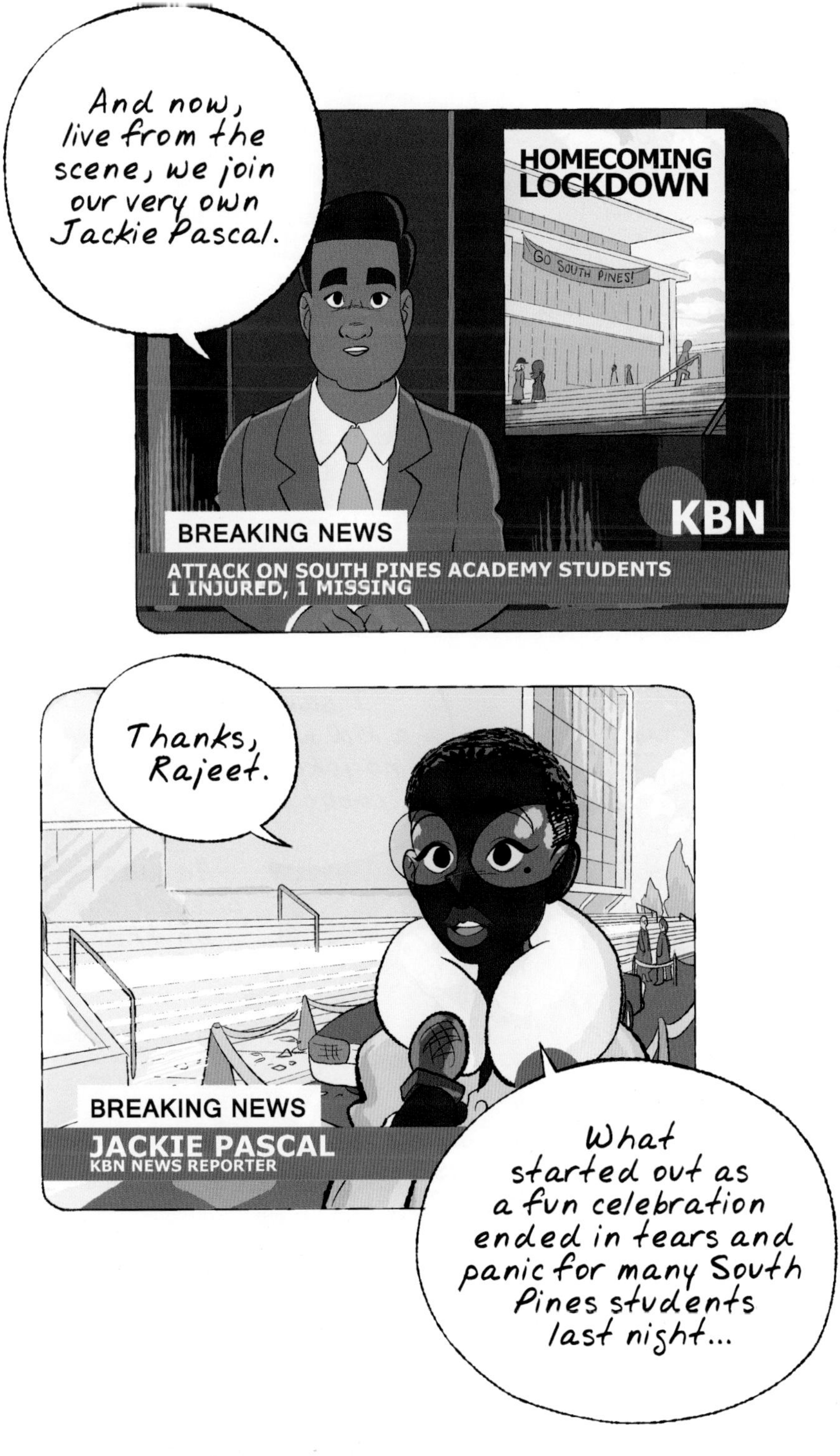
And now, live from the scene, we join our very own Jackie Pascal.
HOMECOMING LOCKDOWN
GO SOUTH PINES!
KBN
BREAKING NEWS
ATTACK ON SOUTH PINES ACADEMY STUDENTS
1 INJURED, 1 MISSING
Thanks, Rajeet.
BREAKING NEWS
JACKIE PASCAL
KBN NEWS REPORTER
What started out as a fun celebration ended in tears and panic for many South Pines students last night...

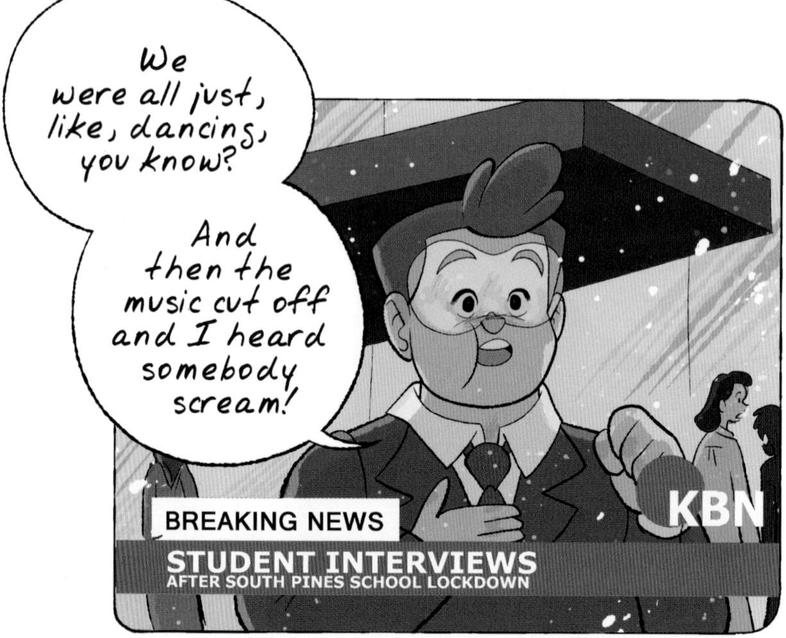
We were all just, like, dancing, you know?
And then the music cut off and I heard somebody scream!
BREAKING NEWS
KBN
STUDENT INTERVIEWS
AFTER SOUTH PINES SCHOOL LOCKDOWN

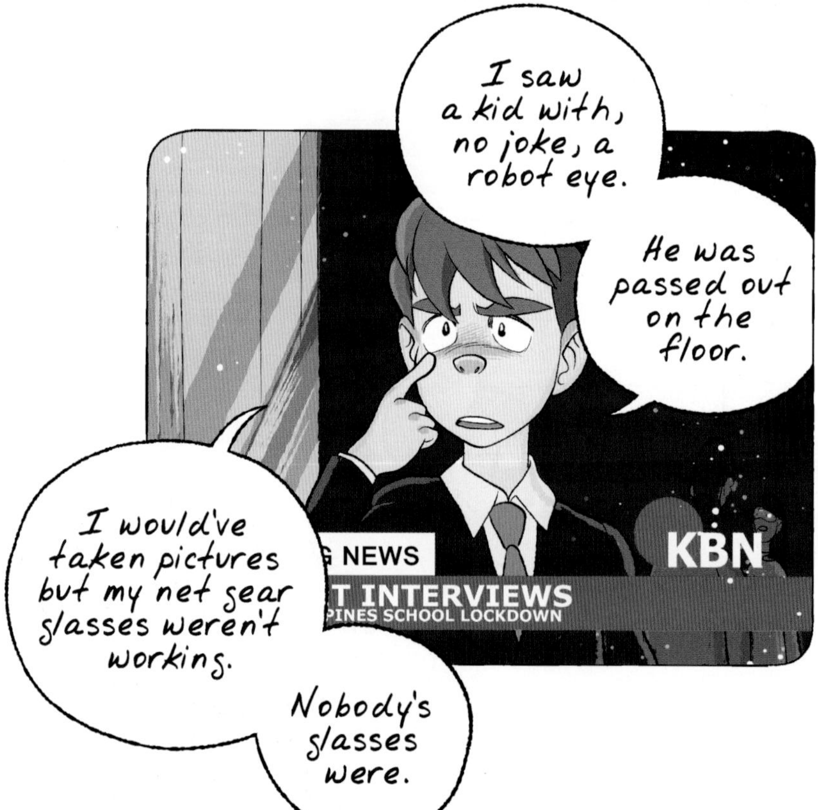
I saw a kid with, no joke, a robot eye.
He was passed out on the floor.
I would've taken pictures but my net gear glasses weren't working.
Nobody's glasses were.
KBN

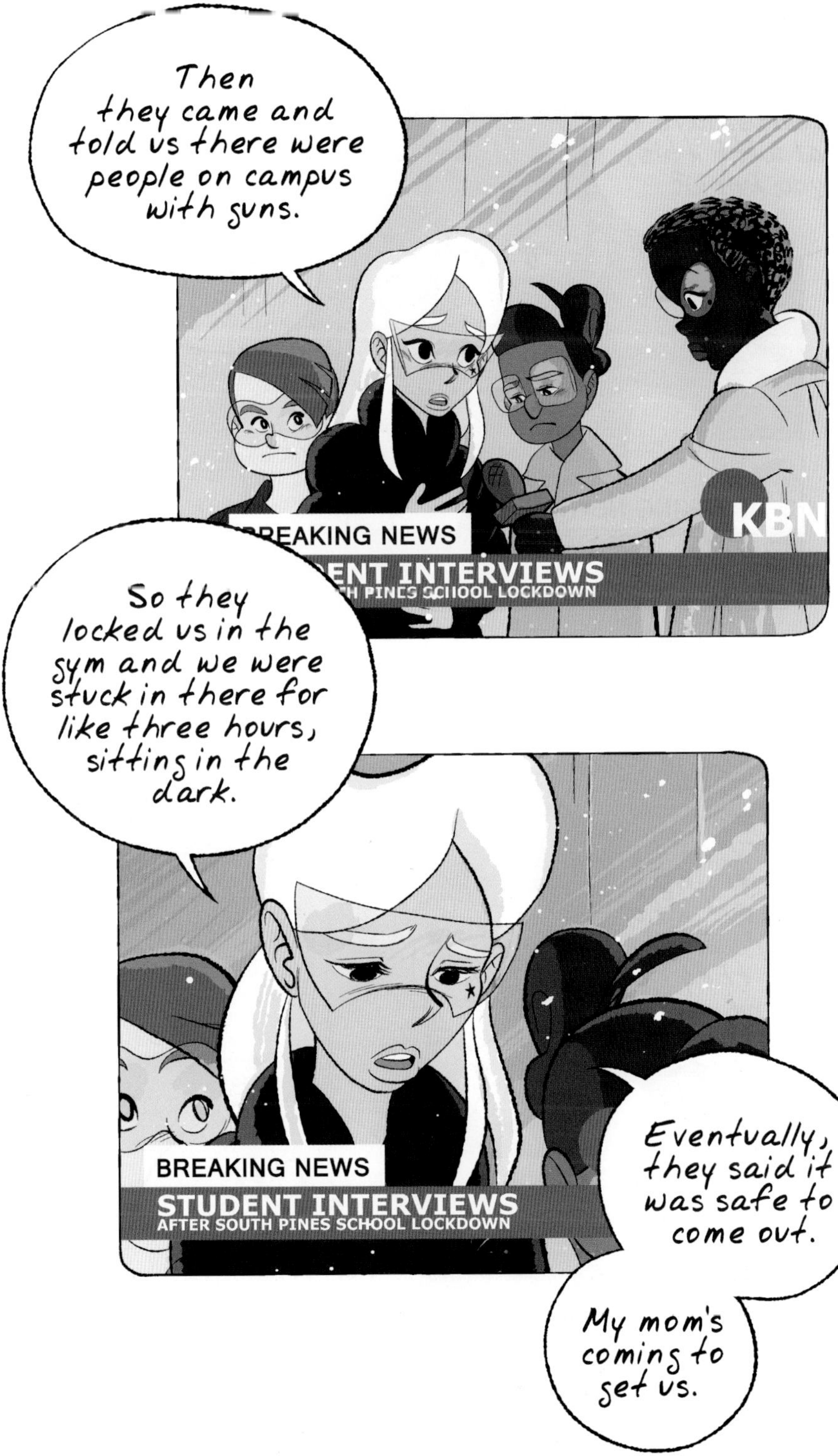

Then they came and told us there were people on campus with guns.
KBN
So they locked us in the gym and we were stuck in there for like three hours, sitting in the dark.
BREAKING NEWS
STUDENT INTERVIEWS
AFTER SOUTH PINES SCHOOL LOCKDOWN
Eventually, they said it was safe to come out.
My mom's coming to get us.

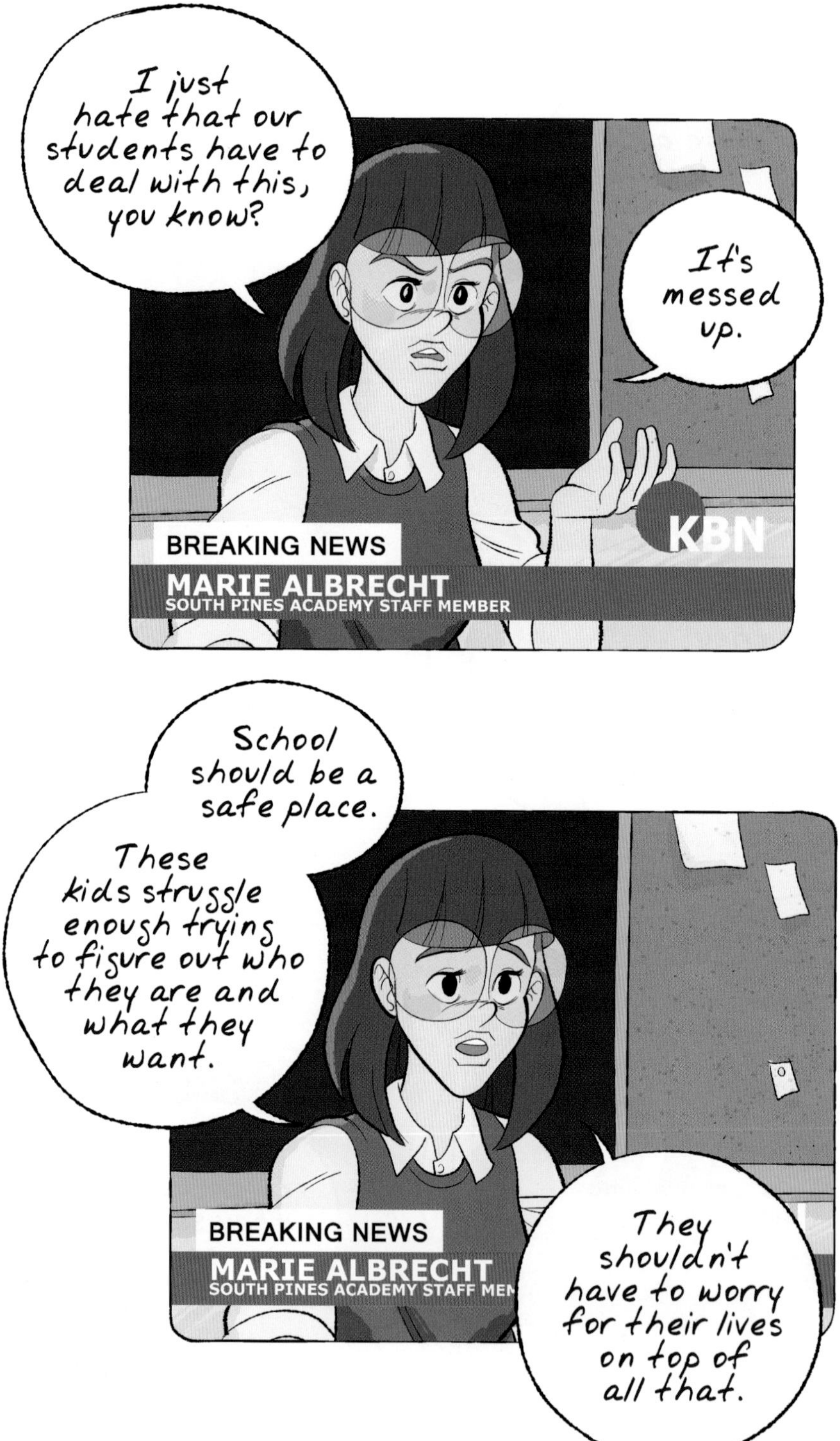
I just hate that our students have to deal with this, you know?
It's messed up.
KBN
BREAKING NEWS
MARIE ALBRECHT
SOUTH PINES ACADEMY STAFF MEMBER
School should be a safe place.
These kids struggle enough trying to figure out who they are and what they want.
BREAKING NEWS
MARIE ALBRECHT
SOUTH PINES ACADEMY STAFF MEM
They shouldn't have to worry for their lives on top of all that.

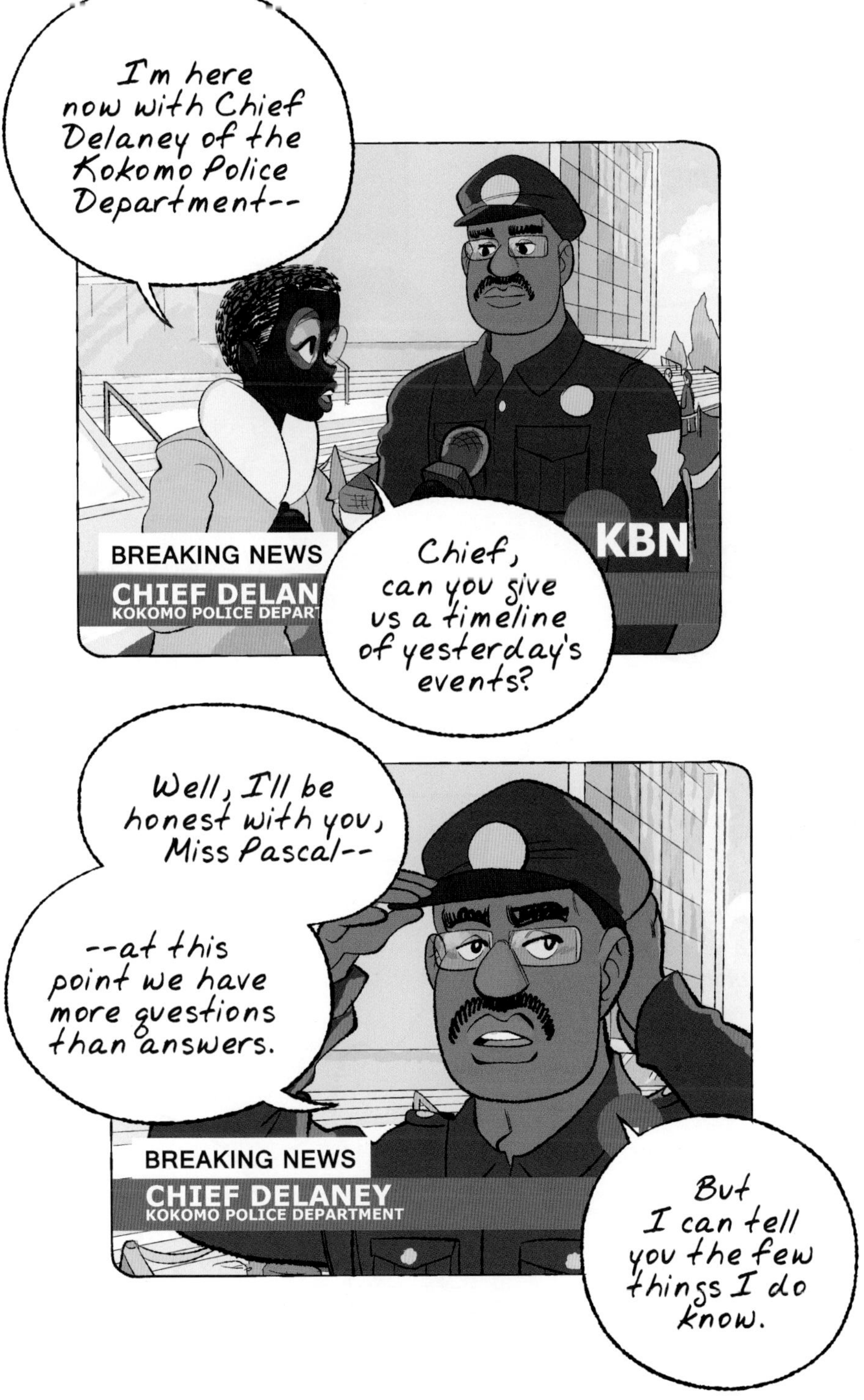
I'm here now with Chief Delaney of the Kokomo Police Department--
BREAKING NEWS
CHIEF DELAN
KOKOMO POLICE DEPART
KBN
Chief, can you give us a timeline of yesterday's events?
Well, I'll be honest with you, Miss Pascal--
--at this point we have more questions than answers.
BREAKING NEWS
CHIEF DELANEY
KOKOMO POLICE DEPARTMENT
But I can tell you the few things I do know.

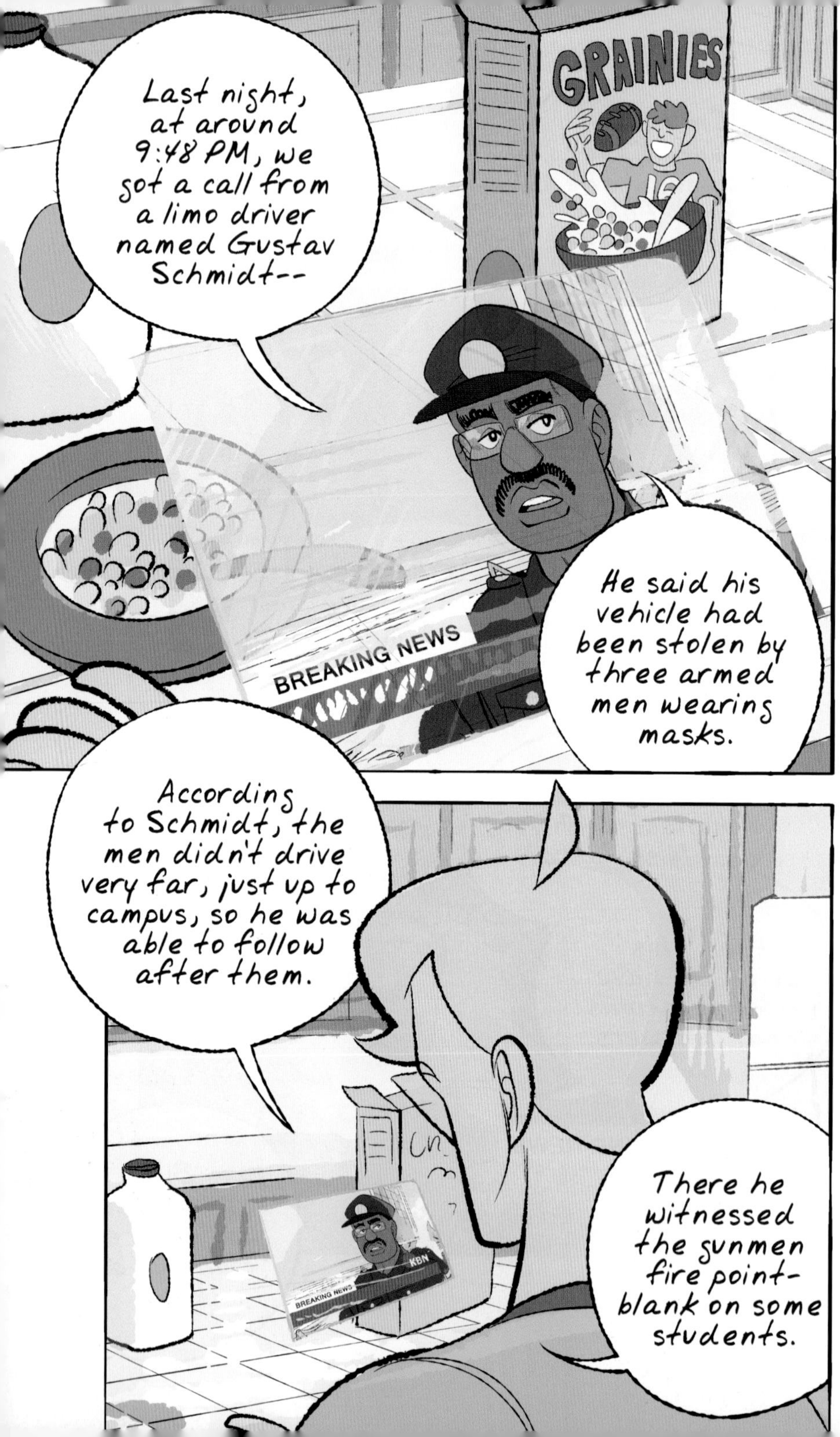

GRAINIES
Last night, at around 9:48 PM, we got a call from a limo driver named Gustav Schmidt--
He said his vehicle had been stolen by three armed men wearing masks.
BREAKING NEWS
Accordins to Schmidt, the men didn't drive very far, just up to campus, so he was able to follow after them.
There he witnessed the gunmen fire point-blank on some students.
KBN
BREAKING NEWS

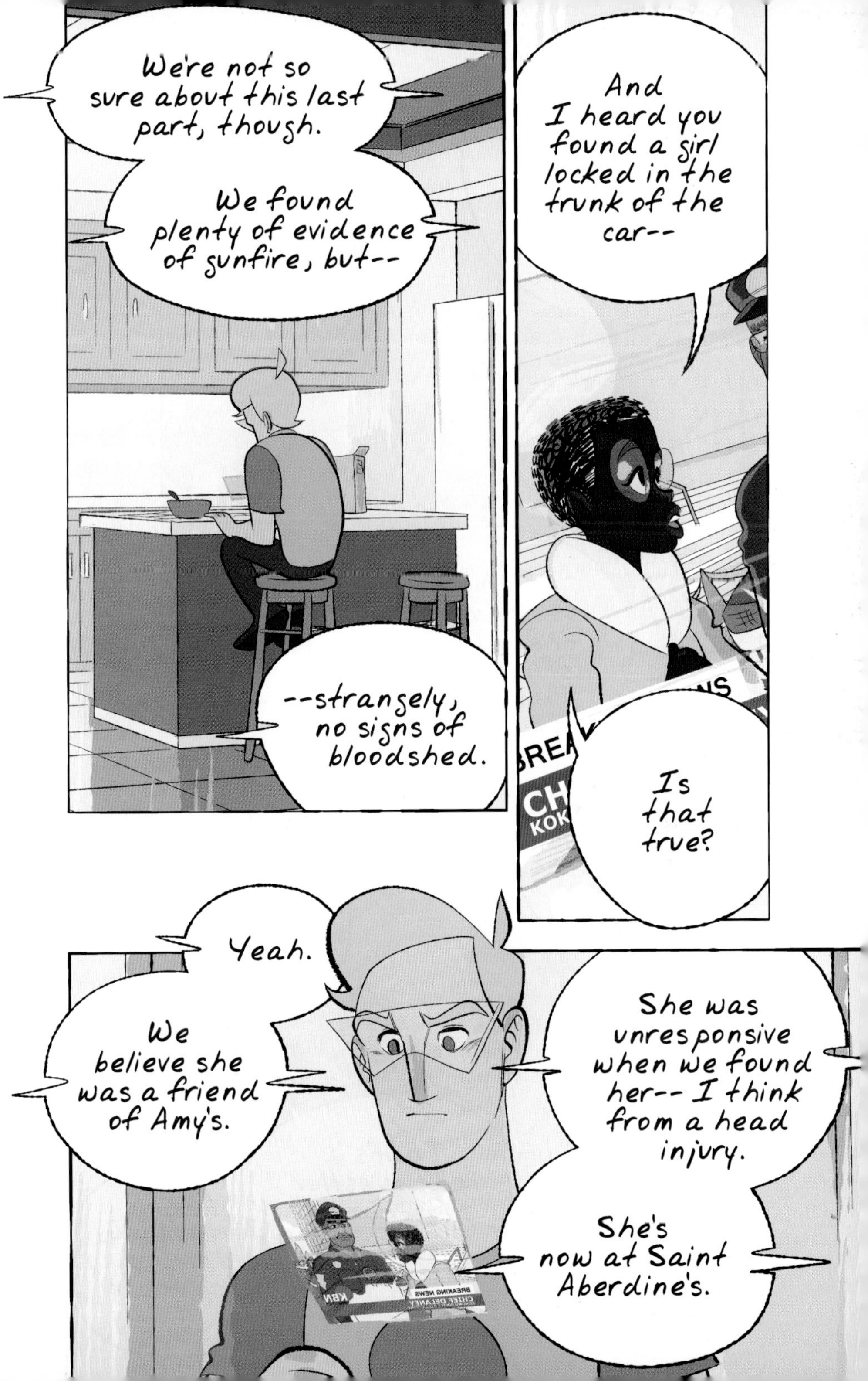

We're not so sure about this last part, though.
We found plenty of evidence of gunfire, but--
--strangely, no signs of bloodshed.
And I heard you found a girl locked in the trunk of the car--
Is that true?
Yeah.
We believe she was a friend of Amy's.
She was unresponsive when we found her-- I think from a head injury.
She's now at Saint Aberdine's.

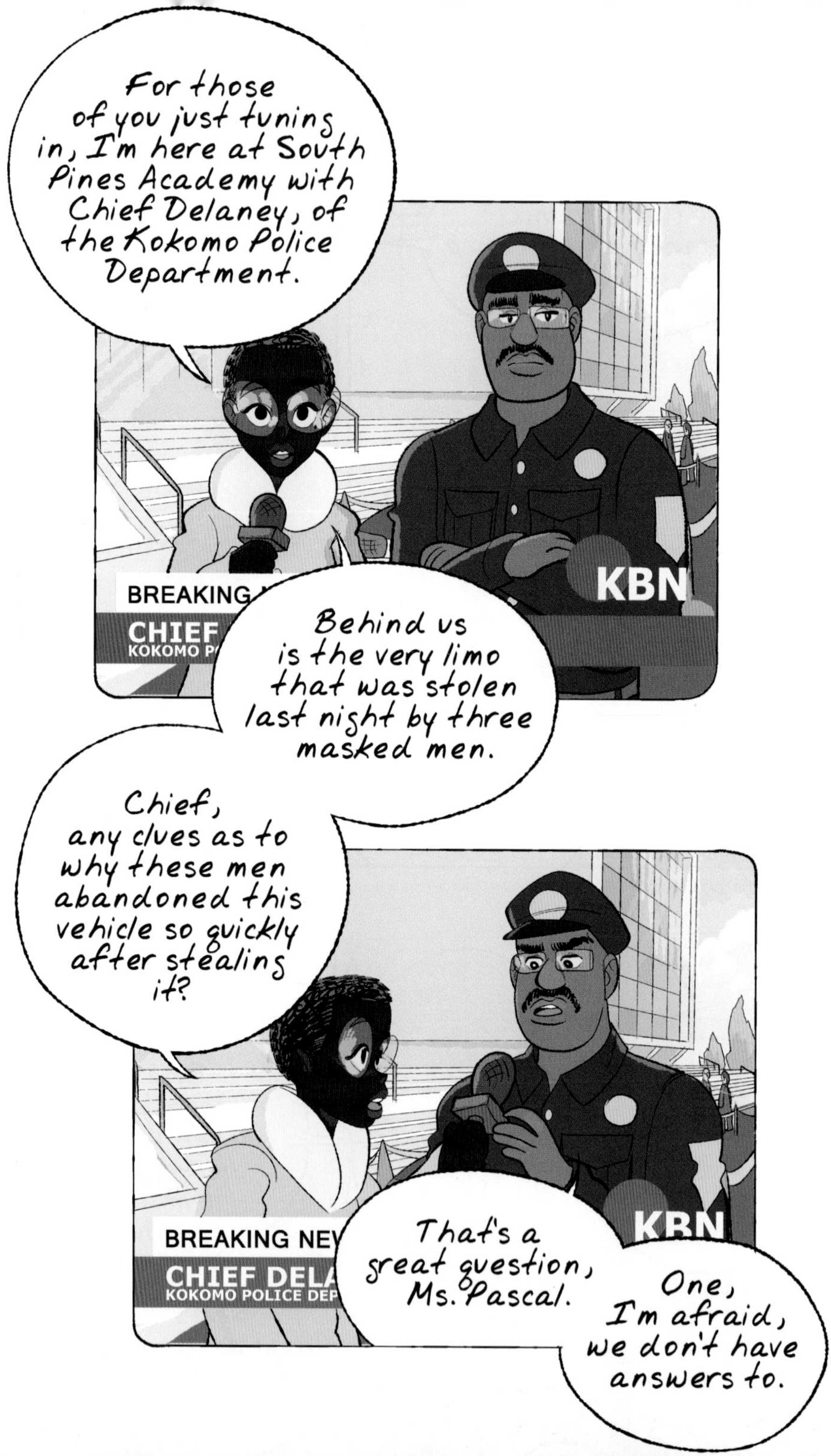
For those of you just tuning in, I'm here at South Pines Academy with Chief Delaney, of the Kokomo Police Department.
BREAKING N
CHIEF
KOKOMO PO
KBN
Behind us is the very limo that was stolen last night by three masked men.
Chief, any clues as to why these men abandoned this vehicle so quickly after stealing it?
BREAKING NEV
CHIEF DELA
KOKOMO POLICE DEP
KBN
That's a great question, Ms. Pascal.
One, I'm afraid, we don't have answers to.

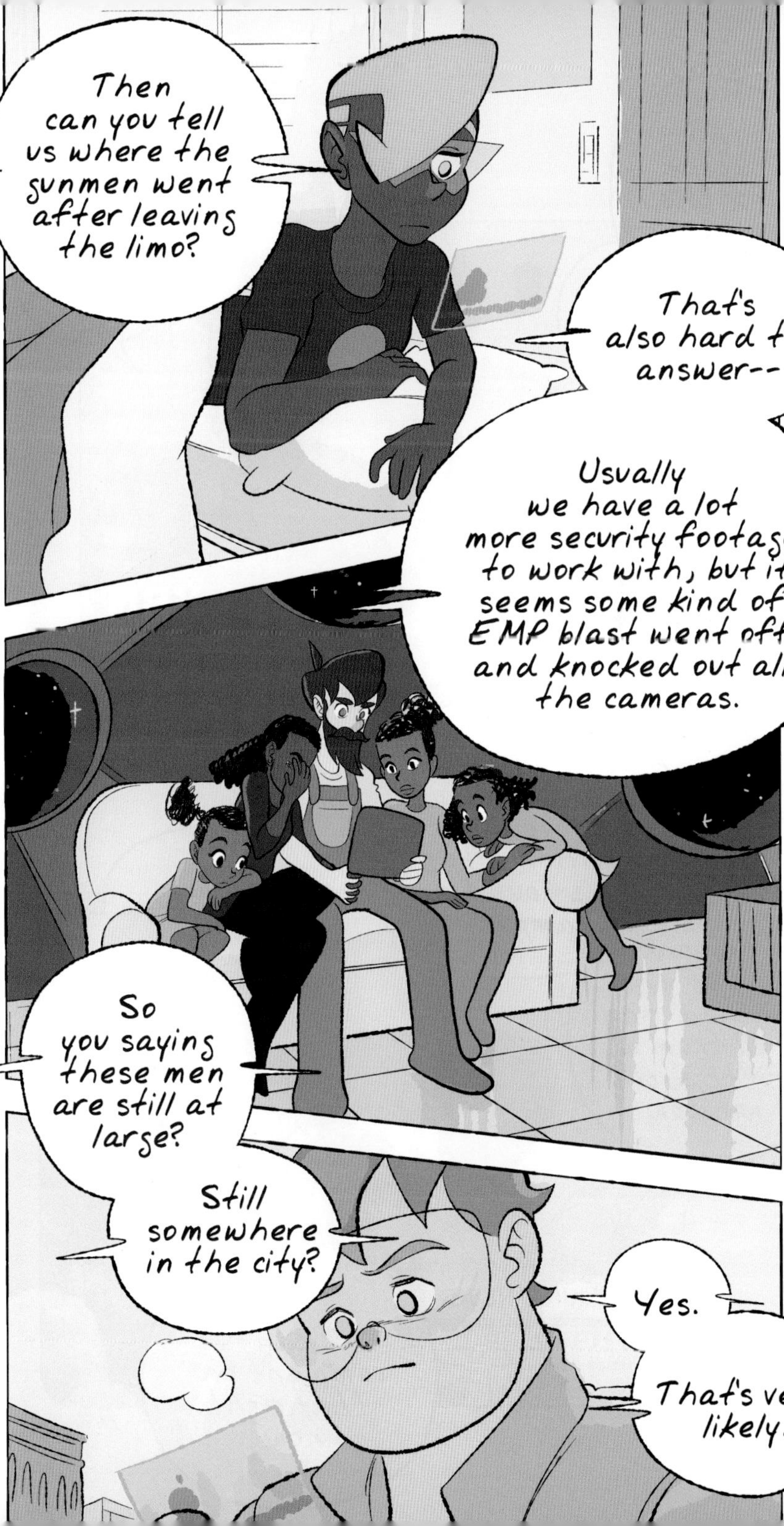
Then can you tell us where the gunmen went after leaving the limo?
That's also hard to answer--
Usually we have a lot more security footage to work with, but it seems some kind of EMP blast went off and knocked out all the cameras.
So you saying these men are still at large?
Still somewhere in the city?
Yes.
That's very likely.

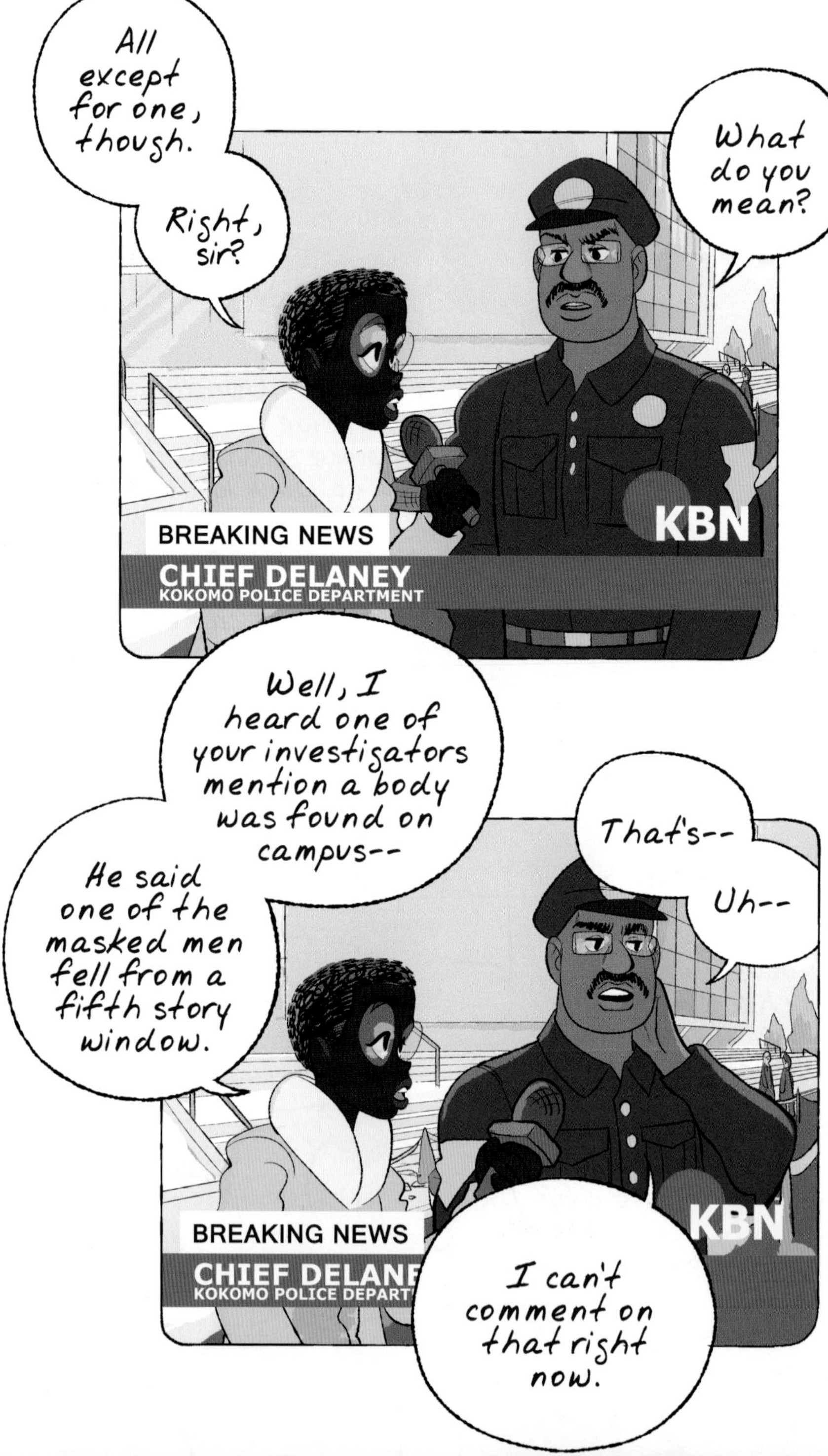
All except for one, though.
Right, sir?
What do you mean?
BREAKING NEWS
CHIEF DELANEY
KOKOMO POLICE DEPARTMENT
KBN
Well, I heard one of your investigators mention a body was found on campus--
He said one of the masked men fell from a fifth story window.
That's--
Uh--
BREAKING NEWS
CHIEF DELANE
KOKOMO POLICE DEPART
KBN
I can't comment on that right now.

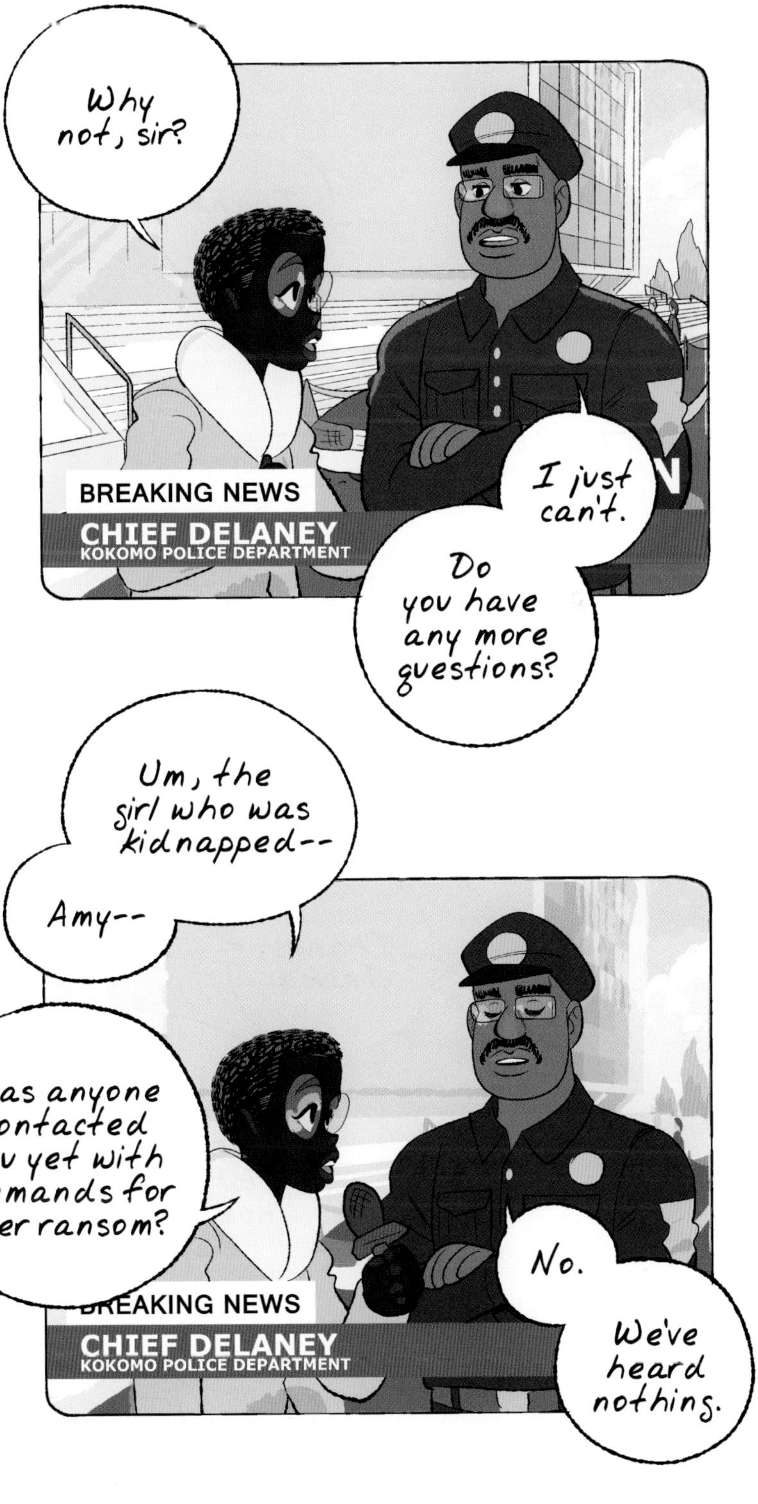
Why not, sir?
BREAKING NEWS
CHIEF DELANEY
KOKOMO POLICE DEPARTMENT
I just can't.
Do you have any more questions?
Um, the girl who was kidnapped--
Amy--
Has anyone contacted you yet with demands for her ransom?
BREAKING NEWS
CHIEF DELANEY
KOKOMO POLICE DEPARTMENT
No.
We've heard nothing.

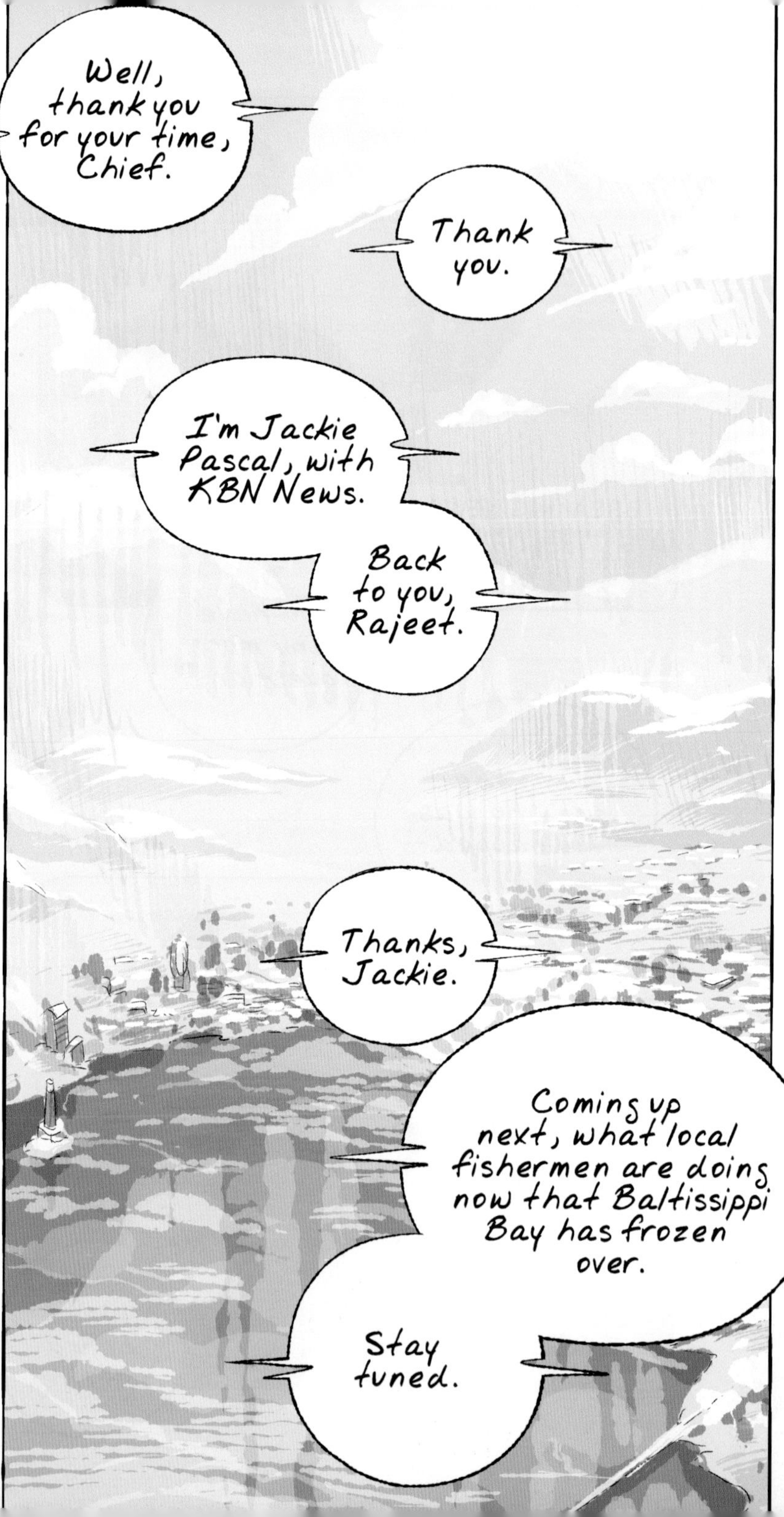
Well, thank you for your time, Chief.
Thank you.
I'm Jackie Pascal, with KBN News.
Back to you, Rajeet.
Thanks, Jackie.
Coming up next, what local fishermen are doing now that Baltissippi Bay has frozen over.
Stay tuned.

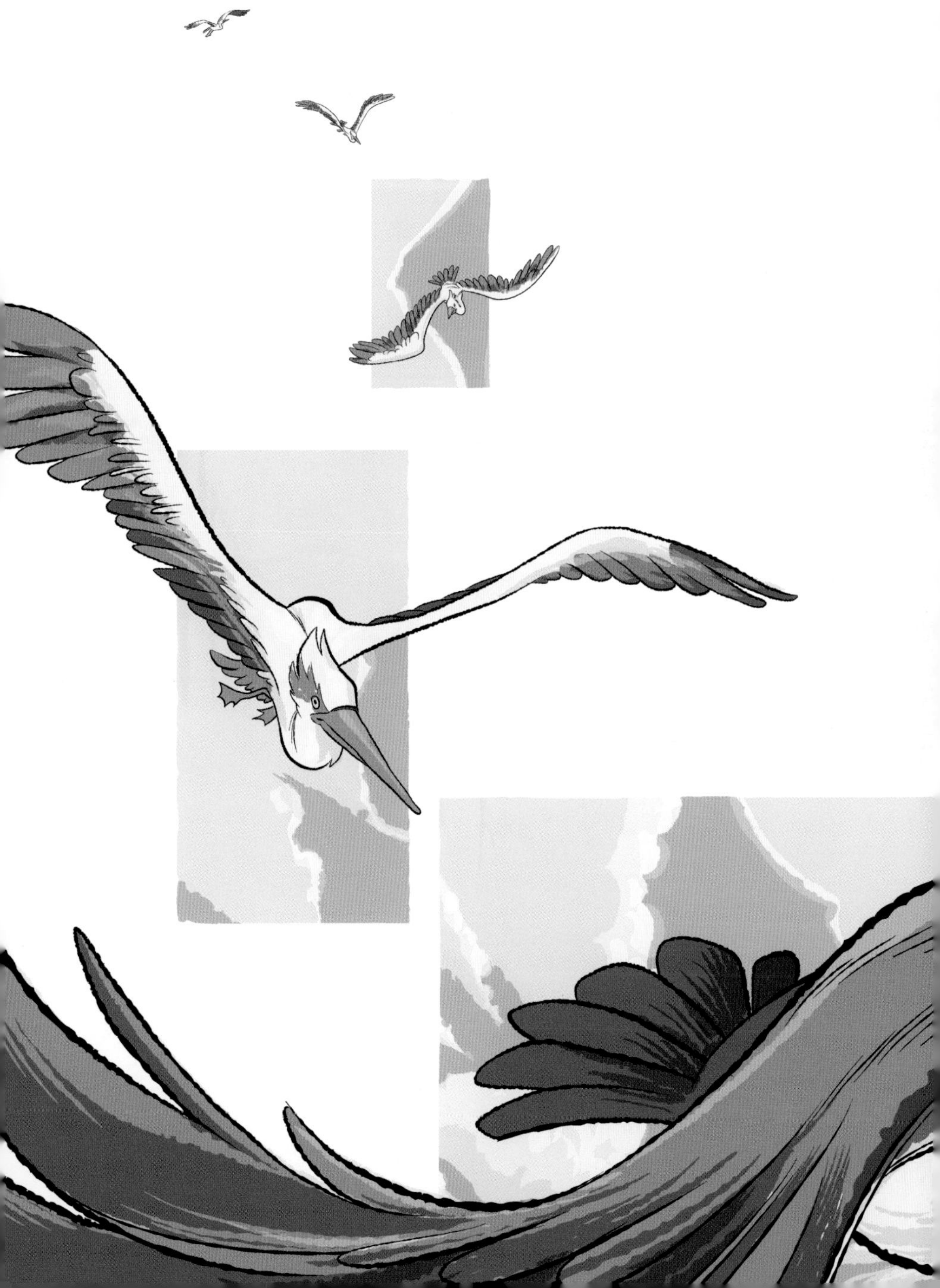

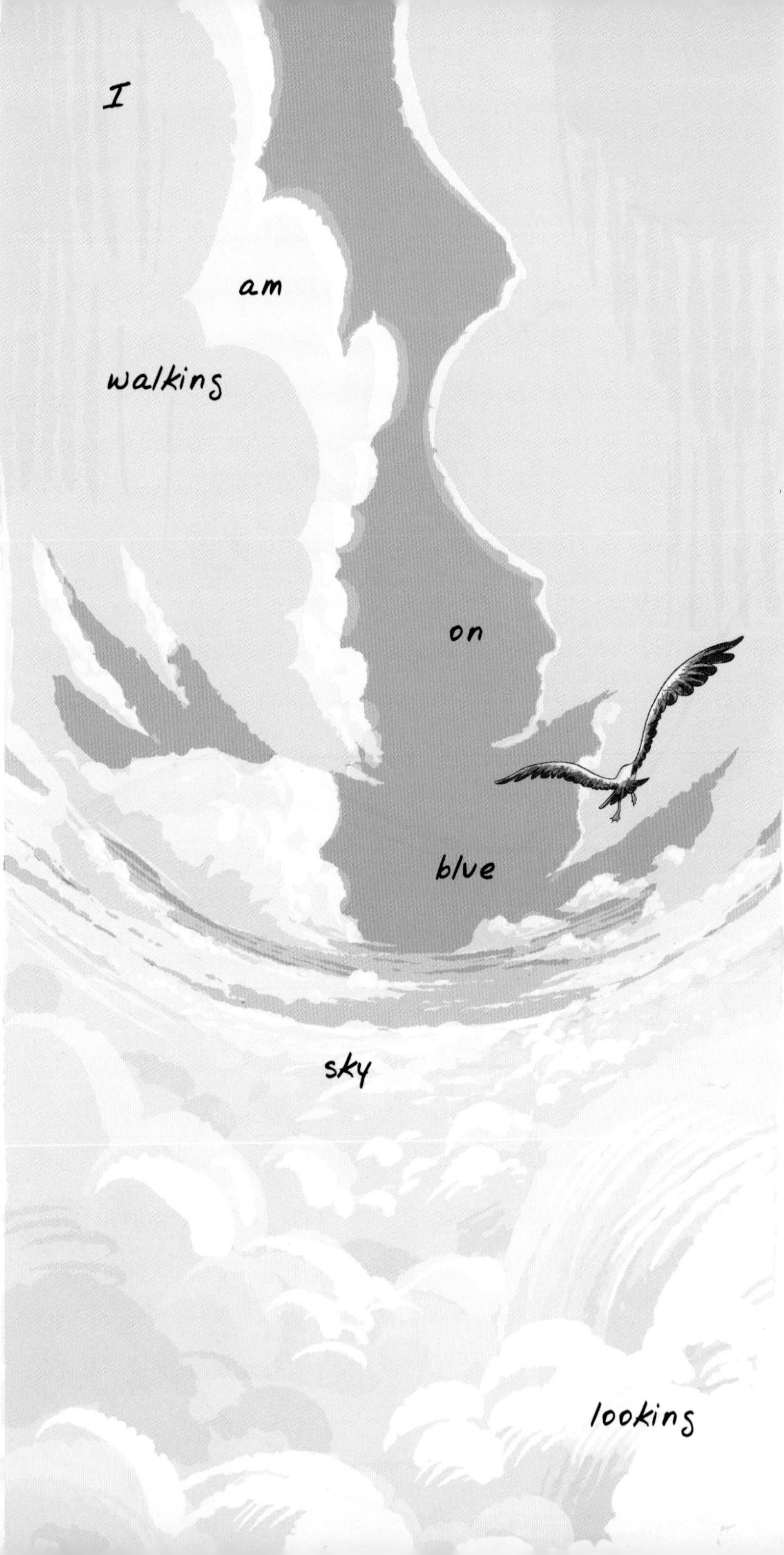
I
am
walking
on
blue
sky
looking

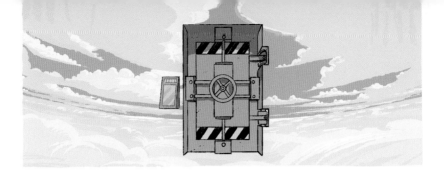

...for
Oliver.

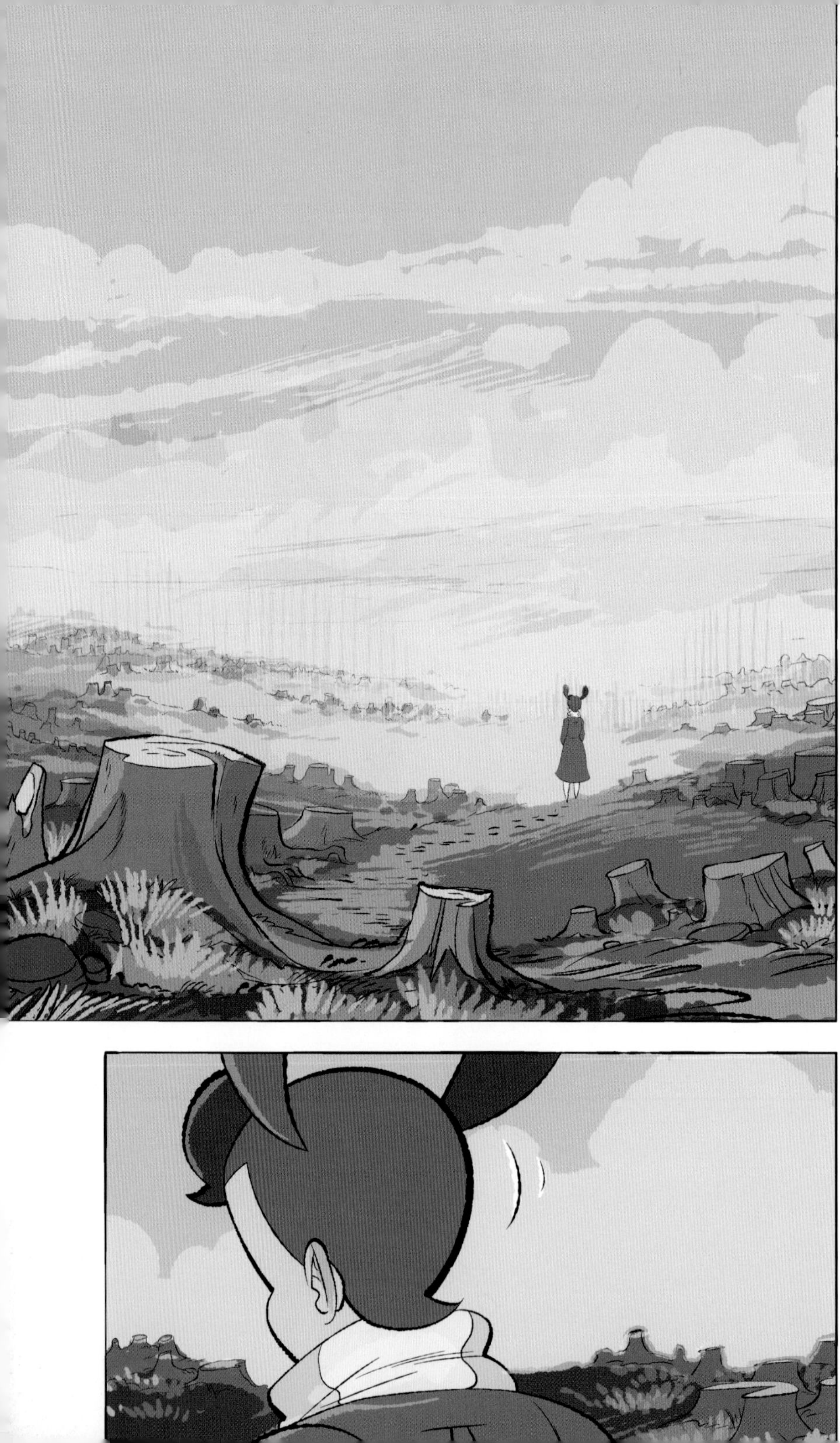

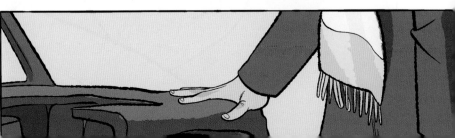

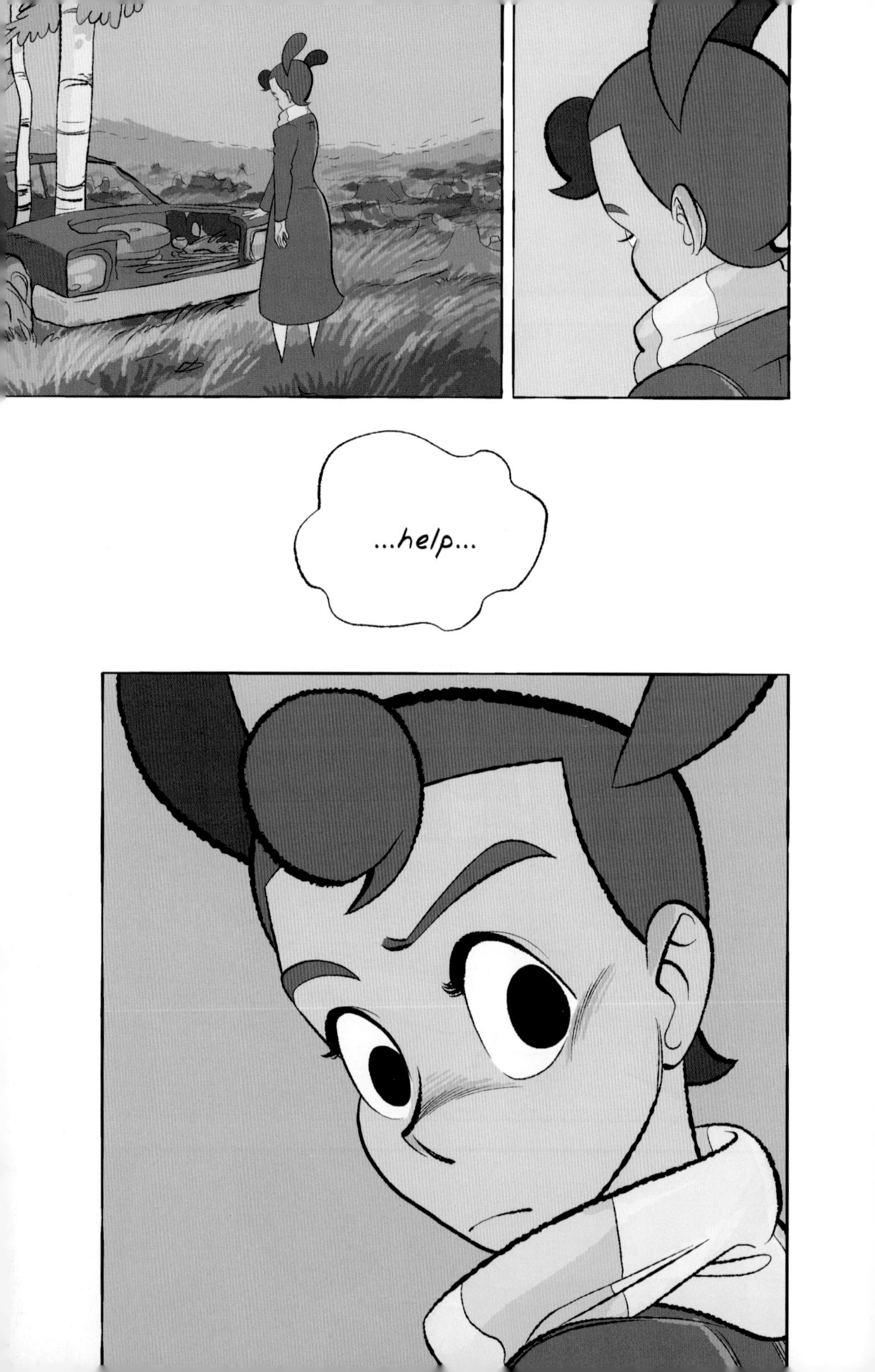
...help...

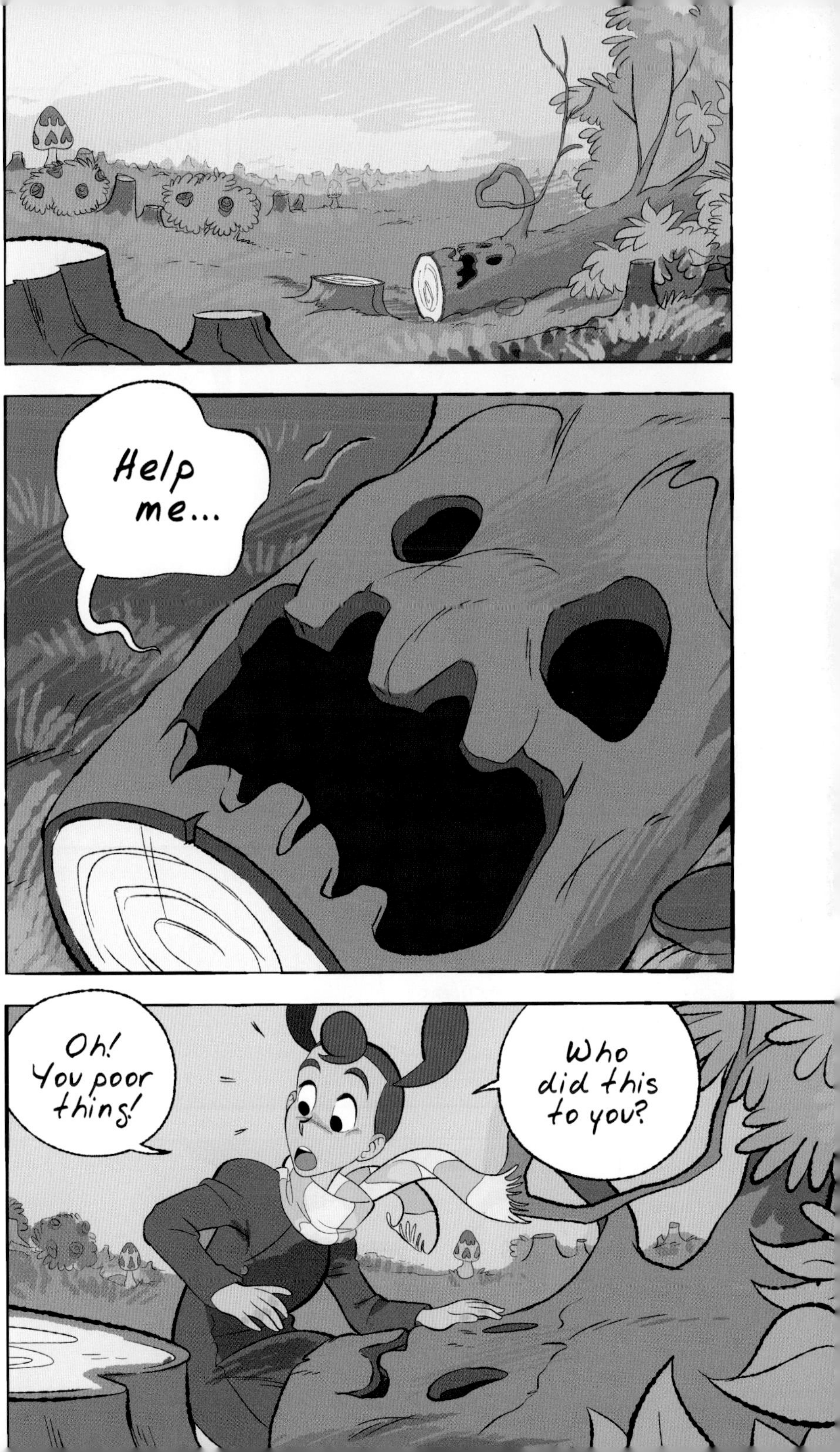
Help me...
Oh! You poor thing!
Who did this to you?

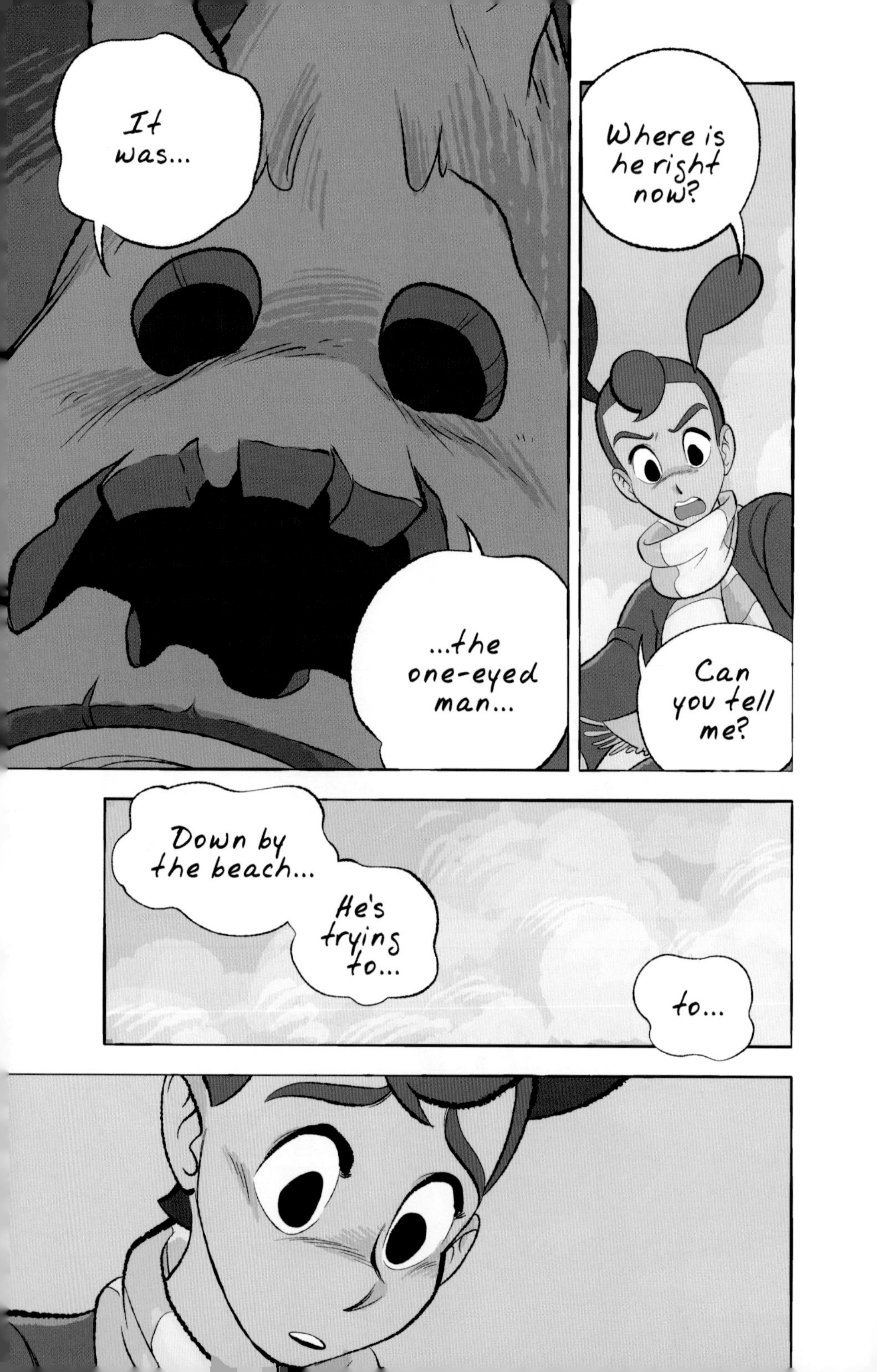
It was...
...the one-eyed man...
Where is he right now?
Can you tell me?
Down by the beach...
He's trying to...
to...

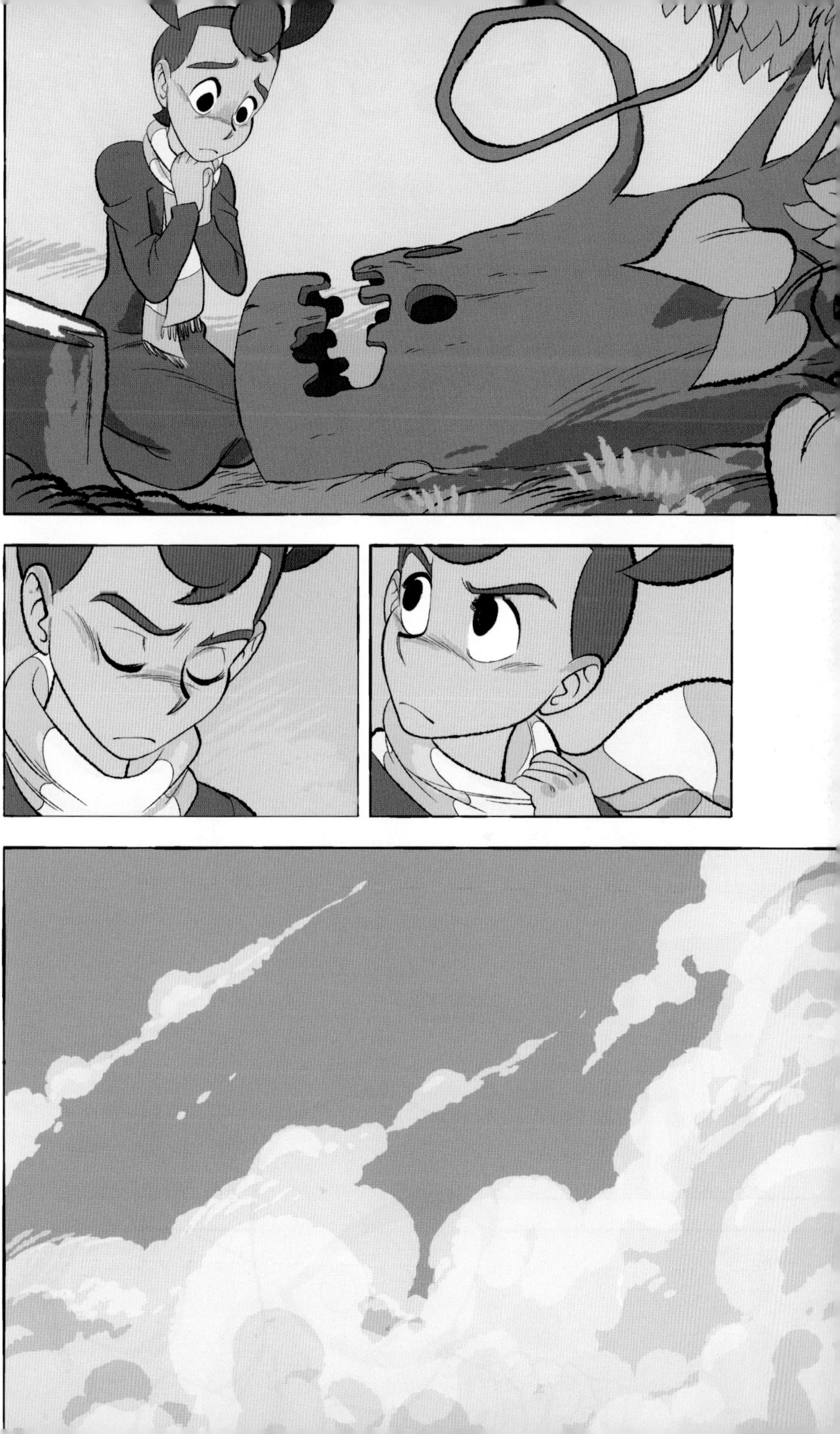

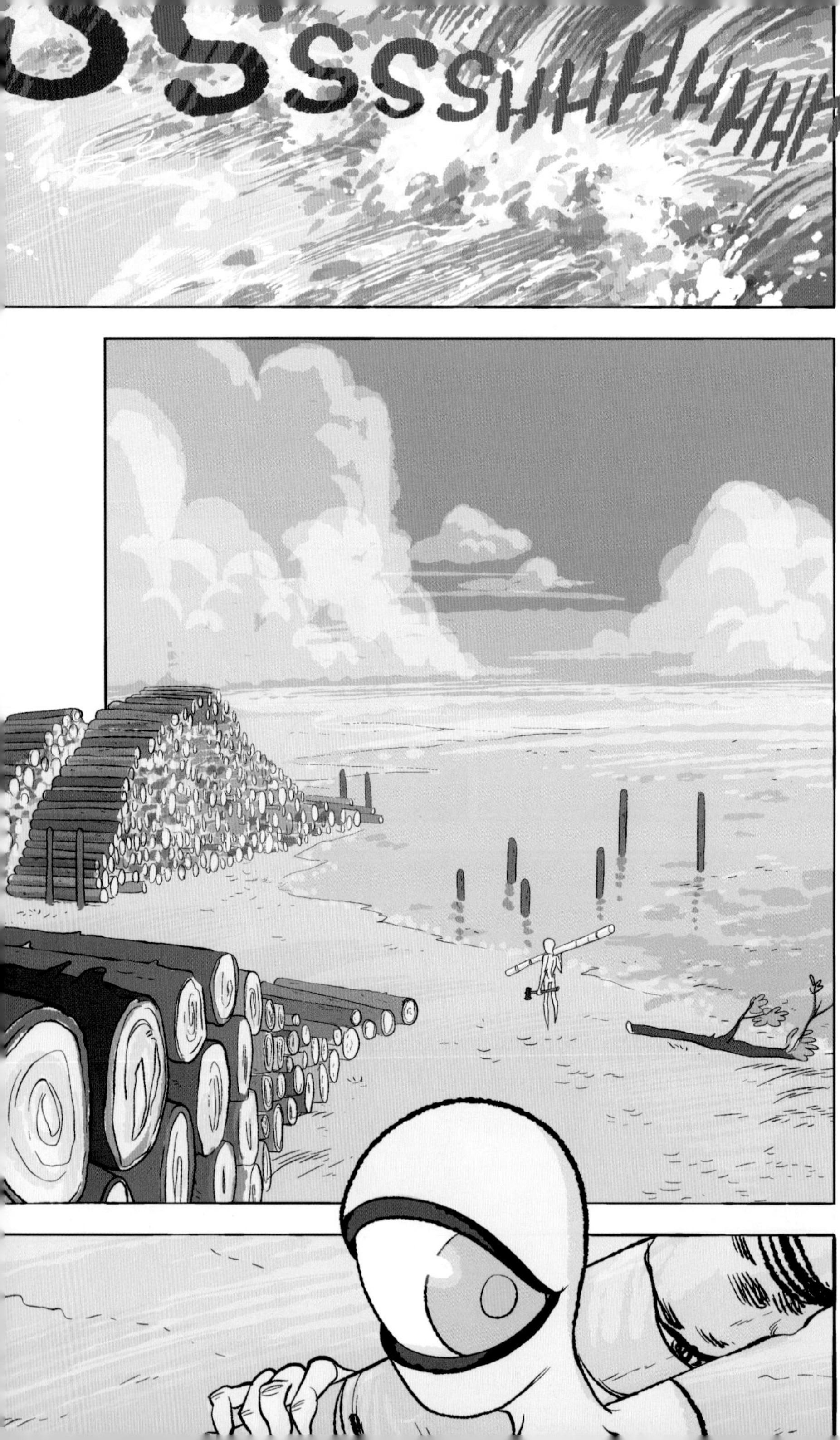
SSSSHHHHHHHH

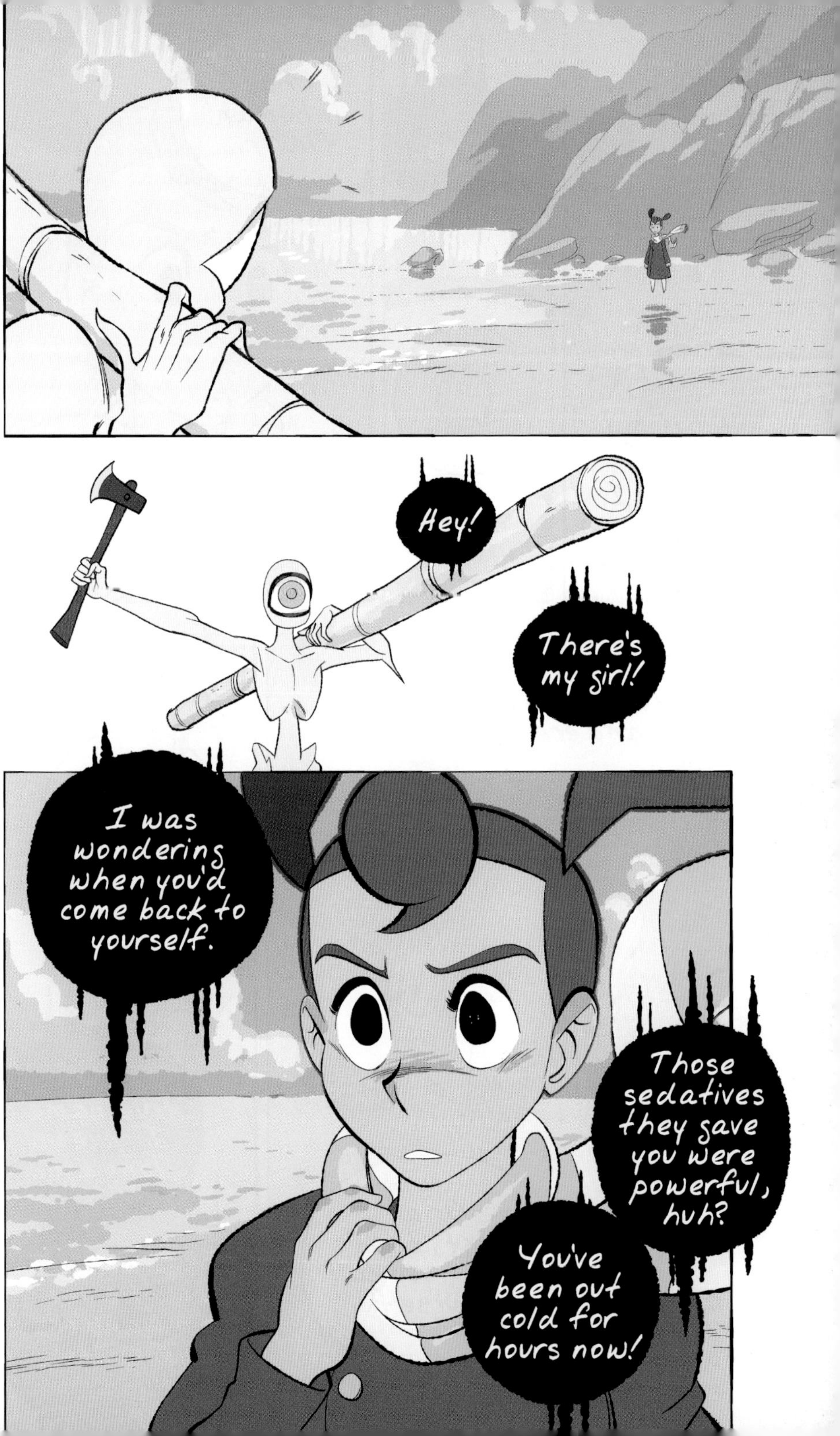
Hey!
There's my girl!
I was wondering when you'd come back to yourself.
Those sedatives they gave you were powerful, huh?
You've been out cold for hours now!

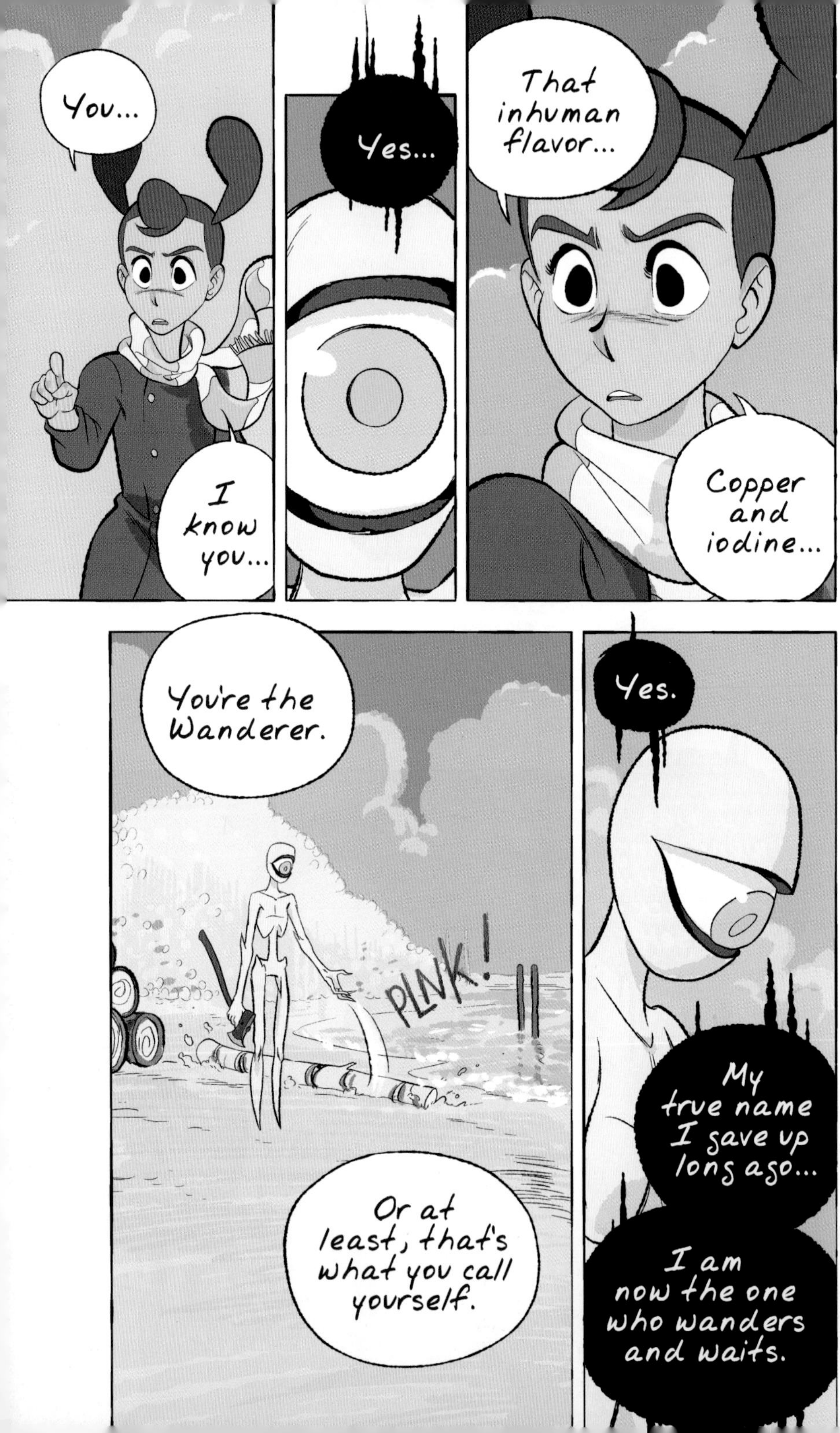
You...
Yes...
That inhuman flavor...
I know you...
Copper and iodine...
You're the Wanderer.
PLINK!
Or at least, that's what you call yourself.
Yes.
My true name I gave up long ago...
I am now the one who wanders and waits.

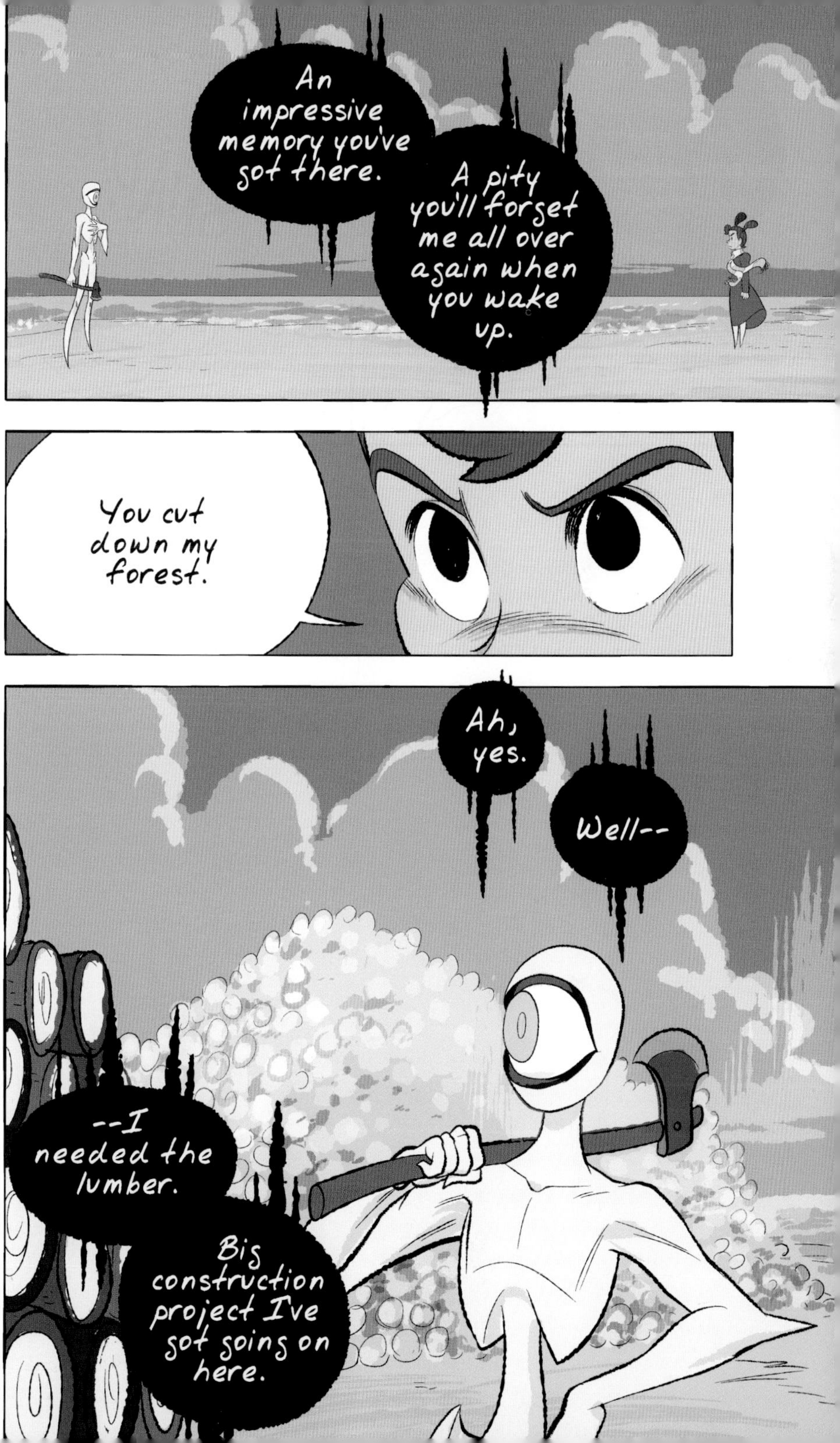
An impressive memory you've got there.
A pity you'll forget me all over again when you wake up.
You cut down my forest.
Ah, yes.
Well--
--I needed the lumber.
Big construction project I've got going on here.

But let's not worry about all that.

SNAP!

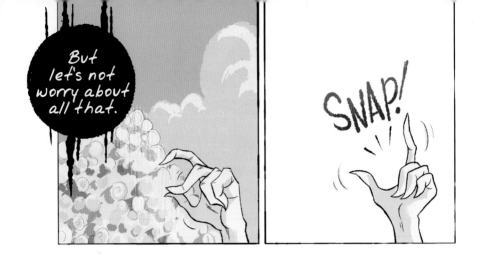

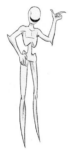

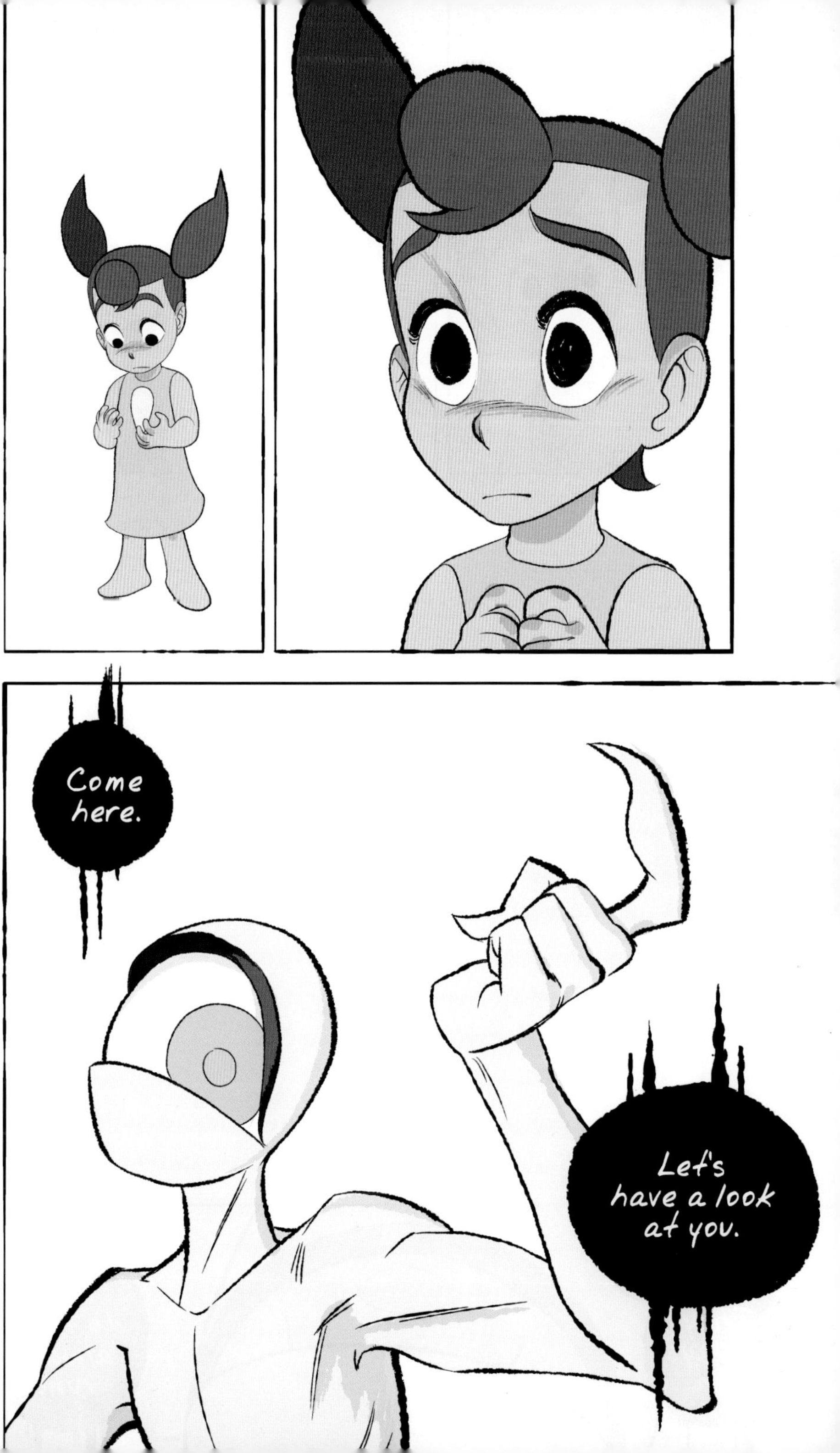
Come here.
Let's have a look at you.

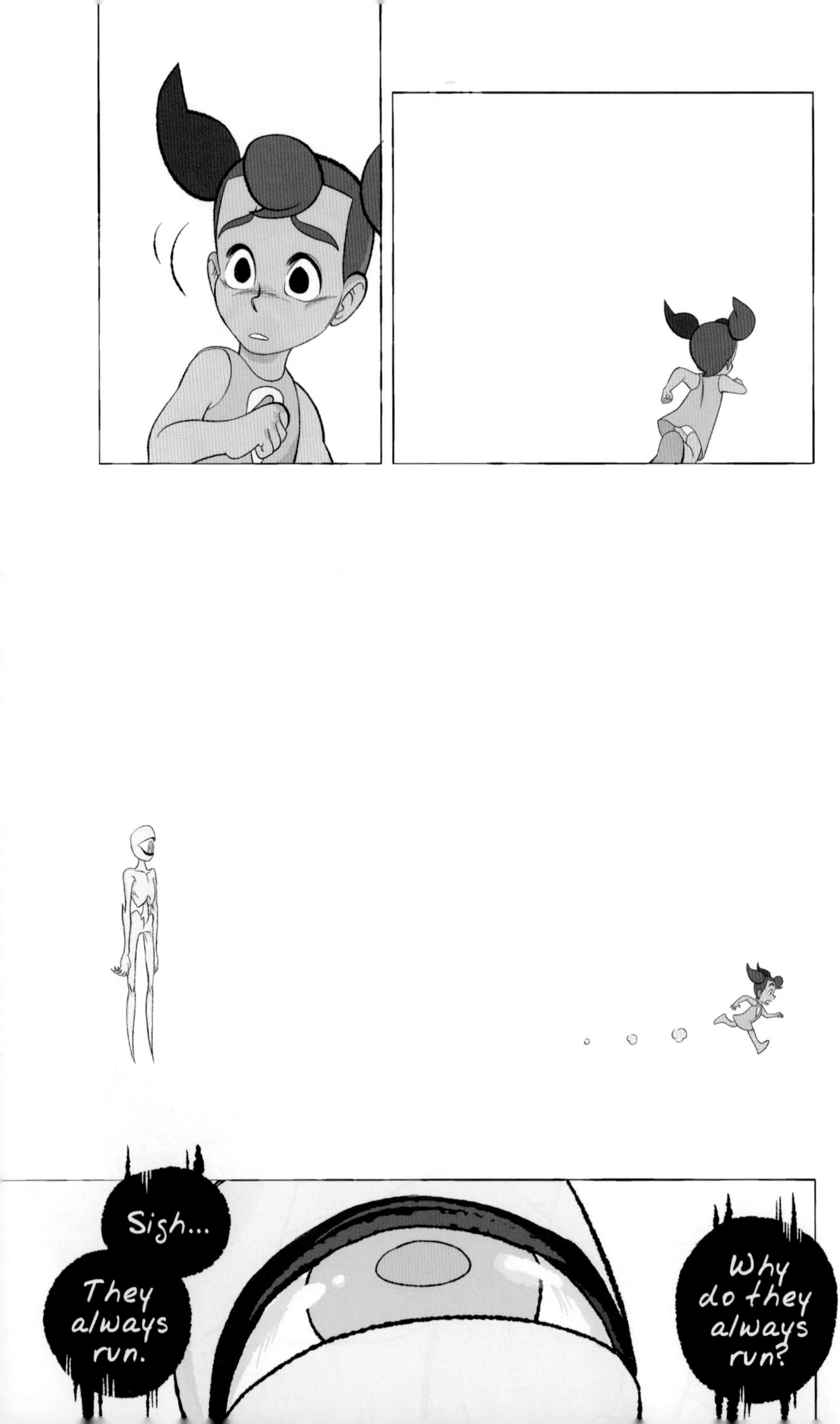
Sigh...
They always run.
Why do they always run?

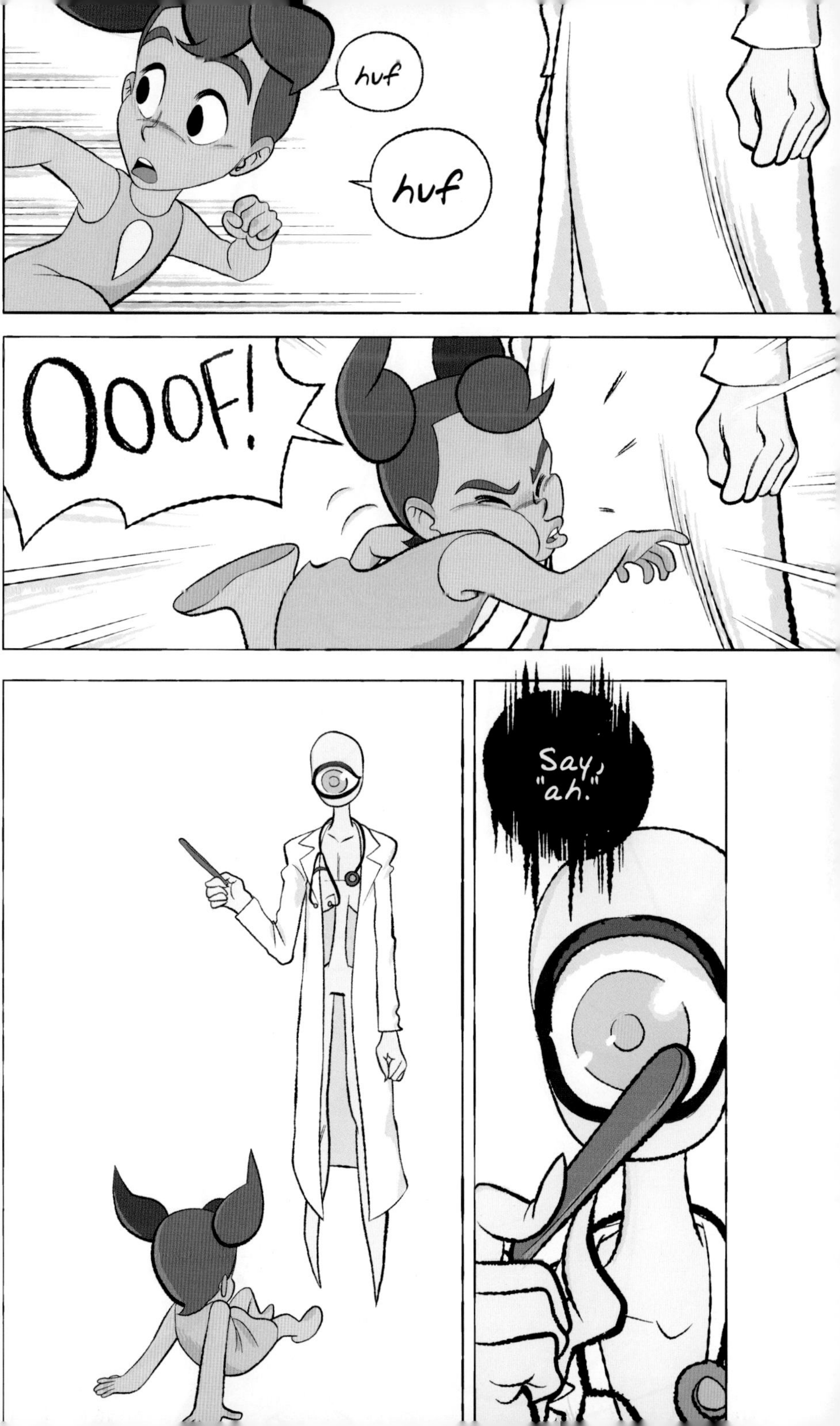
huf
huf
OOOF!
Say, "ah."

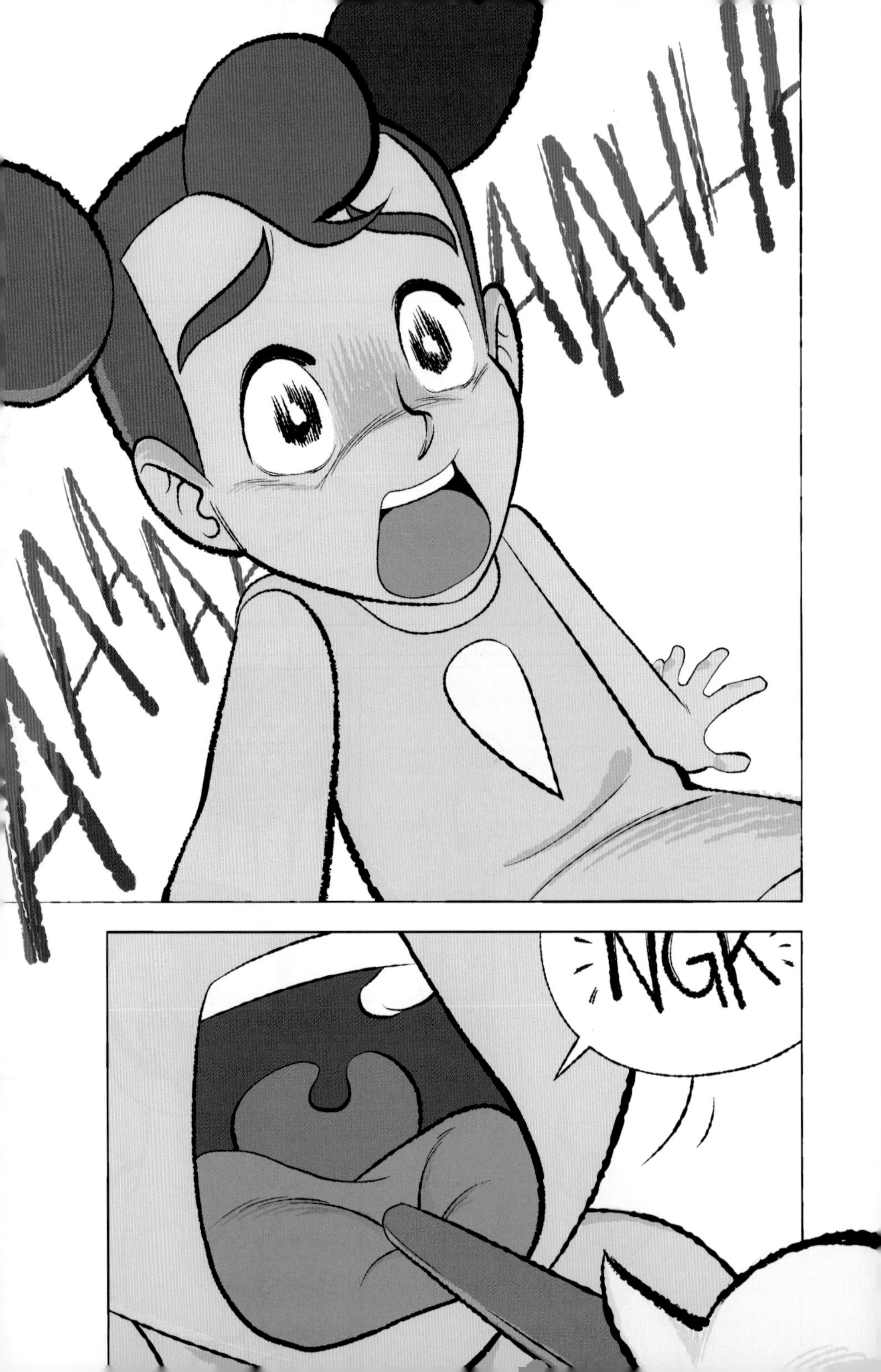
AAAAAAHHH
NGK

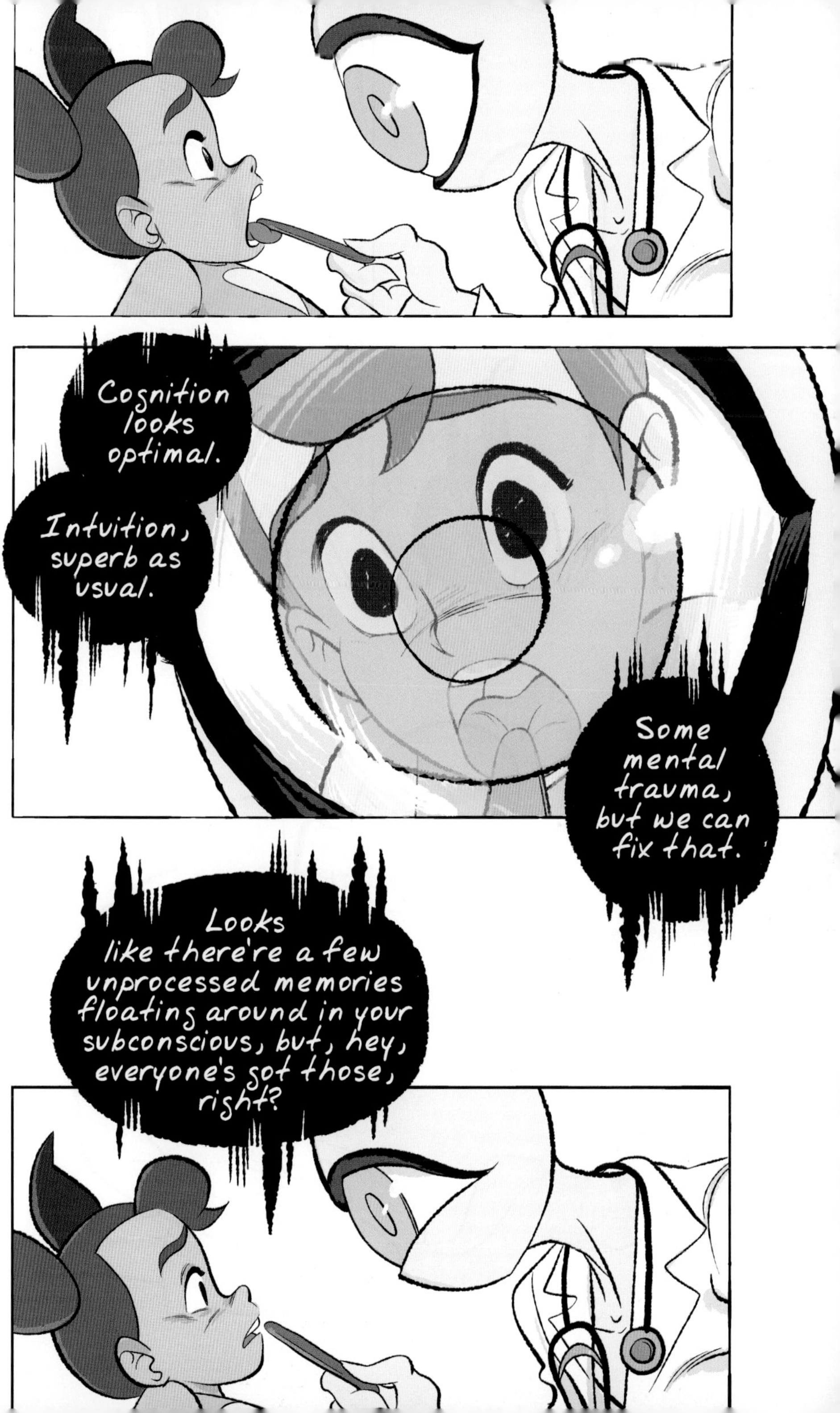
Cognition looks optimal.
Intuition, superb as usual.
Some mental trauma, but we can fix that.
Looks like there're a few unprocessed memories floating around in your subconscious, but, hey, everyone's got those, right?

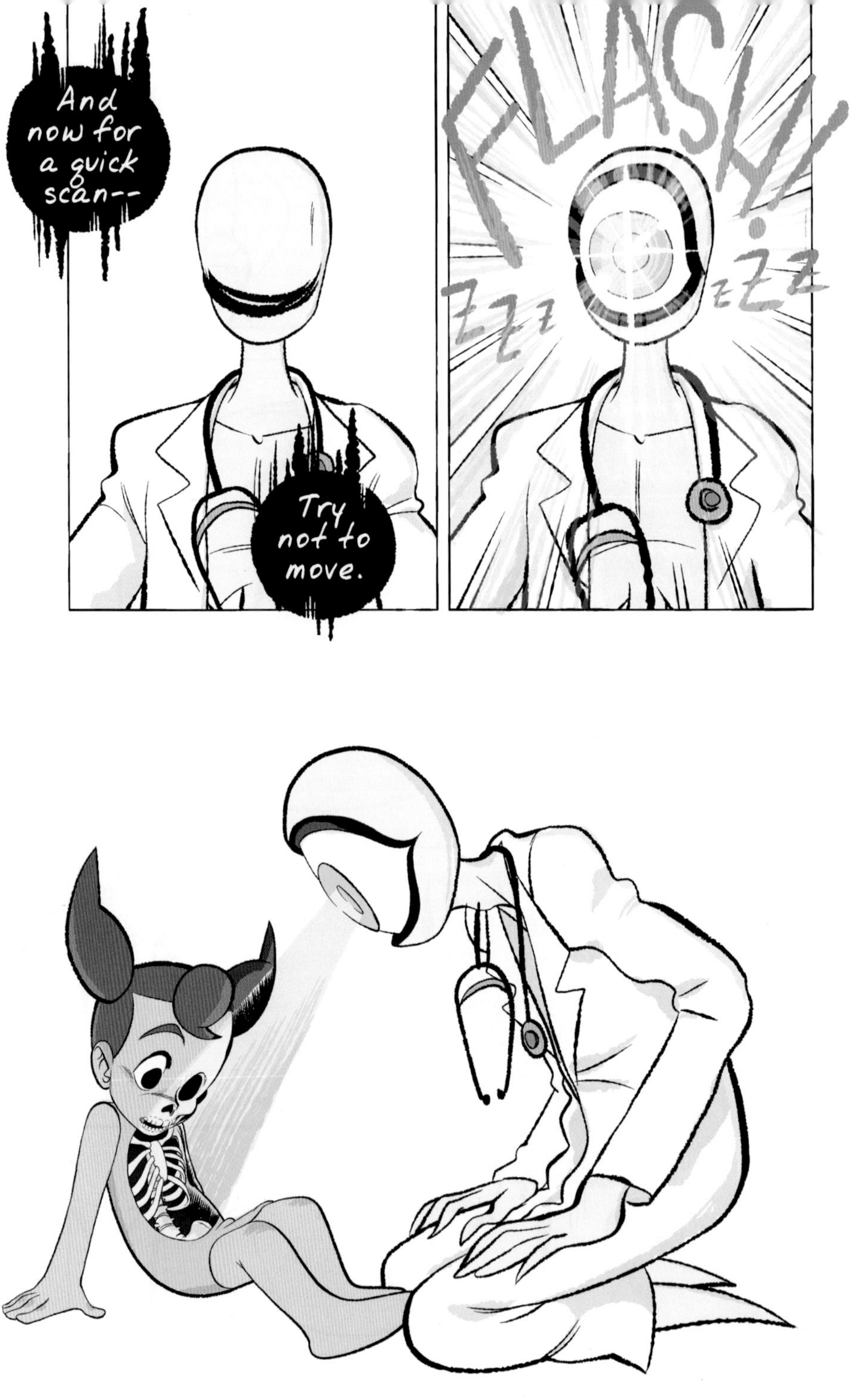

And now for a quick scan--
Try not to move.
FLASH!
ZZZ
zZZZ

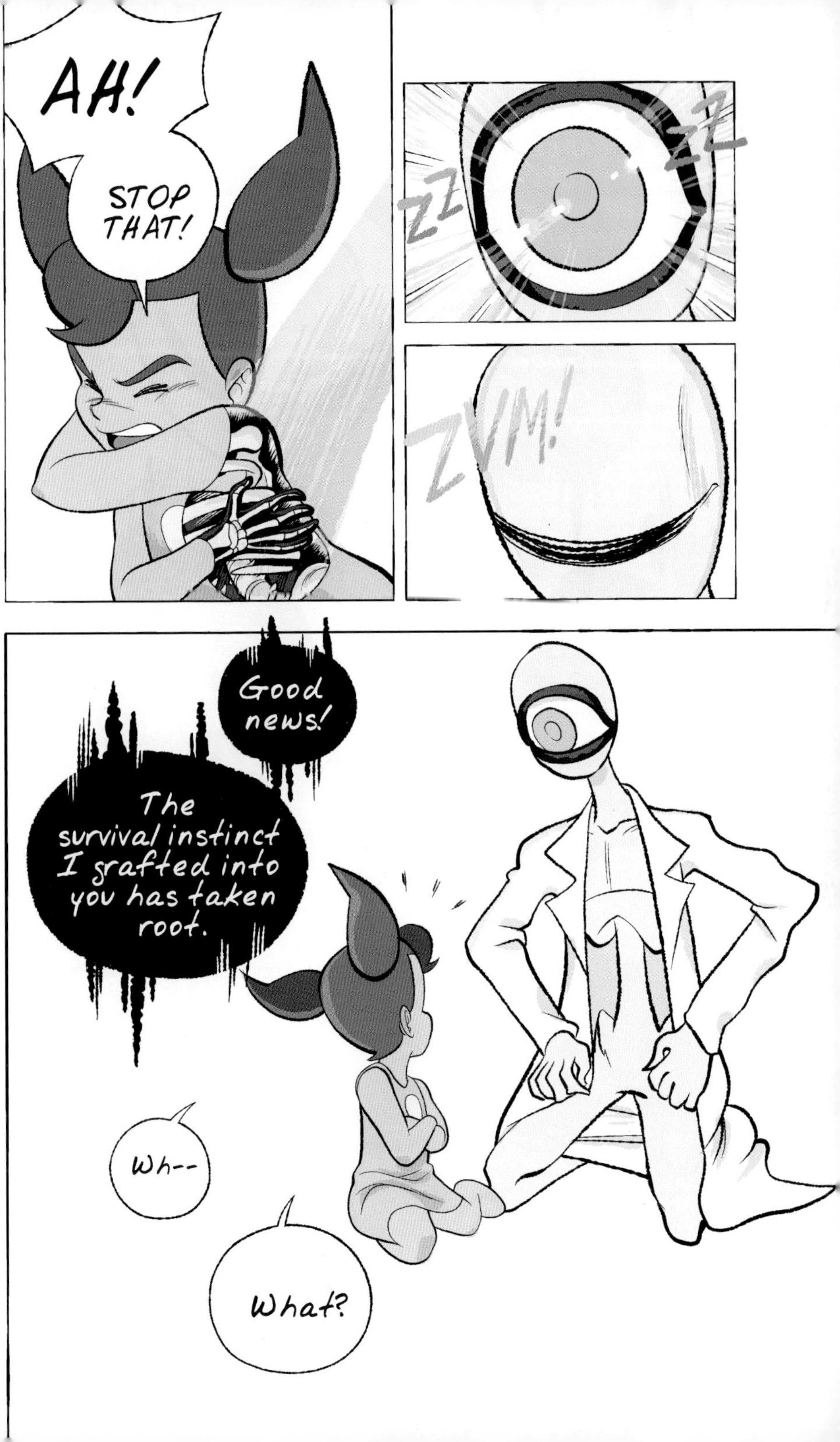
AH!
STOP THAT!
ZZ
ZZ
ZVM!
Good news!
The survival instinct I grafted into you has taken root.
Wh--
What?

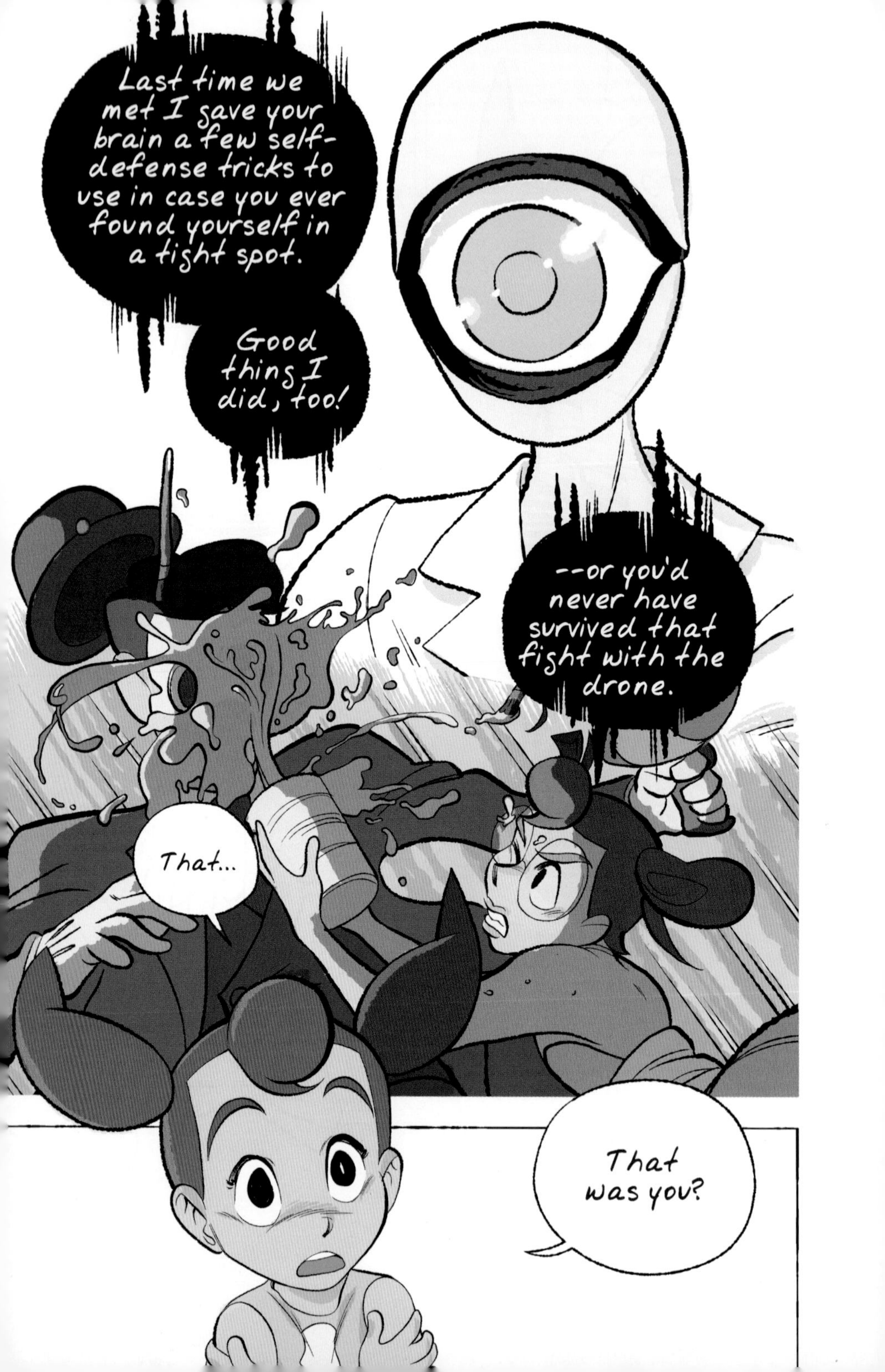
Last time we met I gave your brain a few self-defense tricks to use in case you ever found yourself in a tight spot.
Good thing I did, too!
--or you'd never have survived that fight with the drone.
That...
That was you?

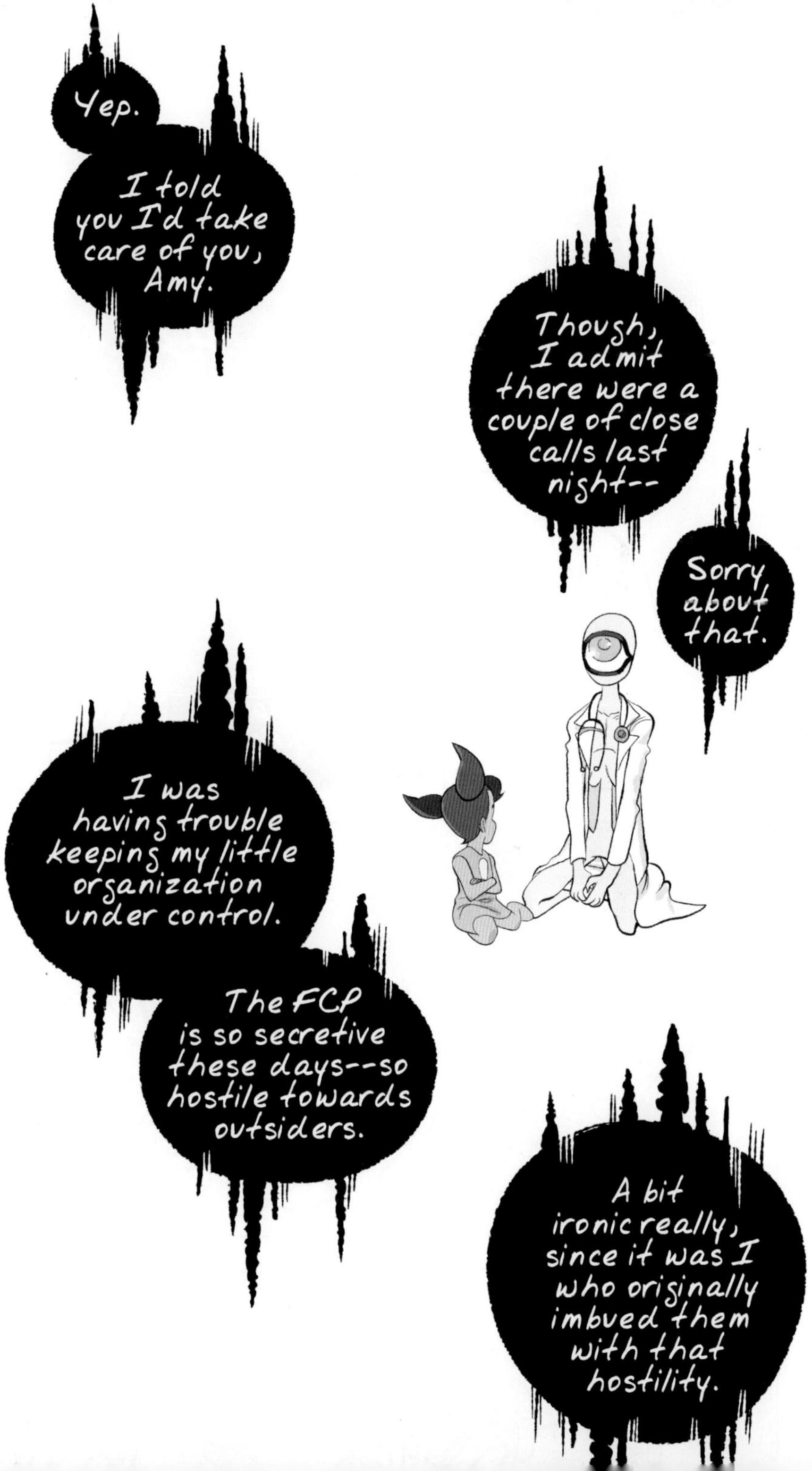
Yep.
I told you I'd take care of you, Amy.
Though, I admit there were a couple of close calls last night--
Sorry about that.
I was having trouble keeping my little organization under control.
The FCP is so secretive these days--so hostile towards outsiders.
A bit ironic really, since it was I who originally imbued them with that hostility.

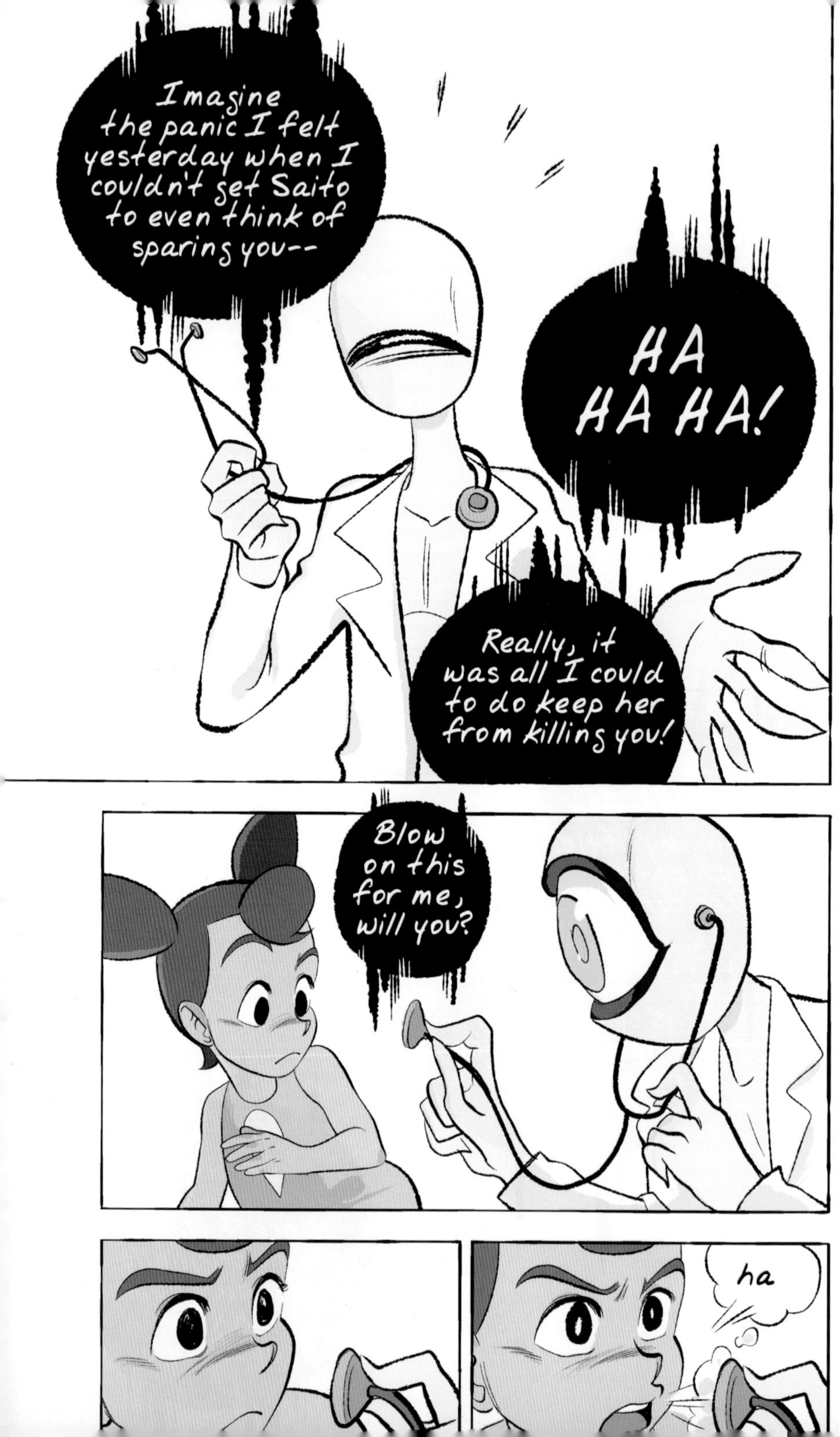
Imagine the panic I felt yesterday when I couldn't get Saito to even think of sparing you--
HA HA HA HA!
Really, it was all I could to do keep her from killing you!
Blow on this for me, will you?
ha

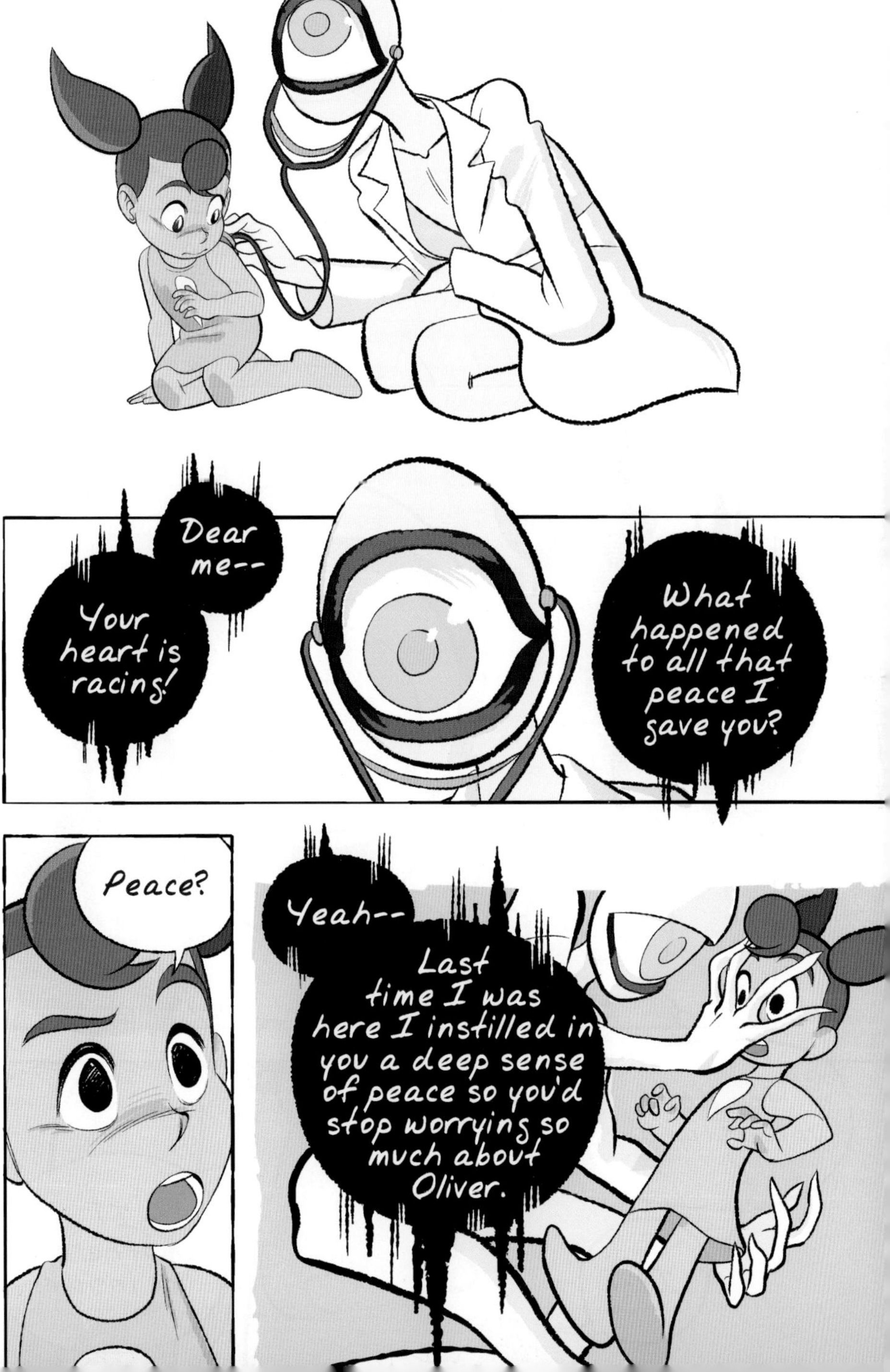
Dear me--
Your heart is racing!
What happened to all that peace I gave you?
Peace?
Yeah--
Last time I was here I instilled in you a deep sense of peace so you'd stop worrying so much about Oliver.

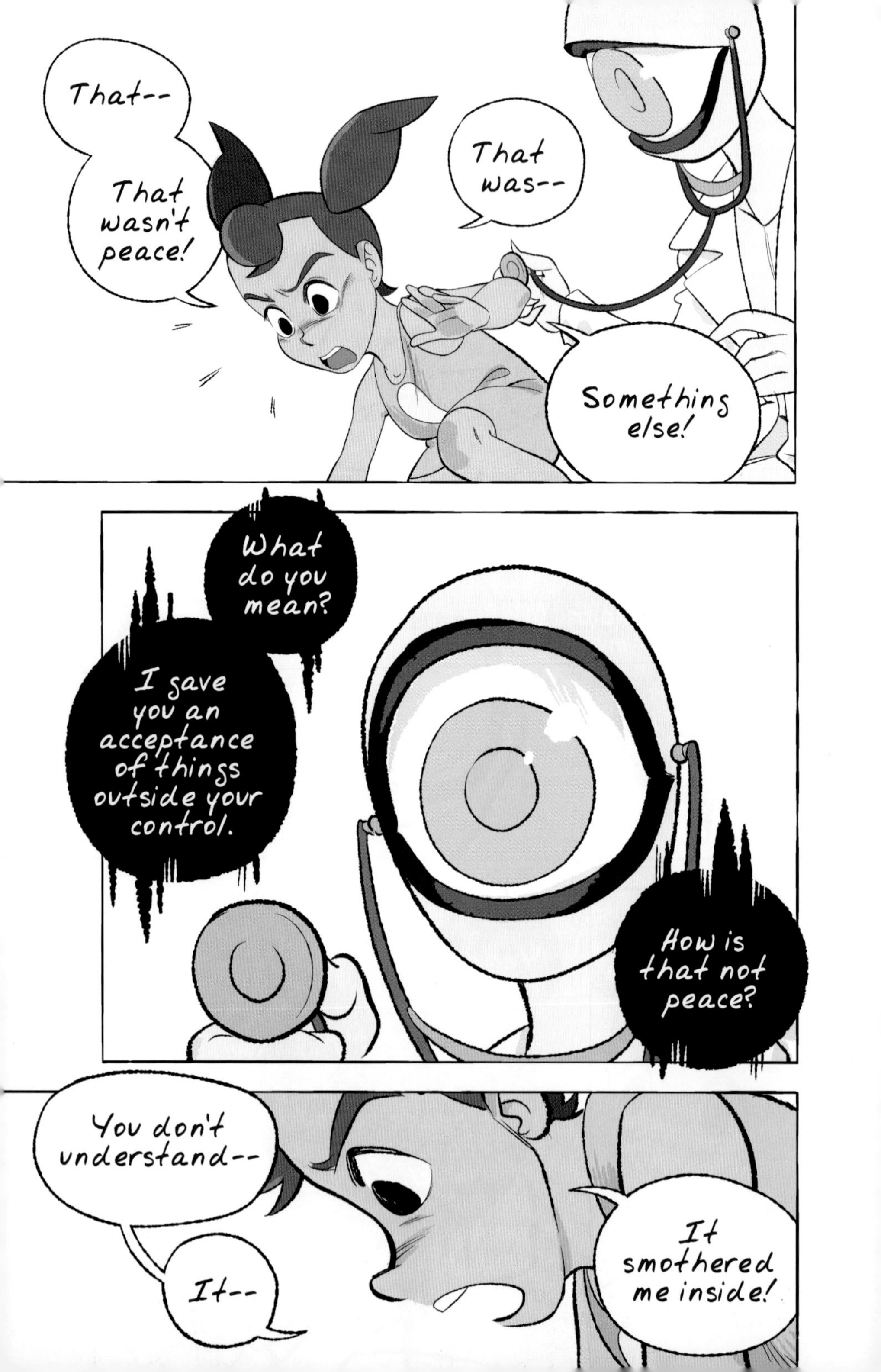
That--
That wasn't peace!
That was--
Something else!
What do you mean?
I gave you an acceptance of things outside your control.
How is that not peace?
You don't understand--
It--
It smothered me inside!

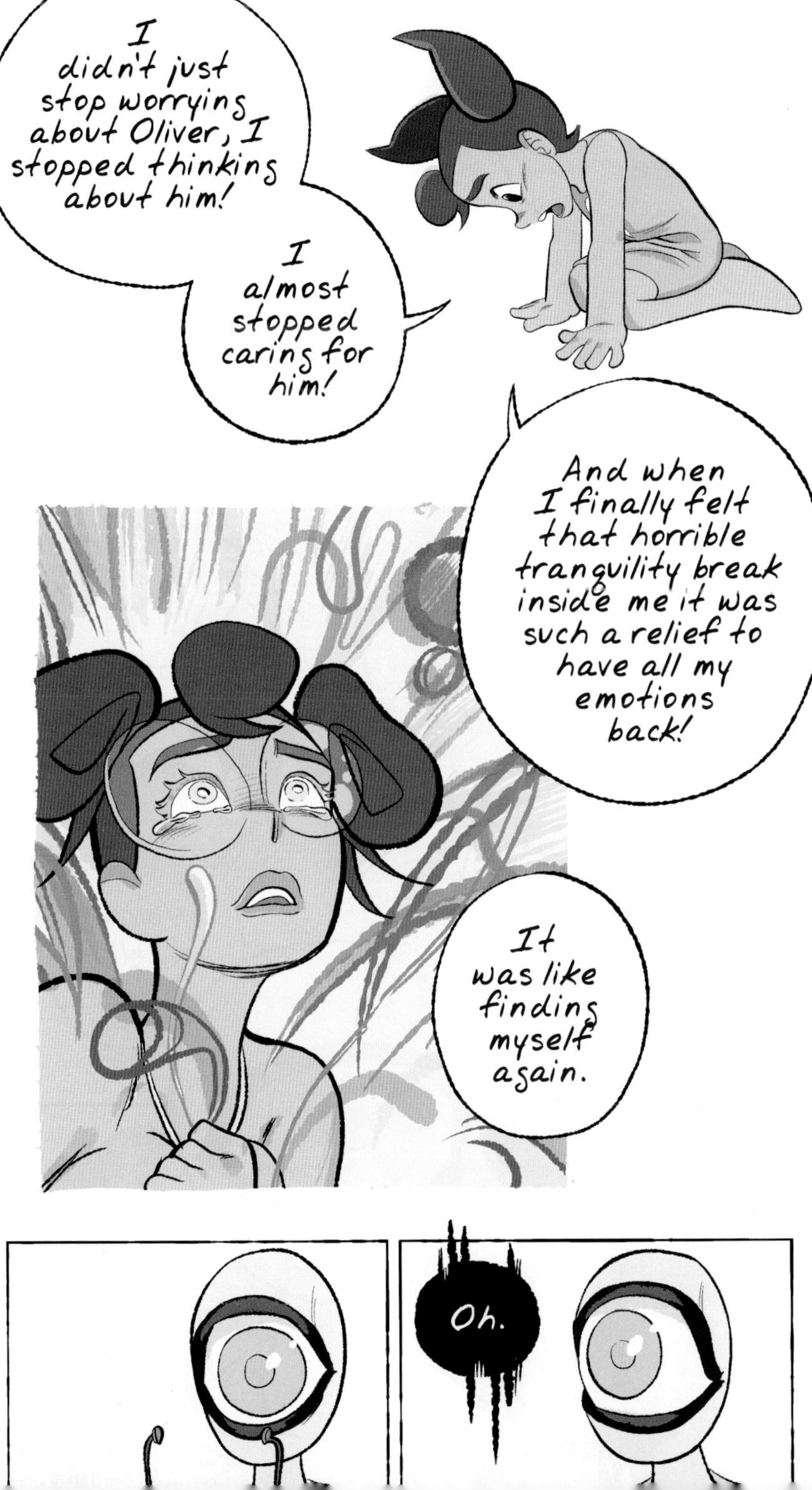
I didn't just stop worrying about Oliver, I stopped thinking about him!
I almost stopped caring for him!
And when I finally felt that horrible tranquility break inside me it was such a relief to have all my emotions back!
It was like finding myself again.
Oh.

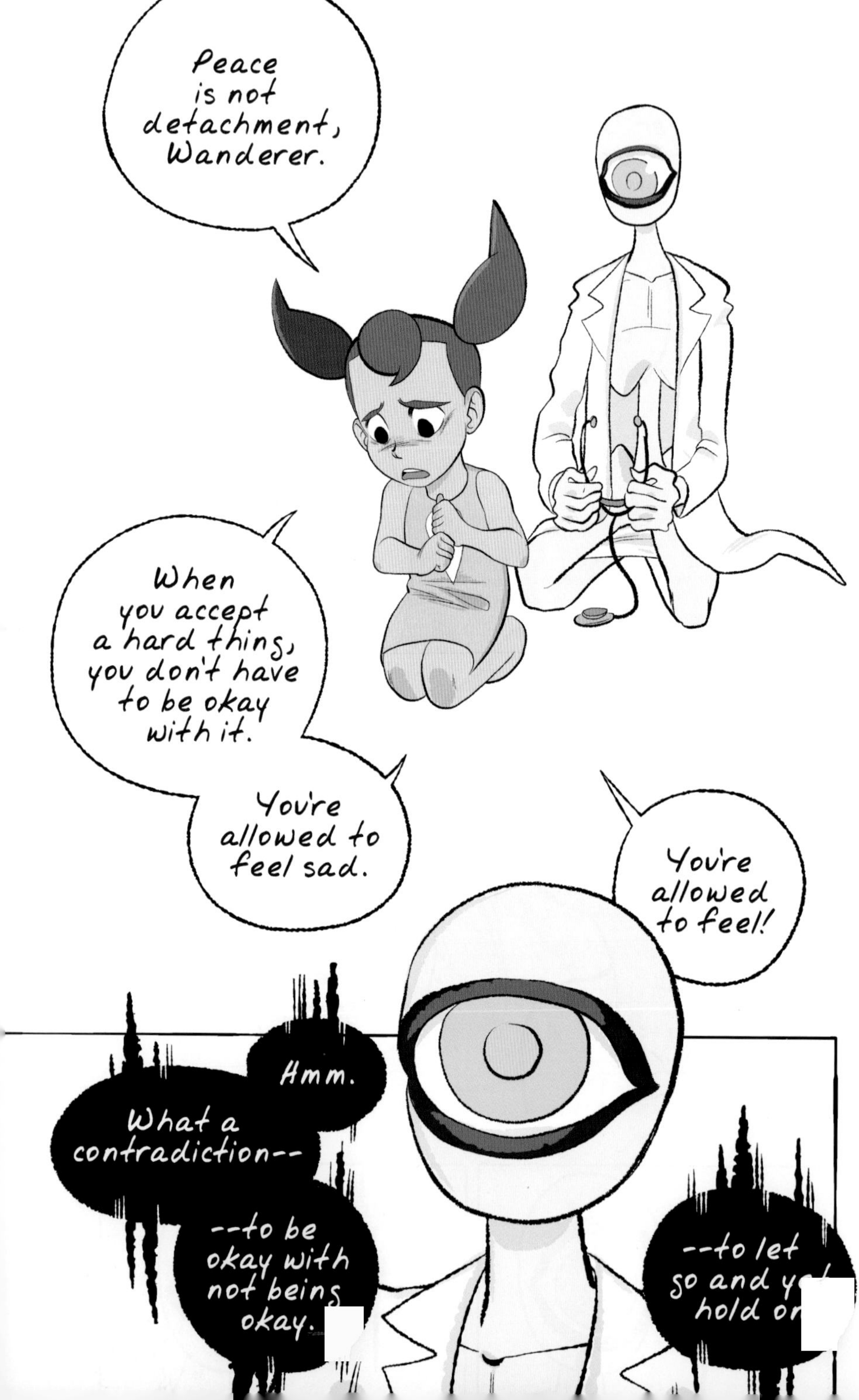
Peace is not detachment, Wanderer.
When you accept a hard thing, you don't have to be okay with it.
You're allowed to feel sad.
You're allowed to feel!
Hmm.
What a contradiction--
--to be okay with not being okay.
--to let go and y
hold o

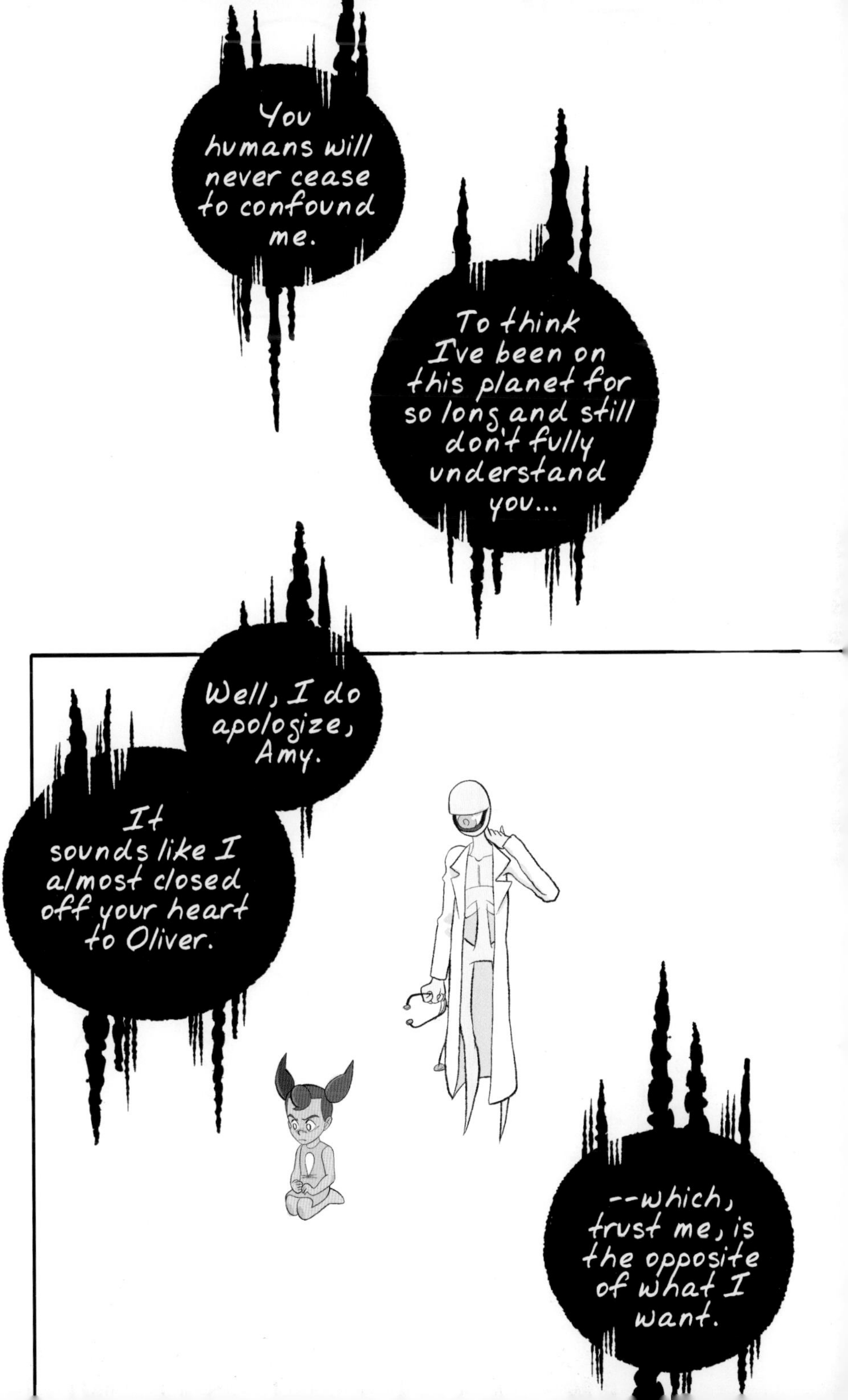
You humans will never cease to confound me.
To think I've been on this planet for so long and still don't fully understand you...
Well, I do apologize, Amy.
It sounds like I almost closed off your heart to Oliver.
--which, trust me, is the opposite of what I want.

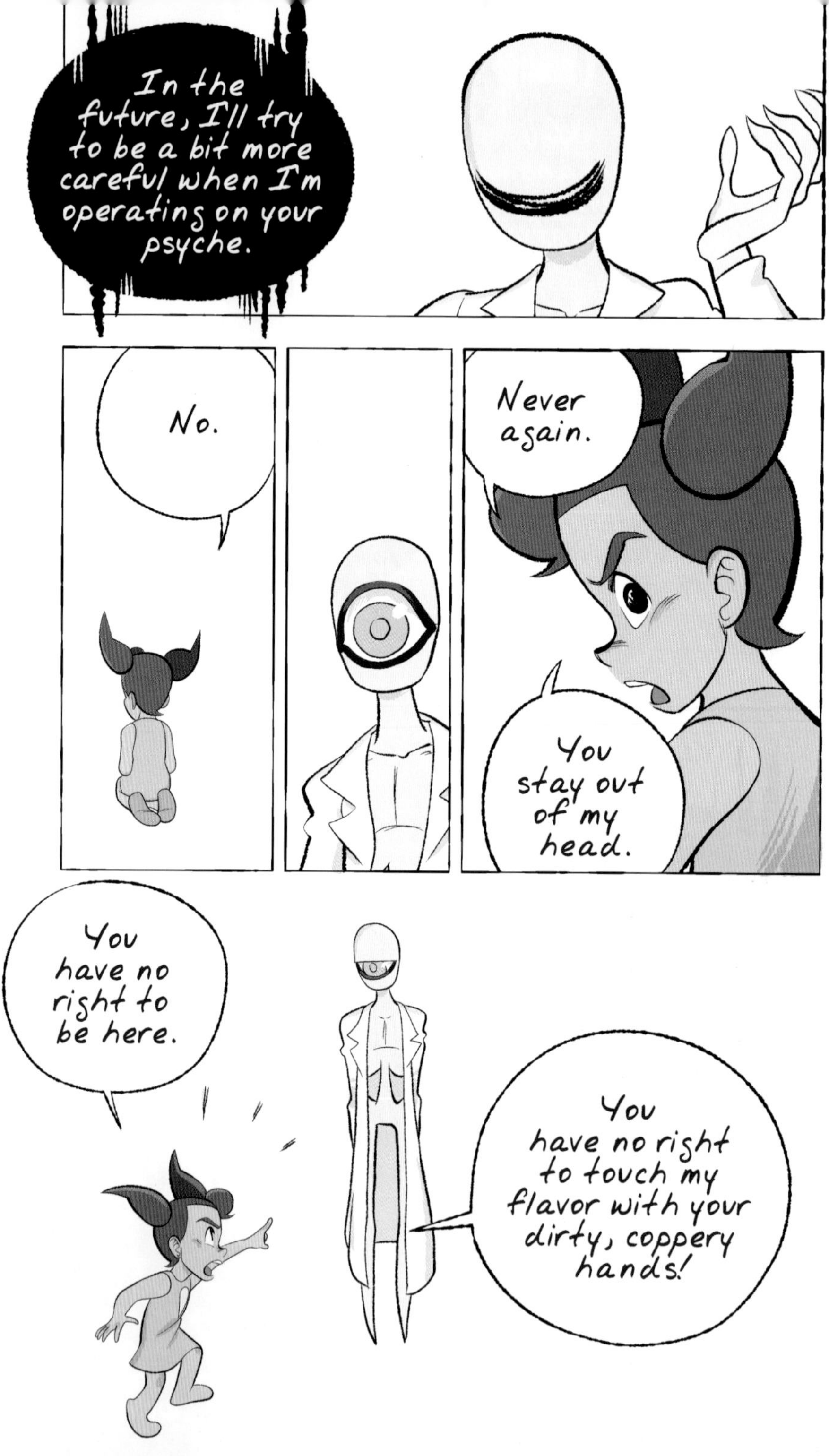
In the future, I'll try to be a bit more careful when I'm operating on your psyche.
No.
Never again.
You stay out of my head.
You have no right to be here.
You have no right to touch my flavor with your dirty, coppery hands!

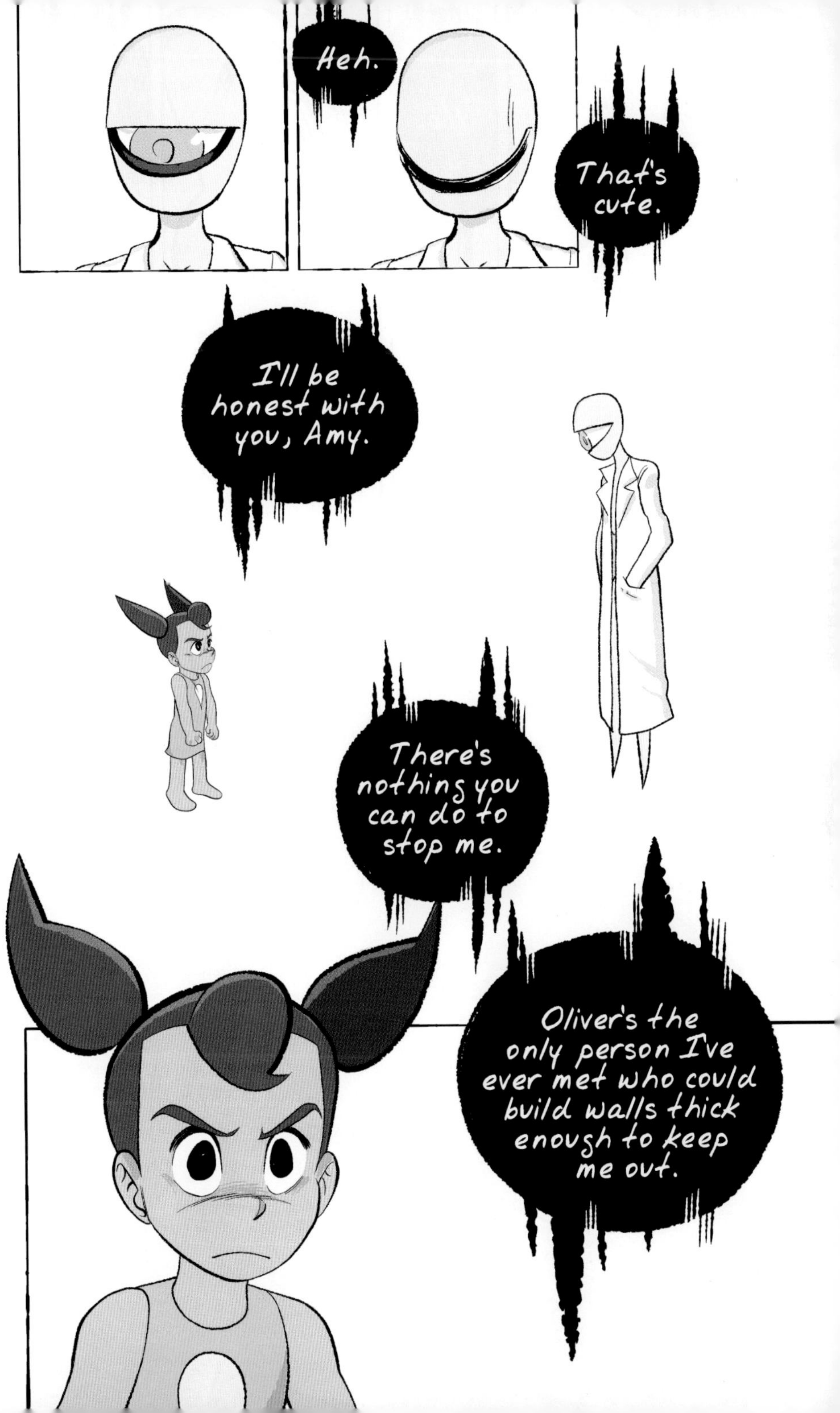
Heh.
That's cute.
I'll be honest with you, Amy.
There's nothing you can do to stop me.
Oliver's the only person Ive ever met who could build walls thick enough to keep me out.

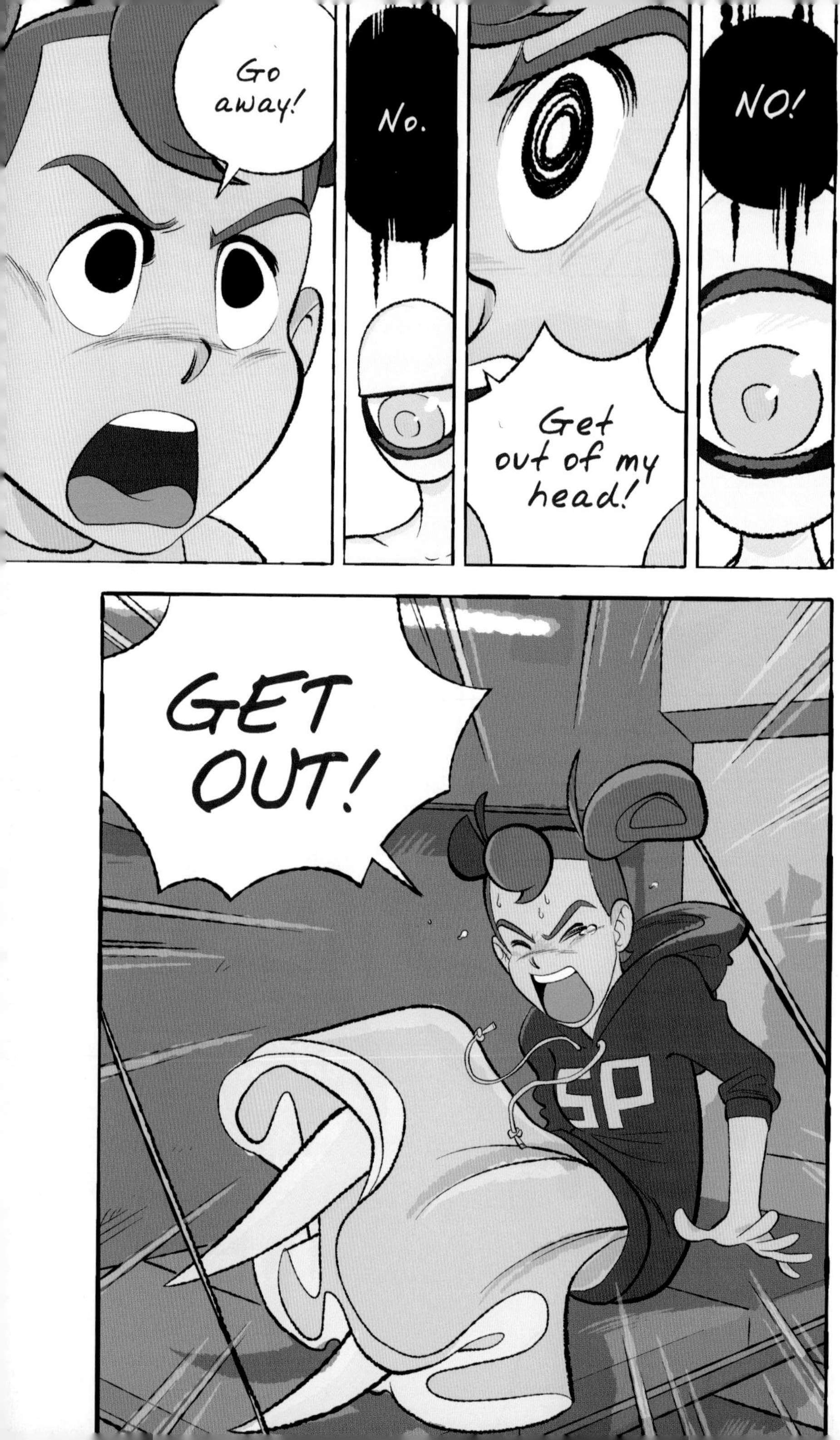
Go away!
No.
Get out of my head!
NO!
GET OUT!
SP

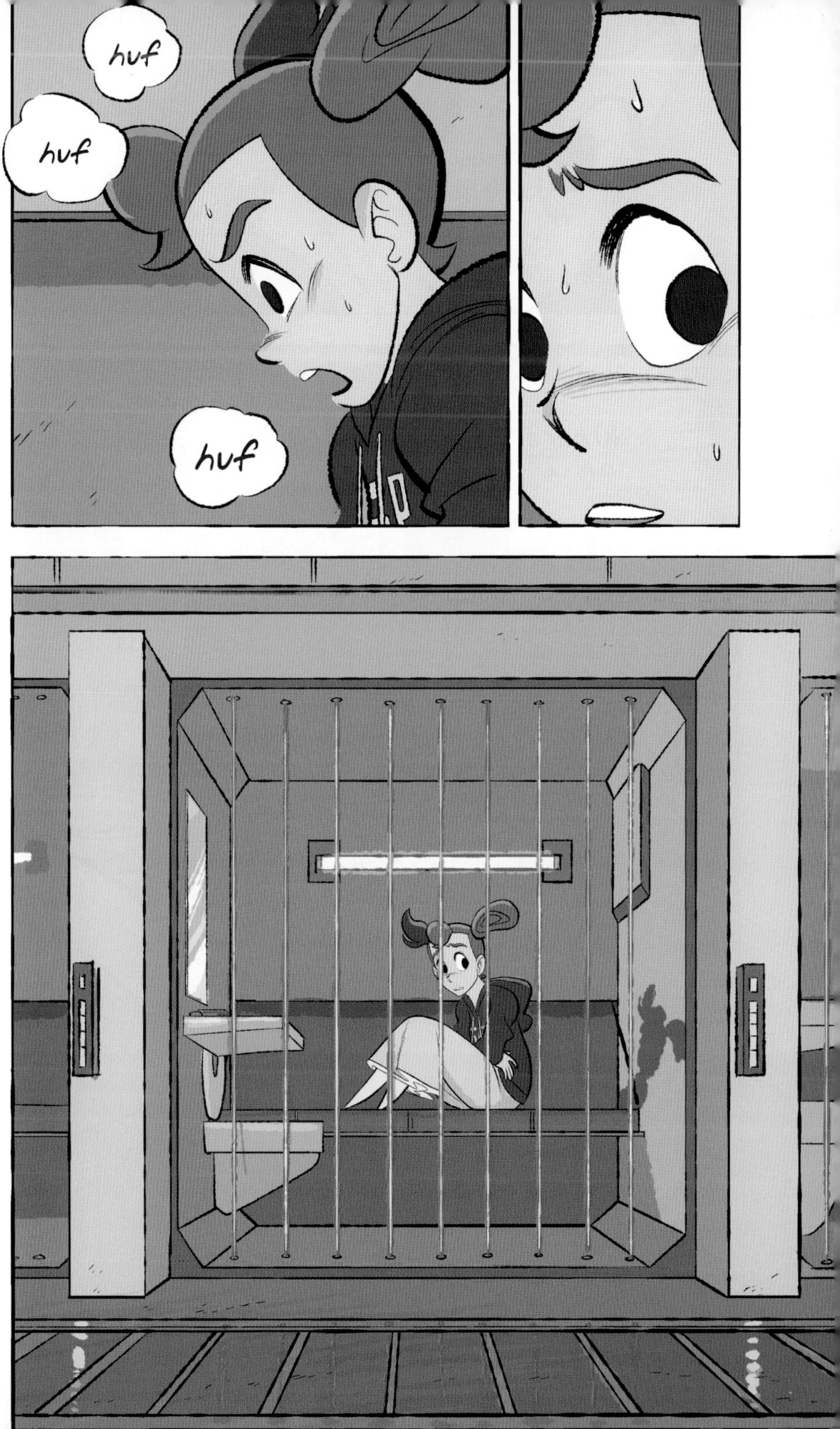
huf
huf
huf

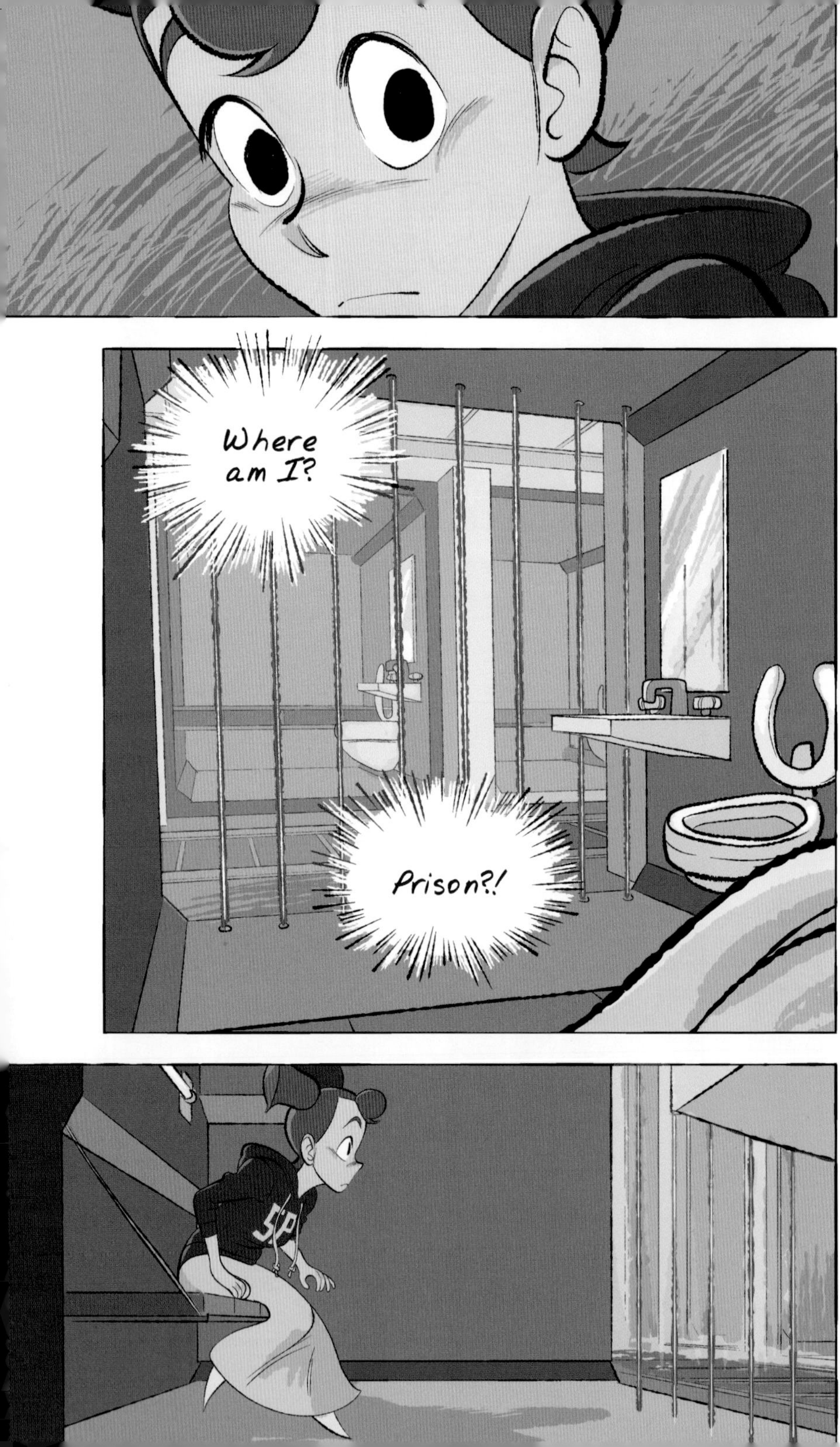
Where am I?
Prison?!

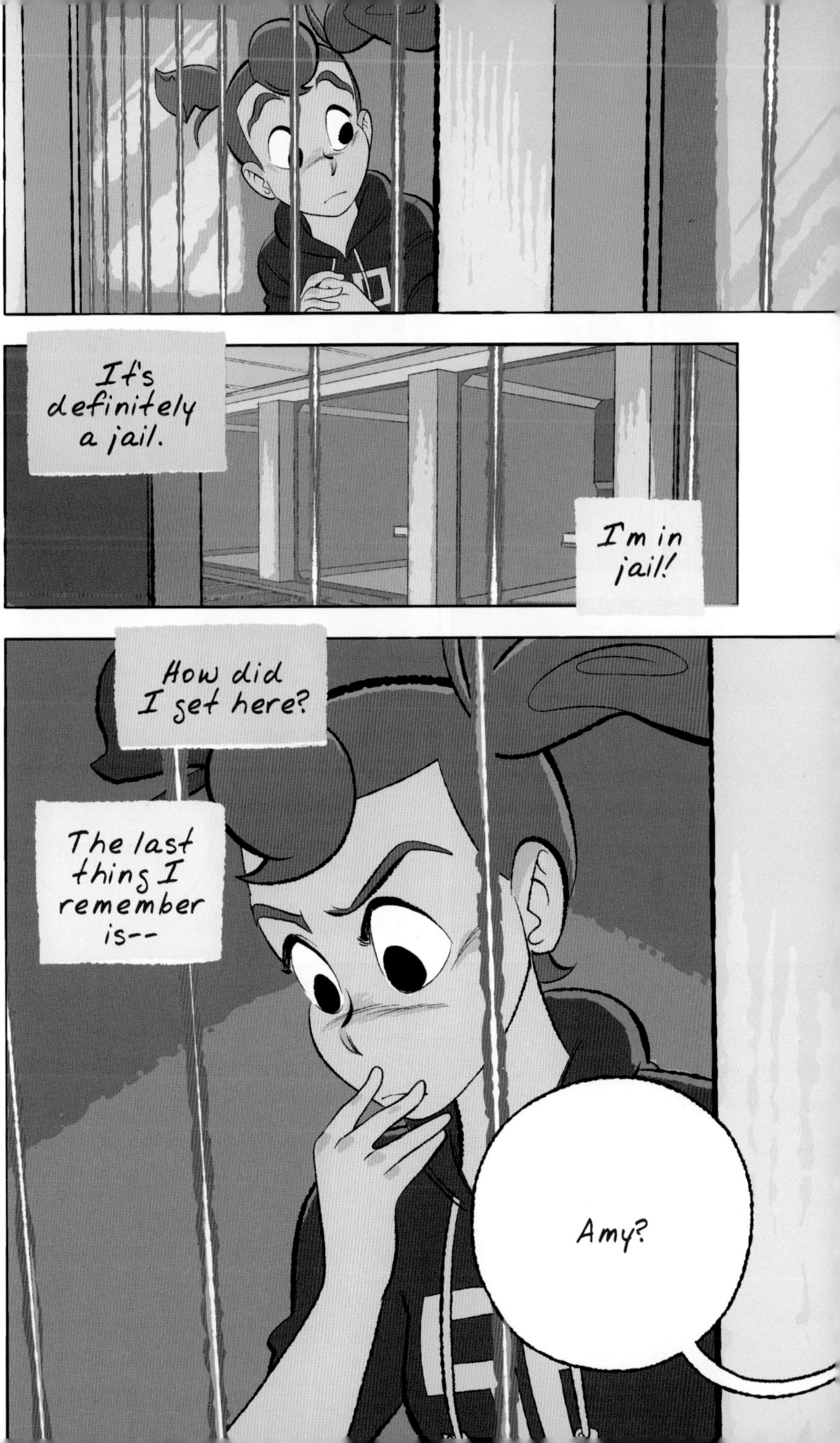
It's definitely a jail.
I'm in jail!
How did I get here?
The last thing I remember is--
Amy?

Amy?

Is that you?

That voice...

T--

Tamara?

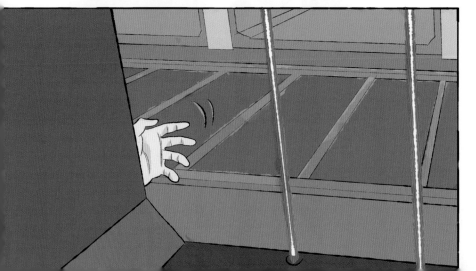

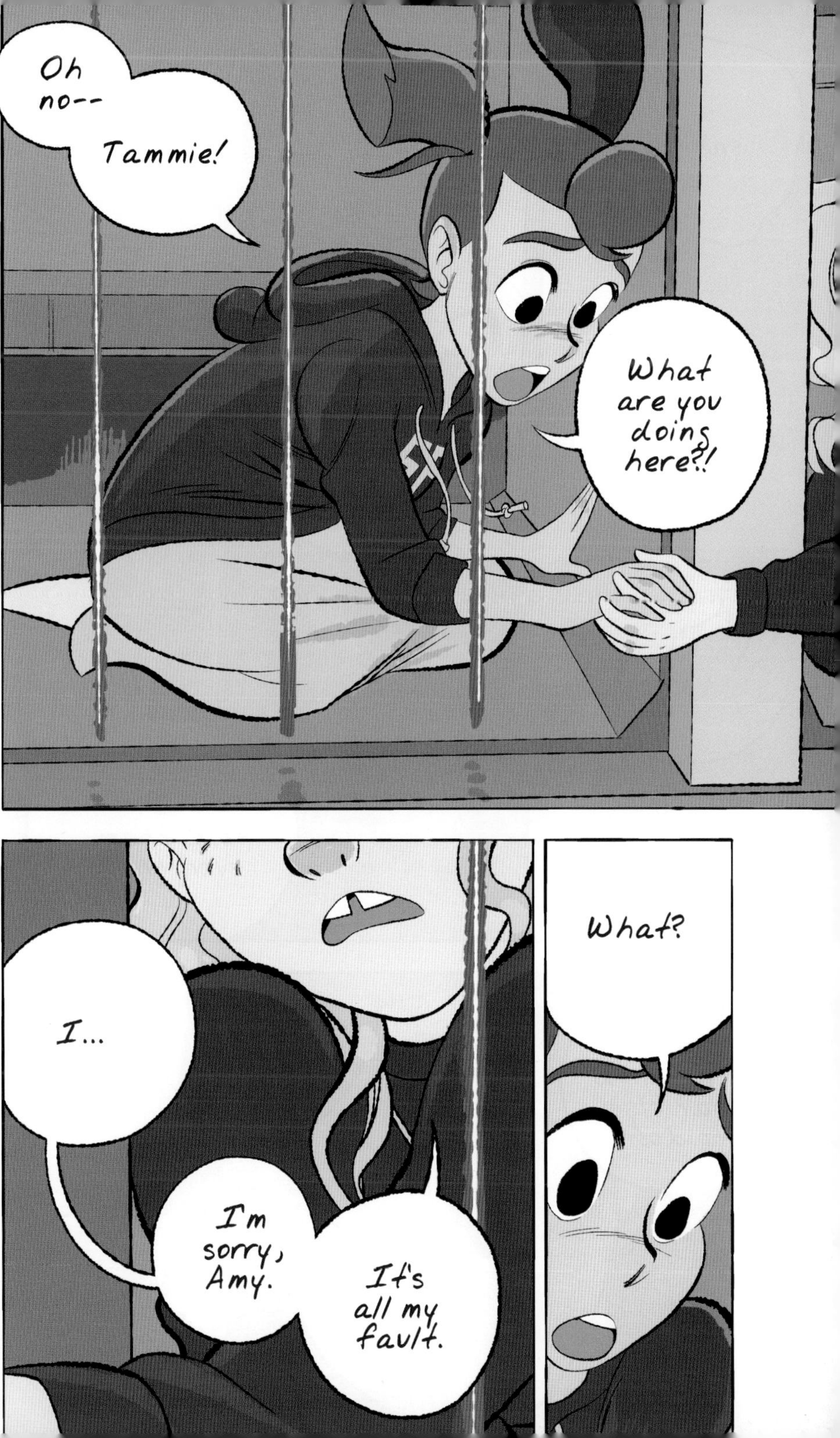
Oh no-- Tammie!
What are you doing here?!
I...
I'm sorry, Amy.
It's all my fault.
What?

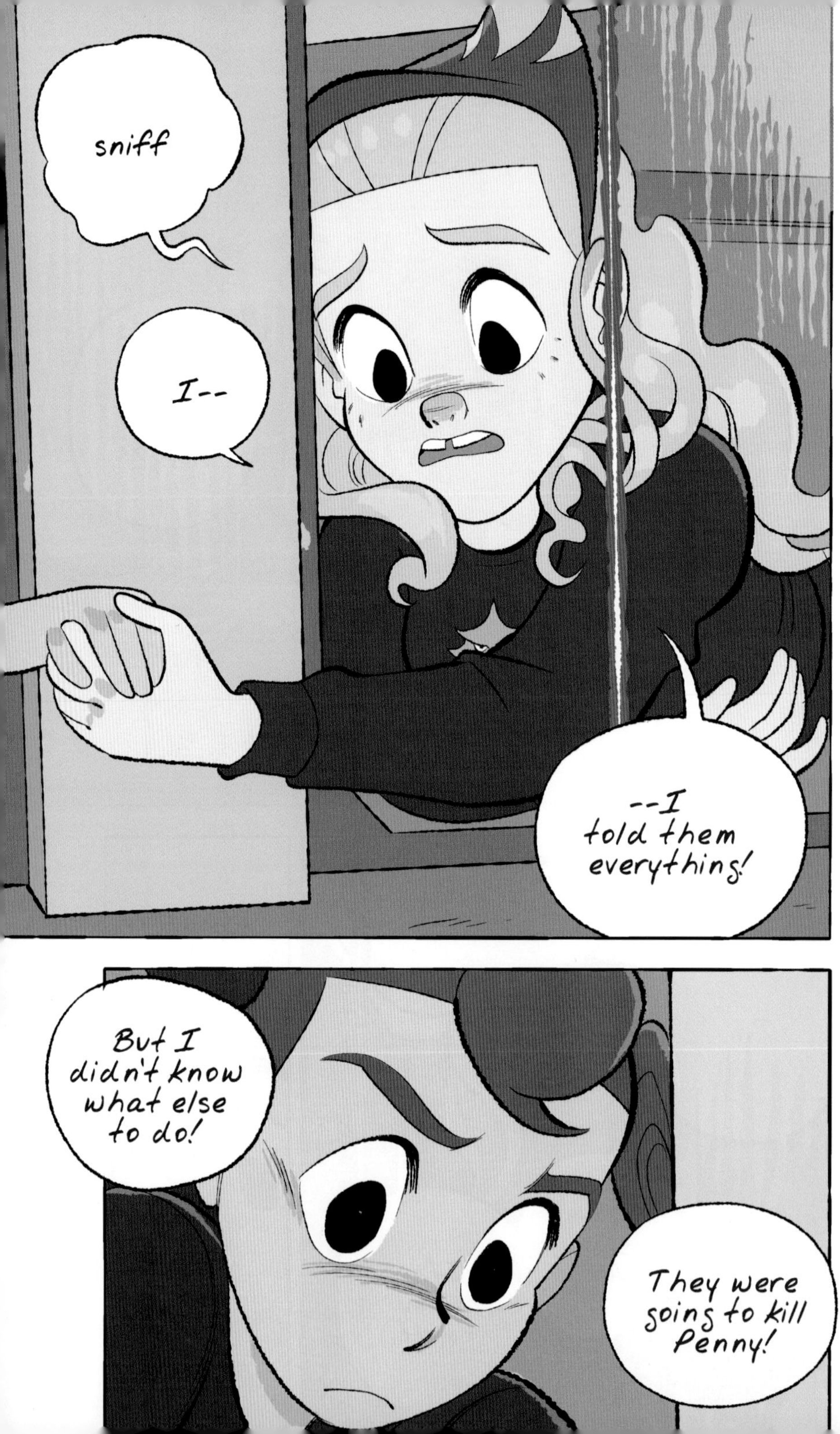
sniff
I--
--I told them everything!
But I didn't know what else to do!
They were going to kill Penny!

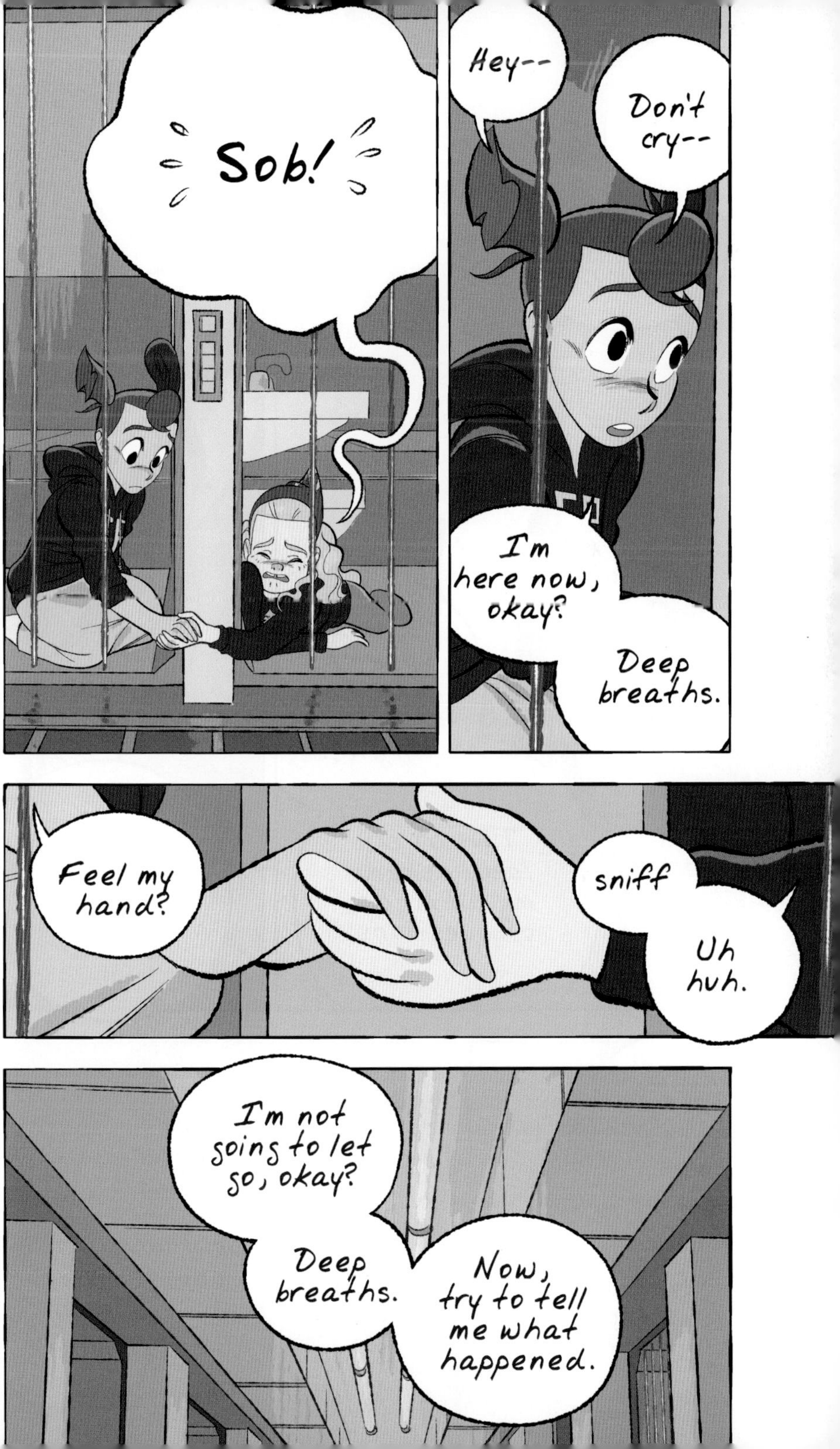
Sob!
Hey--
Don't cry--
I'm here now, okay?
Deep breaths.
Feel my hand?
sniff
Uh huh.
I'm not going to let go, okay?
Deep breaths.
Now, try to tell me what happened.

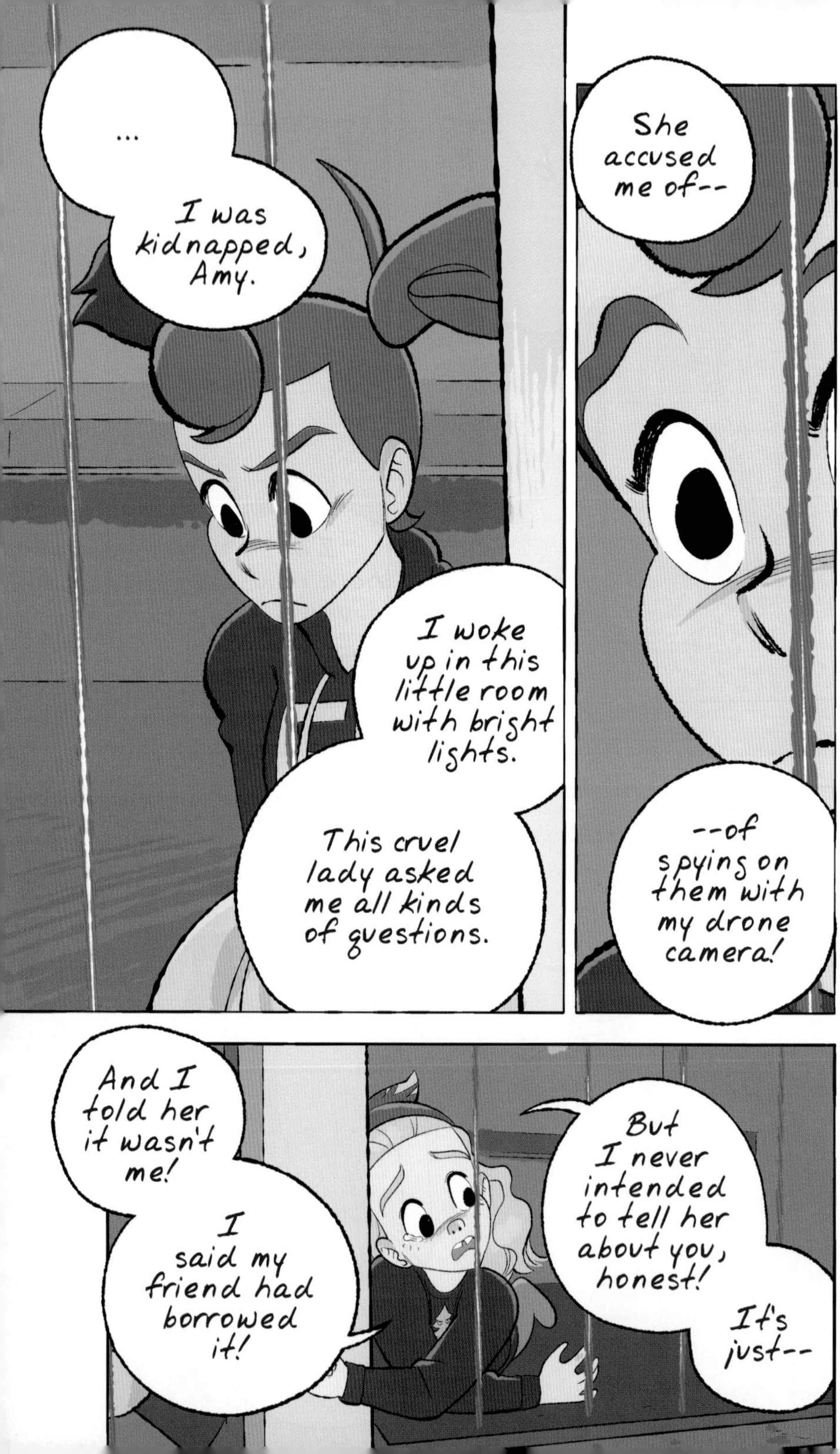
...
I was kidnapped, Amy.
She accused me of--
I woke up in this little room with bright lights.
This cruel lady asked me all kinds of questions.
--of spying on them with my drone camera!
And I told her it wasn't me!
I said my friend had borrowed it!
But I never intended to tell her about you, honest!
It's just--

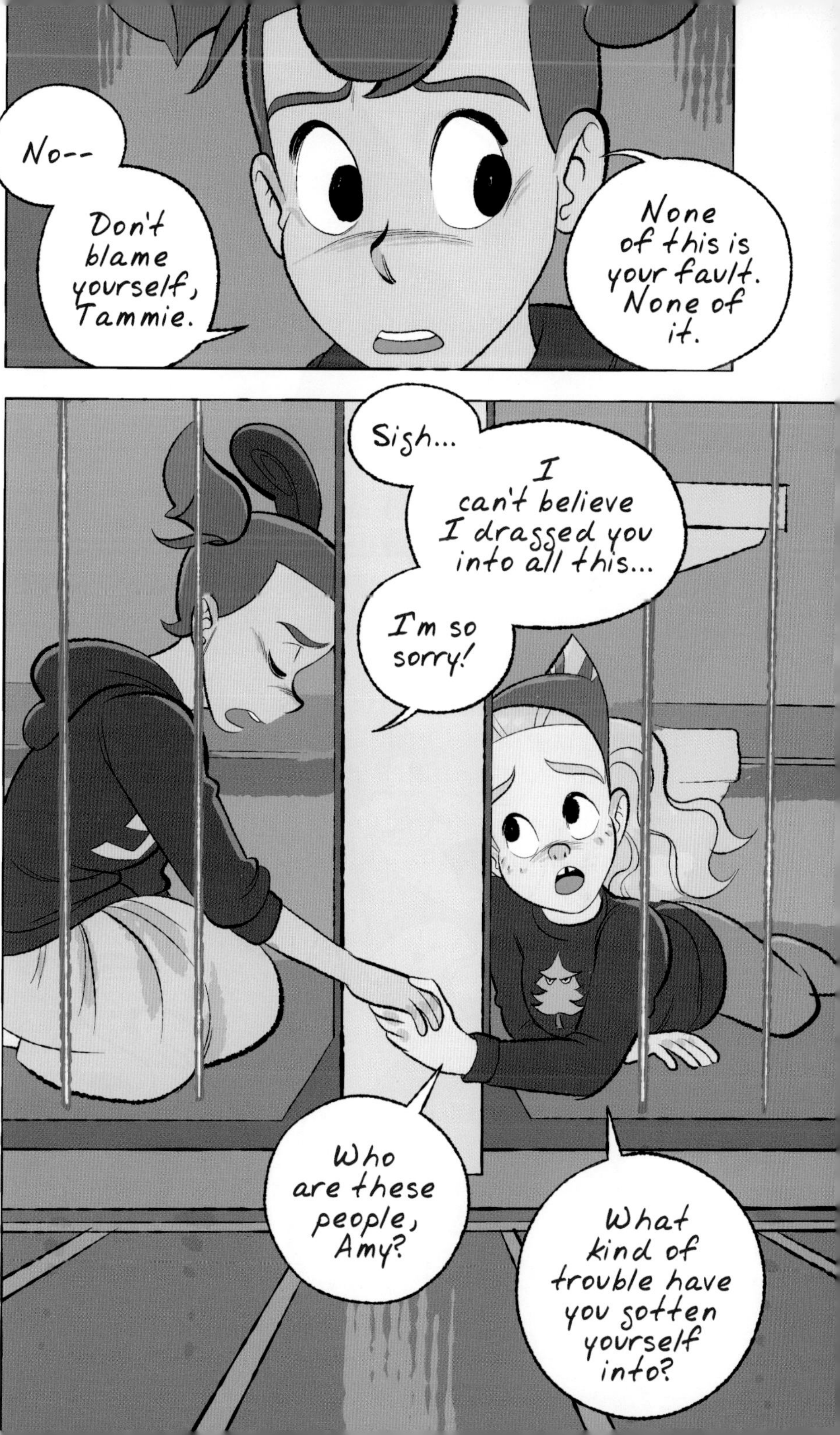
No--
Don't blame yourself, Tammie.
None of this is your fault. None of it.
Sigh...
I can't believe I dragged you into all this...
I'm so sorry!
Who are these people, Amy?
What kind of trouble have you gotten yourself into?

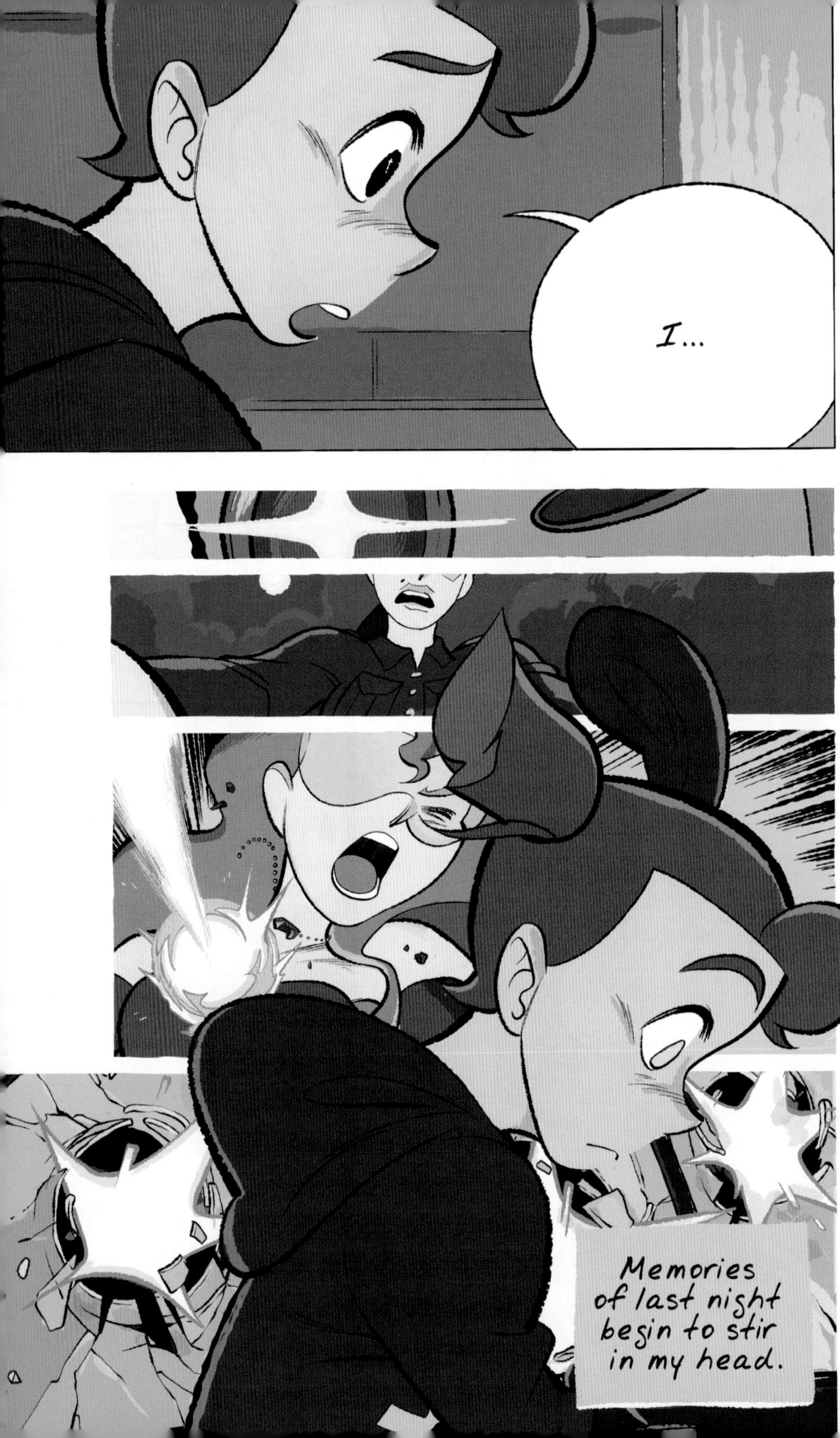
I...
Memories of last night begin to stir in my head.

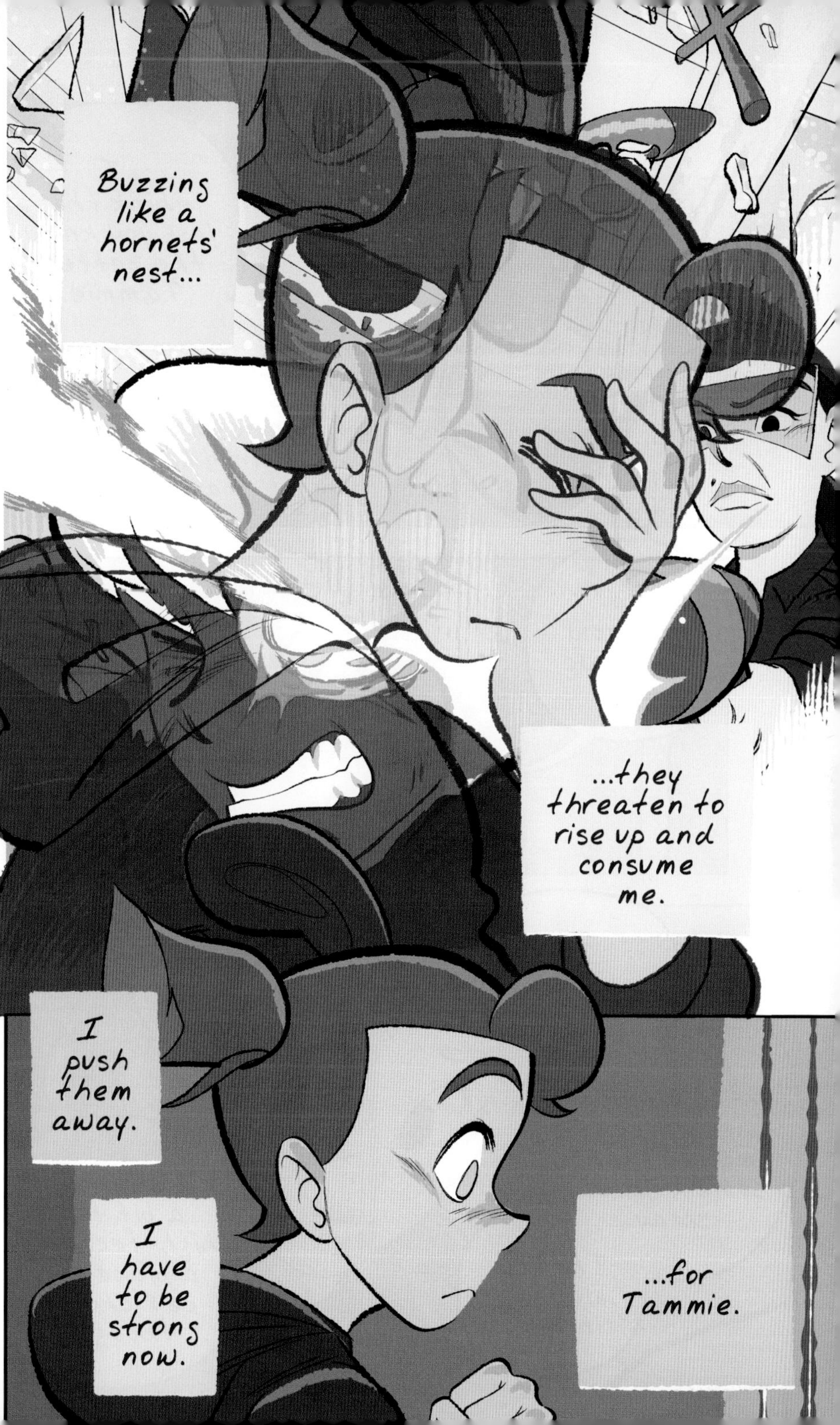
Buzzing like a hornets' nest...
...they threaten to rise up and consume me.
I push them away.
I have to be strong now.
...for Tammie.

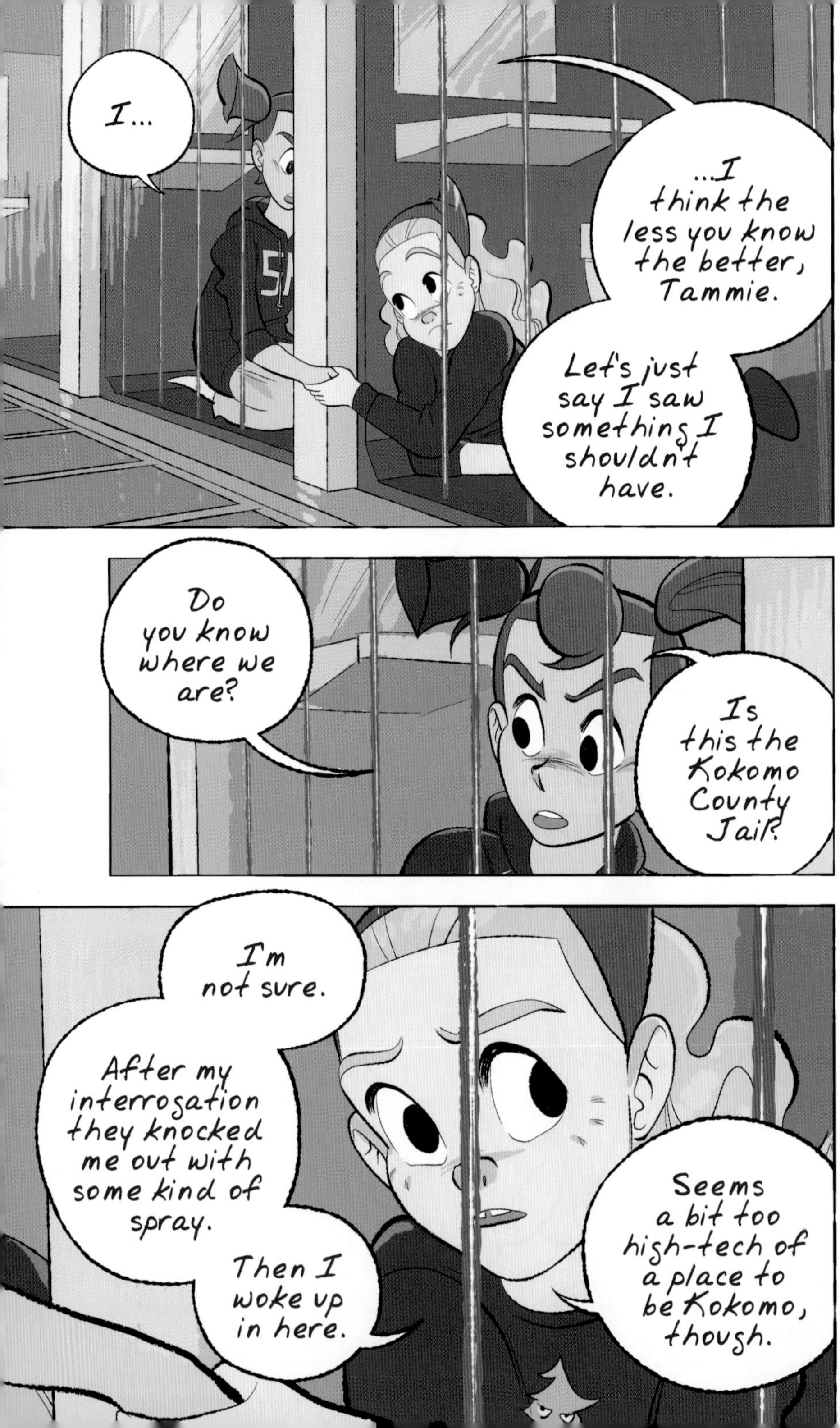
I...
...I think the less you know the better, Tammie.
Let's just say I saw something I shouldn't have.
Do you know where we are?
Is this the Kokomo County Jail?
I'm not sure.
After my interrogation they knocked me out with some kind of spray.
Then I woke up in here.
Seems a bit too high-tech of a place to be Kokomo, though.

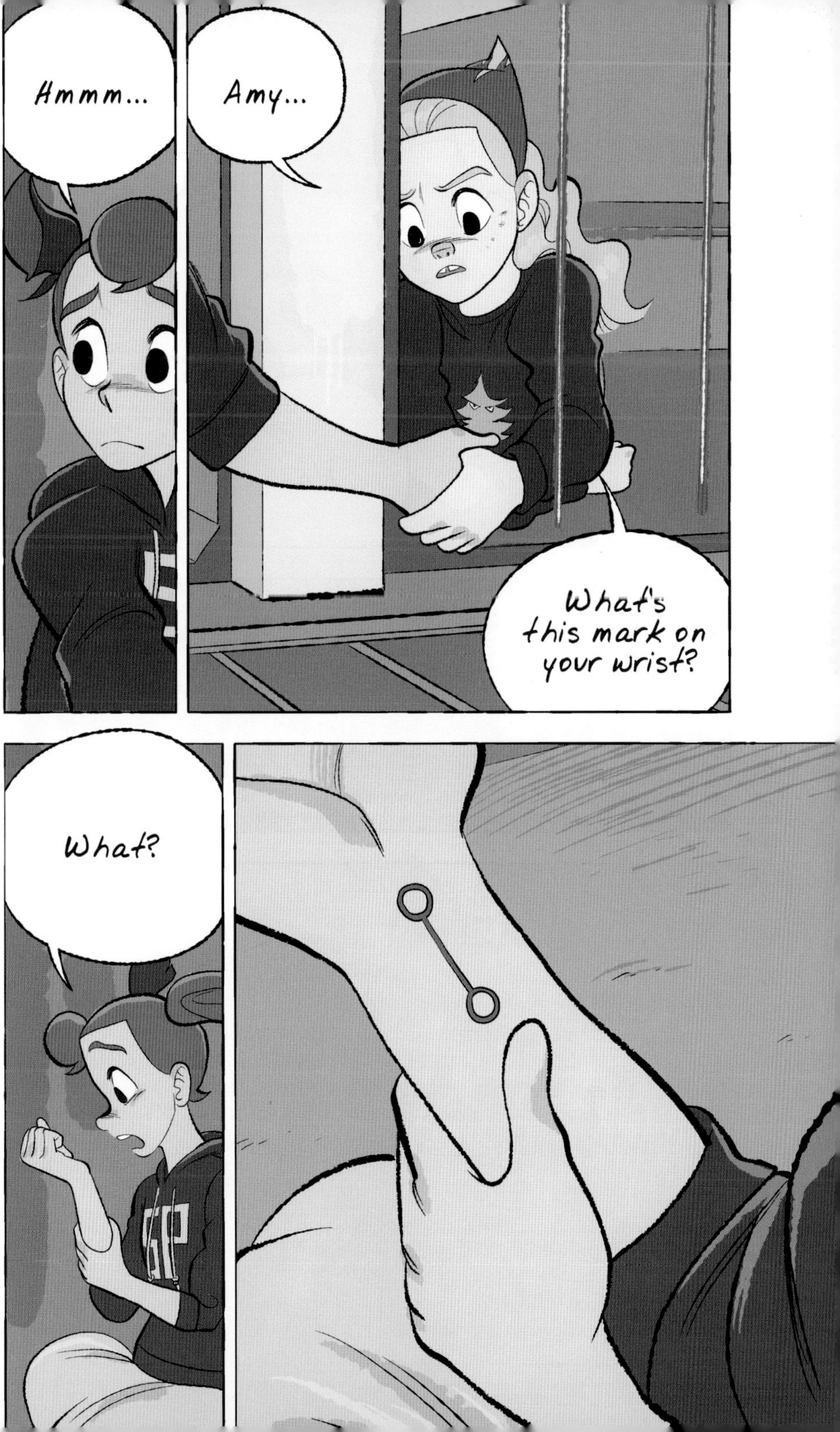
Hmmm...
Amy...
What's this mark on your wrist?
What?

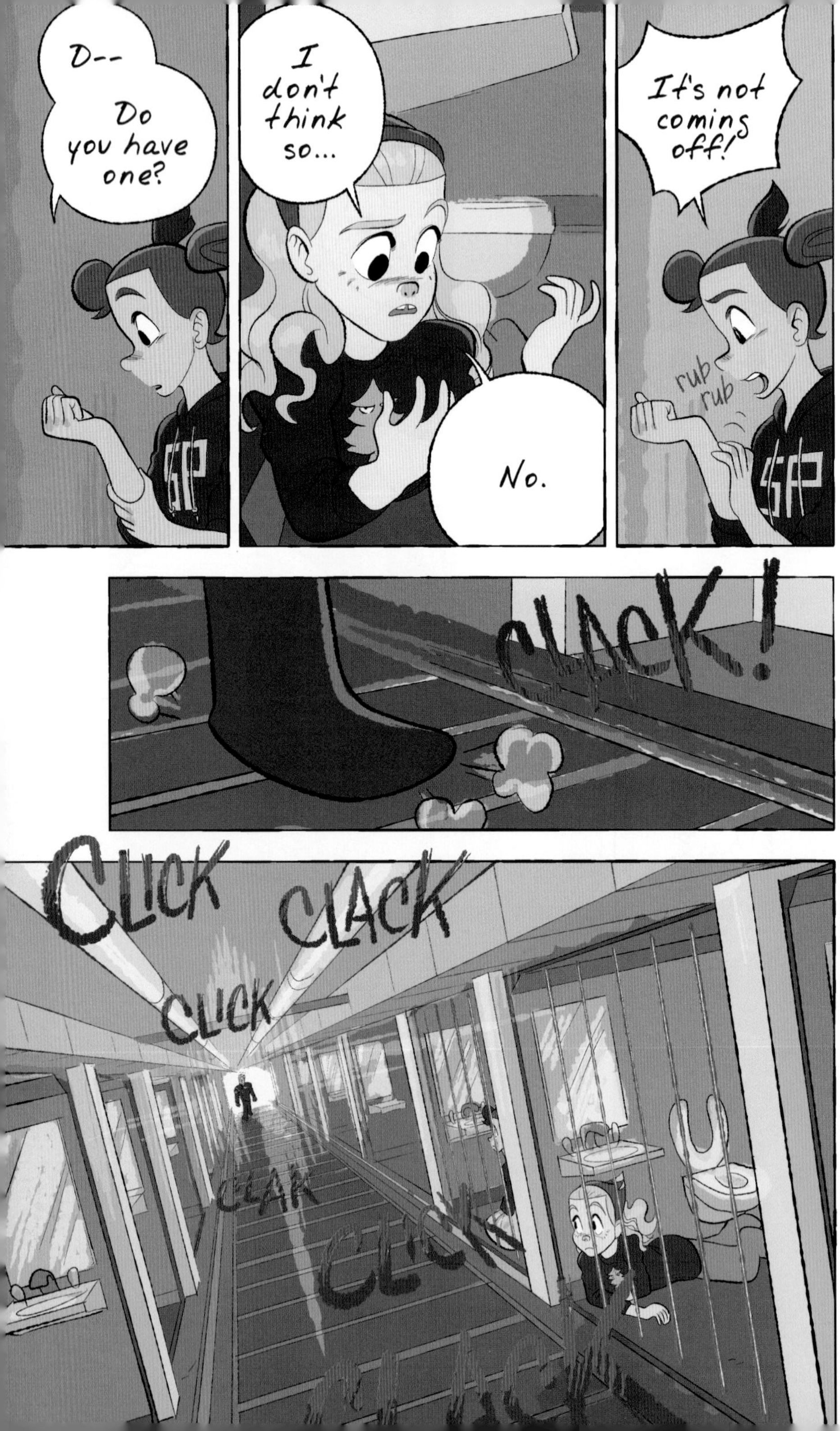
D--
Do you have one?
I don't think so...
No.
It's not coming off!
rub rub
CLACK!
CLICK
CLACK
CLICK
CLAK
CLICK

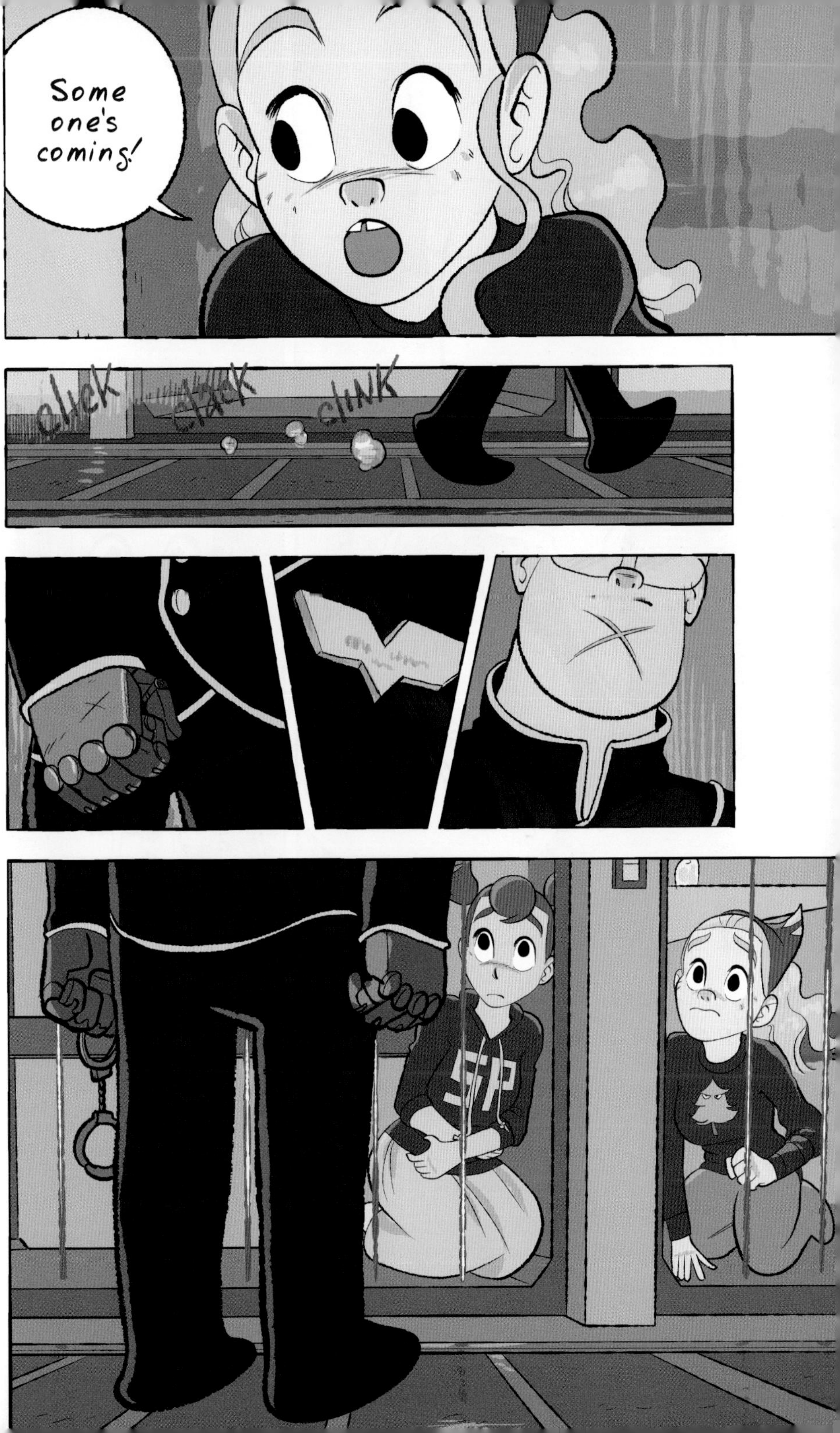
Some one's coming!
click
clack
clink

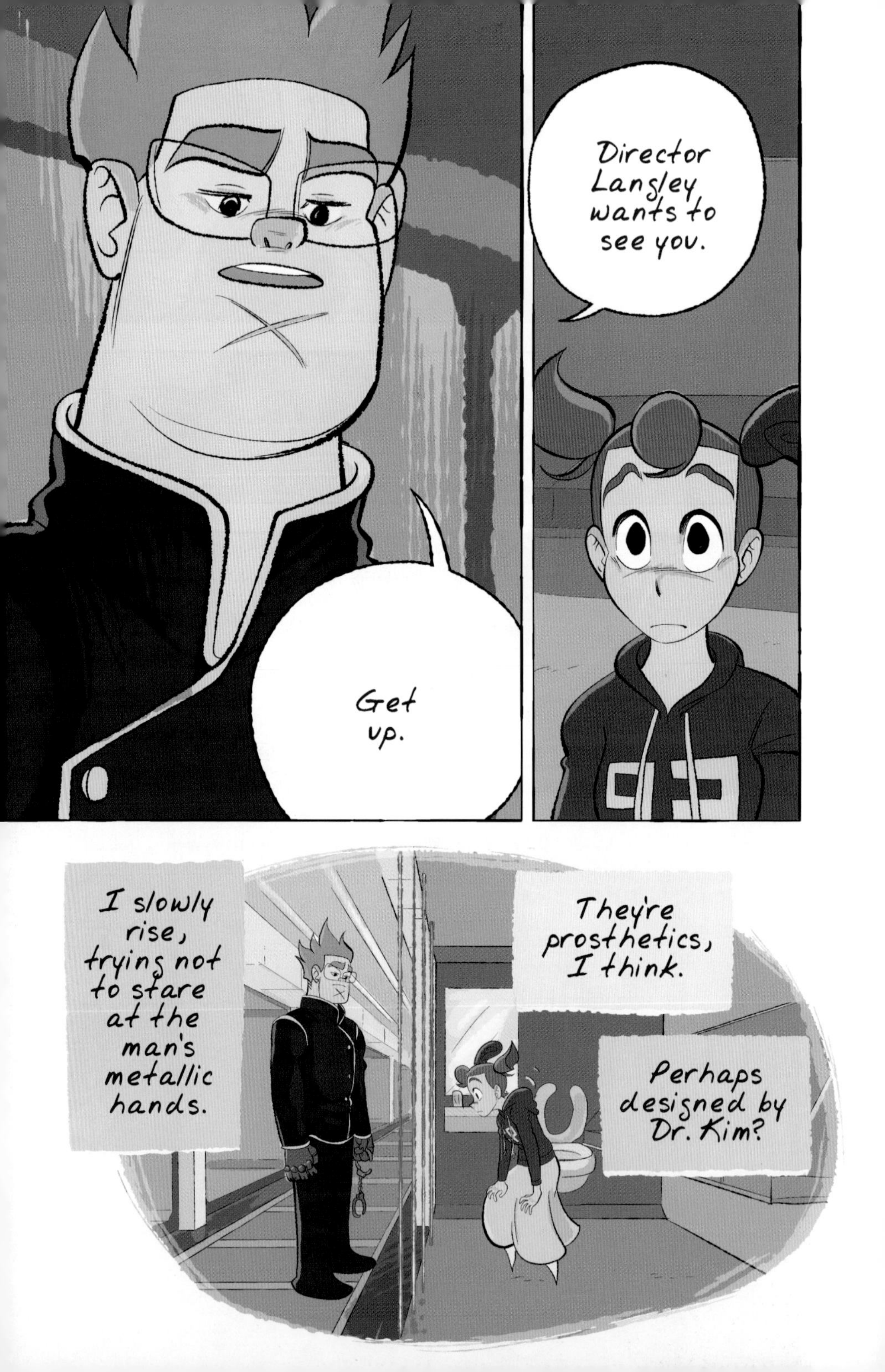
Director Langley wants to see you.
Get up.
I slowly rise, trying not to stare at the man's metallic hands.
They're prosthetics, I think.
Perhaps designed by Dr. Kim?

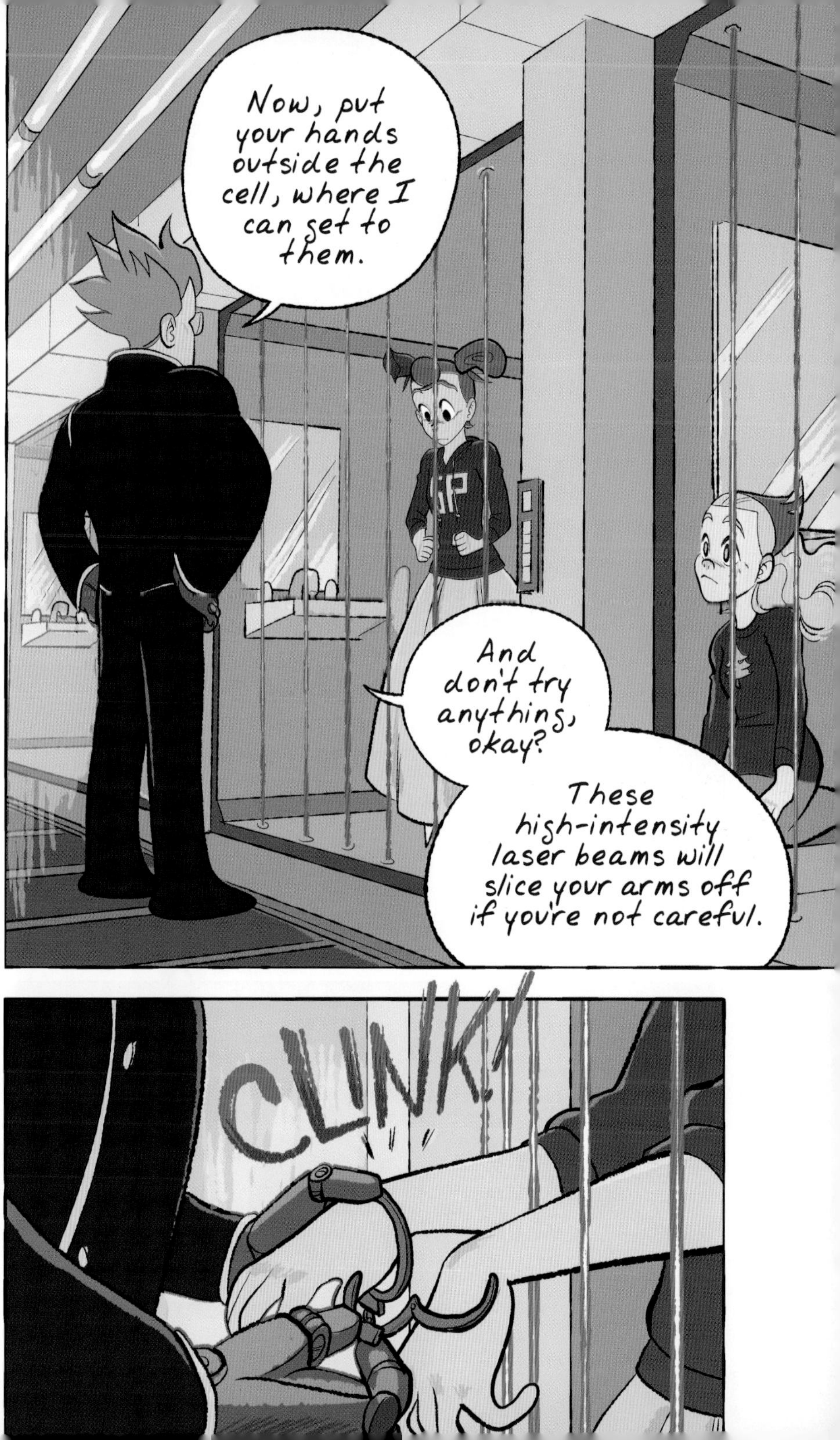
Now, put your hands outside the cell, where I can get to them.
And don't try anything, okay?
These high-intensity laser beams will slice your arms off if you're not careful.
CLINK!

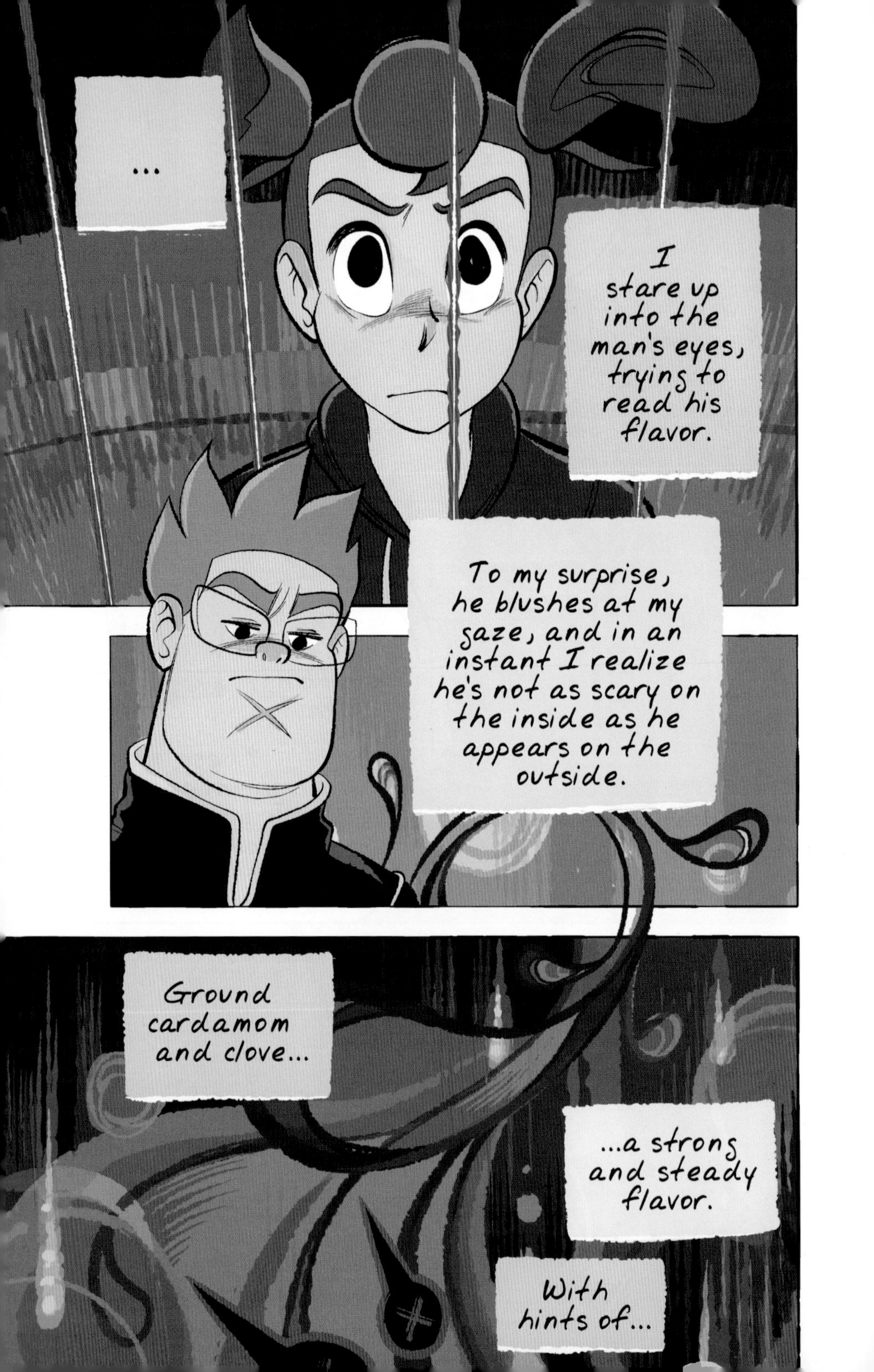
...
I stare up into the man's eyes, trying to read his flavor.
To my surprise, he blushes at my gaze, and in an instant I realize he's not as scary on the inside as he appears on the outside.
Ground cardamom and clove...
...a strong and steady flavor.
With hints of...

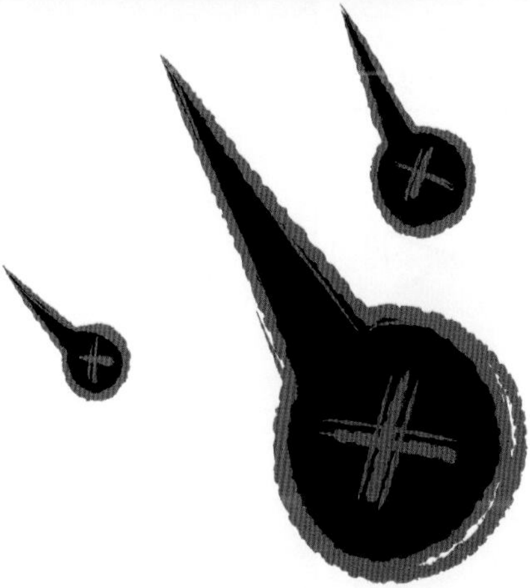
...something else.

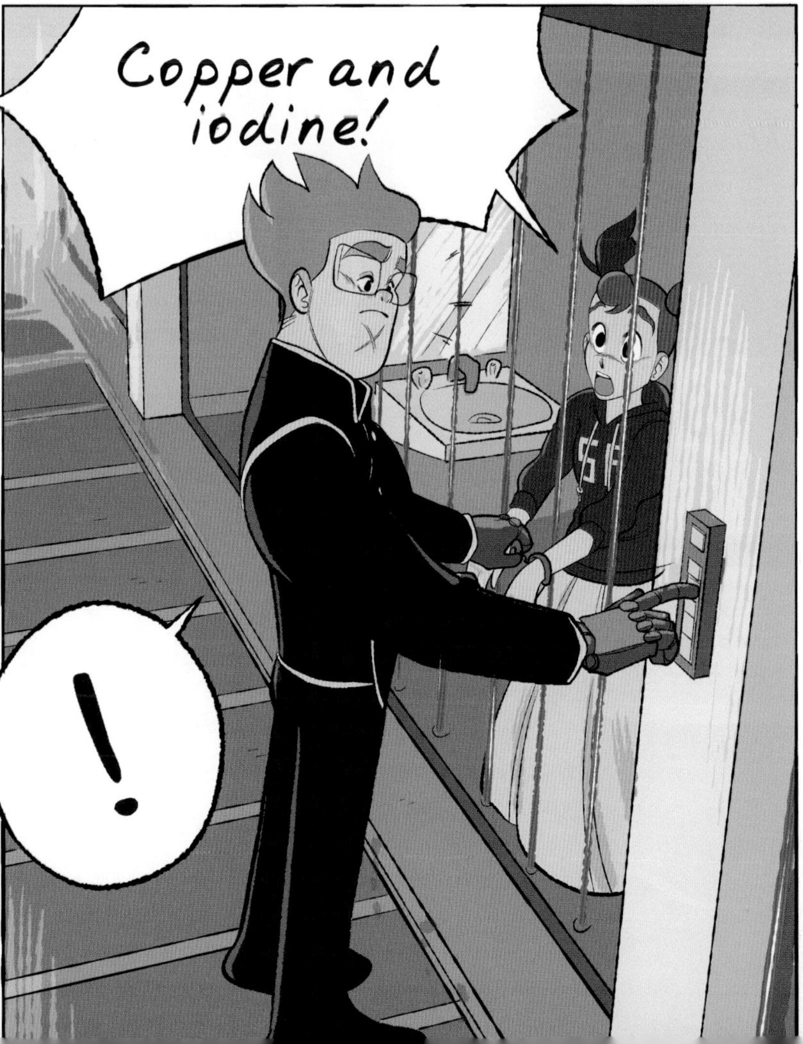
Copper and iodine!
!

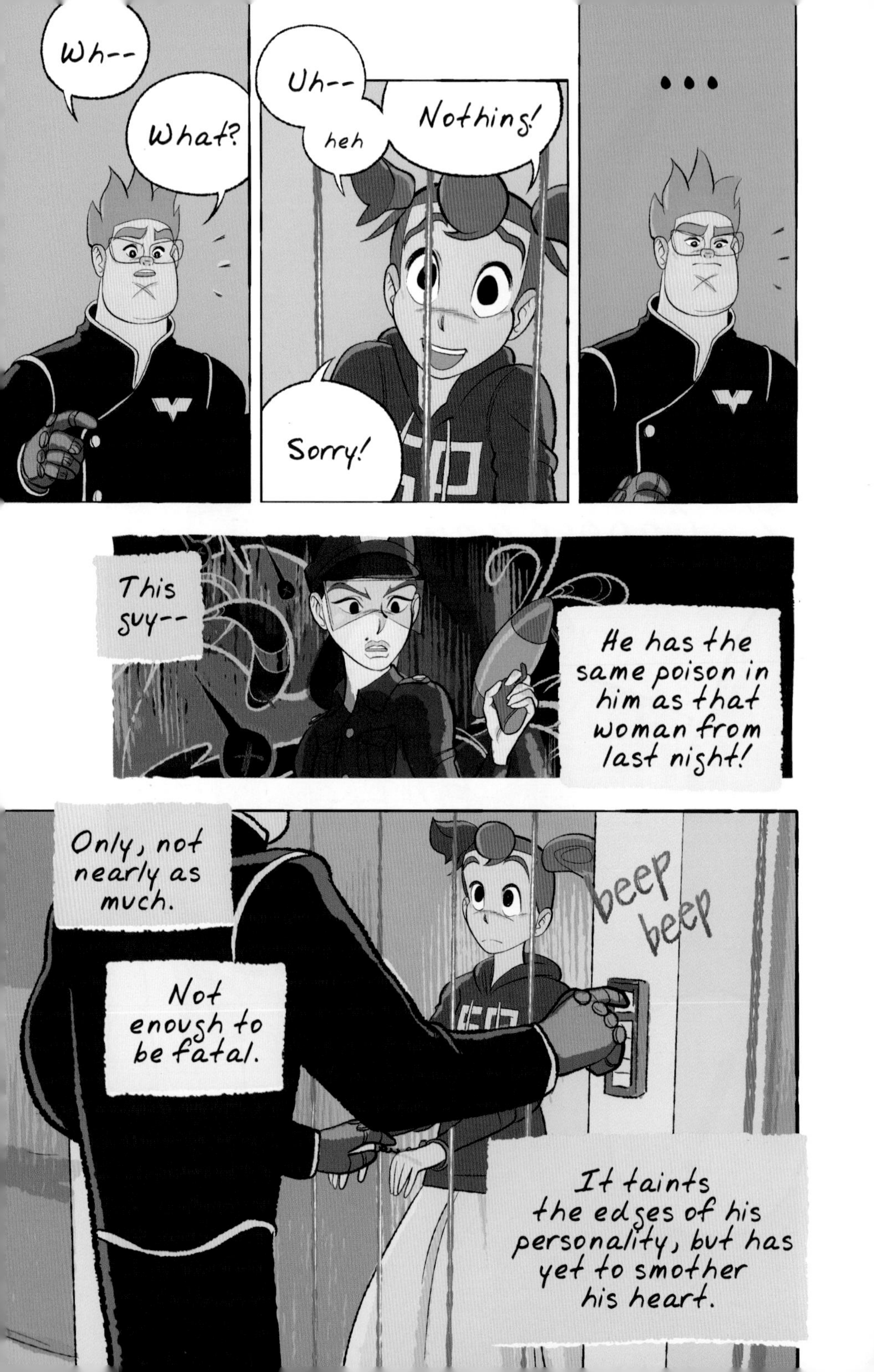
Wh--
What?
Uh--
heh
Nothing!
Sorry!
...
This guy--
He has the same poison in him as that woman from last night!
Only, not nearly as much.
Not enough to be fatal.
beep beep
It taints the edges of his personality, but has yet to smother his heart.

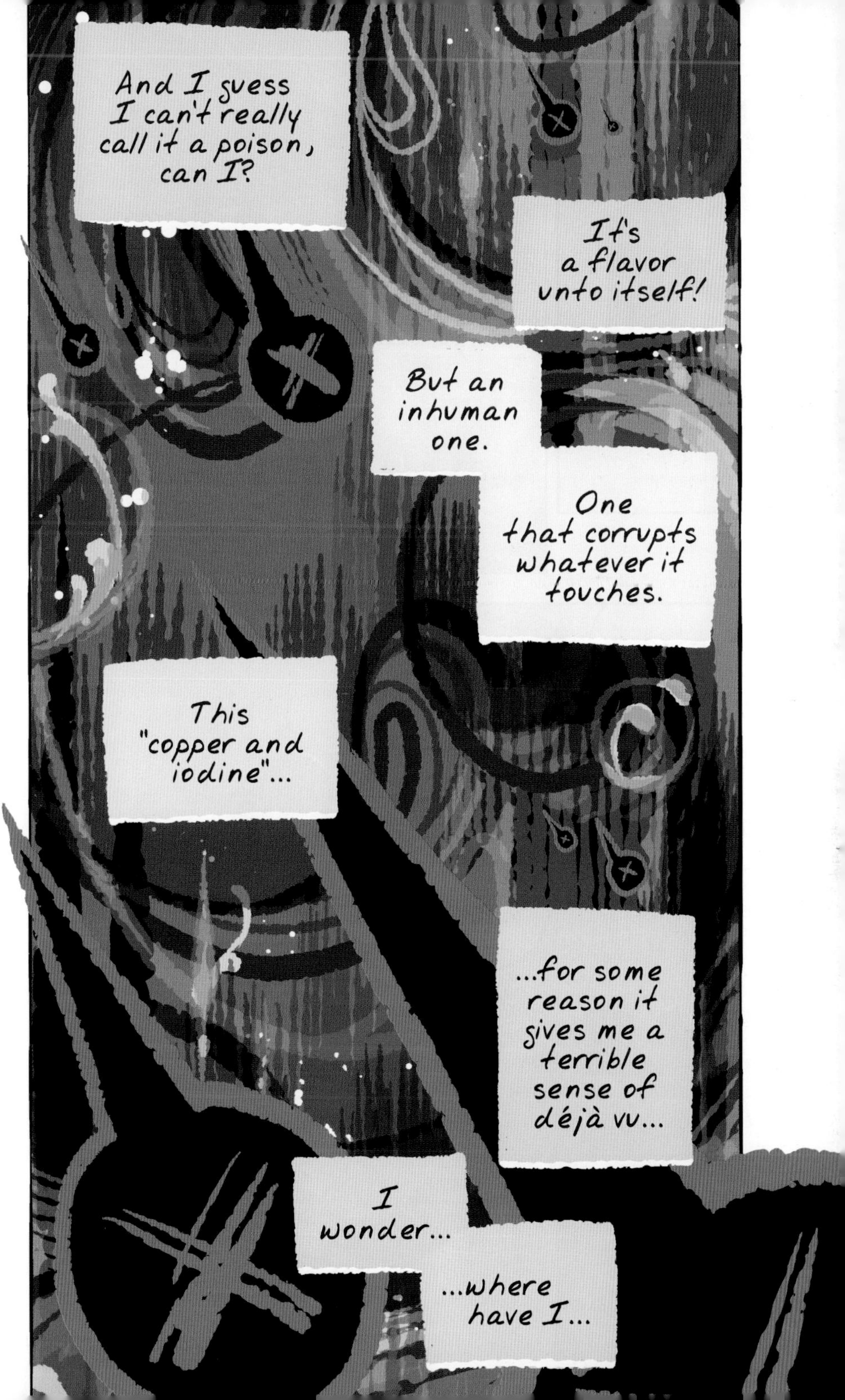
And I guess I can't really call it a poison, can I?
It's a flavor unto itself!
But an inhuman one.
One that corrupts whatever it touches.
This "copper and iodine"...
...for some reason it gives me a terrible sense of déjà vu...
I wonder...
...where have I...

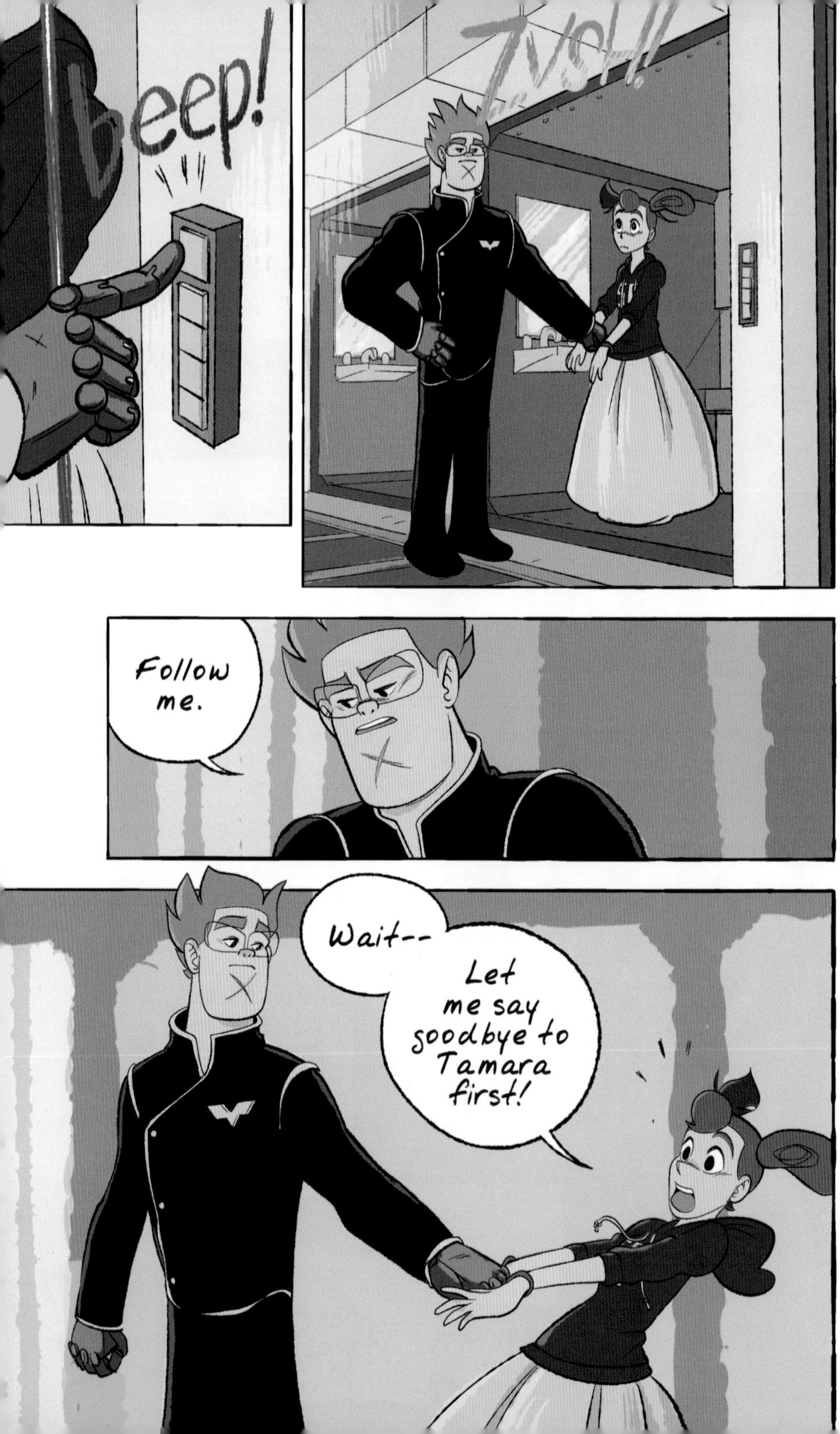
Beep!
ZVSH!!
Follow me.
Wait--
Let me say goodbye to Tamara first!

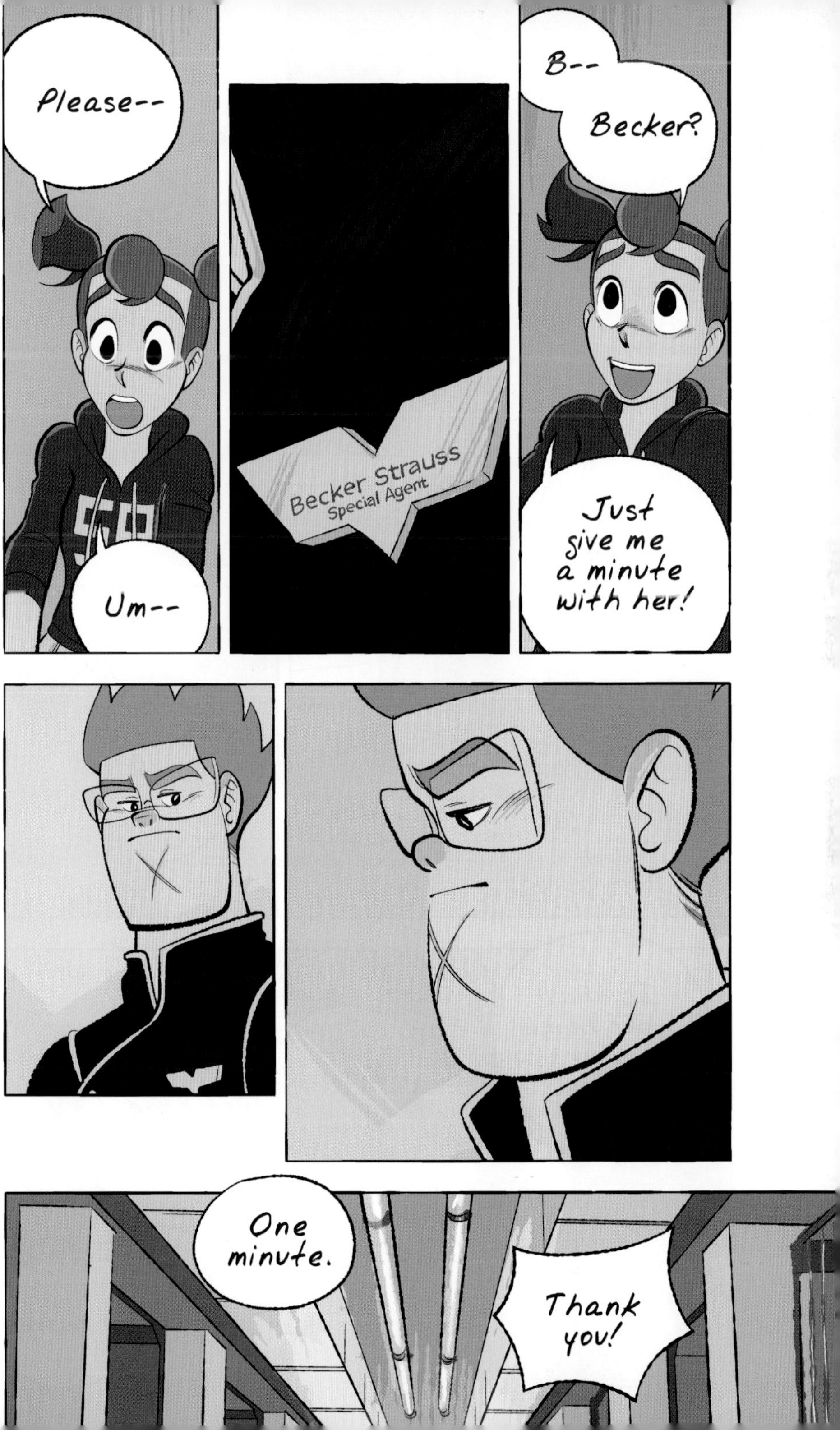
Please--
Um--
Becker Strauss
Special Agent
B--
Becker?
Just give me a minute with her!
One minute.
Thank you!

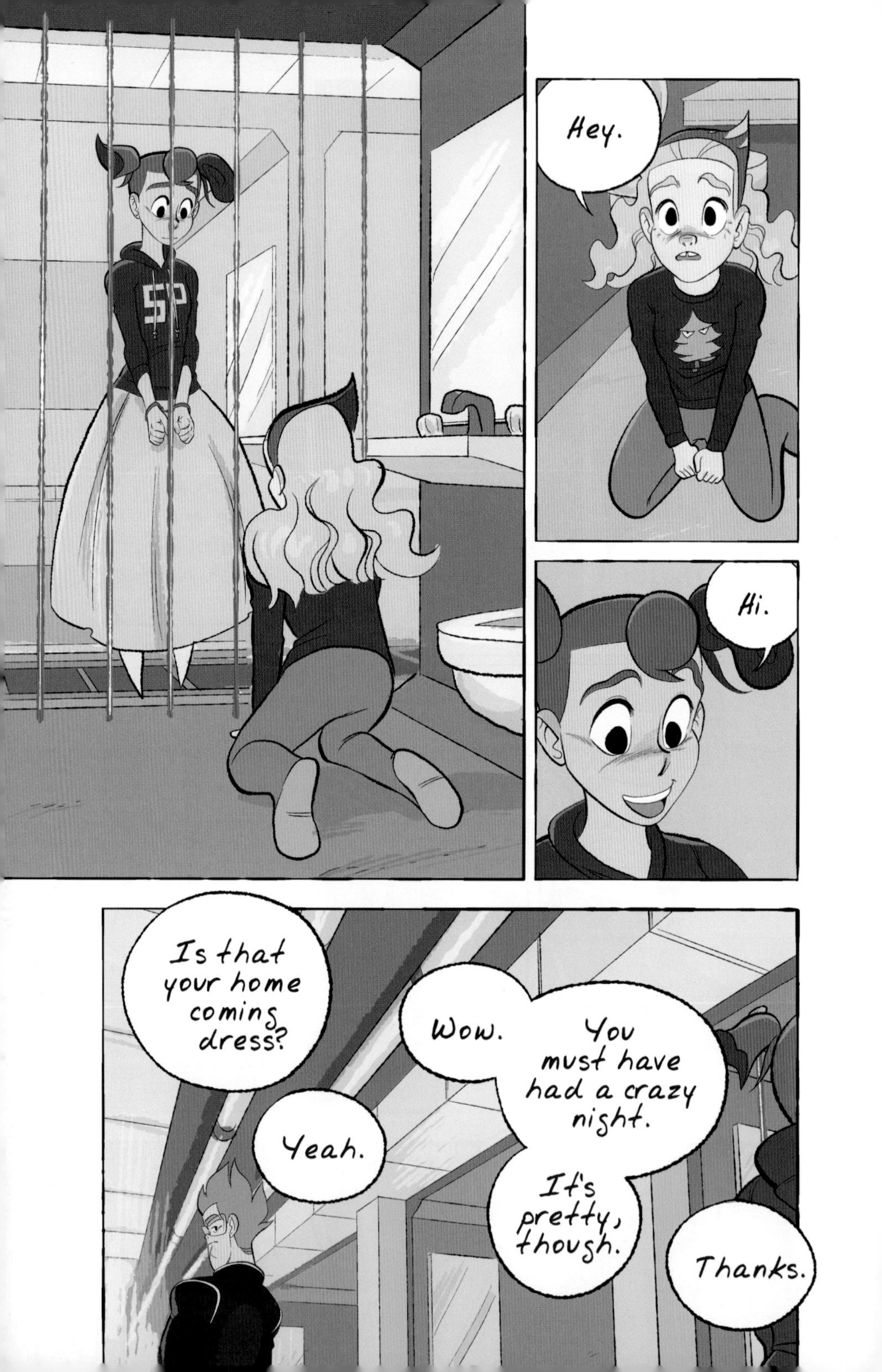
Hey.
Hi.
Is that your home comins dress?
Yeah.
Wow.
You must have had a crazy night.
It's pretty, though.
Thanks.

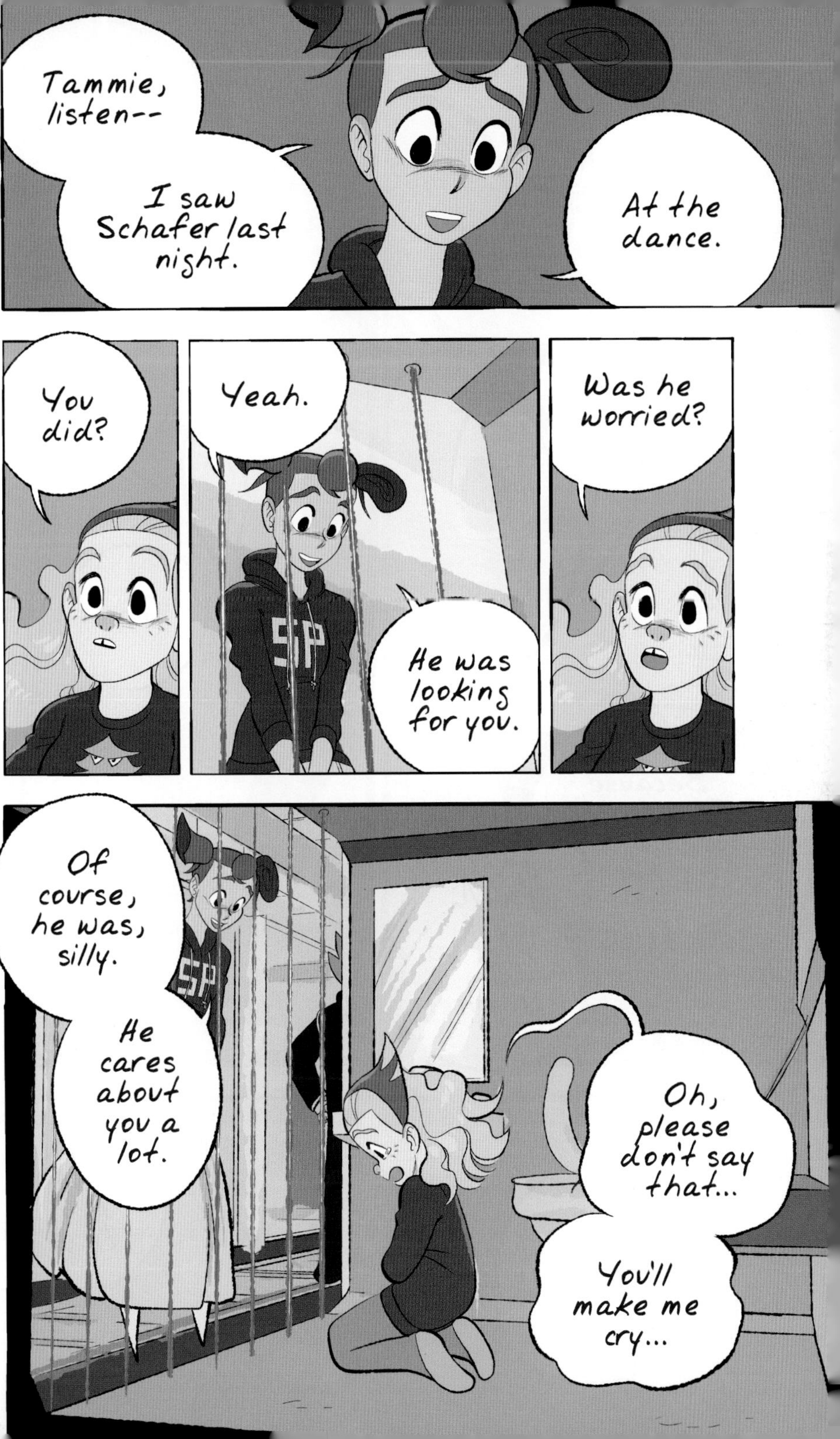
Tammie, listen--
I saw Schafer last night.
At the dance.
You did?
Yeah.
He was looking for you.
Was he worried?
Of course, he was, silly.
He cares about you a lot.
Oh, please don't say that...
You'll make me cry...

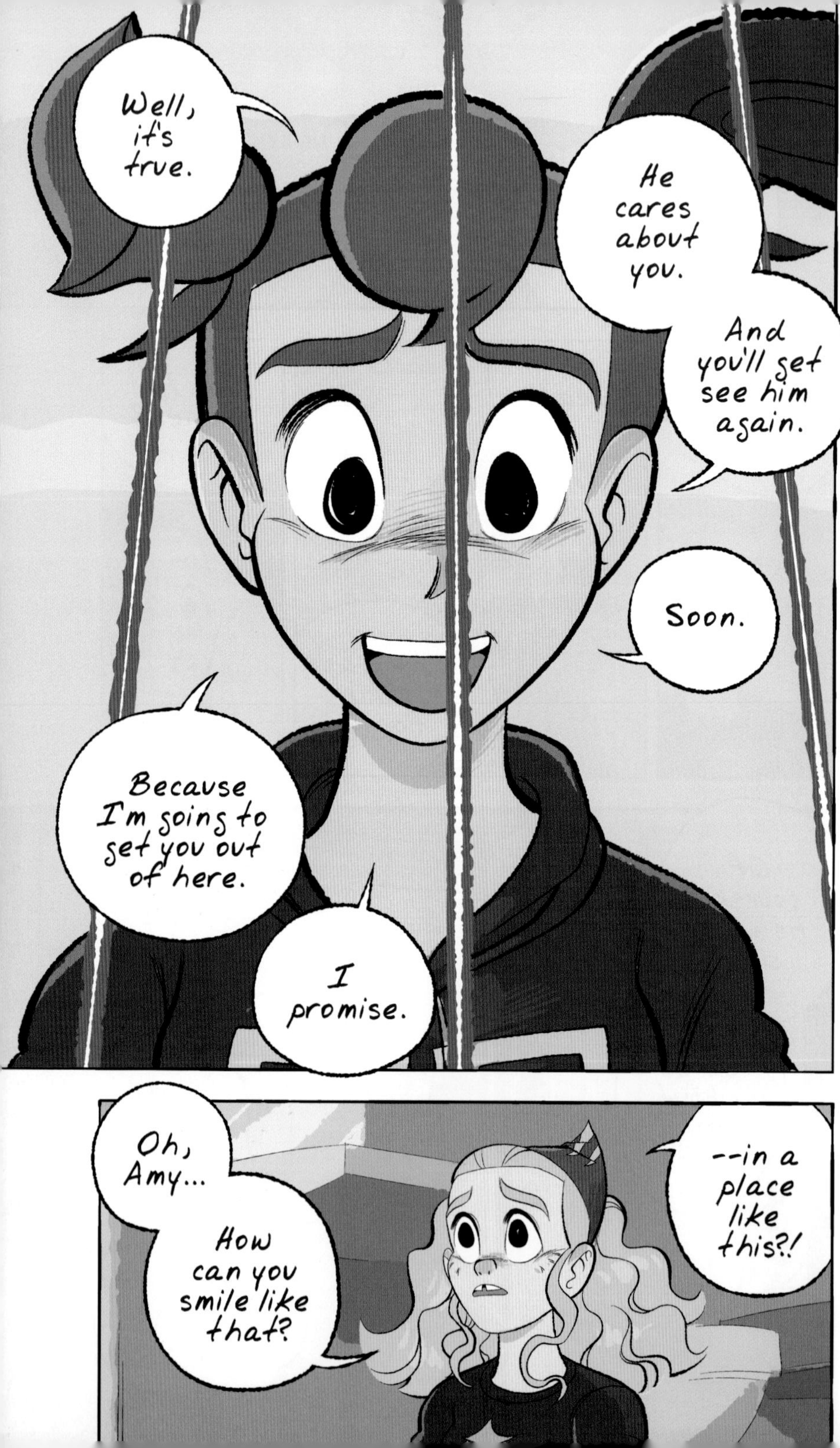
Well, it's true.
He cares about you.
And you'll get see him again.
Soon.
Because I'm going to get you out of here.
I promise.
Oh, Amy...
How can you smile like that?
--in a place like this?!

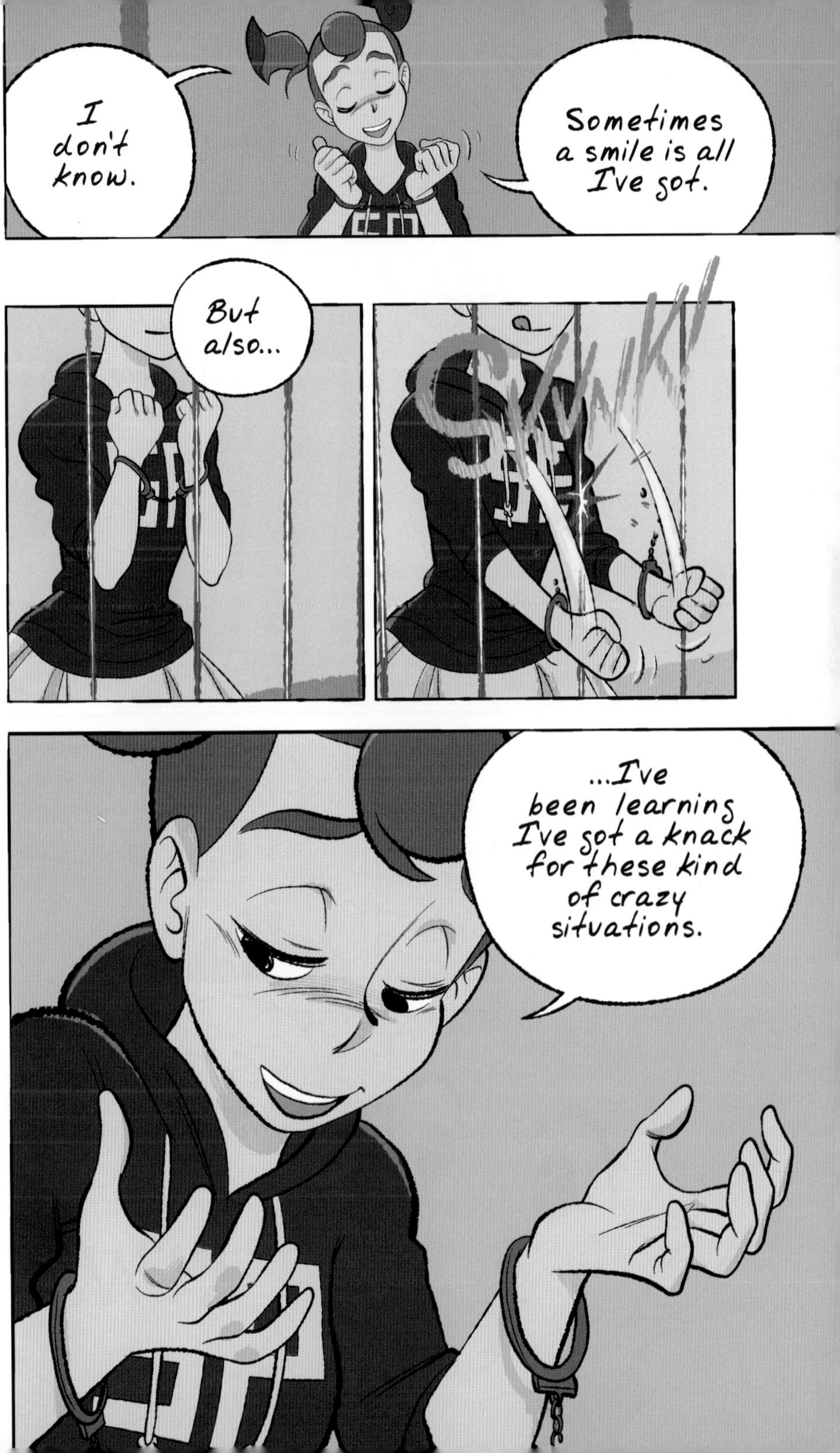
I don't know.
Sometimes a smile is all I've got.
But also...
...I've been learning I've got a knack for these kind of crazy situations.

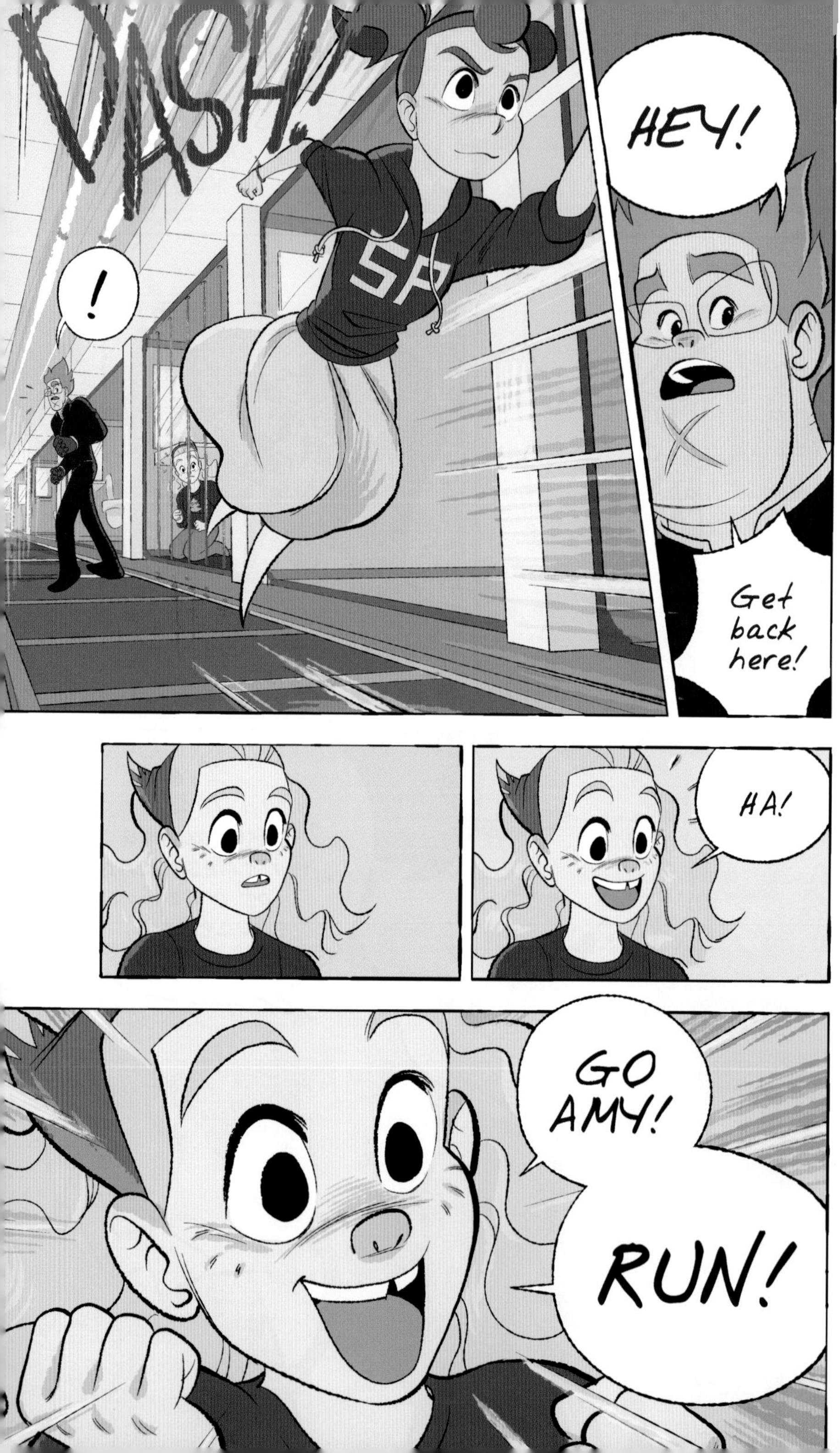
DASH!
!
HEY!
Get back here!
HA!
GO AMY!
RUN!

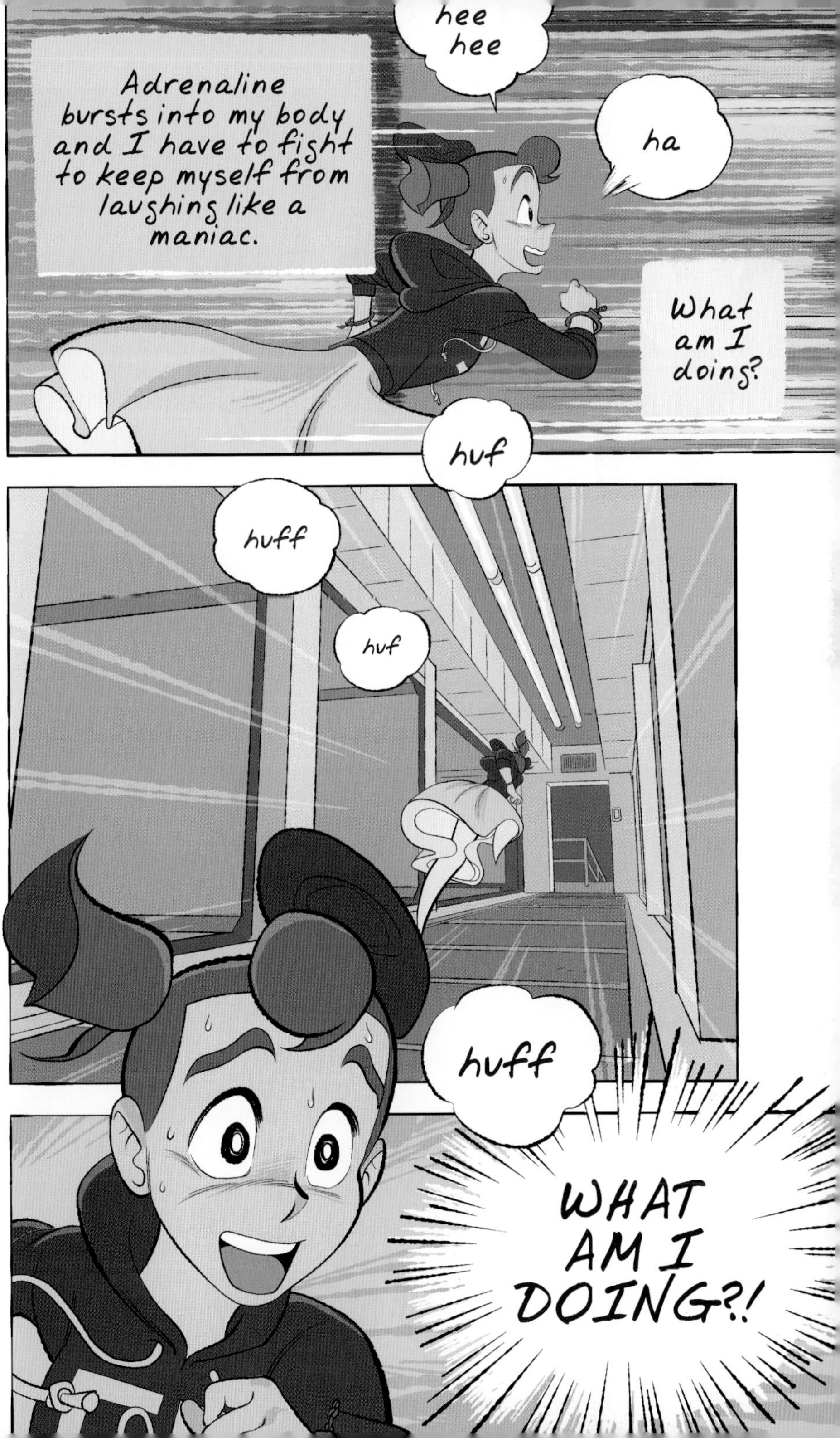
Adrenaline bursts into my body and I have to fight to keep myself from laughing like a maniac.
hee hee
ha
What am I doing?
huf
huff
huf
huff
WHAT AM I DOING?!

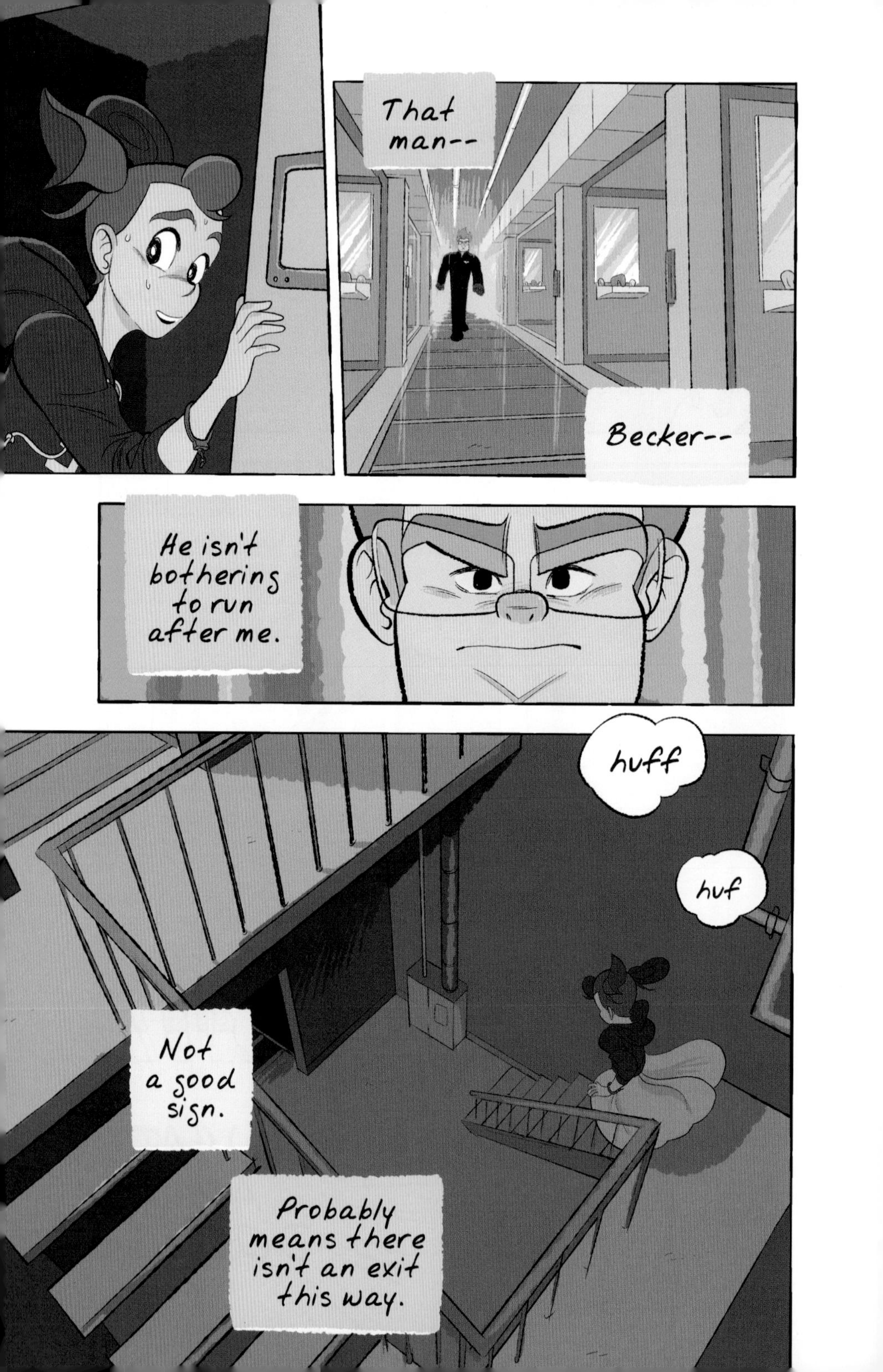
That man--
Becker--
He isn't botherins to run after me.
huff
huf
Not a good sign.
Probably means there isn't an exit this way.

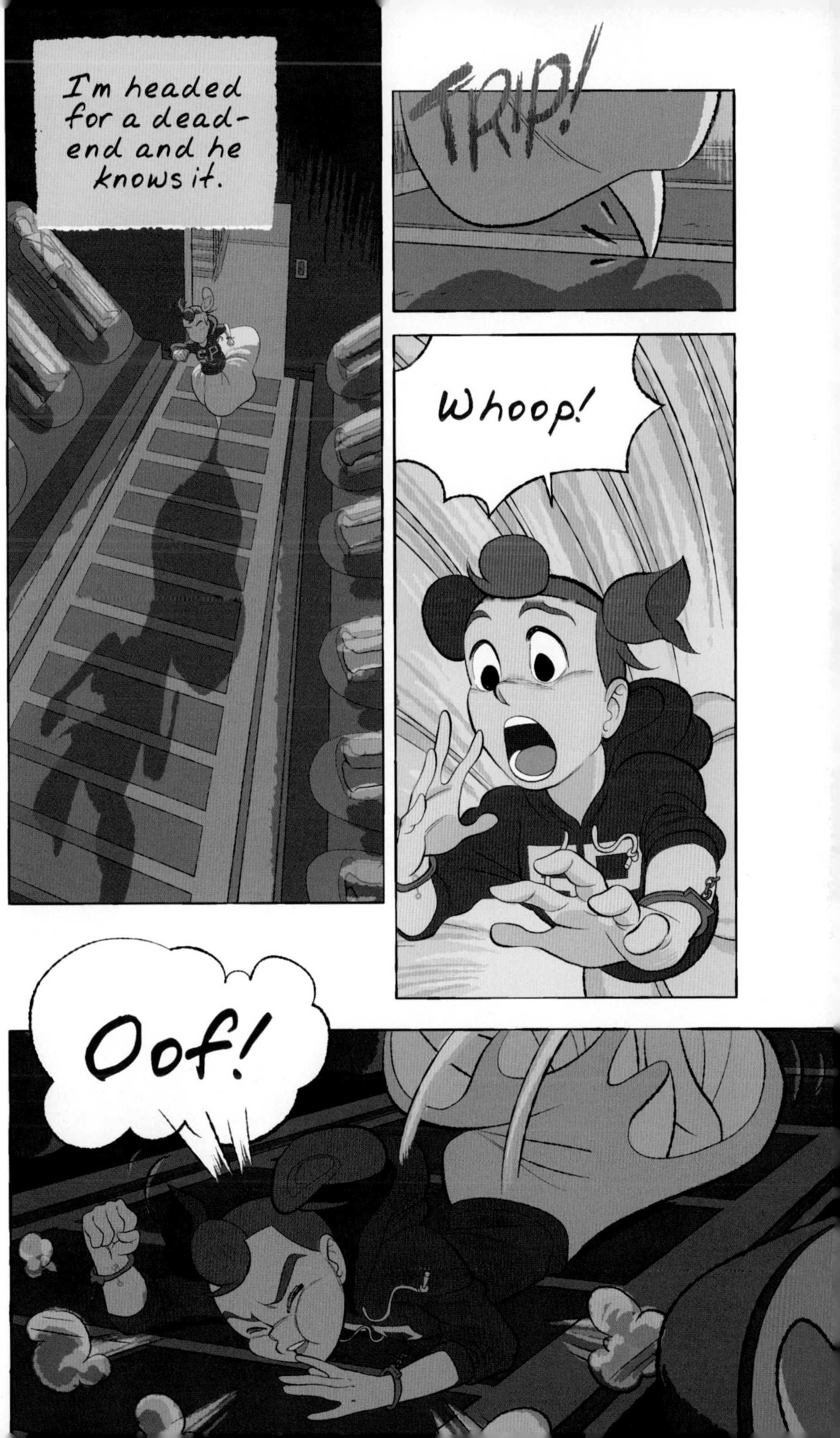
I'm headed for a dead-end and he knows it.
TRIP!
Whoop!
Oof!

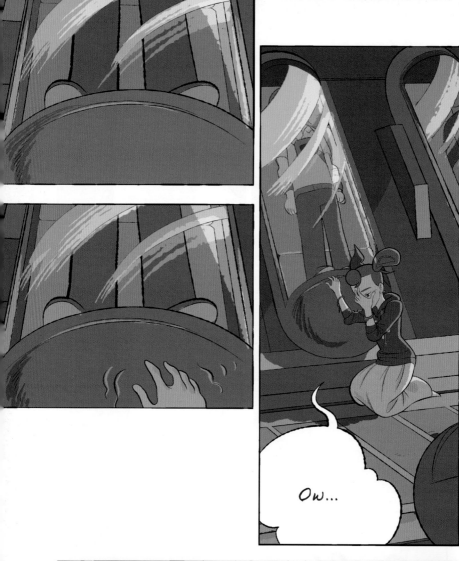

Ow...

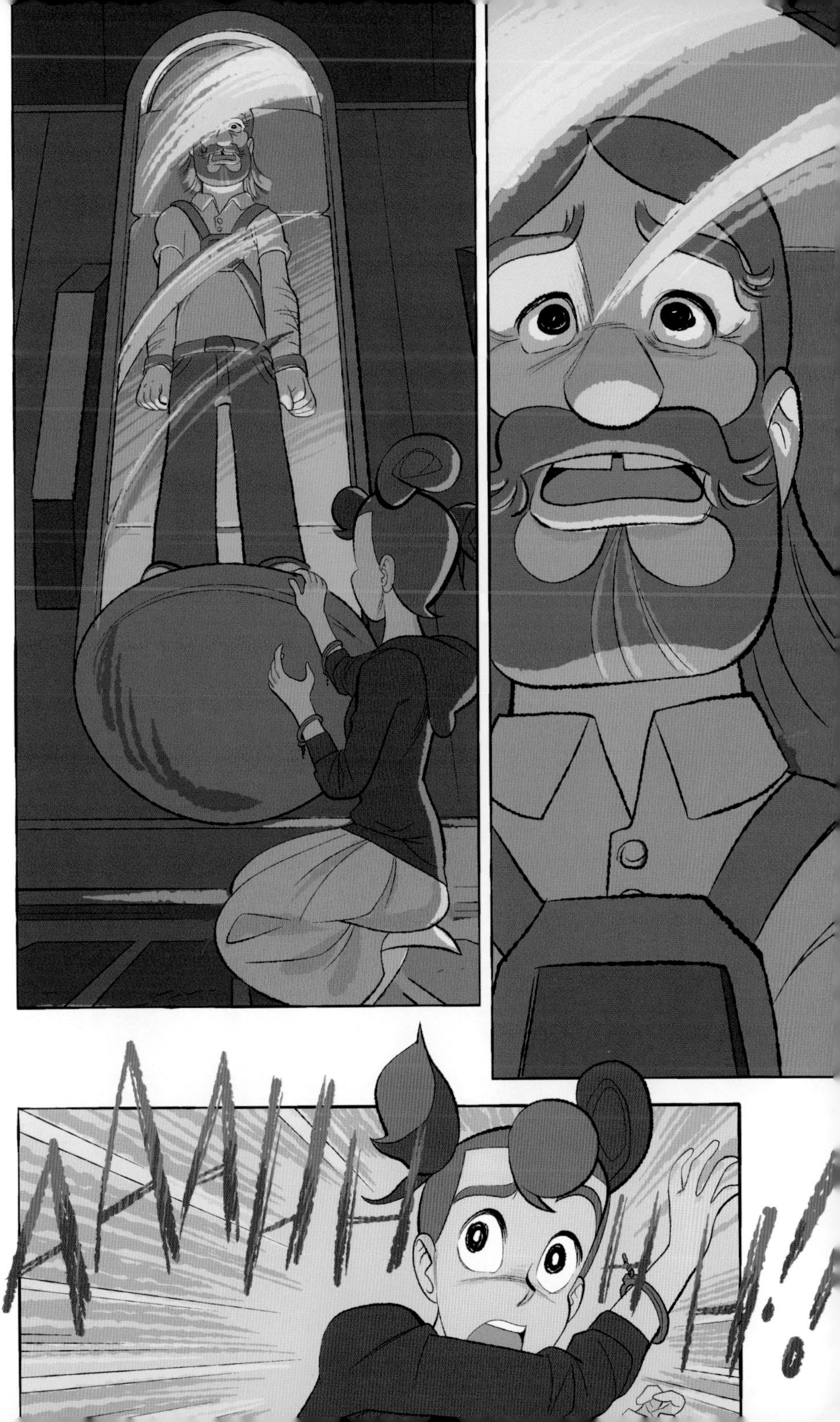
AAHHHHH!!

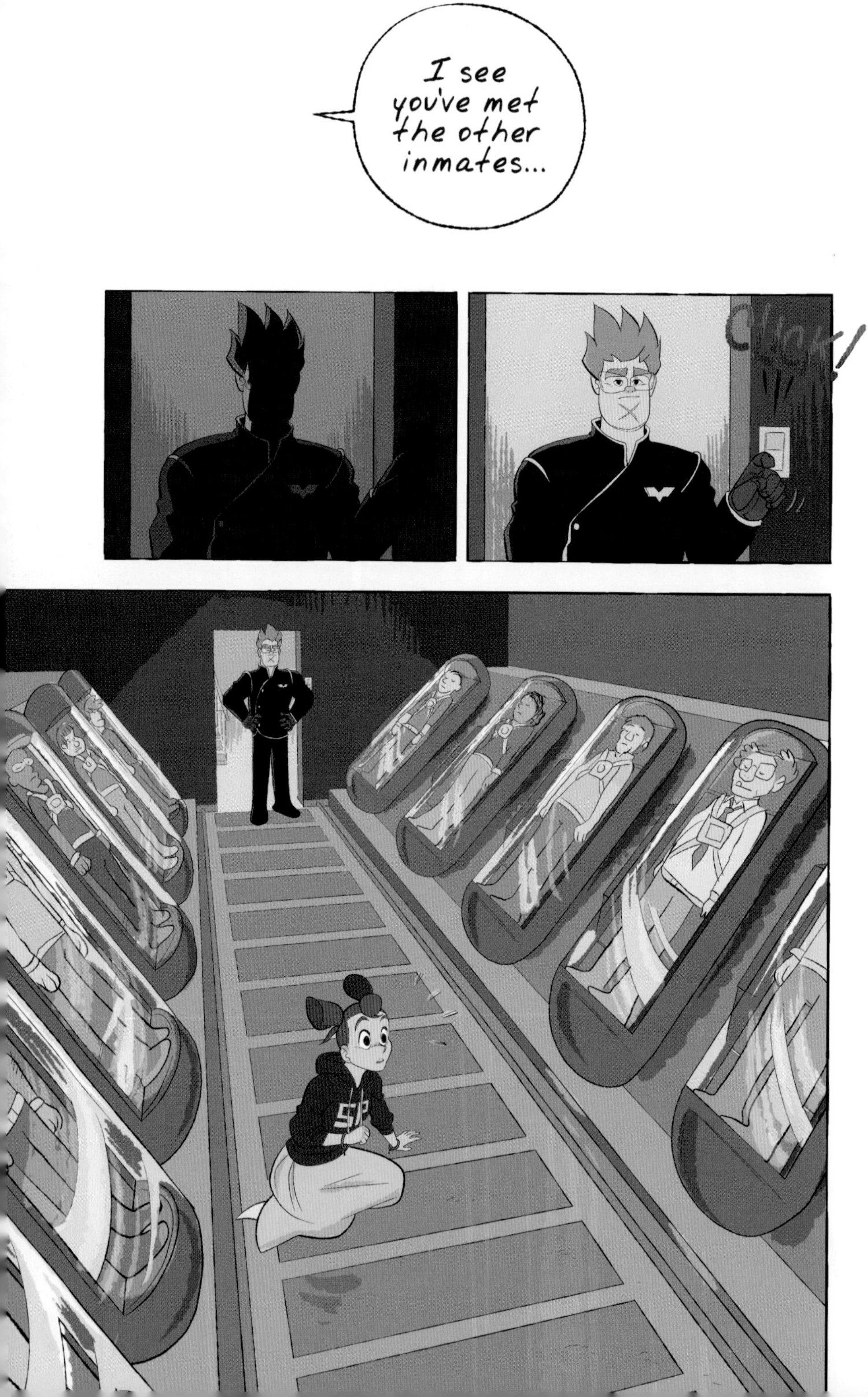
I see you've met the other inmates...

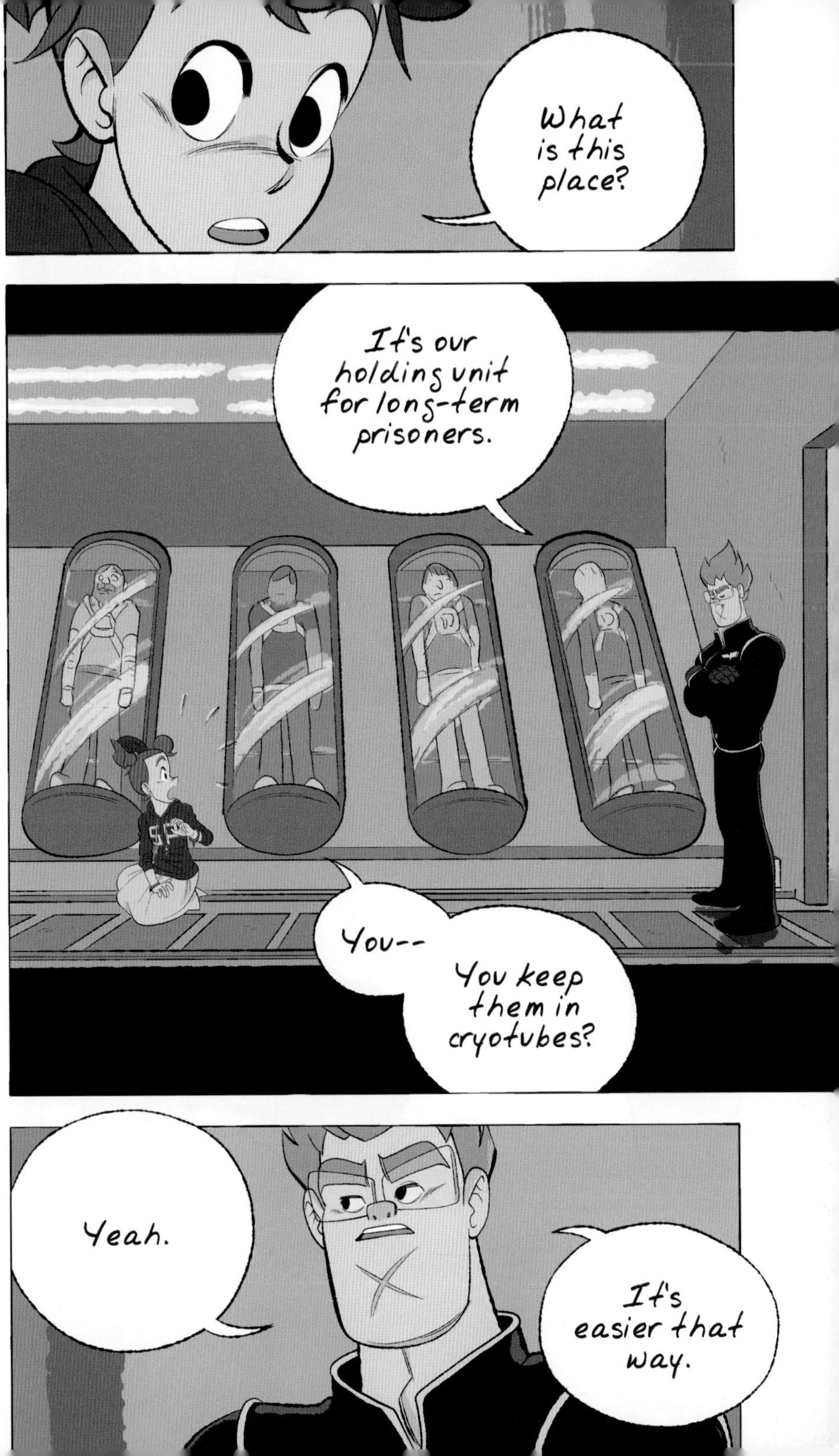
What is this place?
It's our holding unit for long-term prisoners.
You--
You keep them in cryotubes?
Yeah.
It's easier that way.

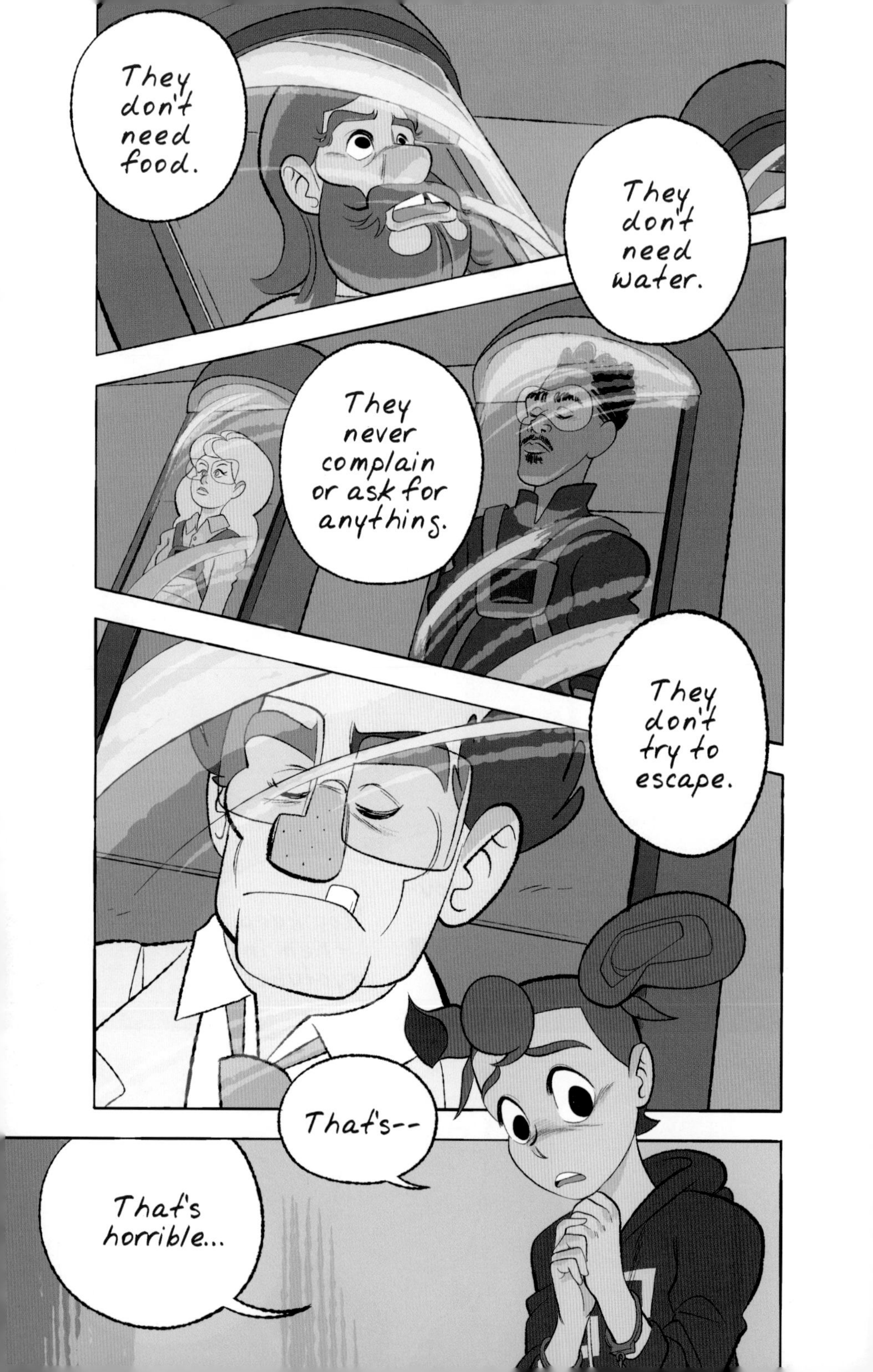
They don't need food.
They don't need water.
They never complain or ask for anything.
They don't try to escape.
That's--
That's horrible...

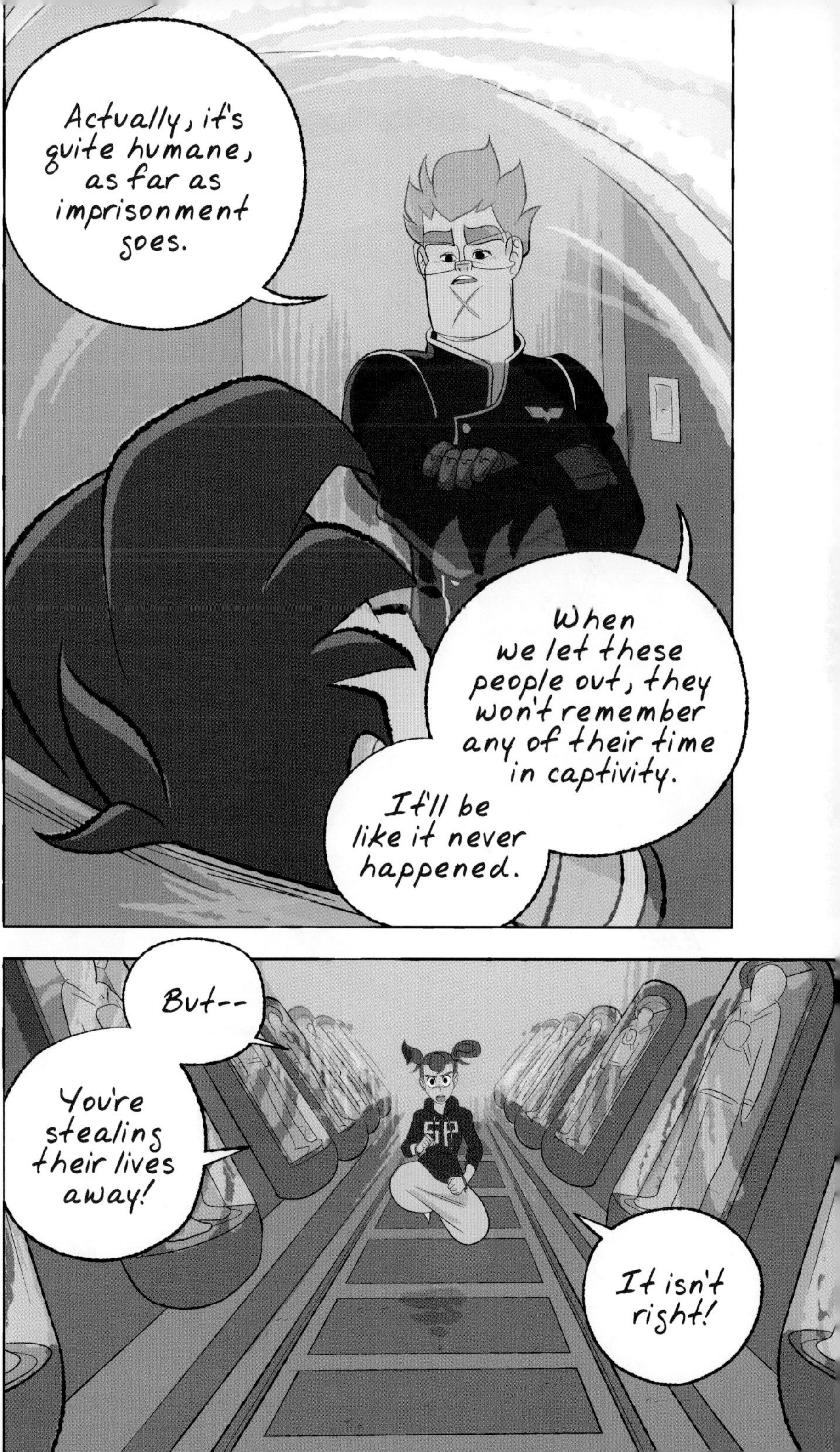
Actually, it's quite humane, as far as imprisonment goes.
When we let these people out, they won't remember any of their time in captivity.
It'll be like it never happened.
But--
You're stealing their lives away!
It isn't right!

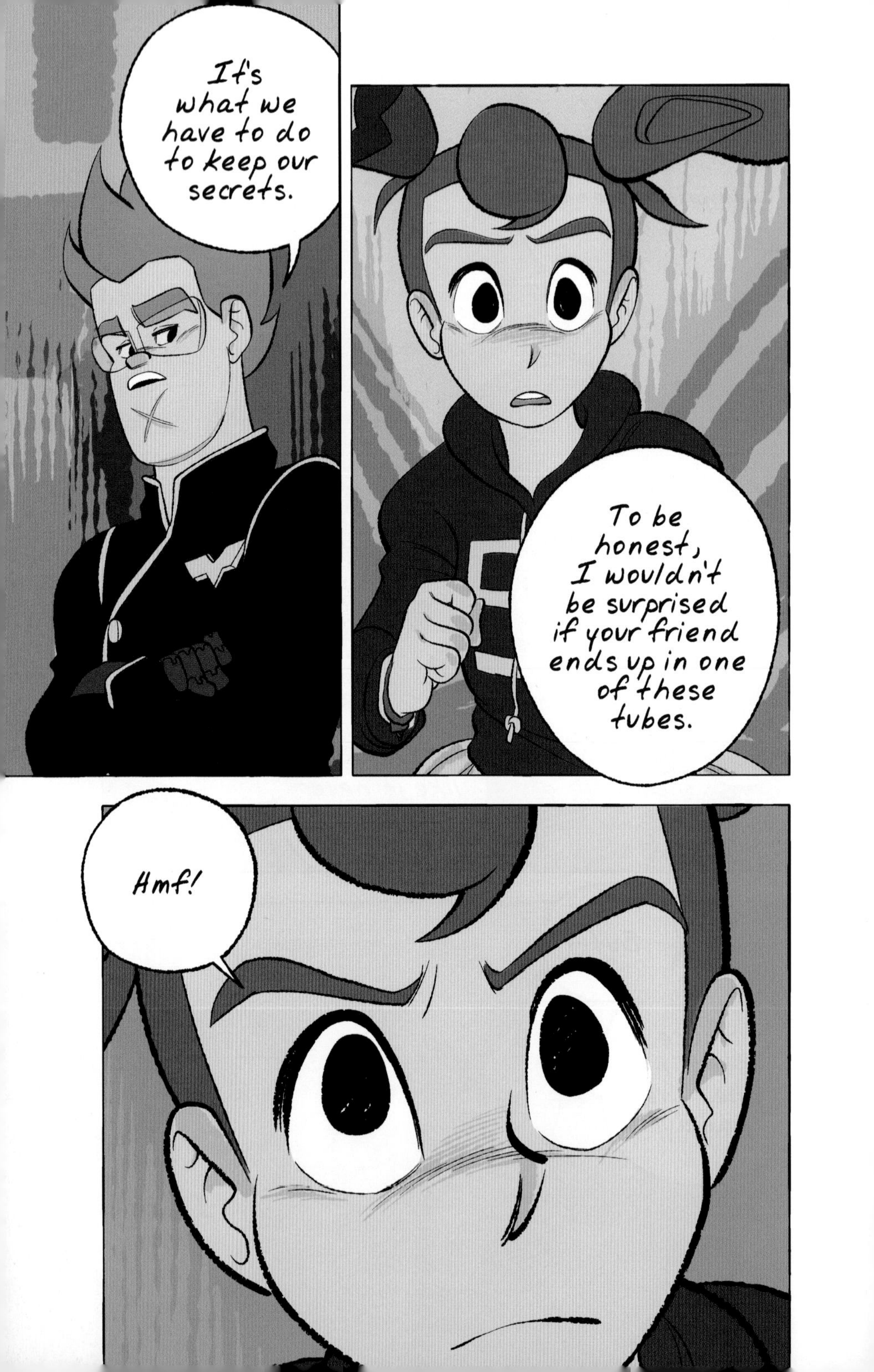
It's what we have to do to keep our secrets.
To be honest, I wouldn't be surprised if your friend ends up in one of these tubes.
Hmf!

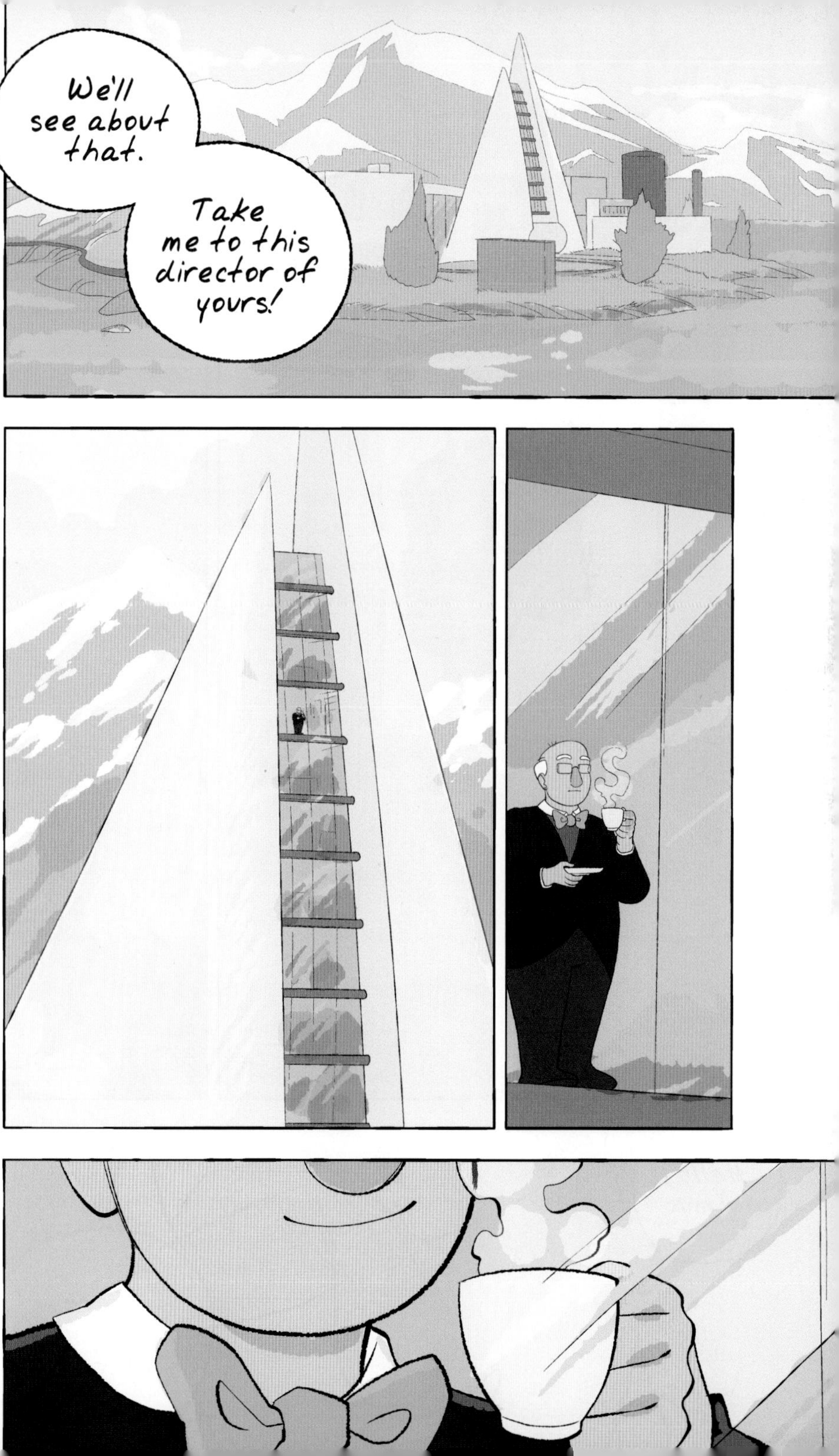
We'll see about that.
Take me to this director of yours!

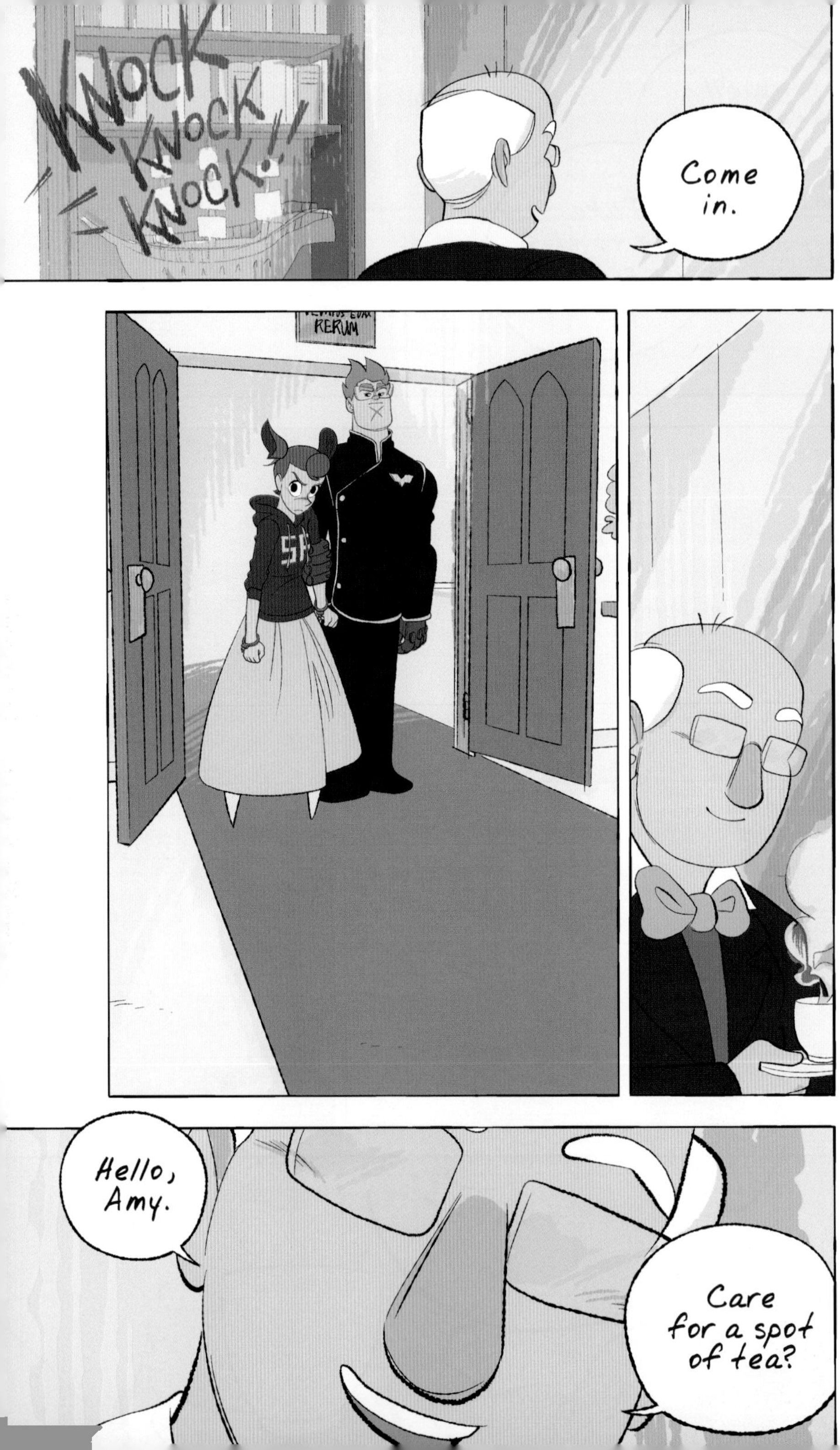
KNOCK KNOCK KNOCK!!
Come in.
RERUM
Hello, Amy.
Care for a spot of tea?

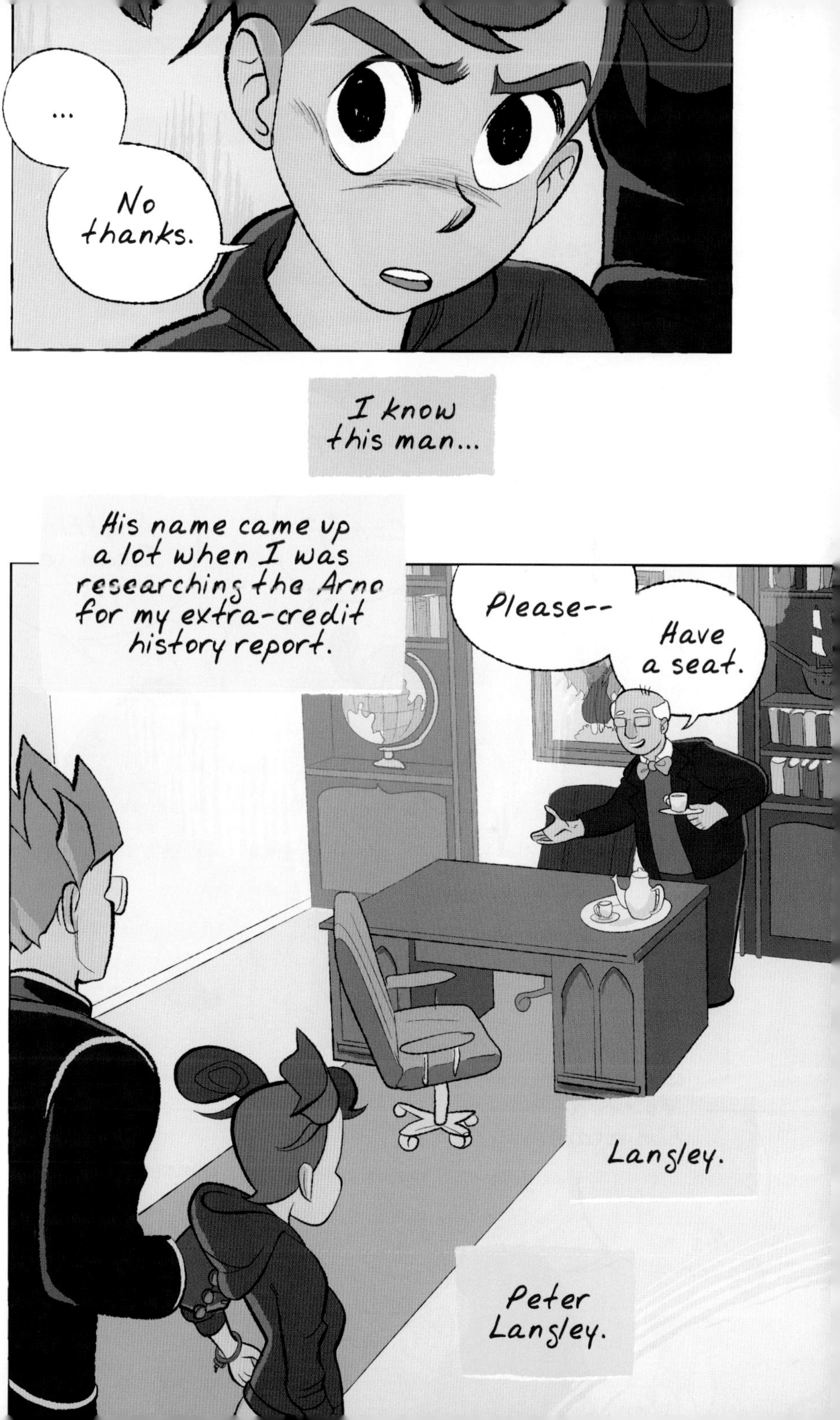
...
No thanks.
I know this man...
His name came up a lot when I was researching the Arno for my extra-credit history report.
Please--
Have a seat.
Langley.
Peter Langley.

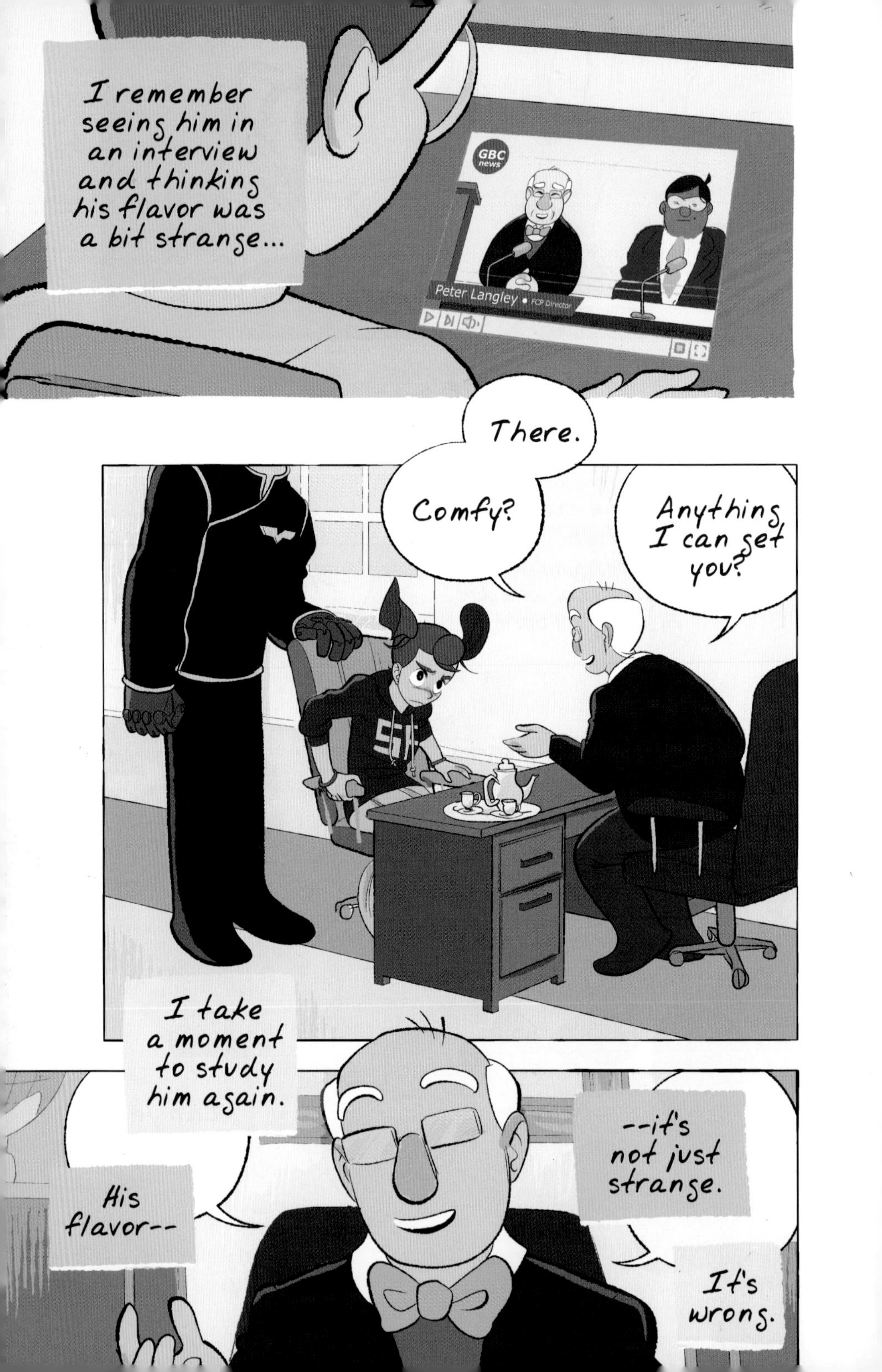
I remember seeing him in an interview and thinking his flavor was a bit strange...
GBC news
Peter Langley • FCP Director
There.
Comfy?
Anything I can get you?
I take a moment to study him again.
His flavor--
--it's not just strange.
It's wrong.

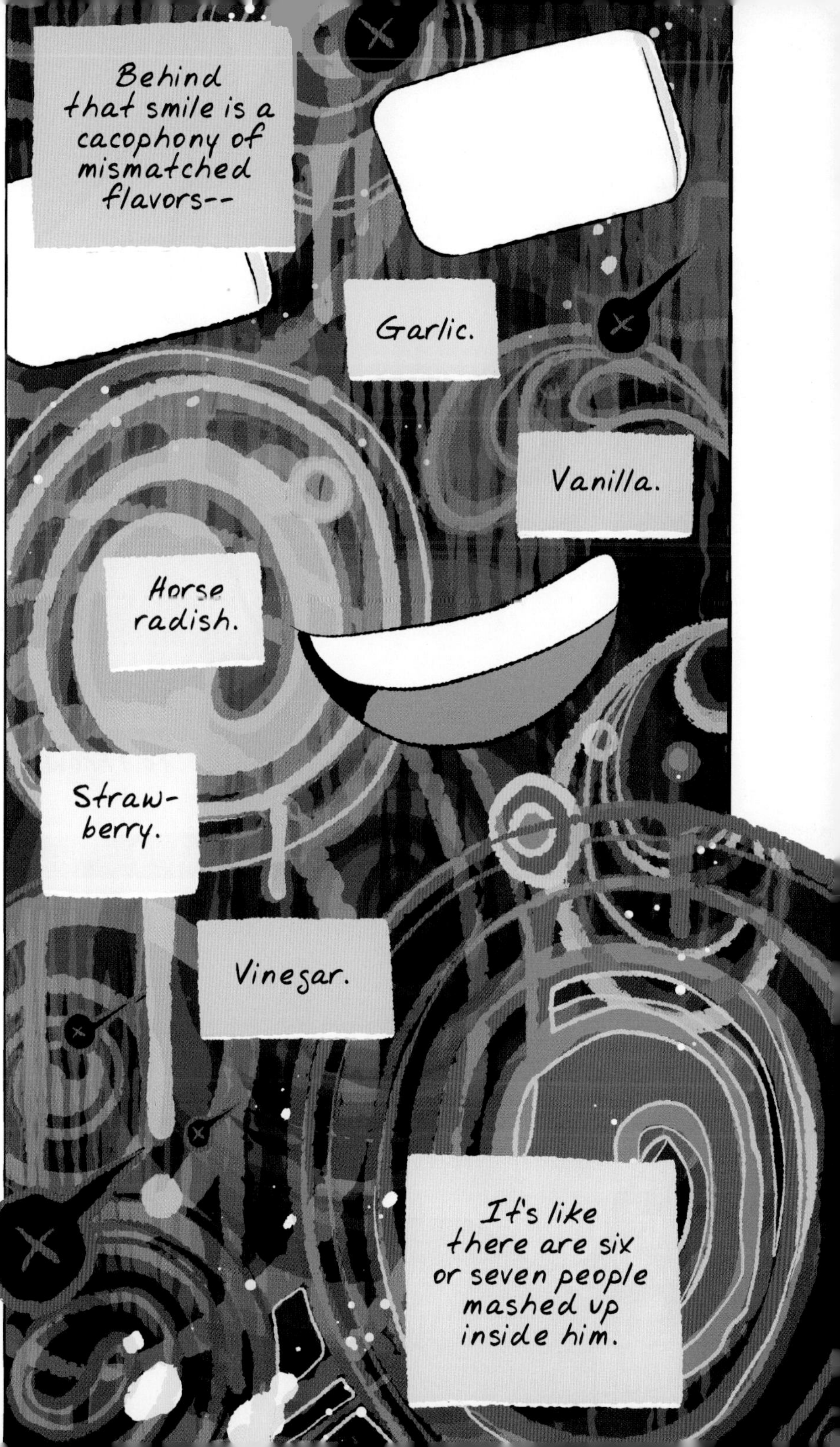
Behind that smile is a cacophony of mismatched flavors--
Garlic.
Vanilla.
Horse radish.
Straw-berry.
Vinegar.
It's like there are six or seven people mashed up inside him.

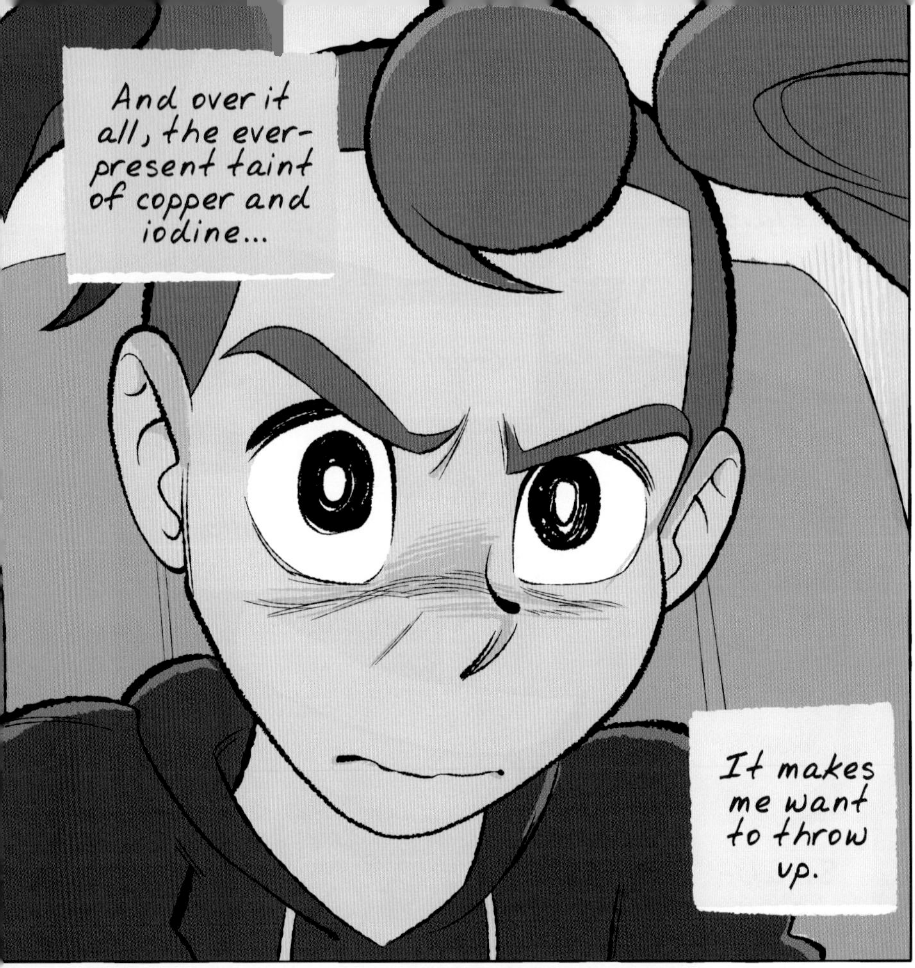
And over it all, the ever-present taint of copper and iodine...
It makes me want to throw up.

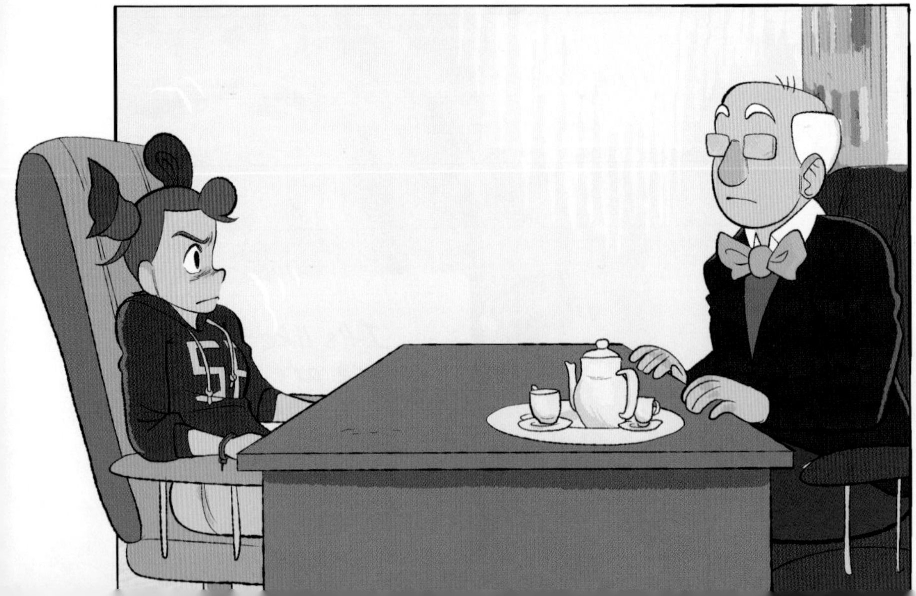

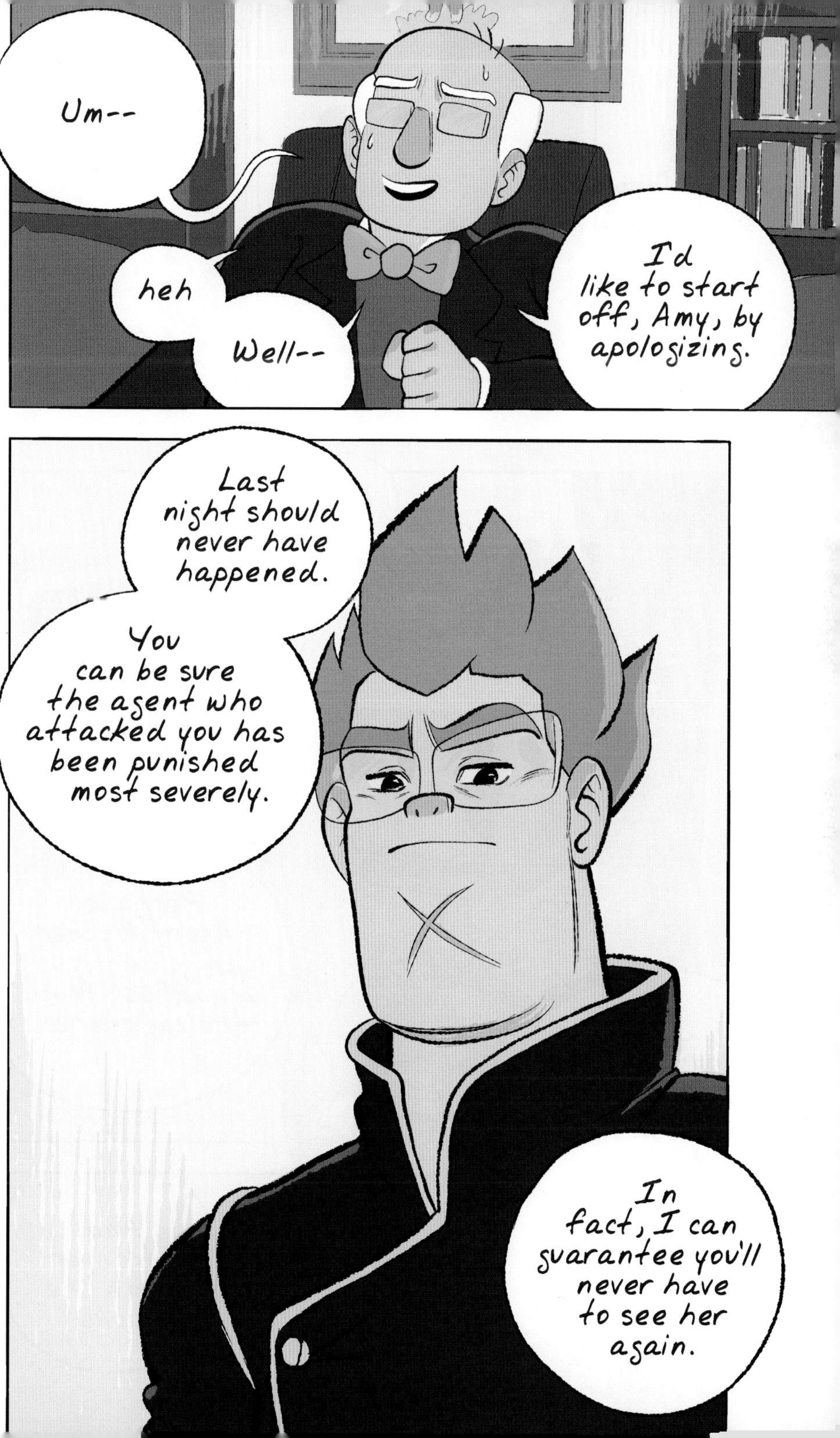
Um--
heh
Well--
I'd like to start off, Amy, by apologizing.
Last night should never have happened.
You can be sure the agent who attacked you has been punished most severely.
In fact, I can guarantee you'll never have to see her again.

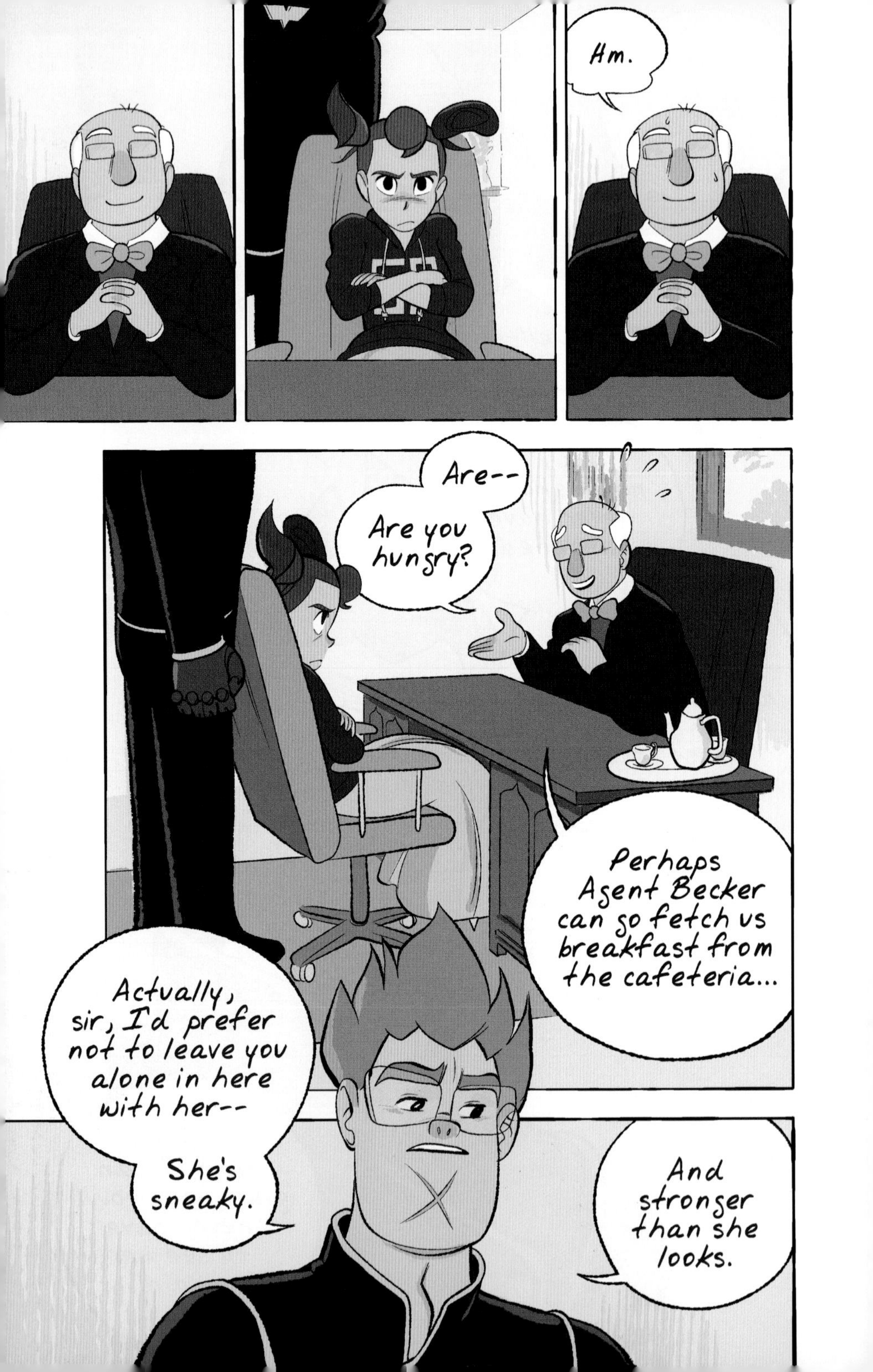
Hm.
Are--
Are you hungry?
Perhaps Agent Becker can go fetch us breakfast from the cafeteria...
Actually, sir, I'd prefer not to leave you alone in here with her--
She's sneaky.
And stronger than she looks.

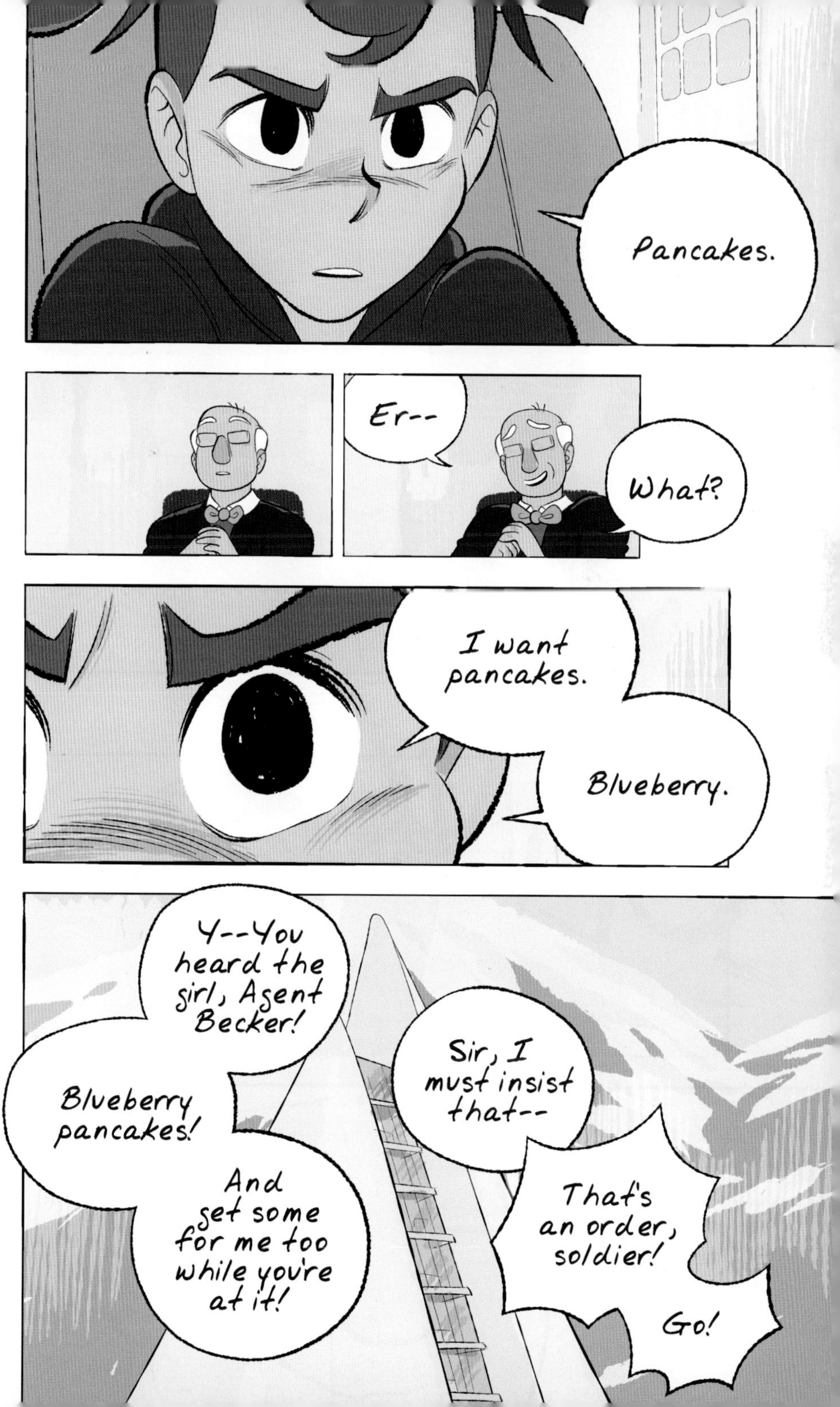
Pancakes.
Er--
What?
I want pancakes.
Blueberry.
Y--You heard the girl, Agent Becker!
Blueberry pancakes!
And get some for me too while you're at it!
Sir, I must insist that--
That's an order, soldier!
Go!

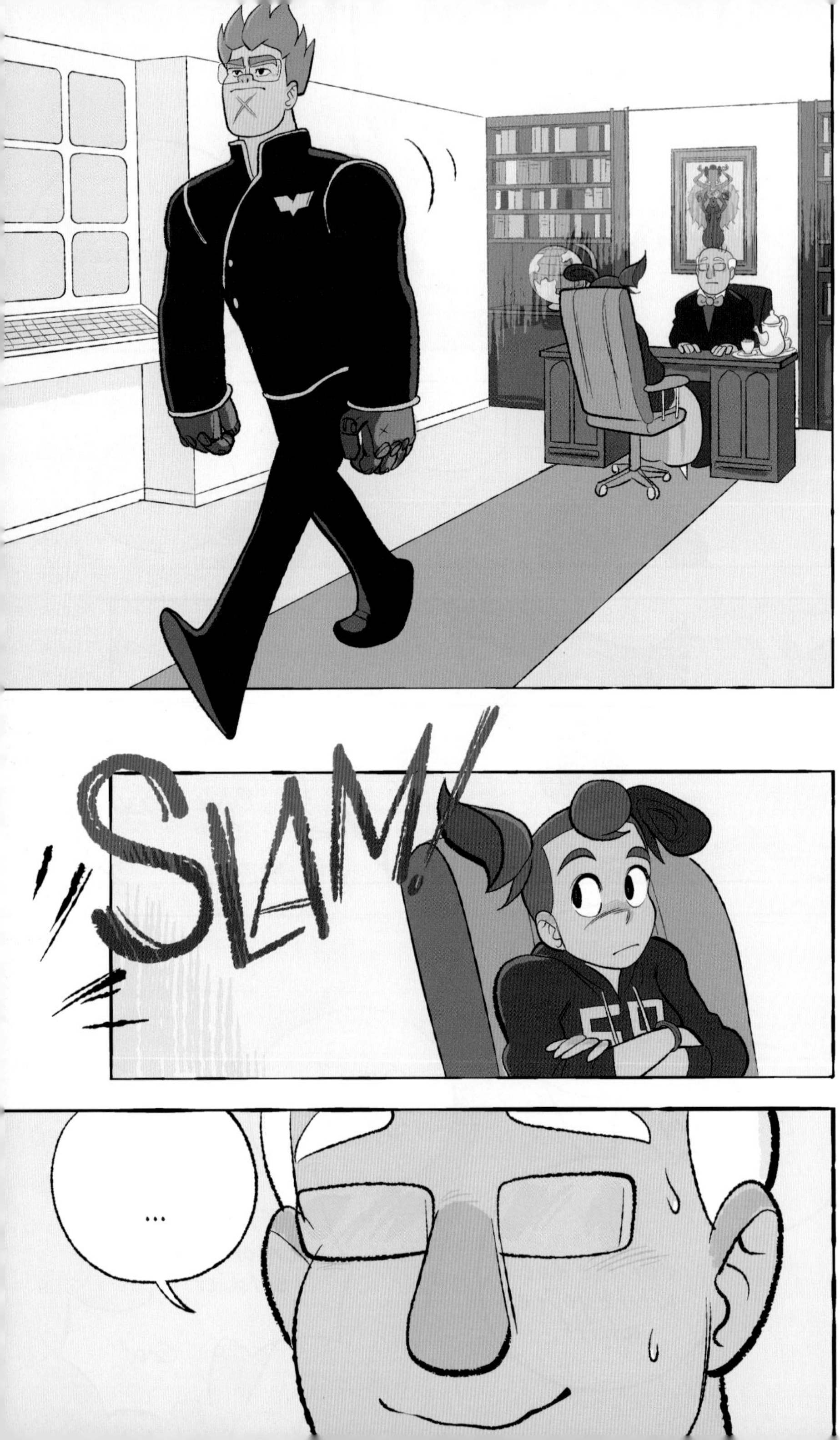
SLAM!
...

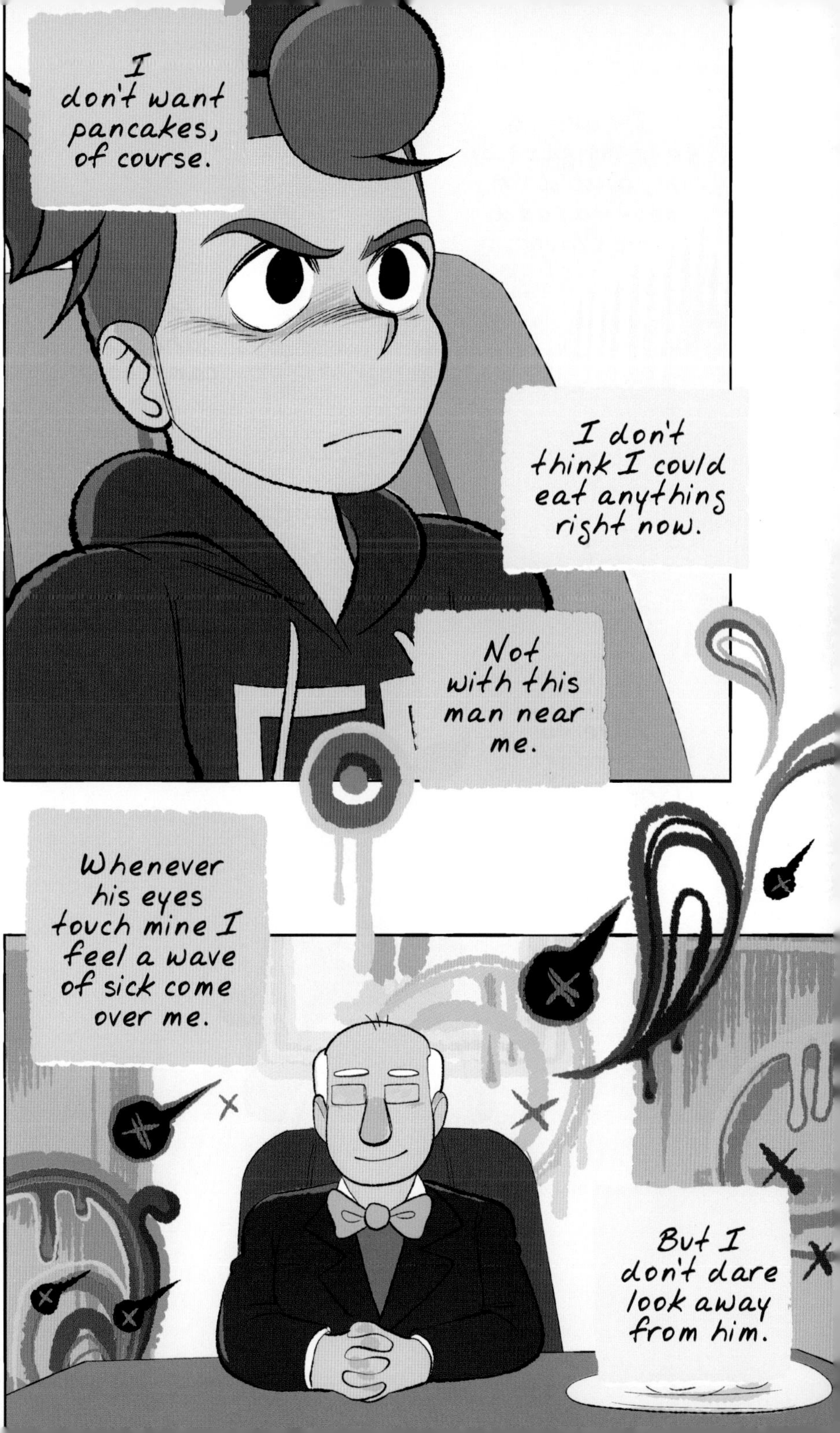
I don't want pancakes, of course.
I don't think I could eat anything right now.
Not with this man near me.
Whenever his eyes touch mine I feel a wave of sick come over me.
But I don't dare look away from him.

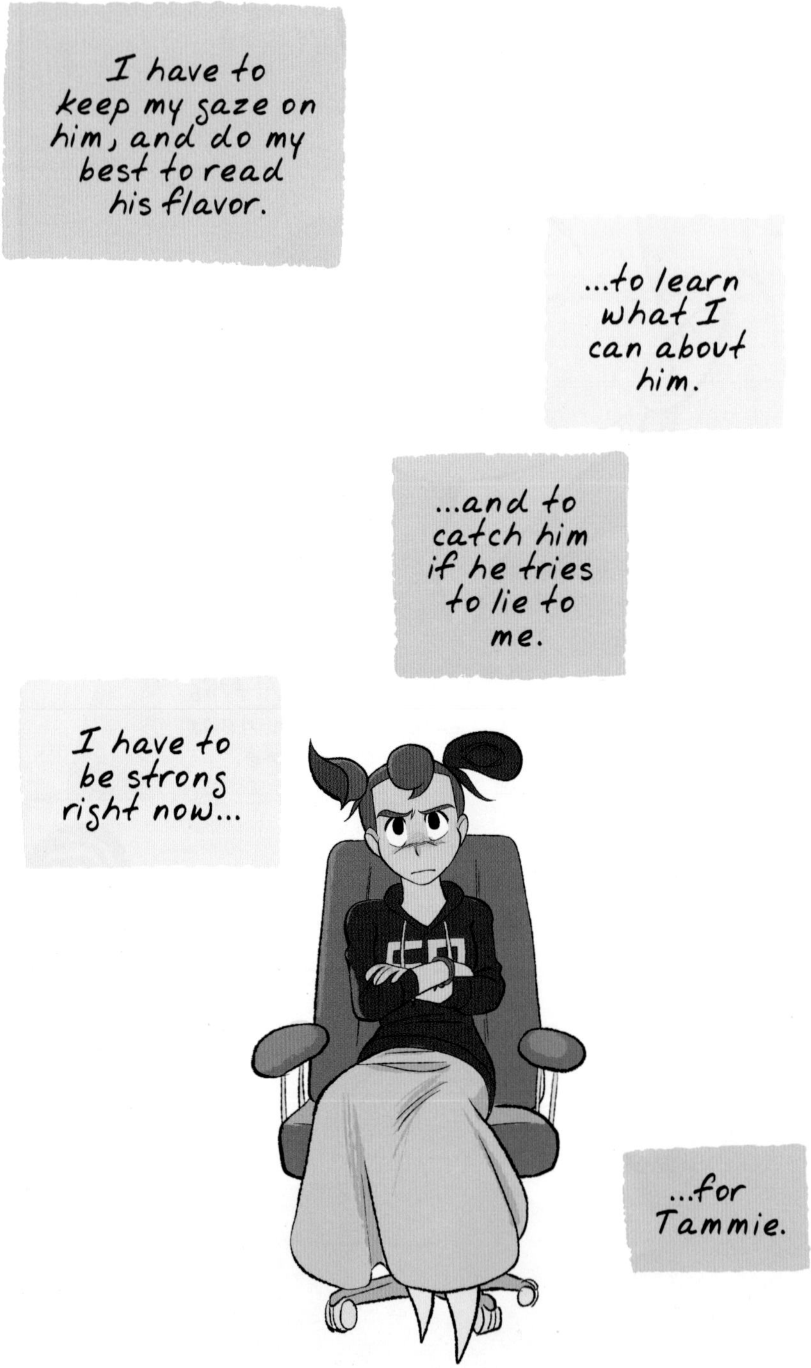
I have to keep my gaze on him, and do my best to read his flavor.
...to learn what I can about him.
...and to catch him if he tries to lie to me.
I have to be strong right now...
...for Tammie.

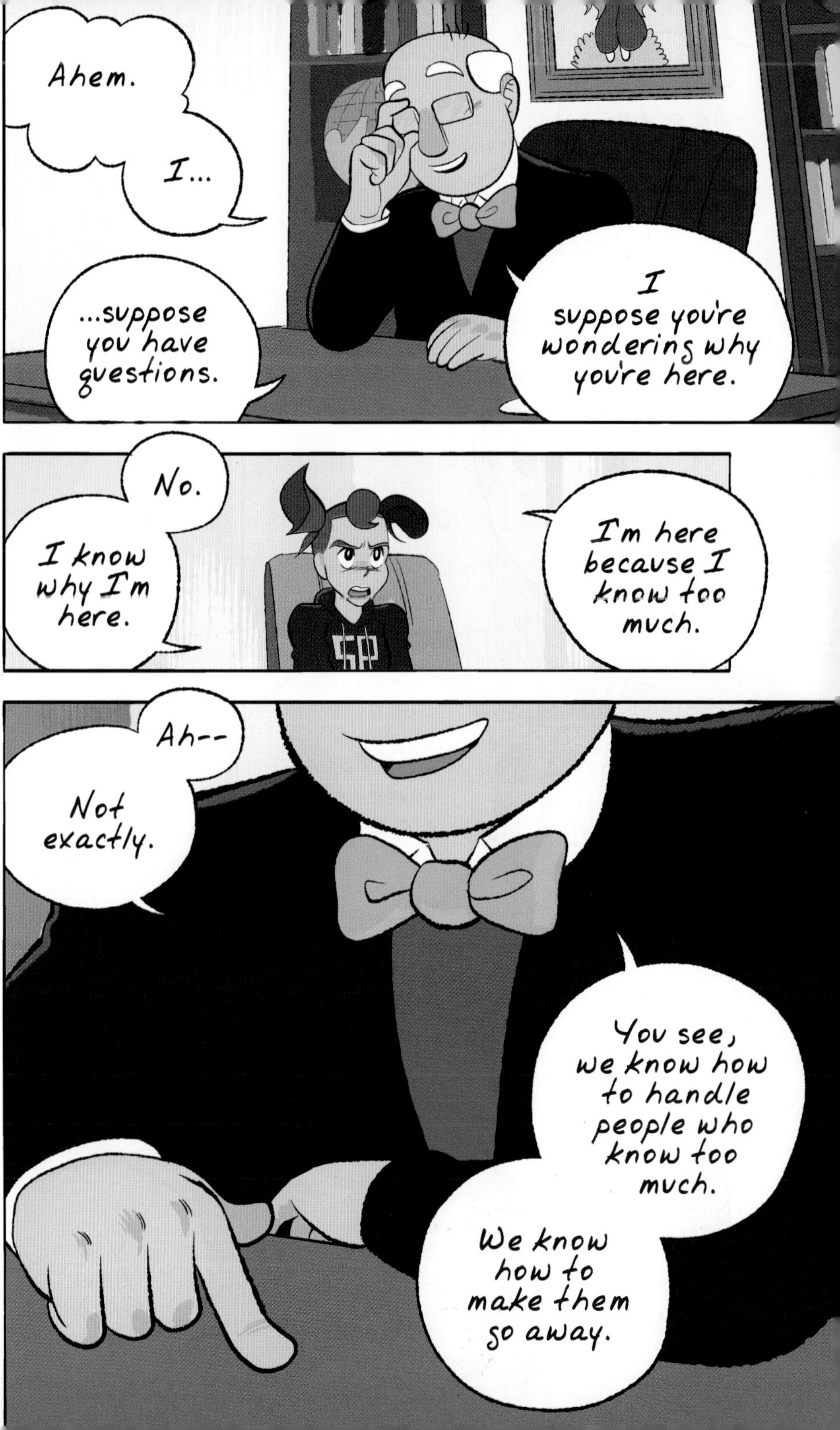

Ahem.
I...
...suppose you have questions.
I suppose you're wondering why you're here.
No.
I know why I'm here.
I'm here because I know too much.
Ah--
Not exactly.
You see, we know how to handle people who know too much.
We know how to make them go away.

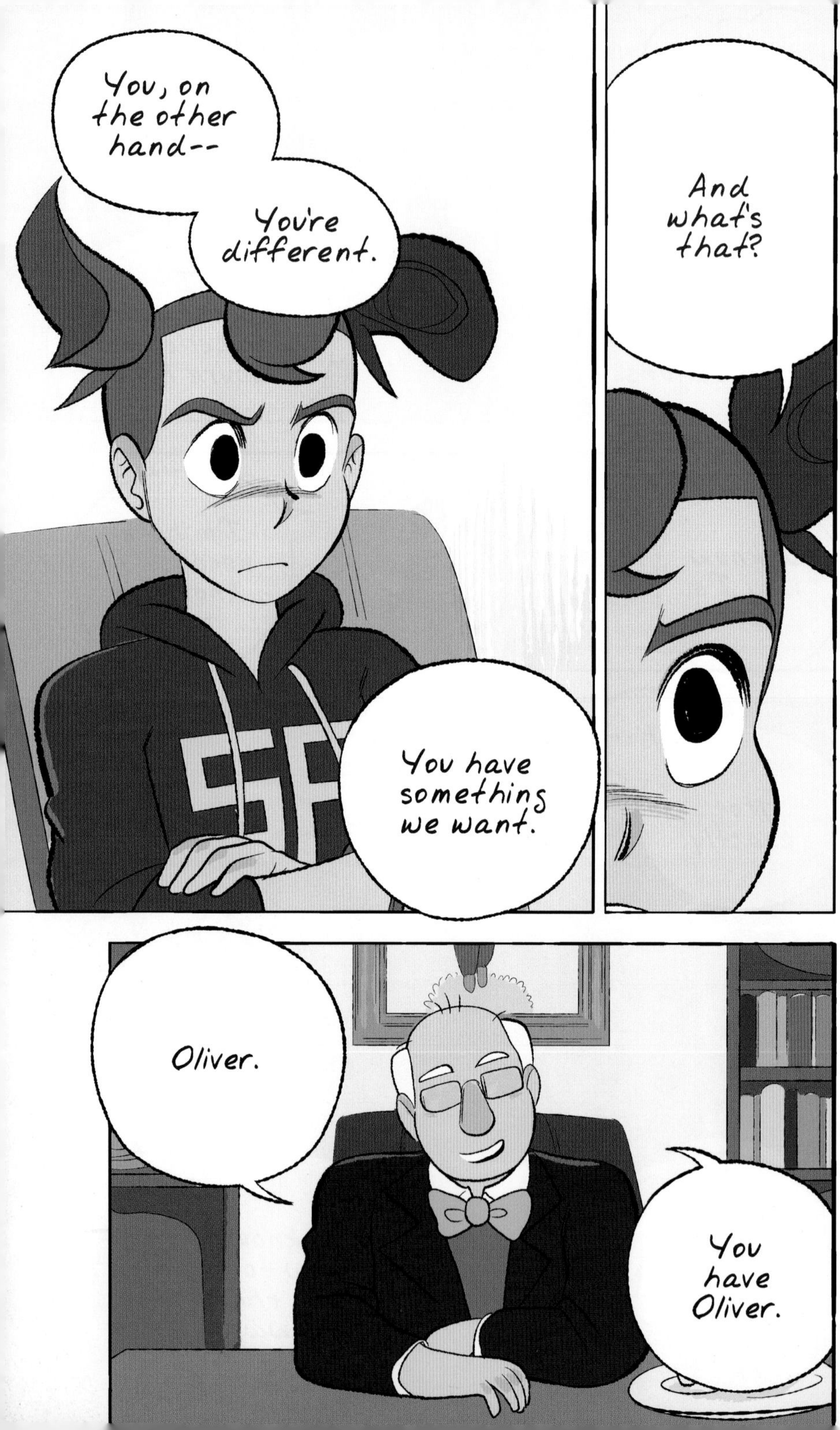
You, on the other hand--
You're different.
And what's that?
You have something we want.
Oliver.
You have Oliver.

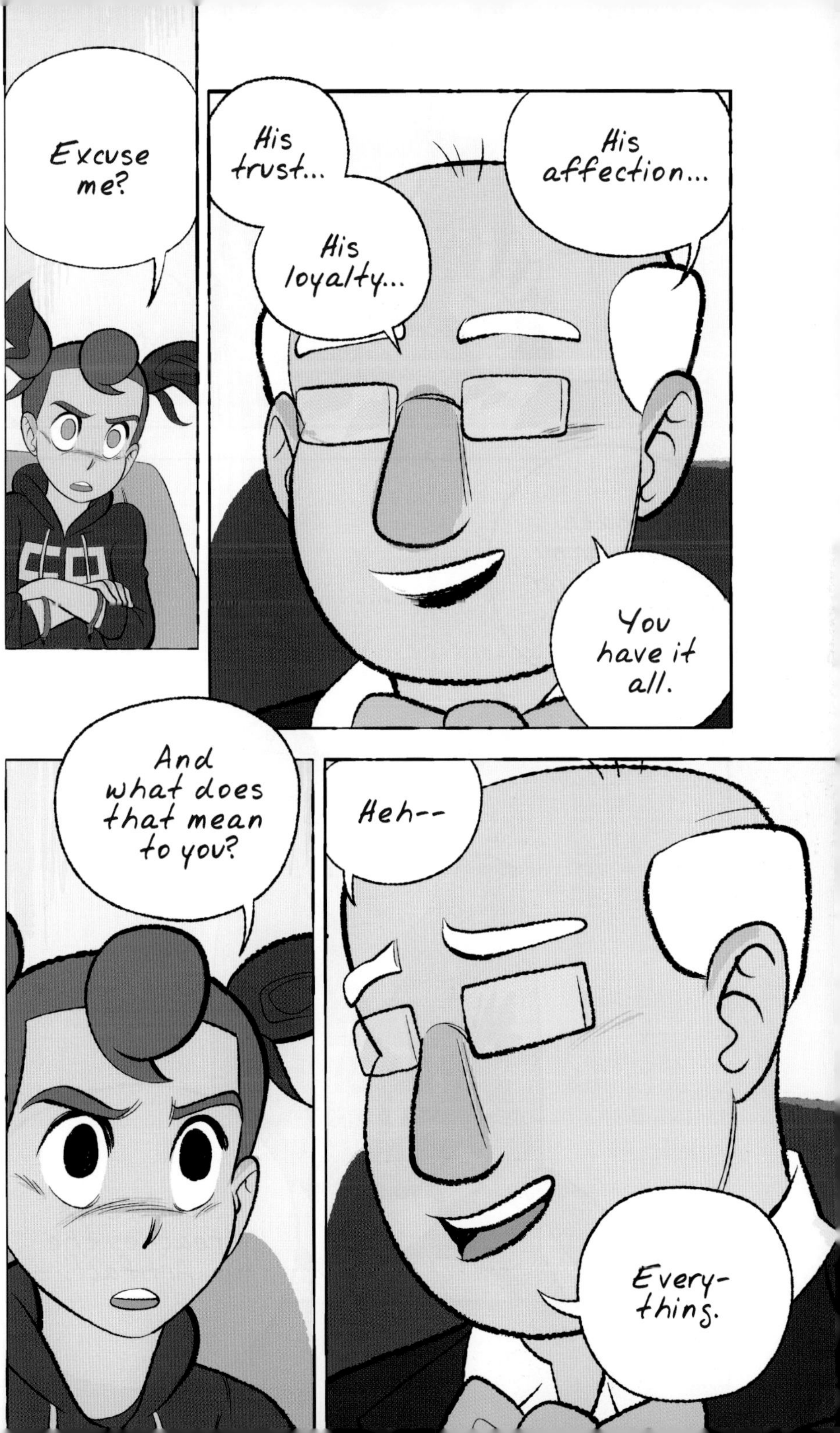
Excuse me?
His trust...
His loyalty...
His affection...
You have it all.
And what does that mean to you?
Heh--
Every-thing.

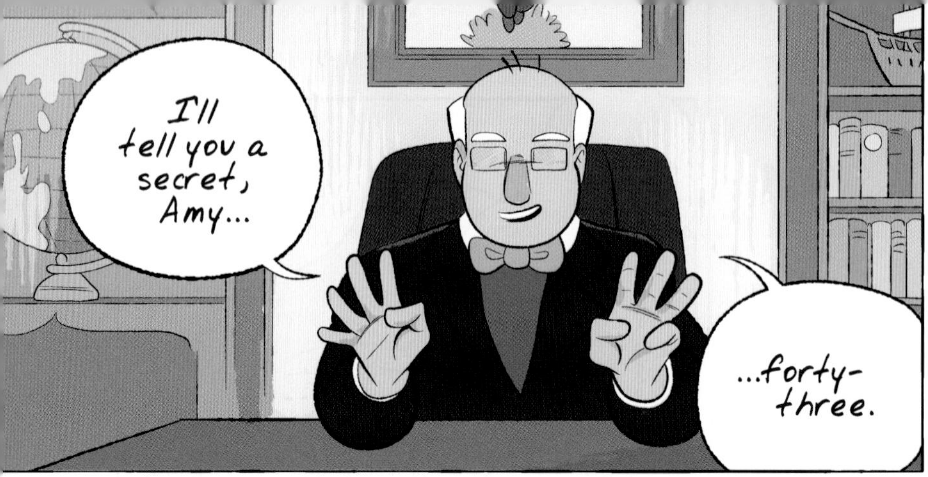
I'll tell you a secret, Amy...
...forty-three.

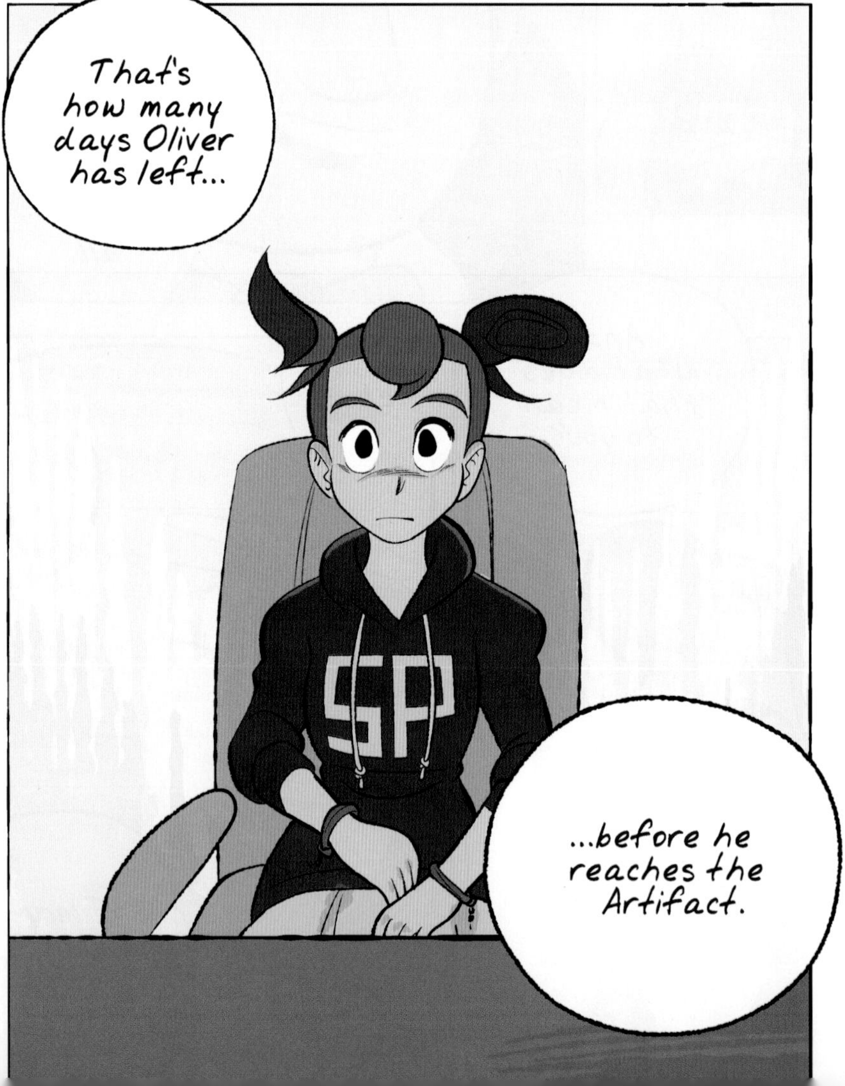
That's how many days Oliver has left...
SP
...before he reaches the Artifact.

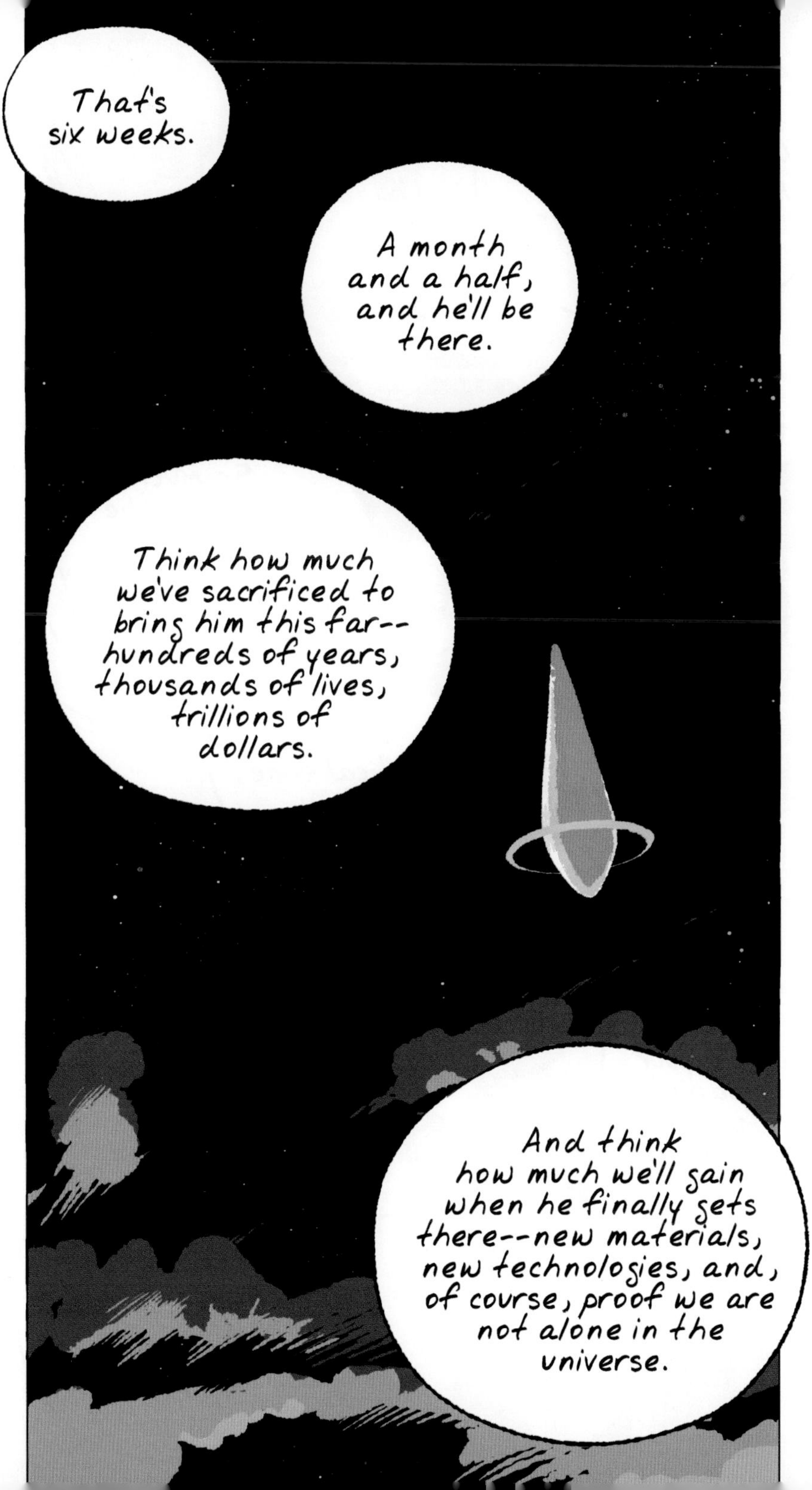
That's six weeks.
A month and a half, and he'll be there.
Think how much we've sacrificed to bring him this far--hundreds of years, thousands of lives, trillions of dollars.
And think how much we'll gain when he finally gets there--new materials, new technologies, and, of course, proof we are not alone in the universe.

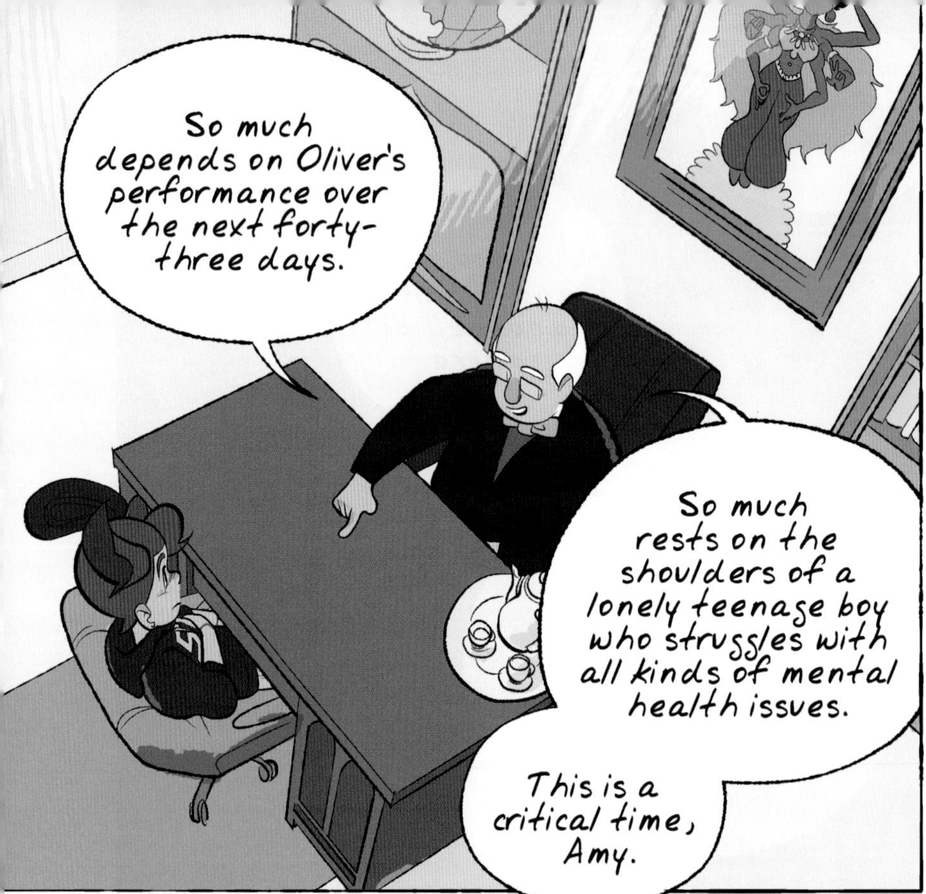
So much depends on Oliver's performance over the next forty-three days.
So much rests on the shoulders of a lonely teenage boy who struggles with all kinds of mental health issues.
This is a critical time, Amy.

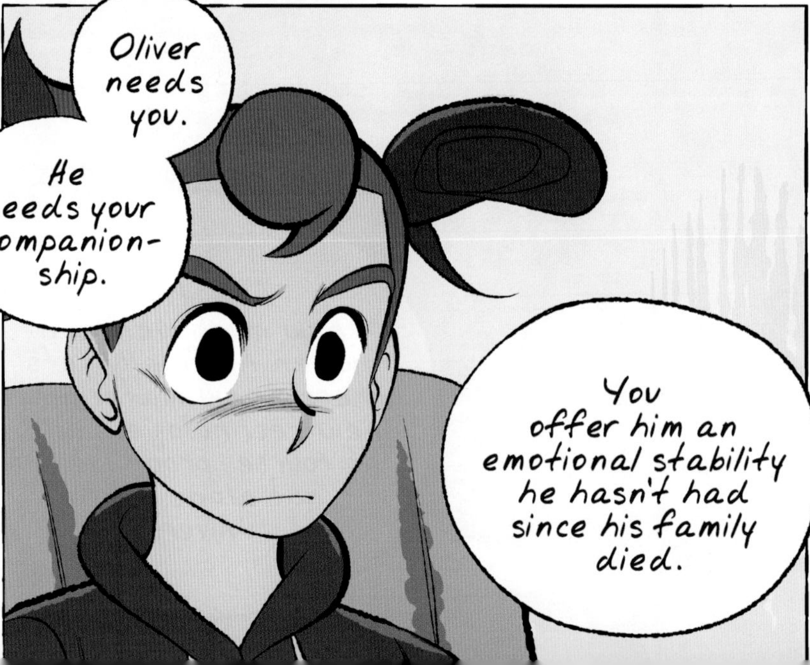
Oliver needs you.
He needs your companion-ship.
You offer him an emotional stability he hasn't had since his family died.

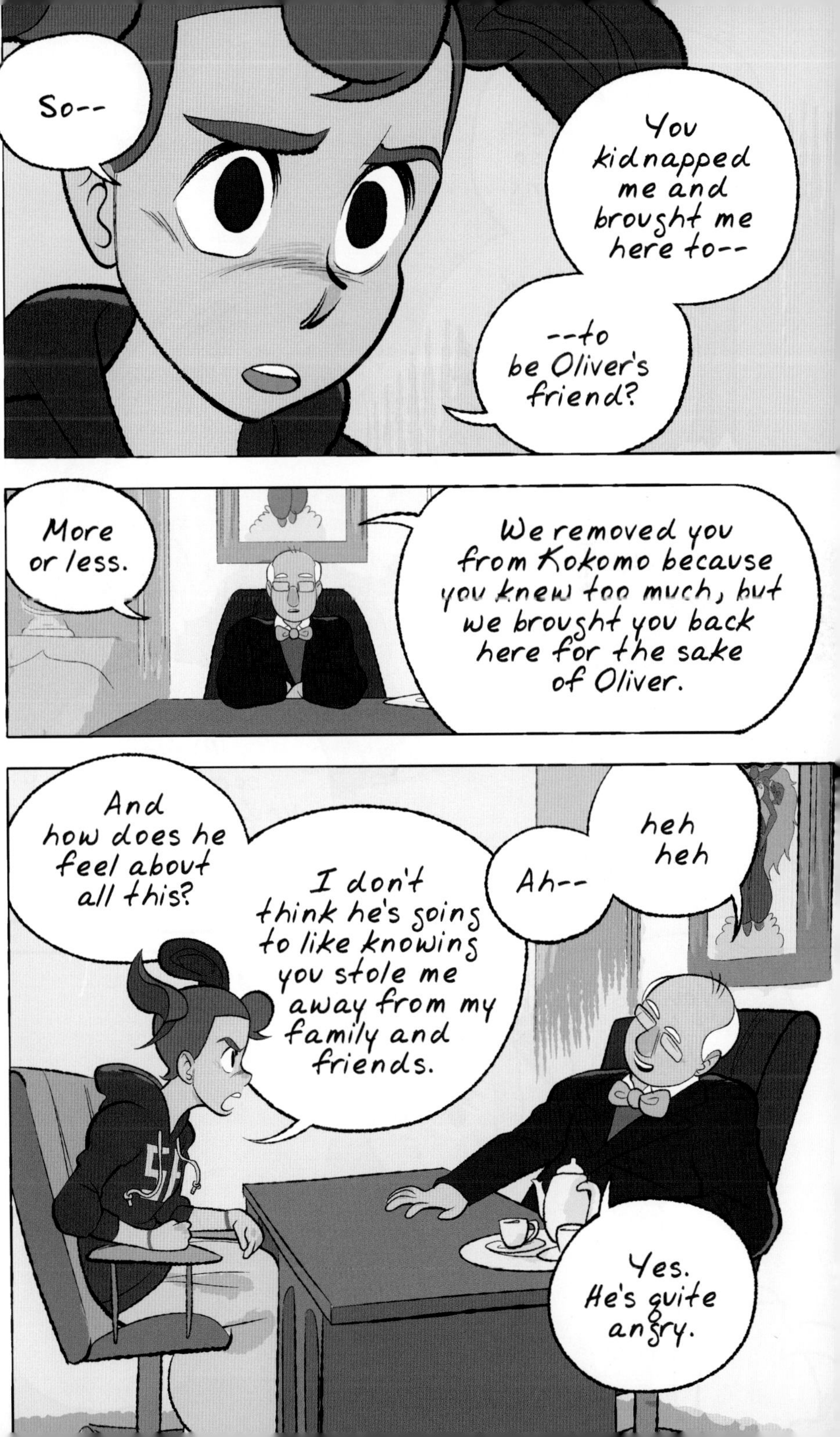
So--
You kidnapped me and brought me here to--
--to be Oliver's friend?
More or less.
We removed you from Kokomo because you knew too much, but we brought you back here for the sake of Oliver.
And how does he feel about all this?
I don't think he's going to like knowing you stole me away from my family and friends.
Ah--
heh heh
Yes. He's quite angry.

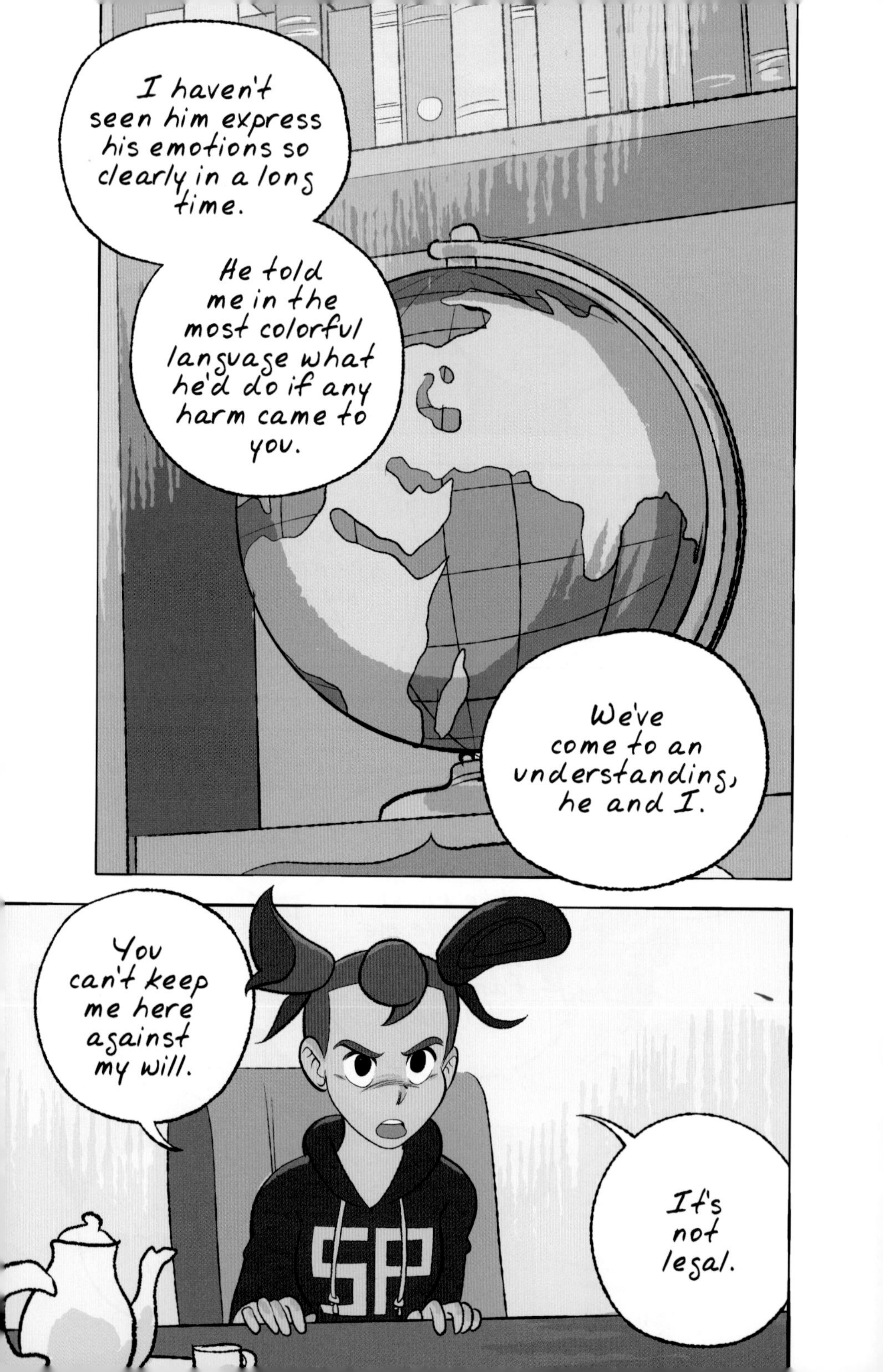
I haven't seen him express his emotions so clearly in a long time.
He told me in the most colorful language what he'd do if any harm came to you.
We've come to an understanding, he and I.
You can't keep me here against my will.
It's not legal.

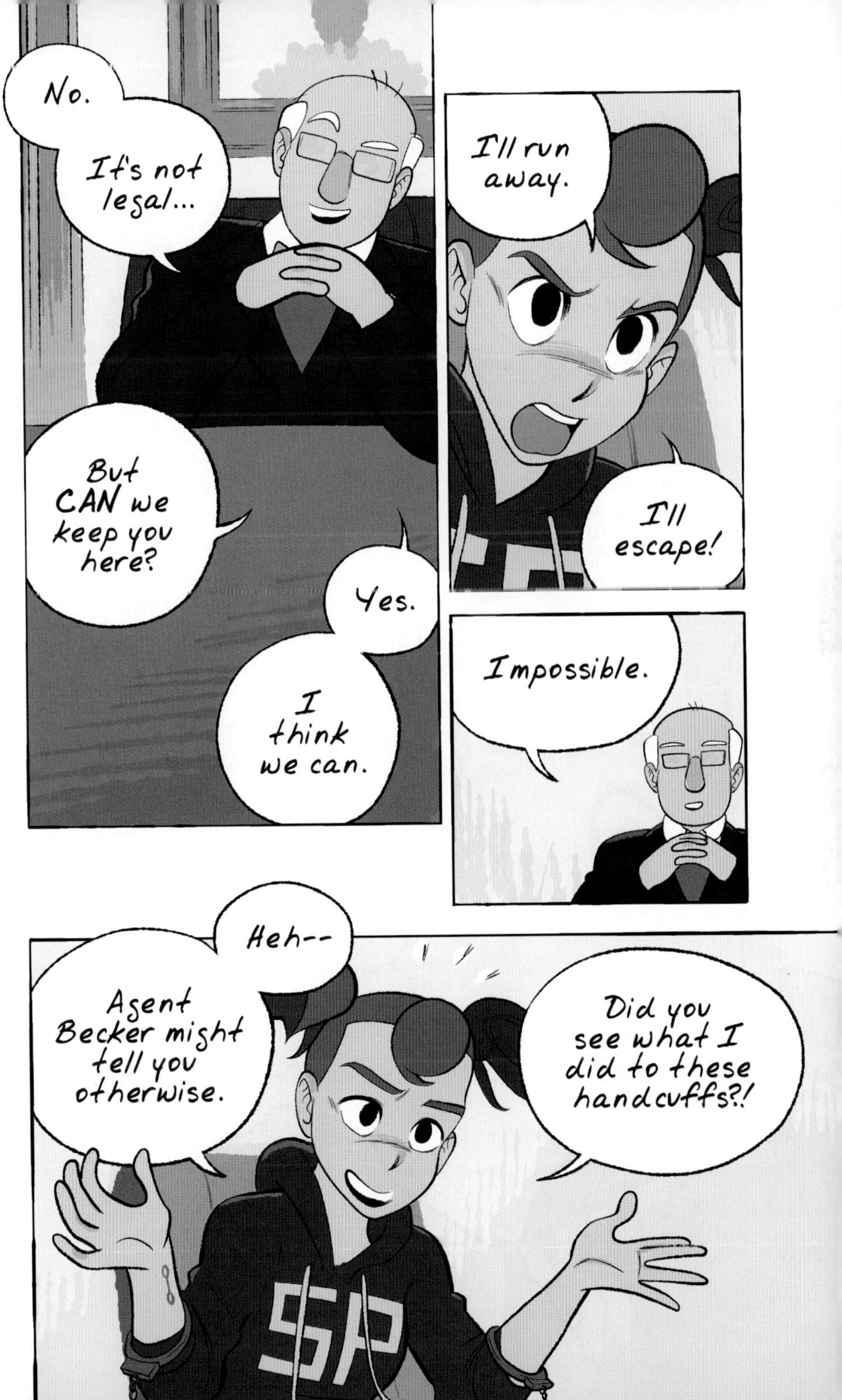
No.
It's not legal...
I'll run away.
I'll escape!
But CAN we keep you here?
Yes.
I think we can.
Impossible.
Heh--
Agent Becker might tell you otherwise.
Did you see what I did to these handcuffs?!

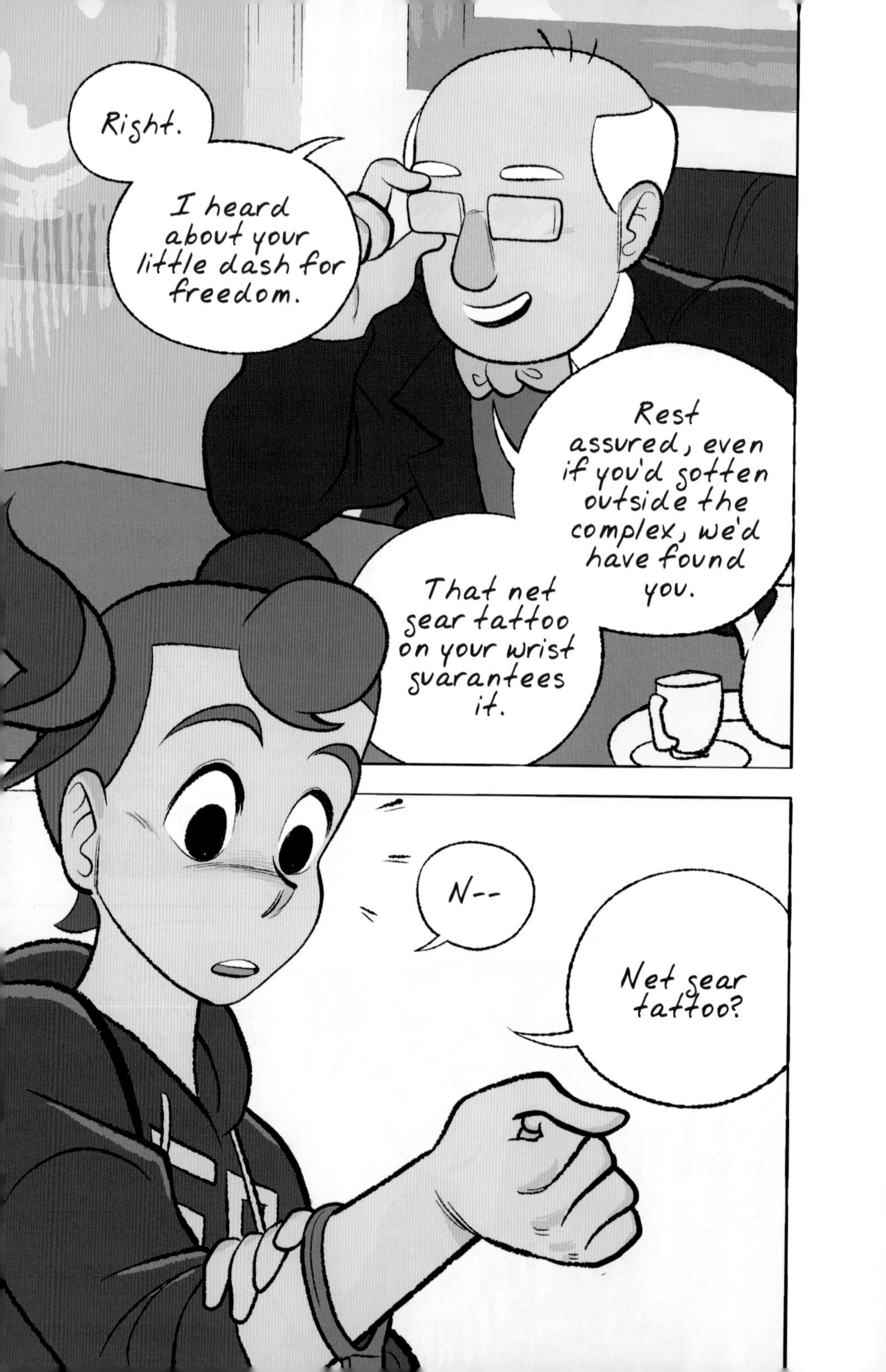
Right.
I heard about your little dash for freedom.
Rest assured, even if you'd gotten outside the complex, we'd have found you.
That net gear tattoo on your wrist guarantees it.
N--
Net gear tattoo?

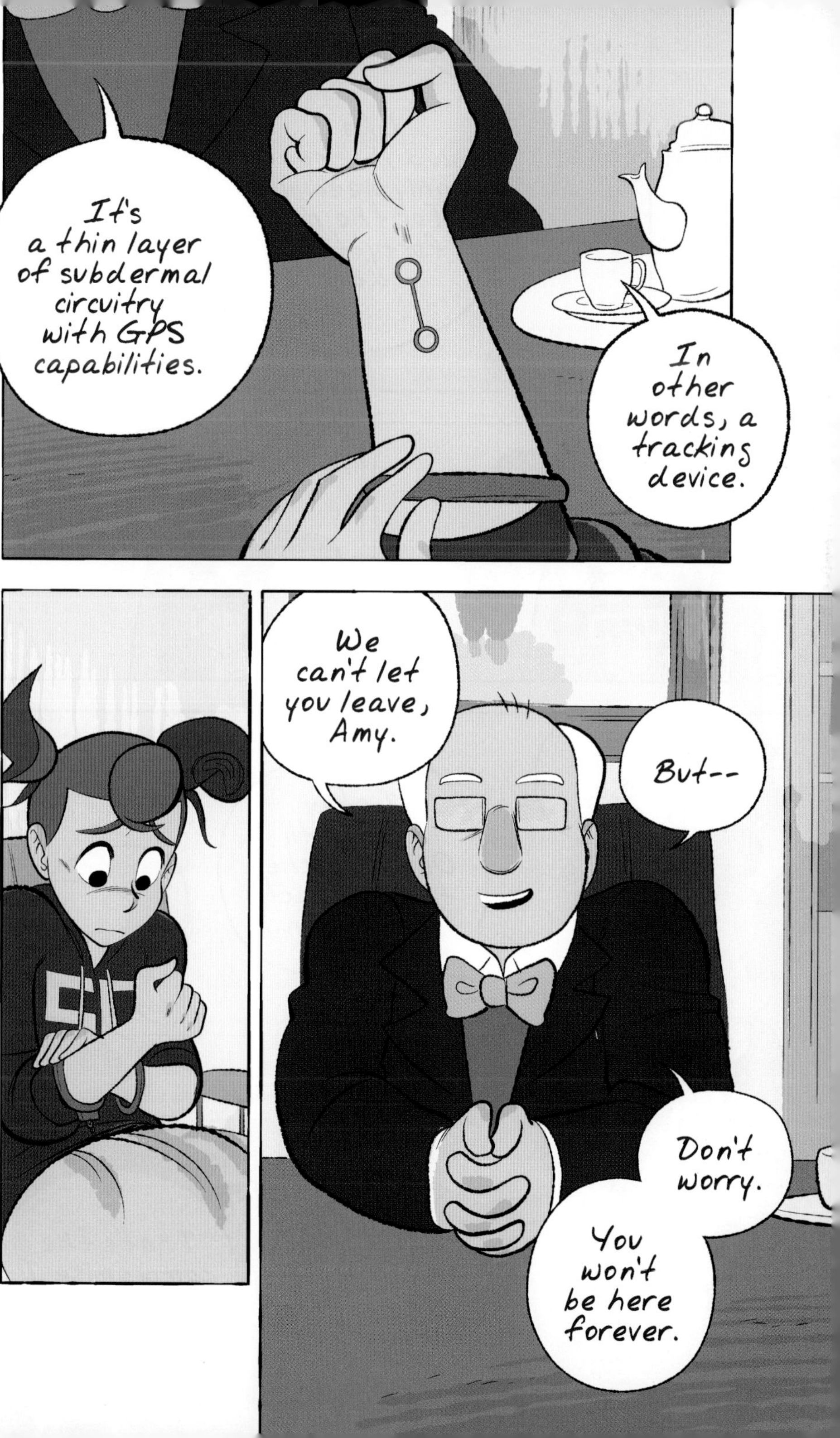
It's a thin layer of subdermal circuitry with GPS capabilities.
In other words, a tracking device.
We can't let you leave, Amy.
But--
Don't worry.
You won't be here forever.

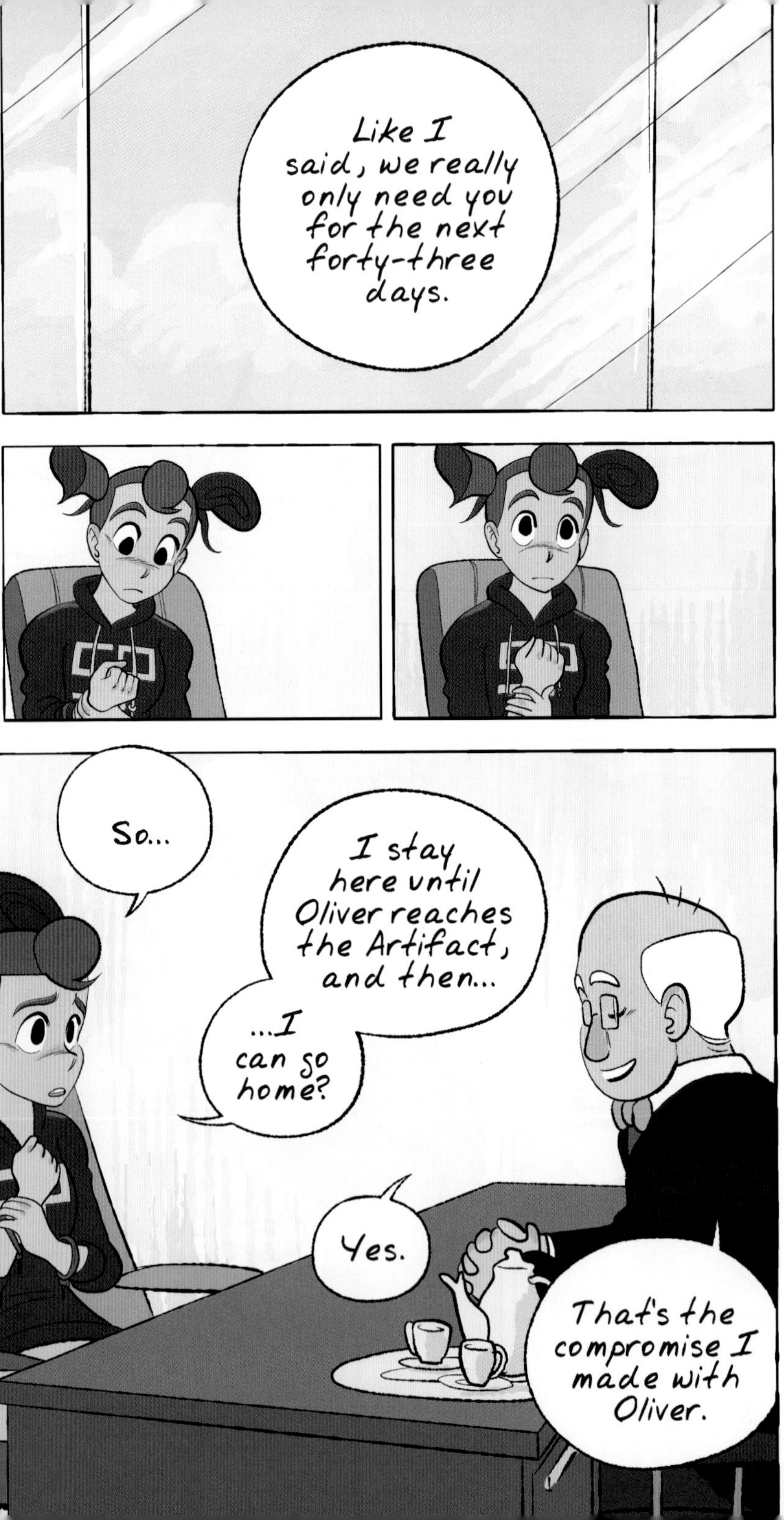
Like I said, we really only need you for the next forty-three days.
So...
I stay here until Oliver reaches the Artifact, and then...
...I can go home?
Yes.
That's the compromise I made with Oliver.

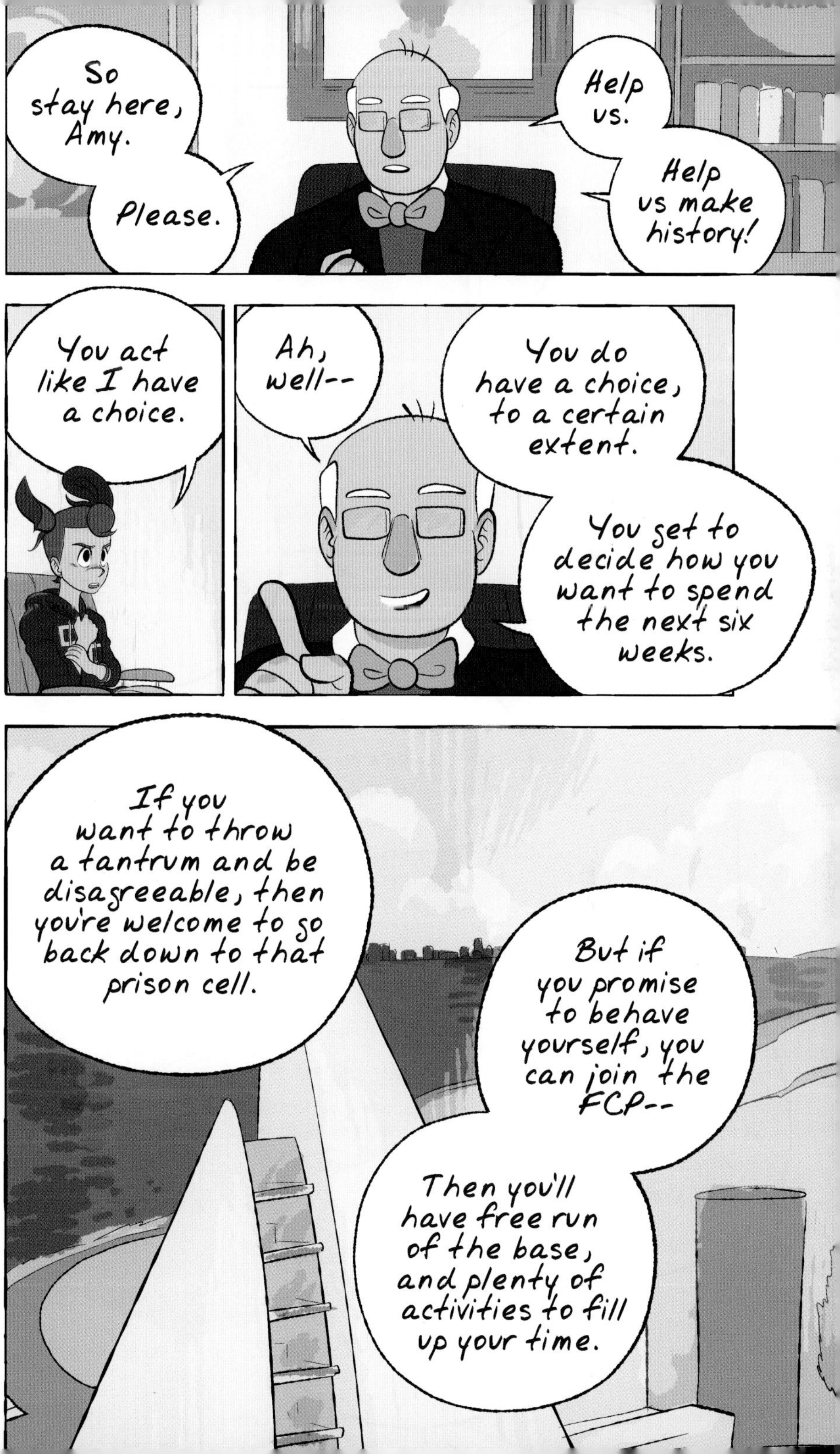
So stay here, Amy.
Please.
Help us.
Help us make history!
You act like I have a choice.
Ah, well--
You do have a choice, to a certain extent.
You get to decide how you want to spend the next six weeks.
If you want to throw a tantrum and be disagreeable, then you're welcome to go back down to that prison cell.
But if you promise to behave yourself, you can join the FCP--
Then you'll have free run of the base, and plenty of activities to fill up your time.

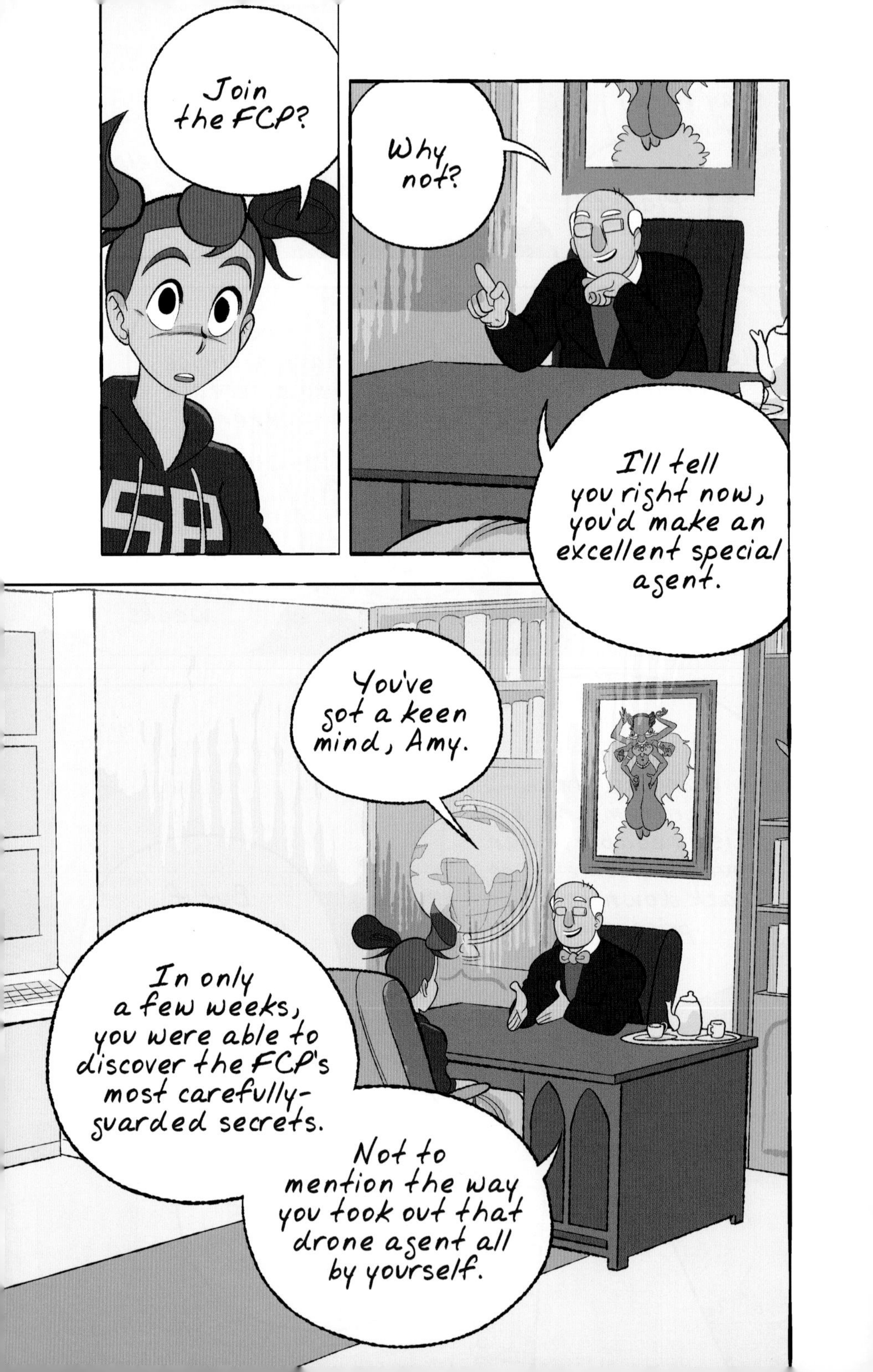
Join the FCP?
Why not?
I'll tell you right now, you'd make an excellent special agent.
You've got a keen mind, Amy.
In only a few weeks, you were able to discover the FCP's most carefully-guarded secrets.
Not to mention the way you took out that drone agent all by yourself.

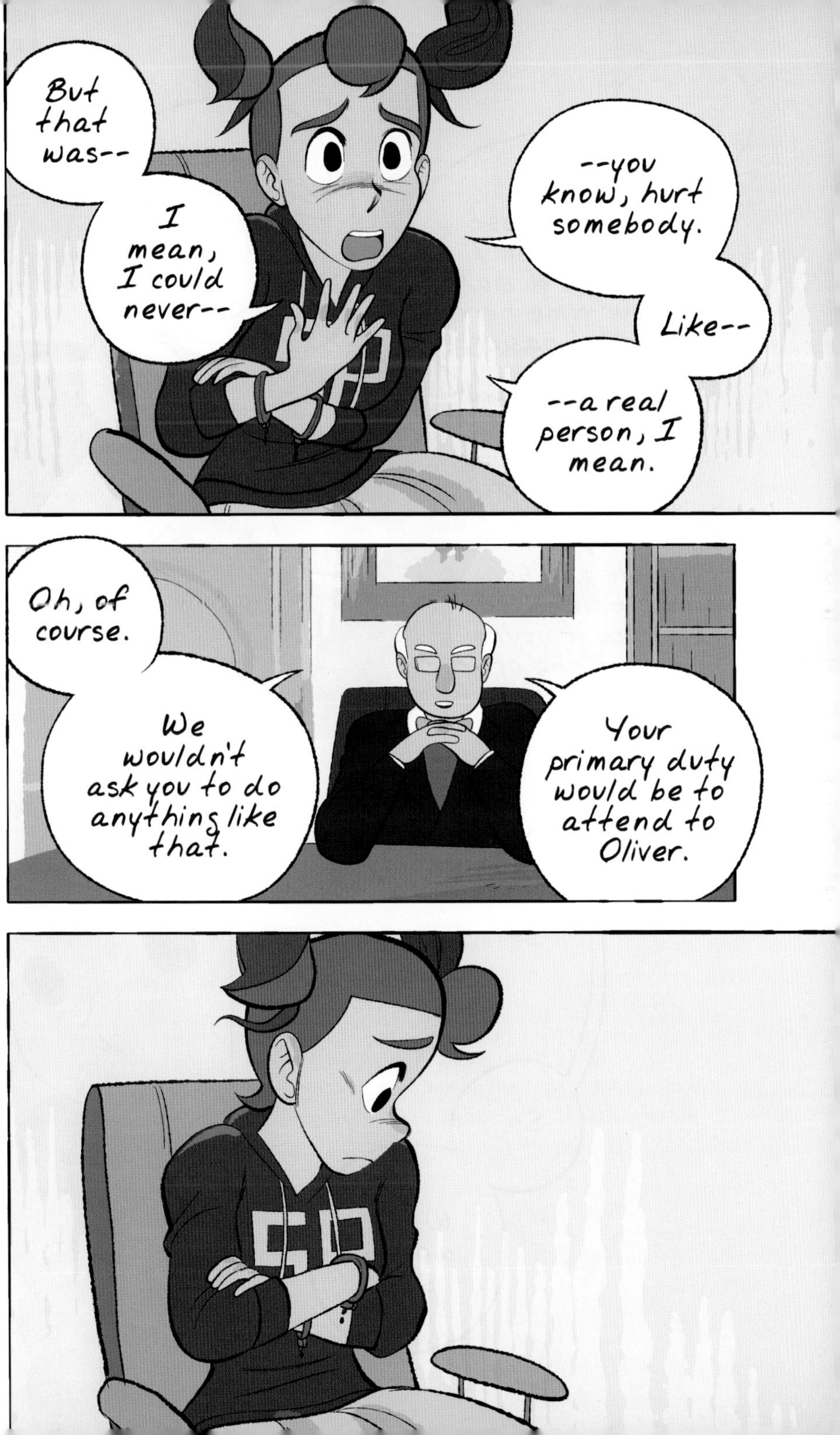
But that was--
I mean, I could never--
--you know, hurt somebody.
Like--
--a real person, I mean.
Oh, of course.
We wouldn't ask you to do anything like that.
Your primary duty would be to attend to Oliver.

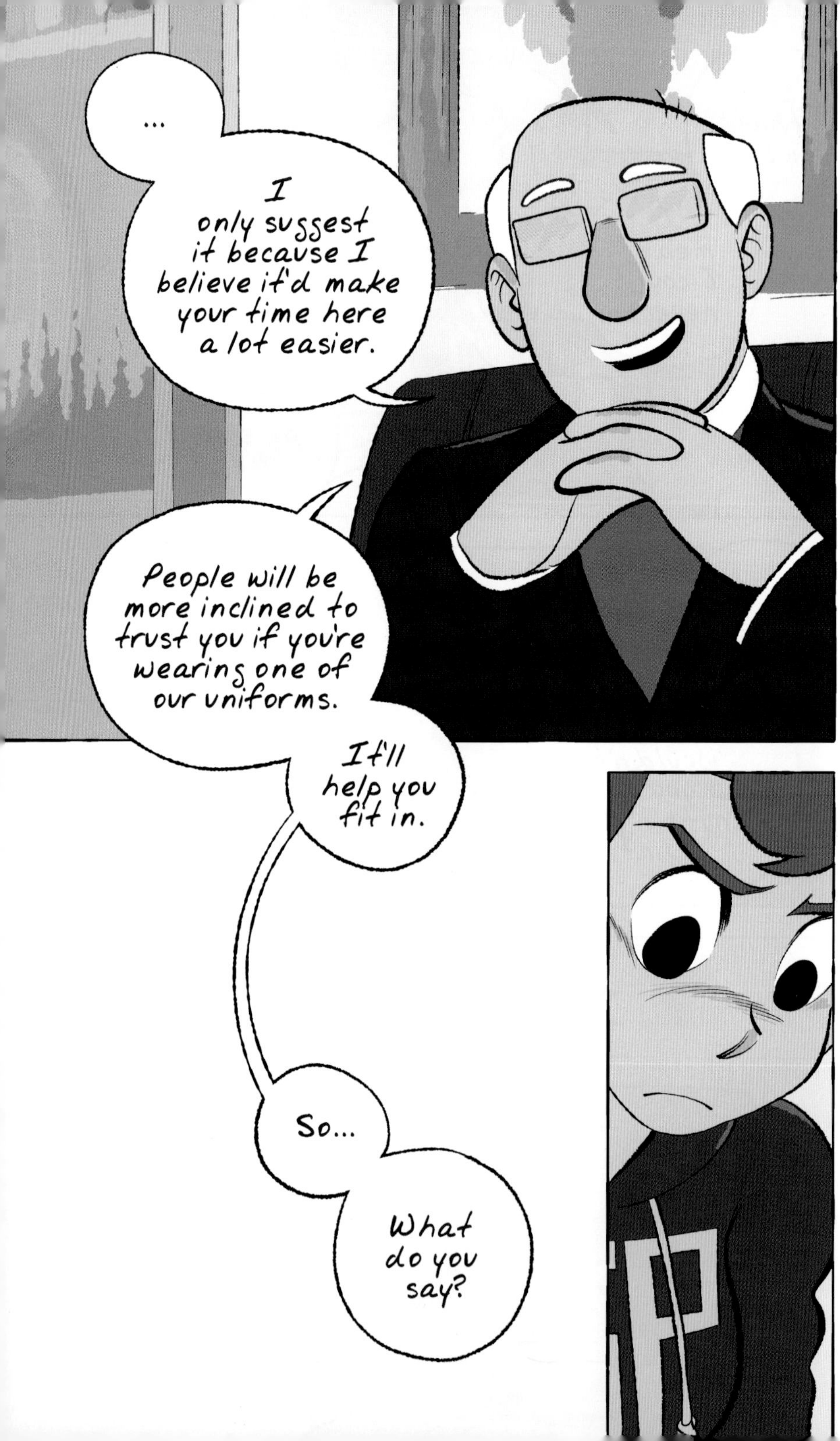
...
I only suggest it because I believe it'd make your time here a lot easier.
People will be more inclined to trust you if you're wearing one of our uniforms.
It'll help you fit in.
So...
What do you say?

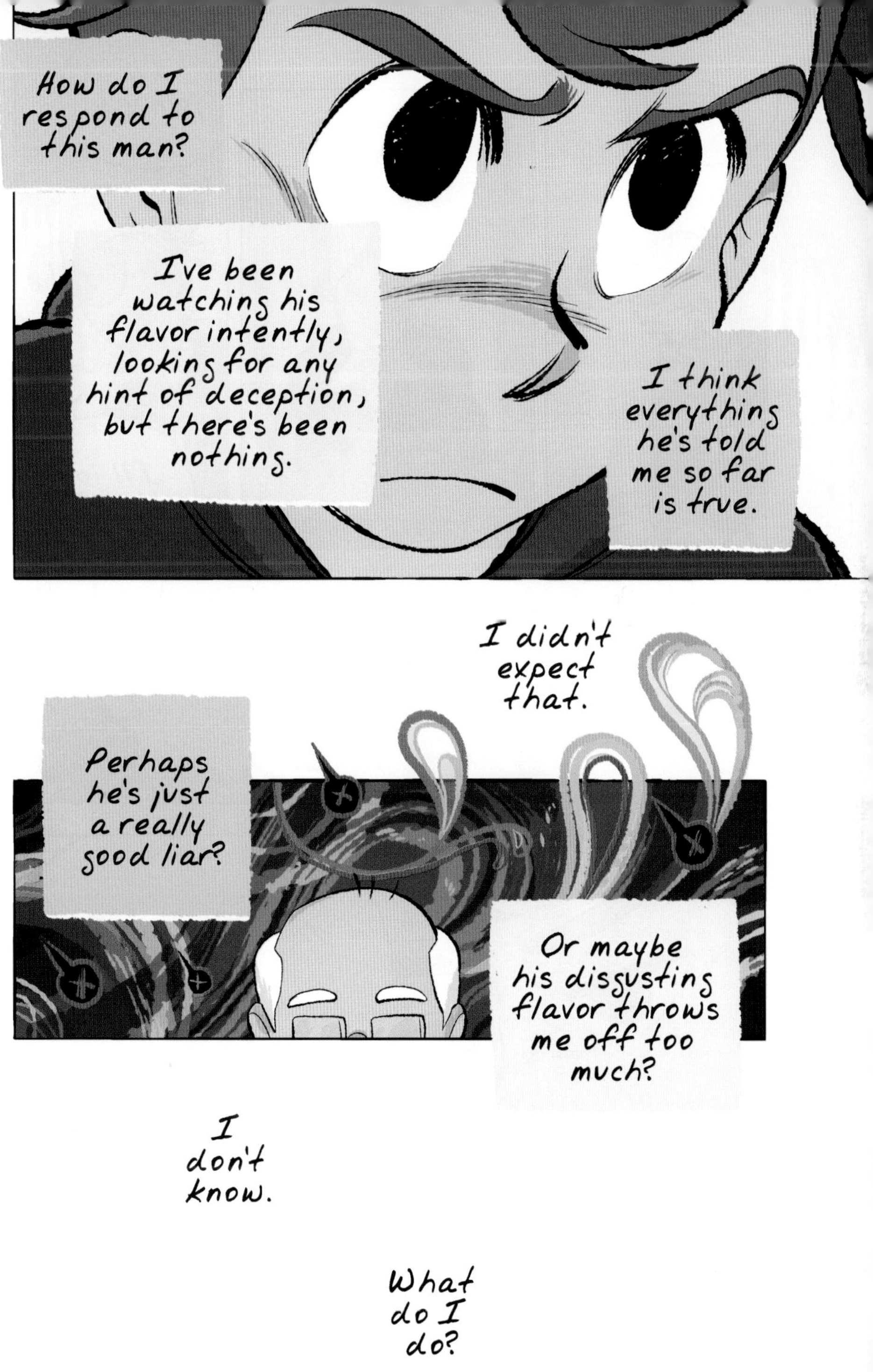
How do I respond to this man?
I've been watching his flavor intently, looking for any hint of deception, but there's been nothing.
I think everything he's told me so far is true.
I didn't expect that.
Perhaps he's just a really good liar?
Or maybe his disgusting flavor throws me off too much?
I don't know.
What do I do?

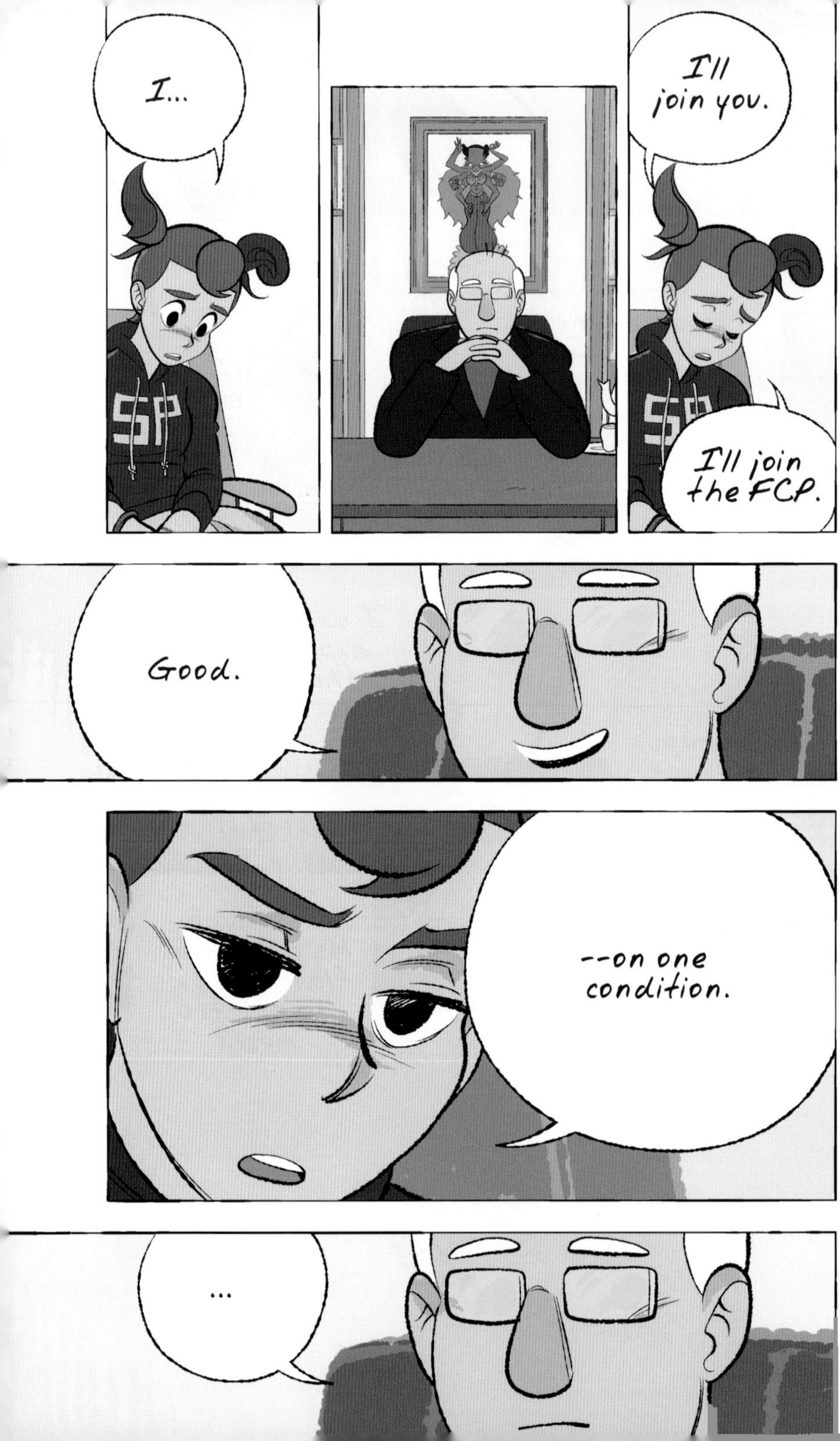
I...
I'll join you.
I'll join the FCP.
Good.
--on one condition.
...

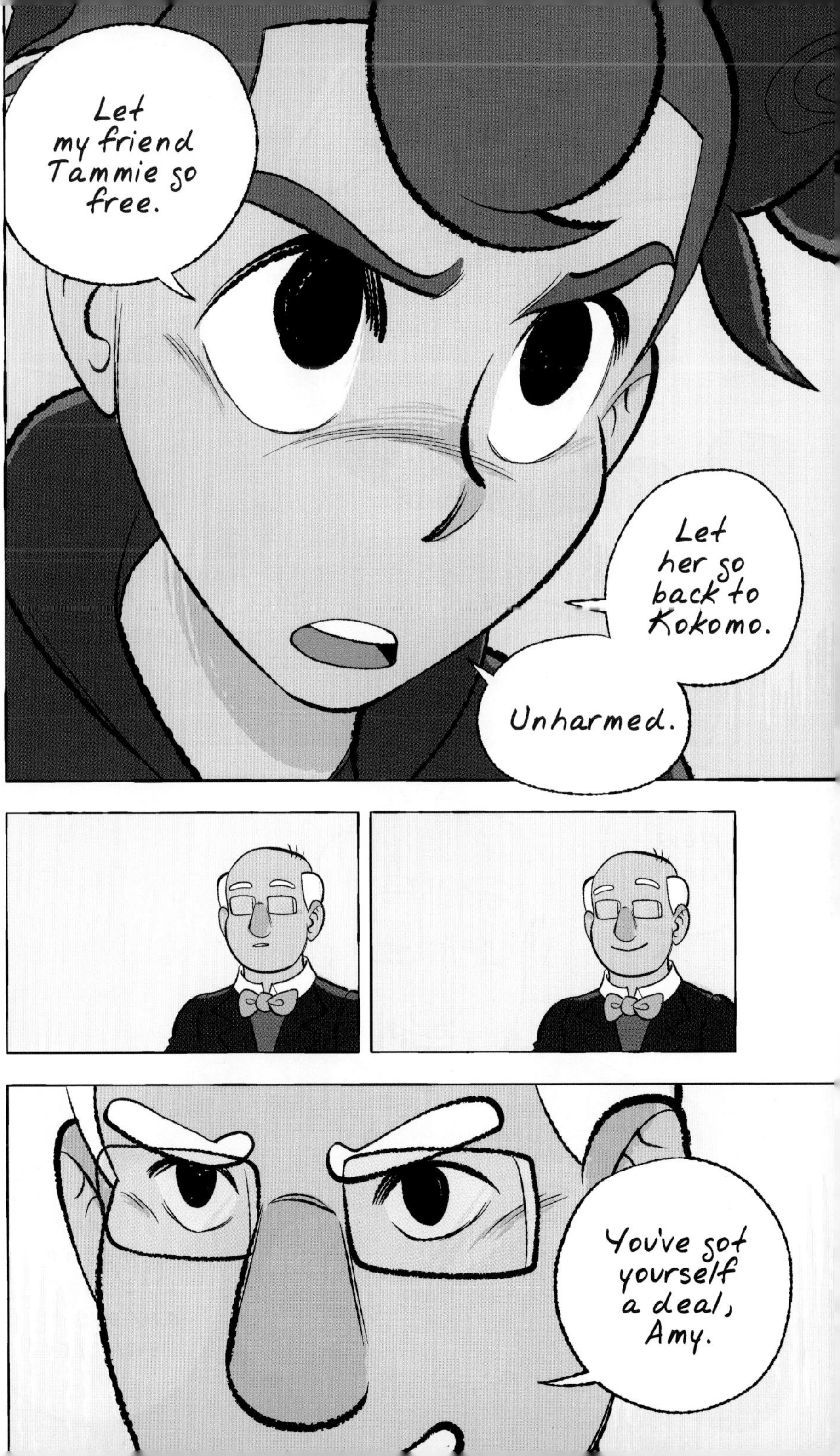
Let my friend Tammie go free.
Let her go back to Kokomo.
Unharmed.
You've got yourself a deal, Amy.

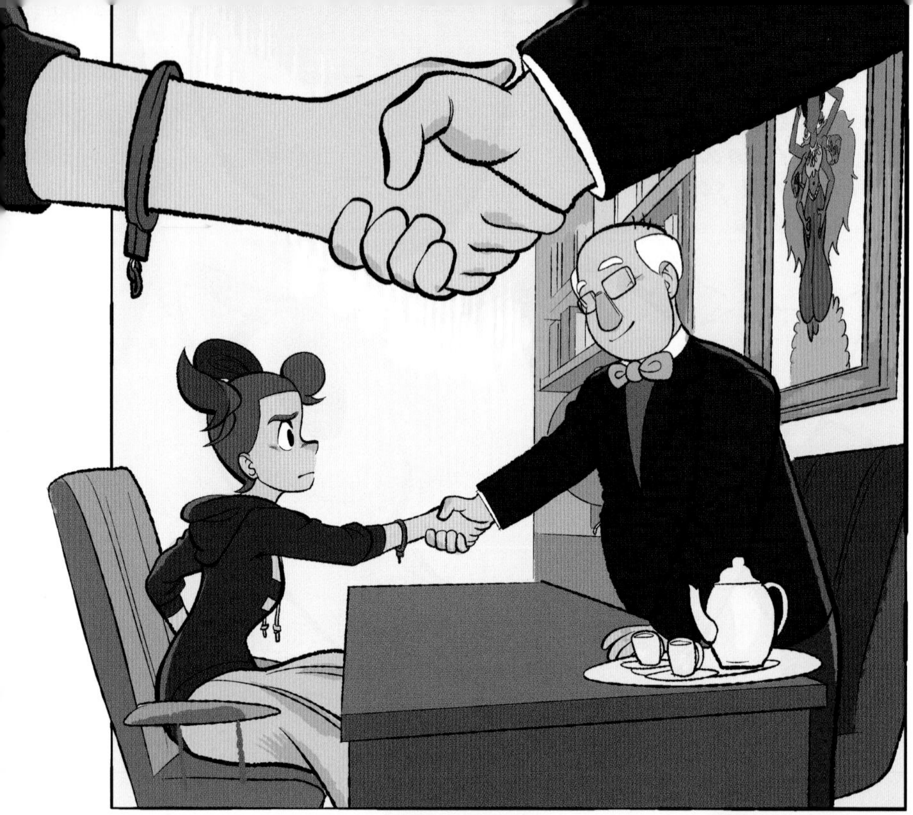

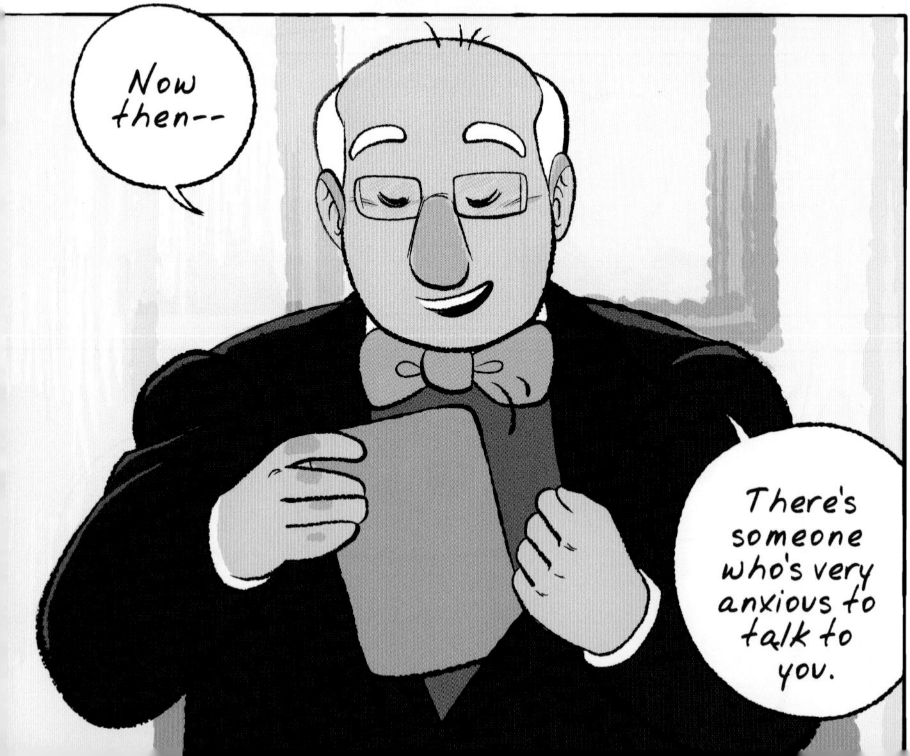
Now then--
There's someone who's very anxious to talk to you.

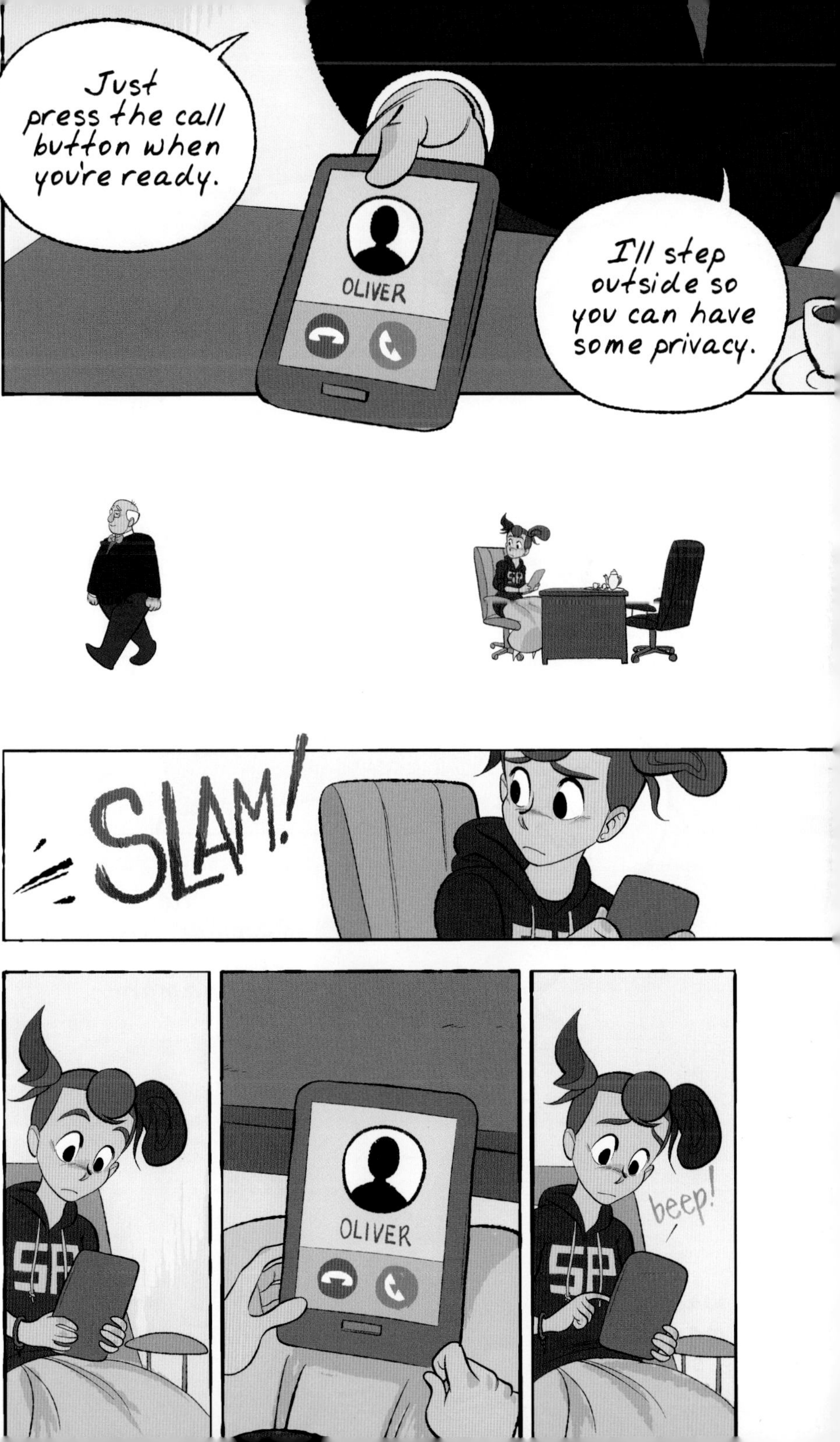
Just press the call button when you're ready.
OLIVER
I'll step outside so you can have some privacy.
SLAM!
SP
OLIVER
SP
beep!

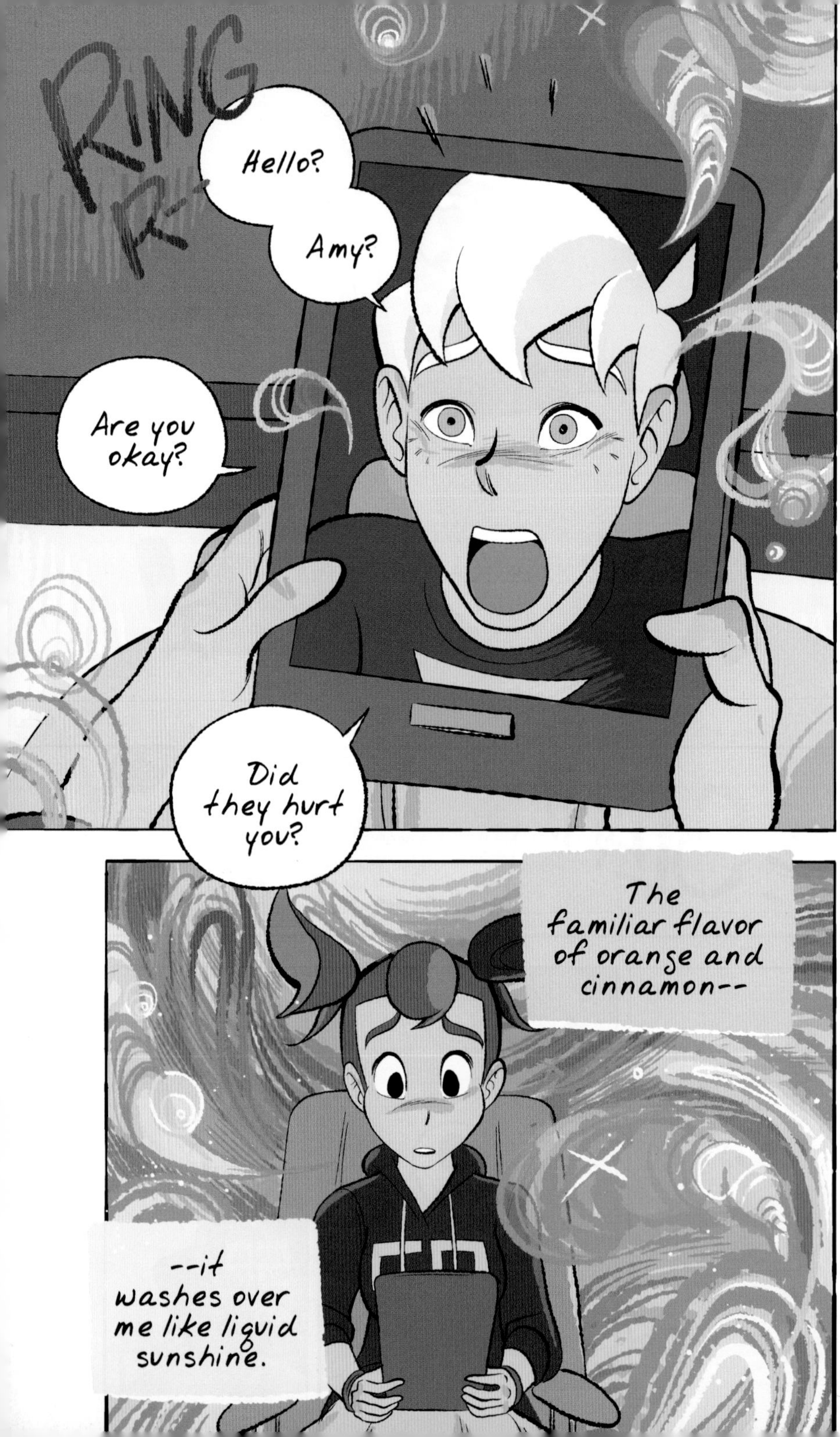
RING
R-
Hello?
Amy?
Are you okay?
Did they hurt you?
The familiar flavor of orange and cinnamon--
--it washes over me like liquid sunshine.

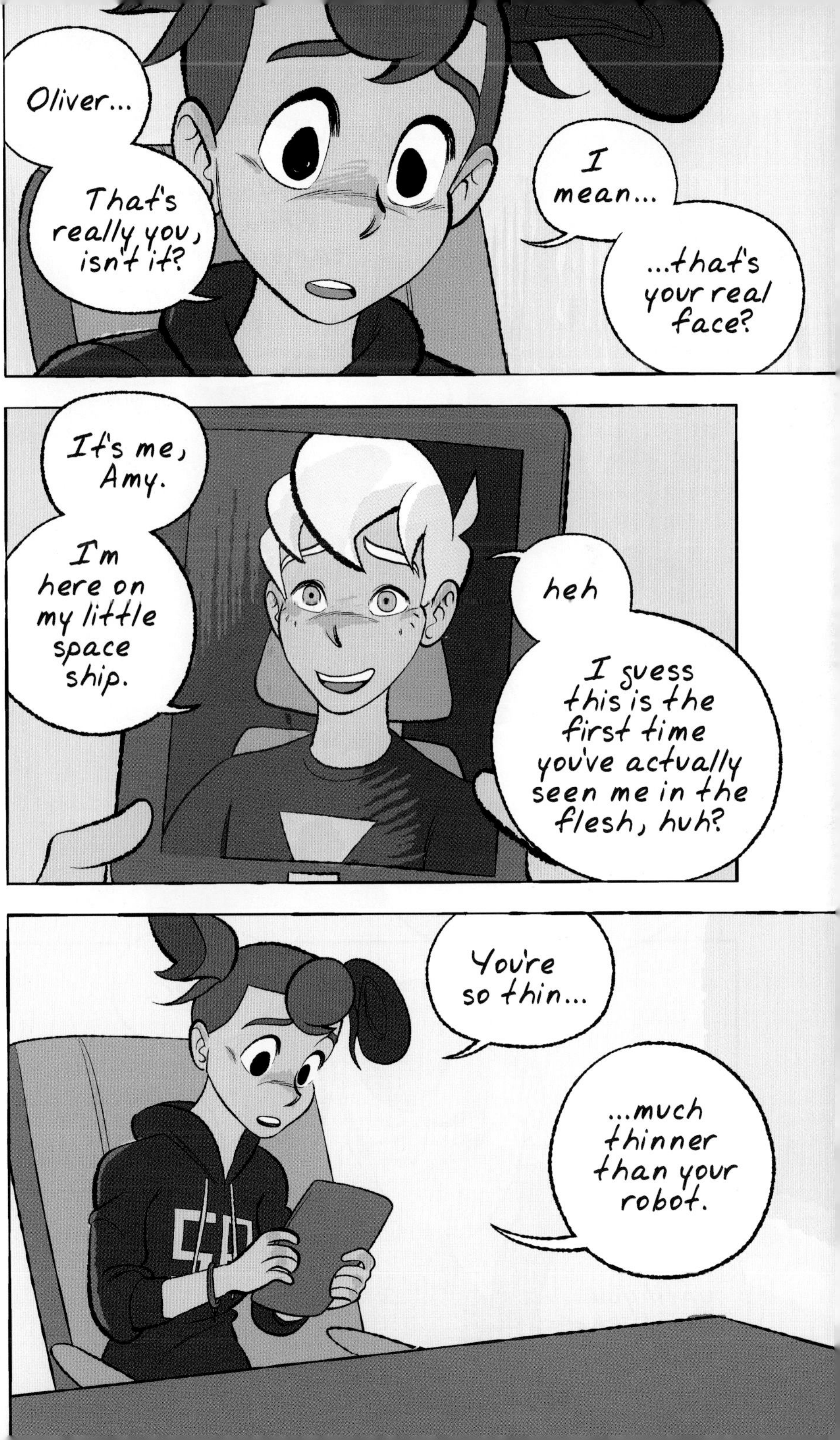
Oliver...
That's really you, isn't it?
I mean...
...that's your real face?
It's me, Amy.
I'm here on my little space ship.
heh
I guess this is the first time you've actually seen me in the flesh, huh?
You're so thin...
...much thinner than your robot.

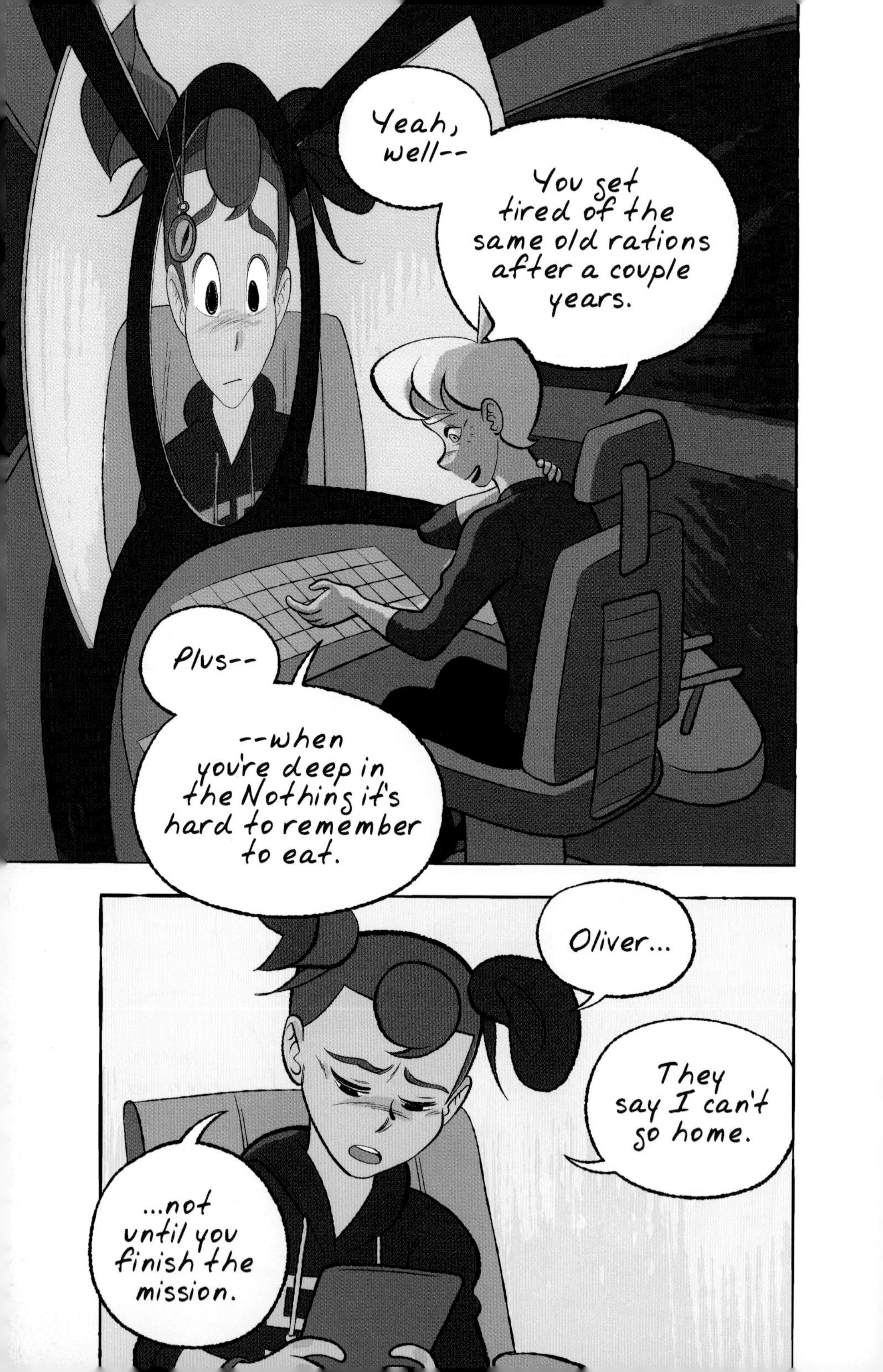
Yeah, well--
You get tired of the same old rations after a couple years.
Plus--
--when you're deep in the Nothing it's hard to remember to eat.
Oliver...
They say I can't go home.
...not until you finish the mission.

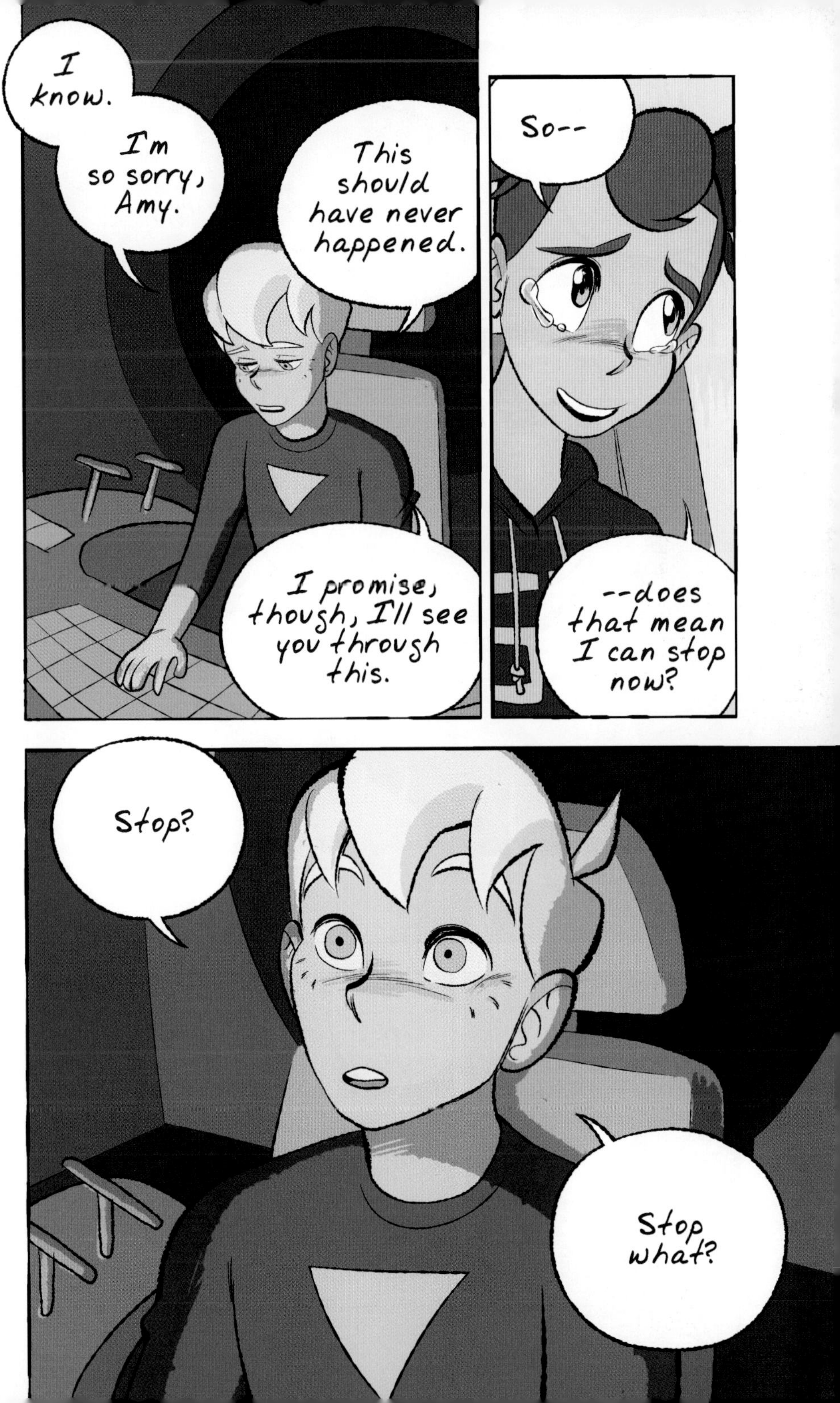
I know.
I'm so sorry, Amy.
This should have never happened.
I promise, though, I'll see you through this.
So--
--does that mean I can stop now?
Stop?
Stop what?

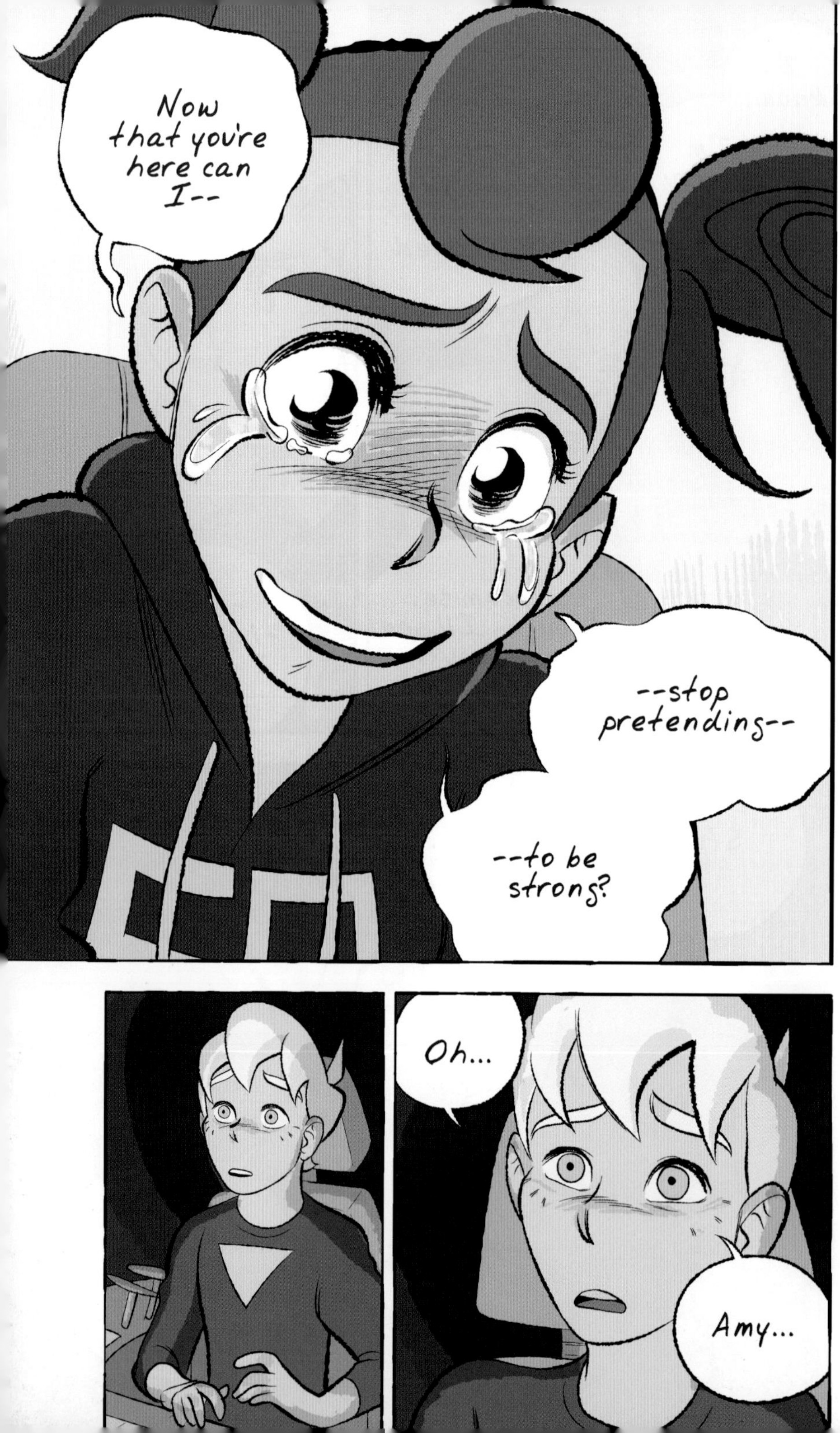
Now that you're here can I--
--stop pretending--
--to be strong?
Oh...
Amy...

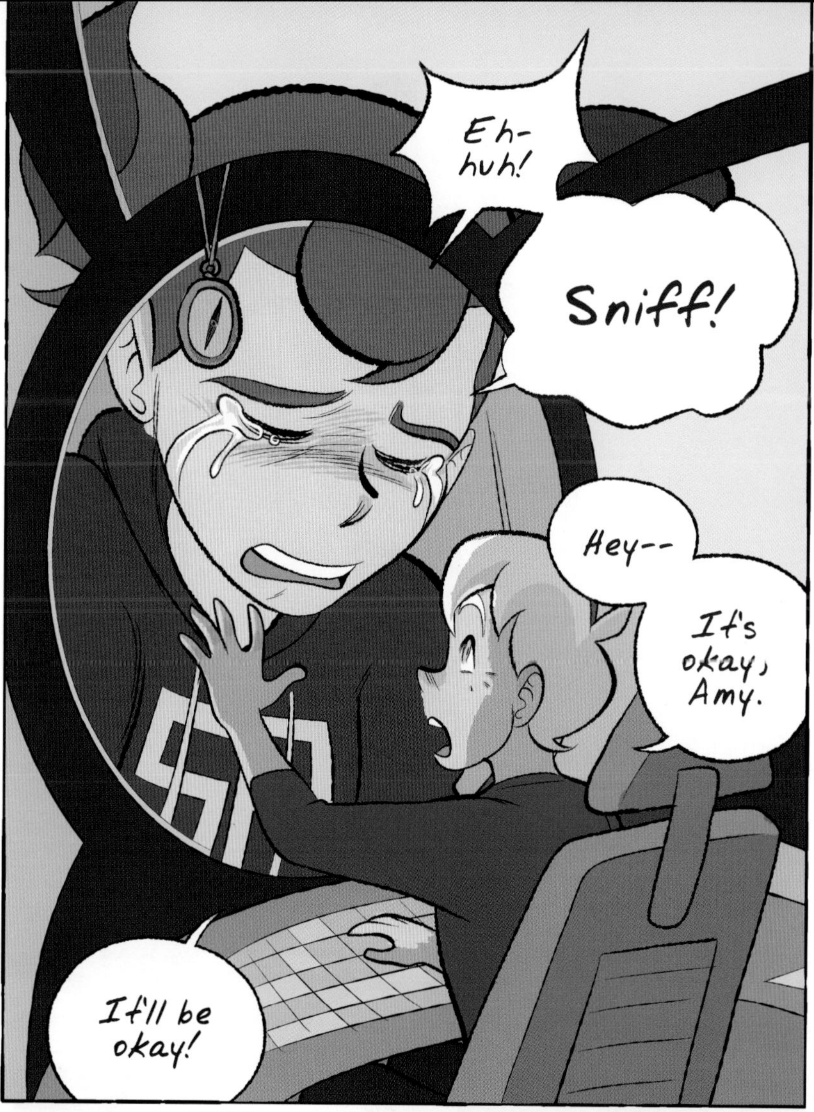
Eh-huh!
Sniff!
Hey--
It's okay, Amy.
It'll be okay!

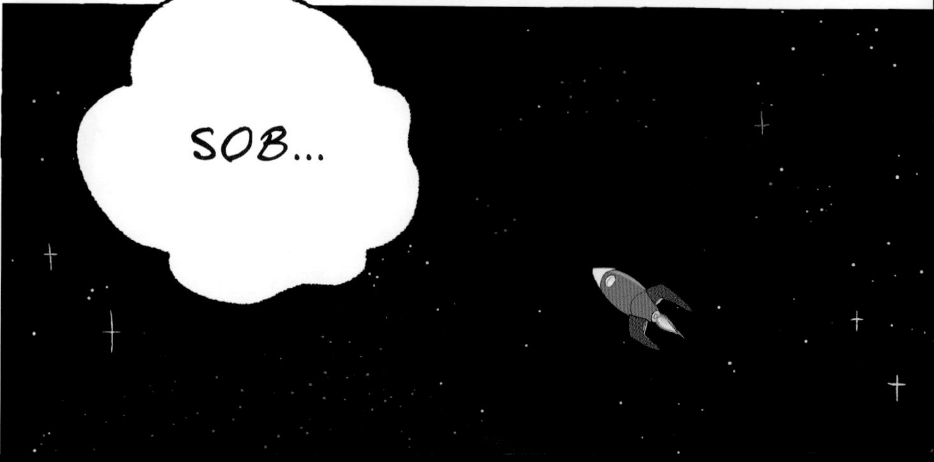
SOB...

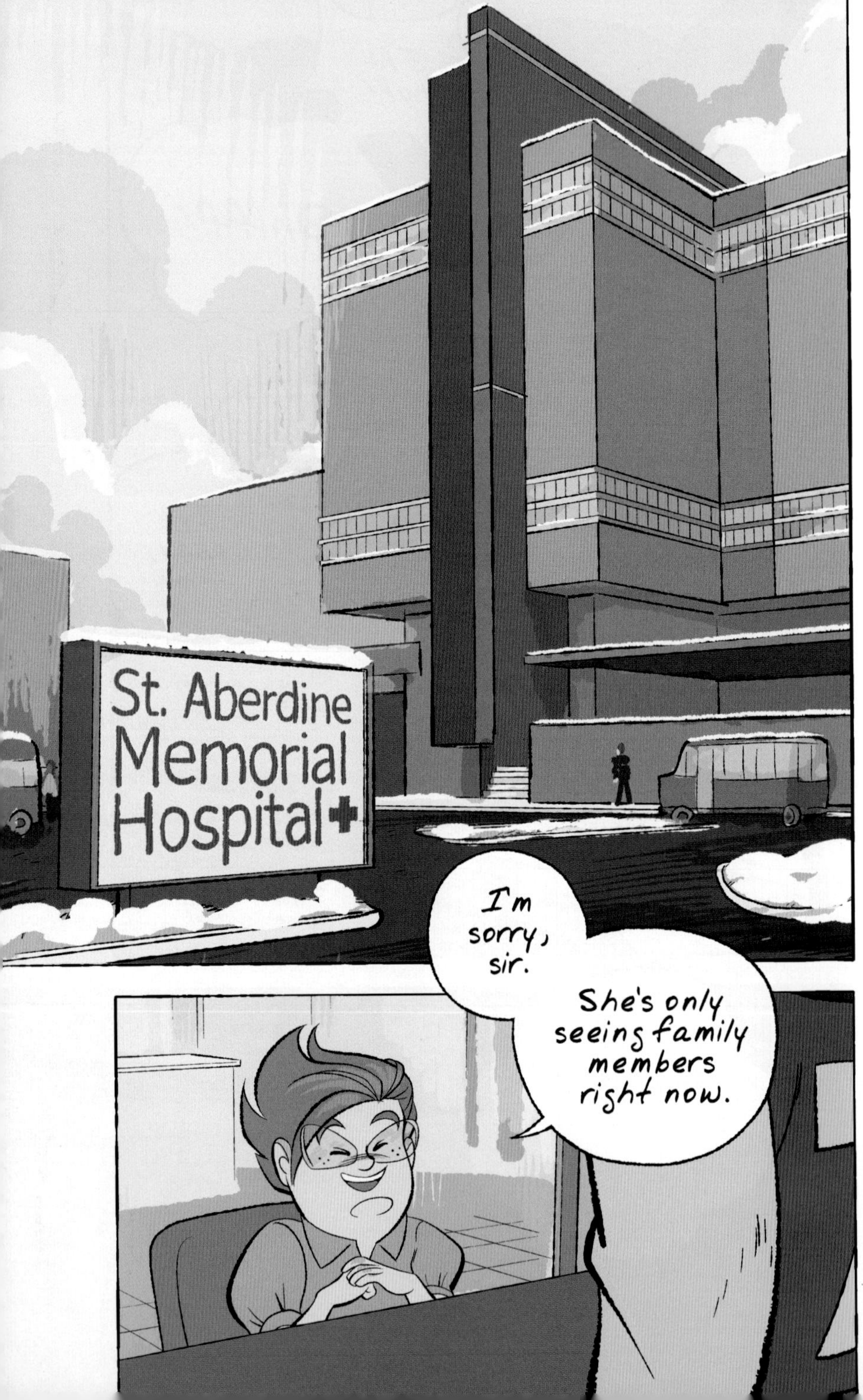
St. Aberdine Memorial Hospital
I'm sorry, sir.
She's only seeing family members right now.

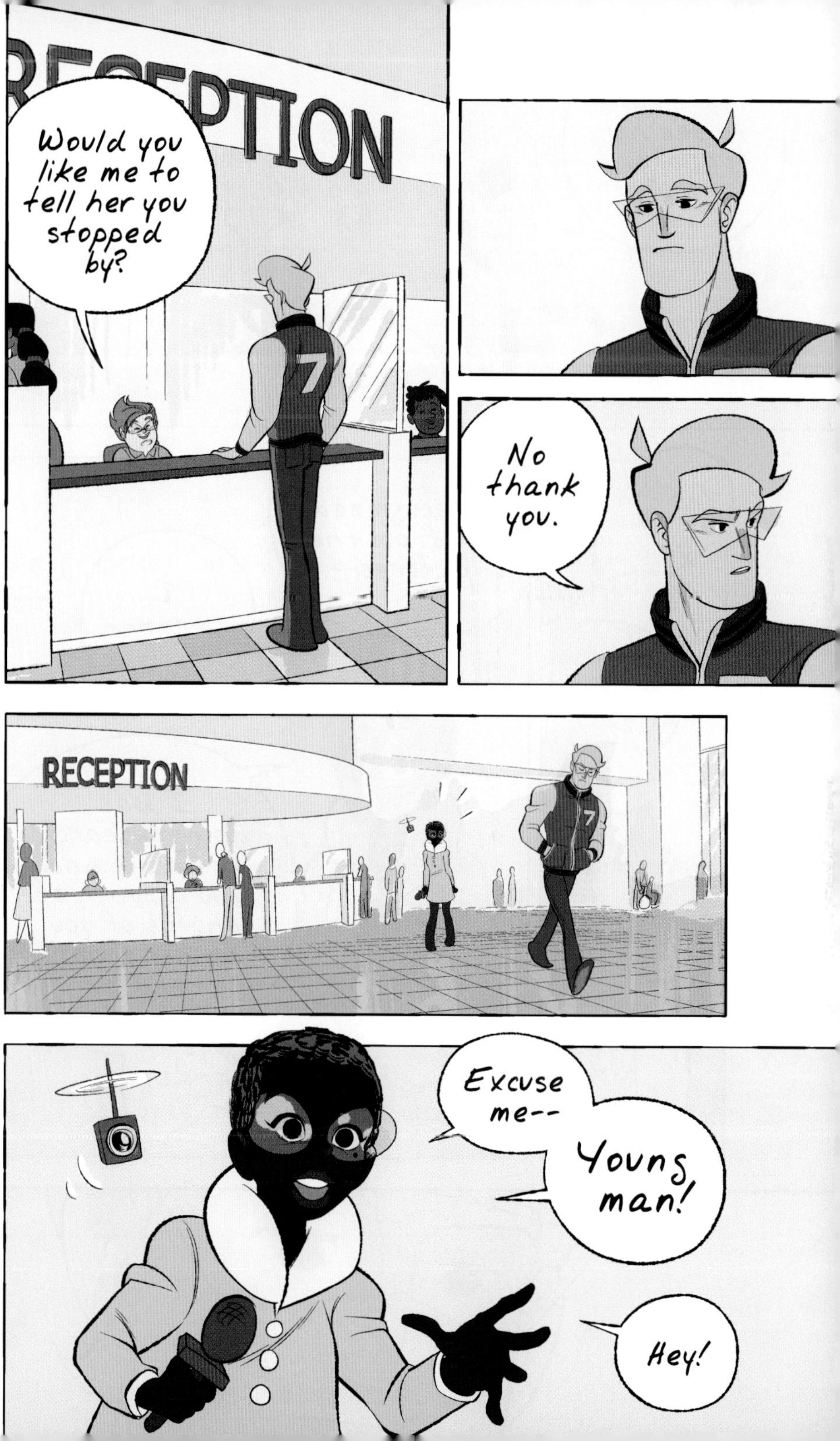
RECEPTION
Would you like me to tell her you stopped by?
No thank you.
RECEPTION
Excuse me--
Young man!
Hey!

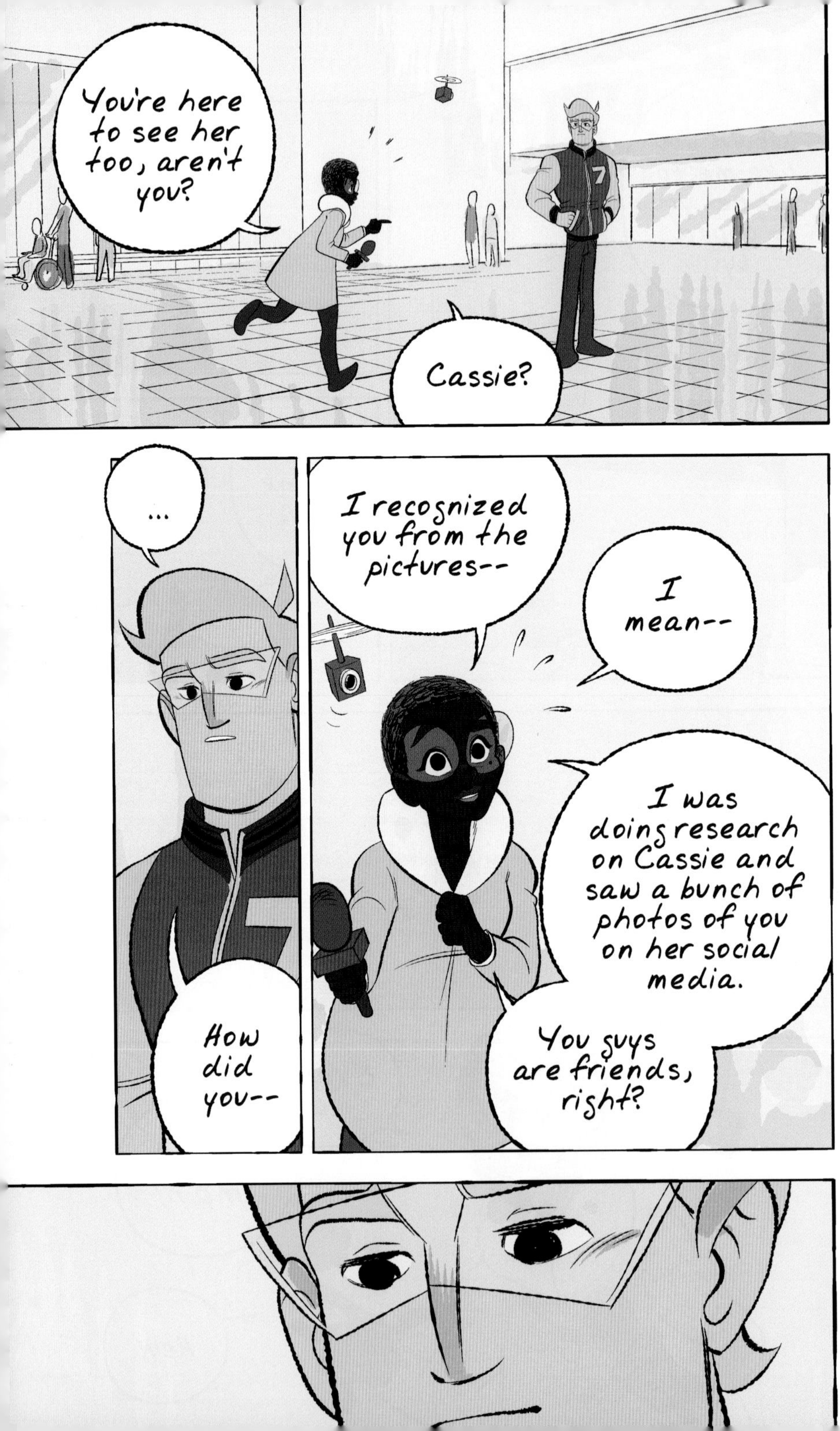
You're here to see her too, aren't you?
Cassie?
...
I recognized you from the pictures--
I mean--
I was doing research on Cassie and saw a bunch of photos of you on her social media.
How did you--
You guys are friends, right?

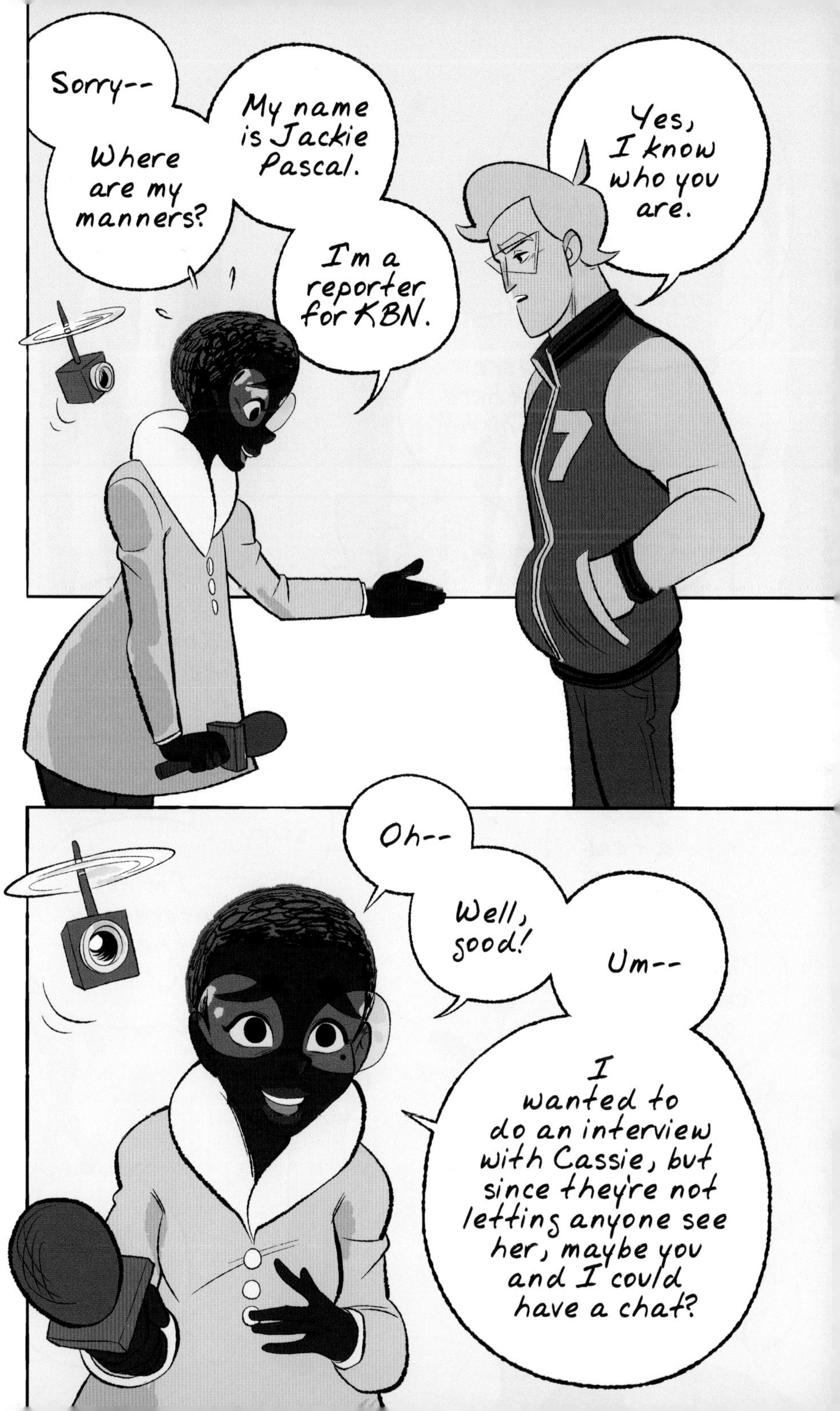
Sorry--
Where are my manners?
My name is Jackie Pascal.
I'm a reporter for KBN.
Yes, I know who you are.
Oh--
Well, good!
Um--
I wanted to do an interview with Cassie, but since they're not letting anyone see her, maybe you and I could have a chat?

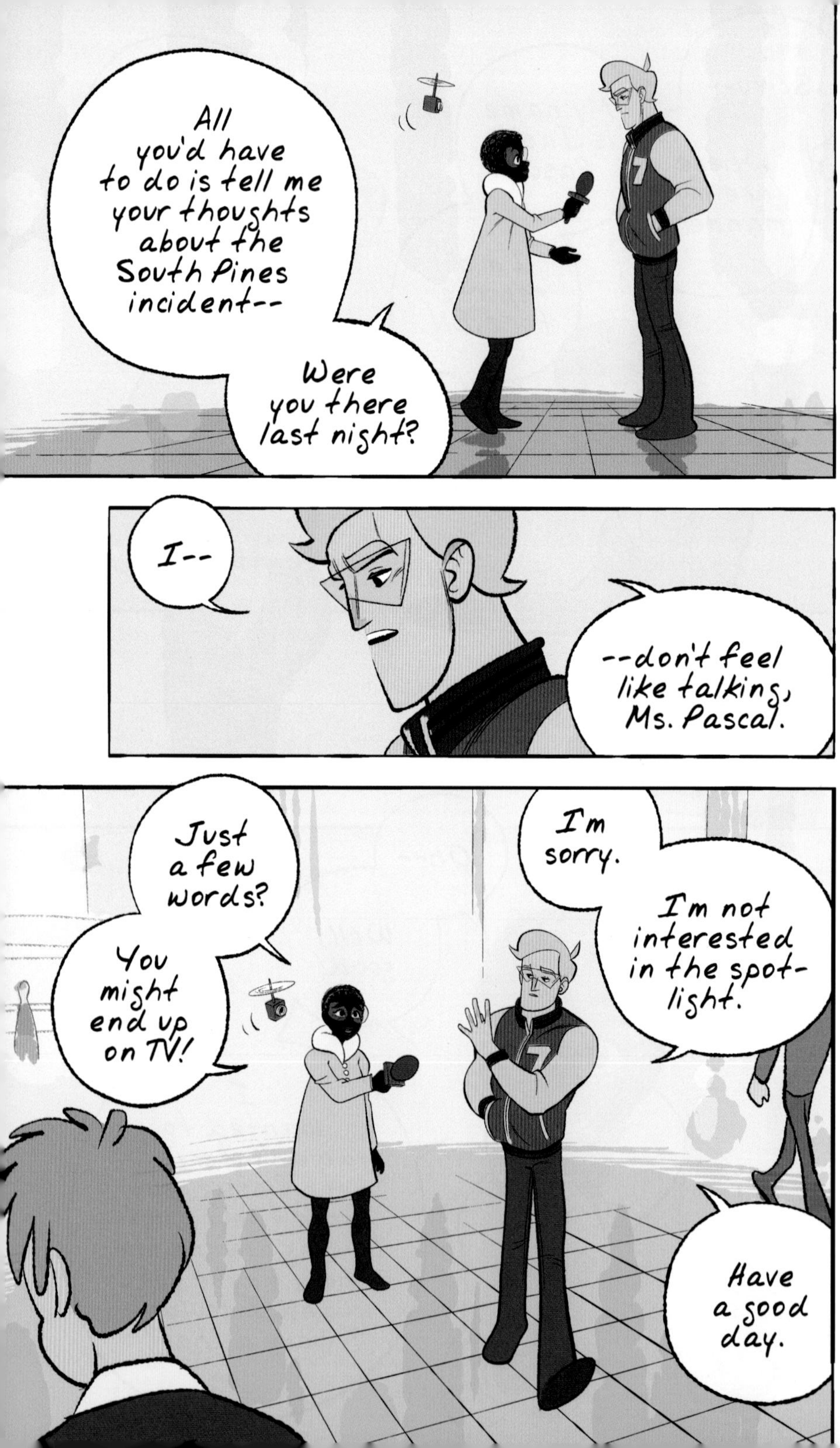
All you'd have to do is tell me your thoughts about the South Pines incident--
Were you there last night?
I--
--don't feel like talking, Ms. Pascal.
Just a few words?
You might end up on TV!
I'm sorry.
I'm not interested in the spot-light.
Have a good day.

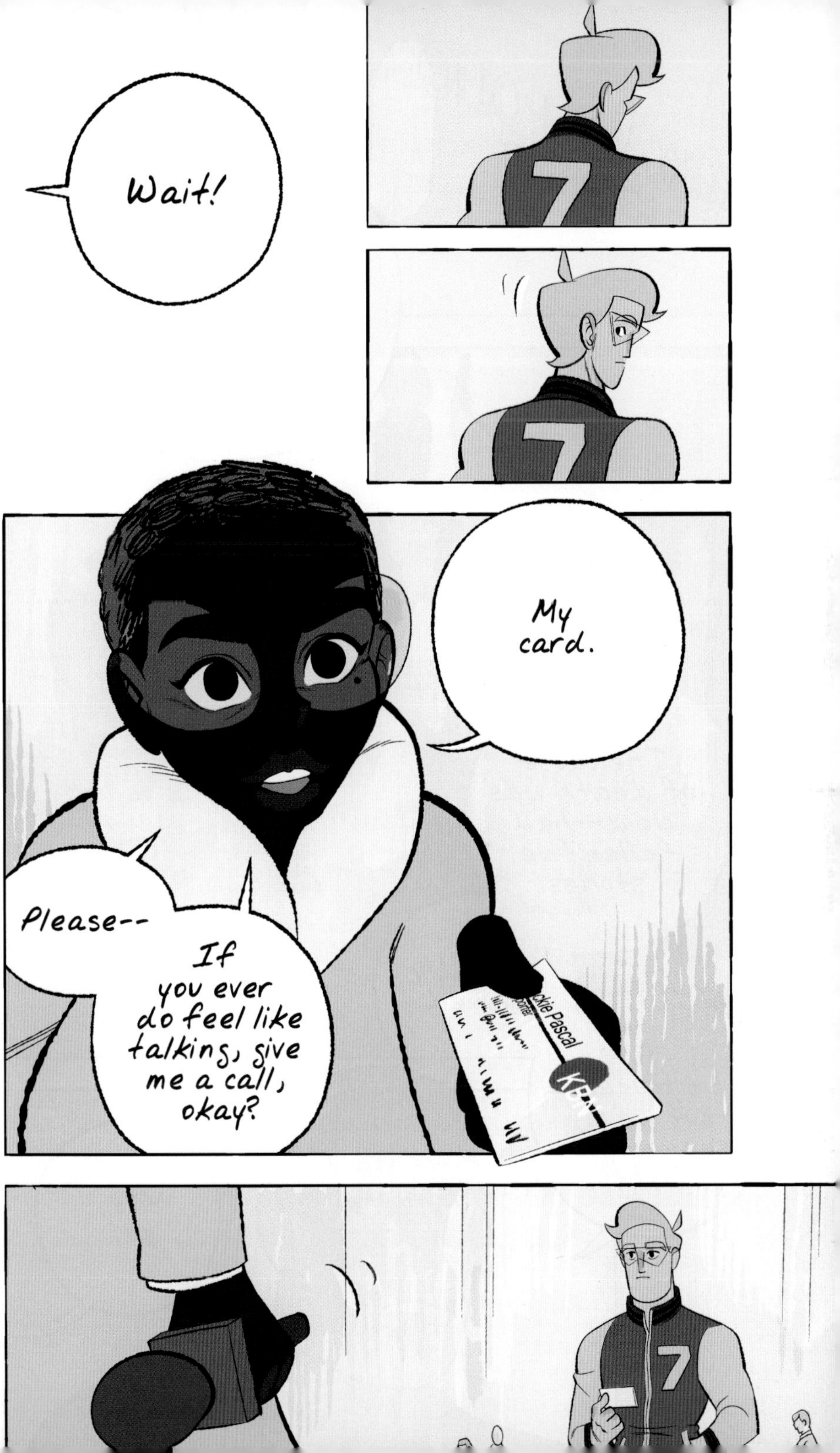
Wait!
My card.
Please--
If you ever do feel like talking, give me a call, okay?

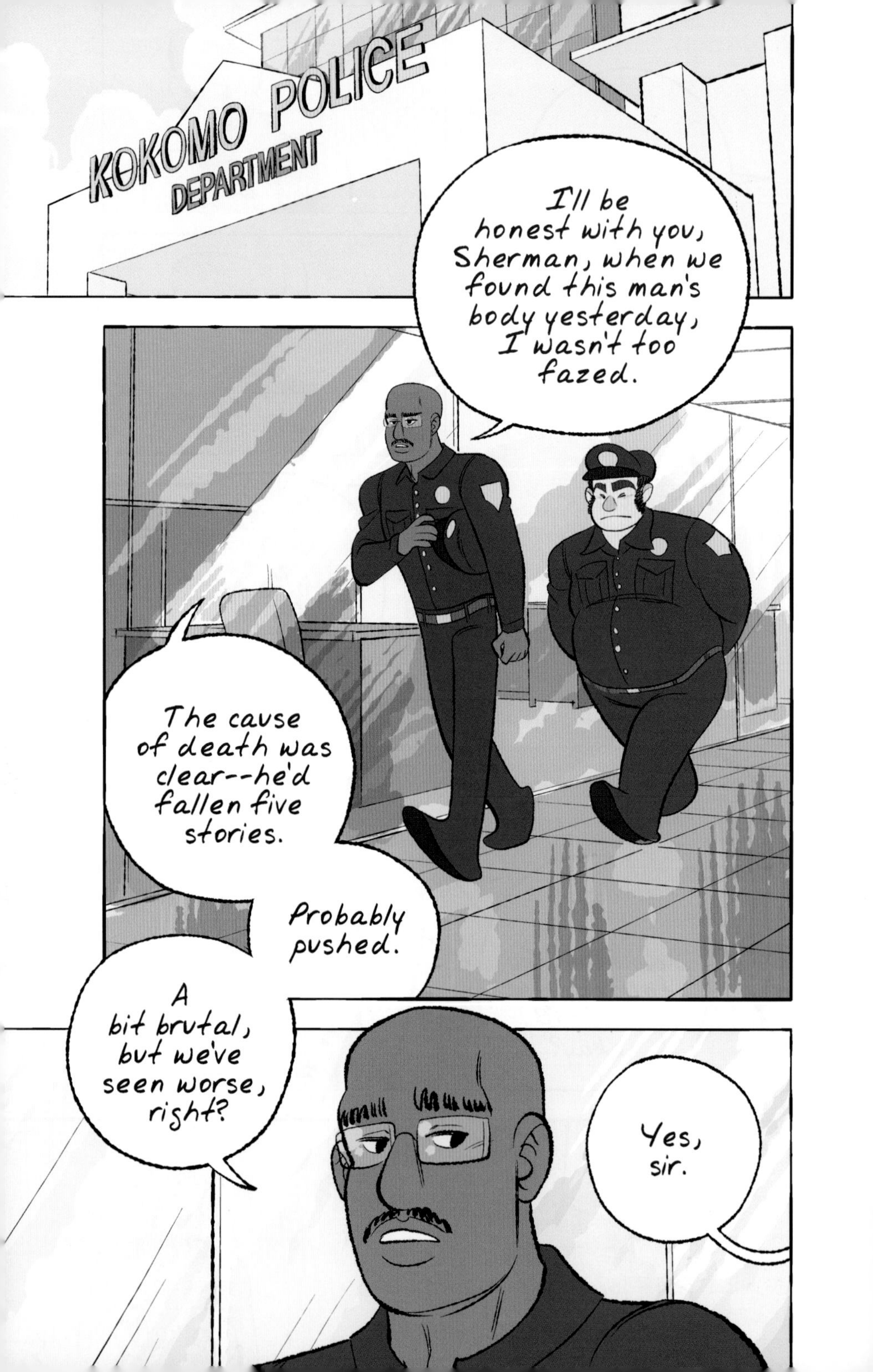
KOKOMO POLICE DEPARTMENT
I'll be honest with you, Sherman, when we found this man's body yesterday, I wasn't too fazed.
The cause of death was clear--he'd fallen five stories.
Probably pushed.
A bit brutal, but we've seen worse, right?
Yes, sir.

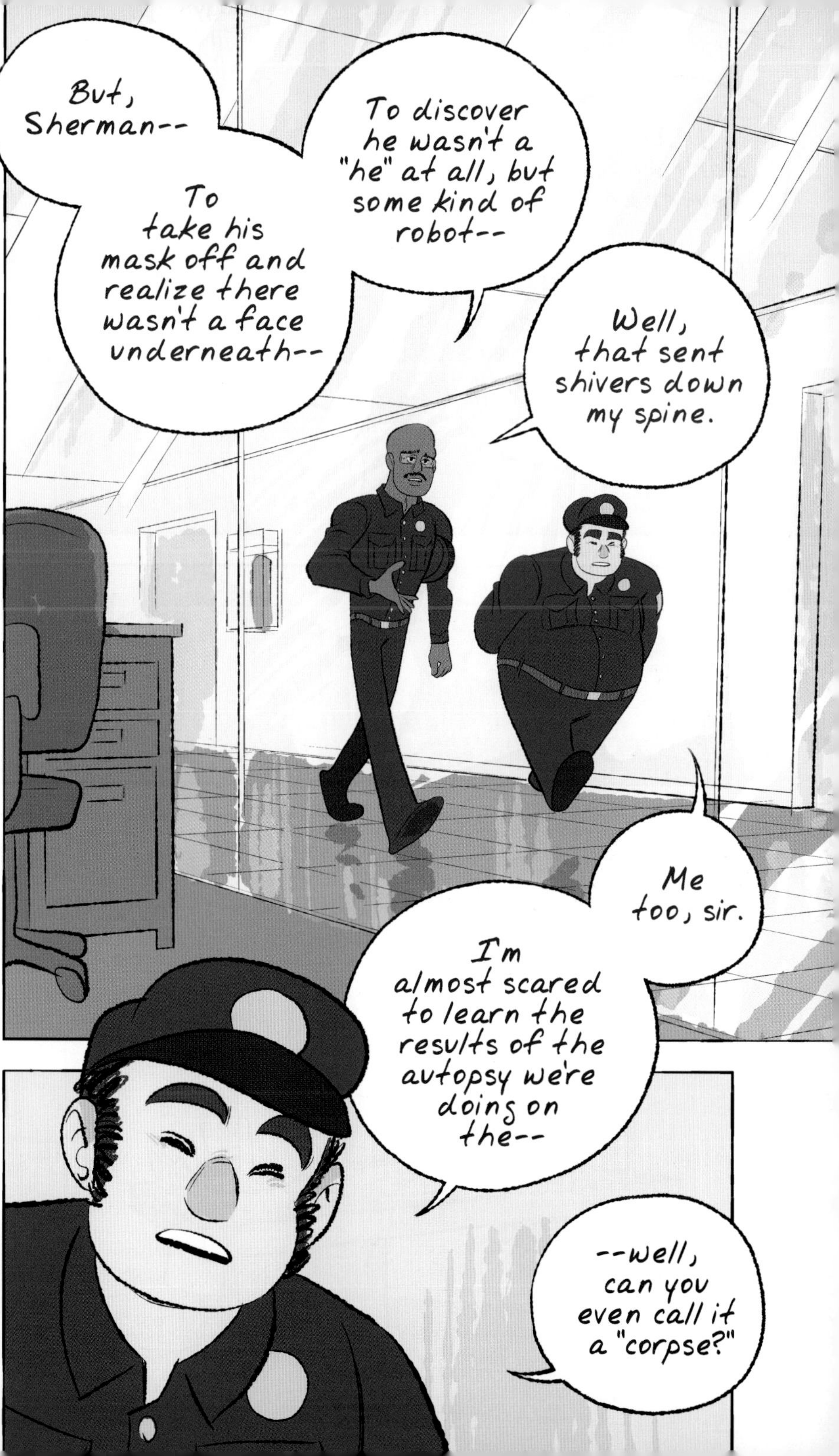
But, Sherman--
To take his mask off and realize there wasn't a face underneath--
To discover he wasn't a "he" at all, but some kind of robot--
Well, that sent shivers down my spine.
Me too, sir.
I'm almost scared to learn the results of the autopsy we're doing on the--
--well, can you even call it a "corpse?"

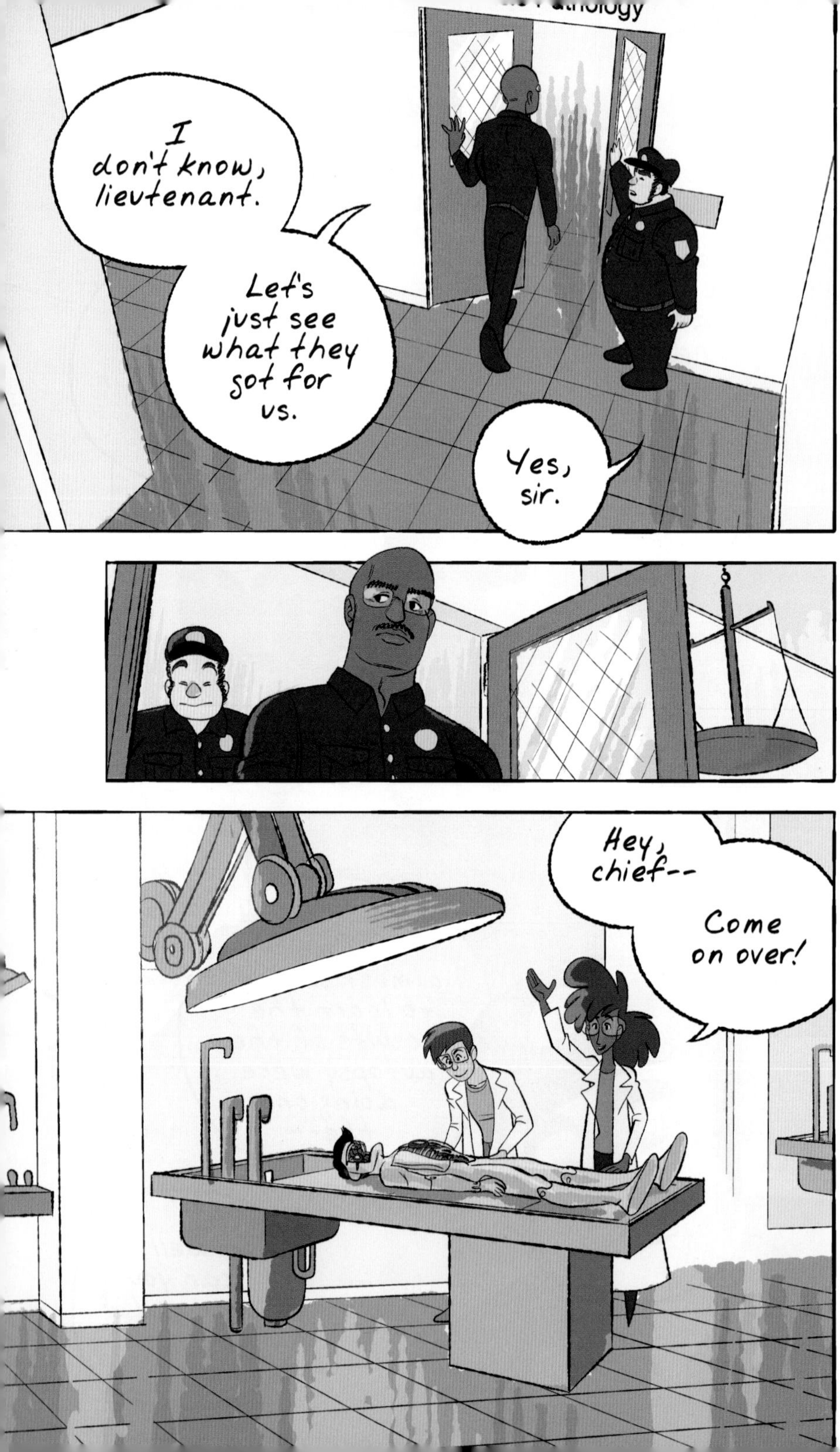

I don't know, lieutenant.
Let's just see what they got for us.
Yes, sir.
Hey, chief--
Come on over!

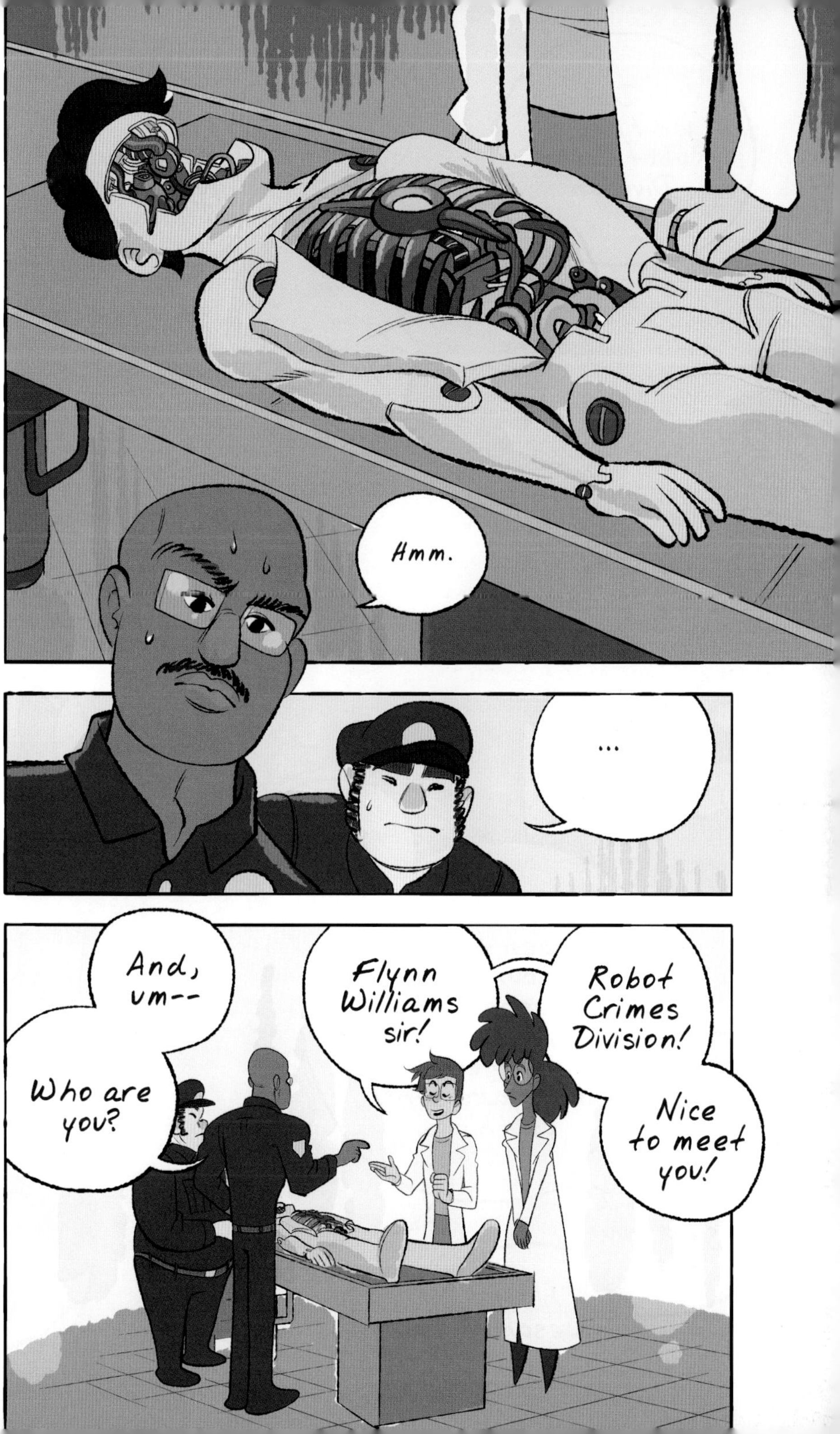
Hmm.
...
Who are you?
And, um--
Flynn Williams sir!
Robot Crimes Division!
Nice to meet you!

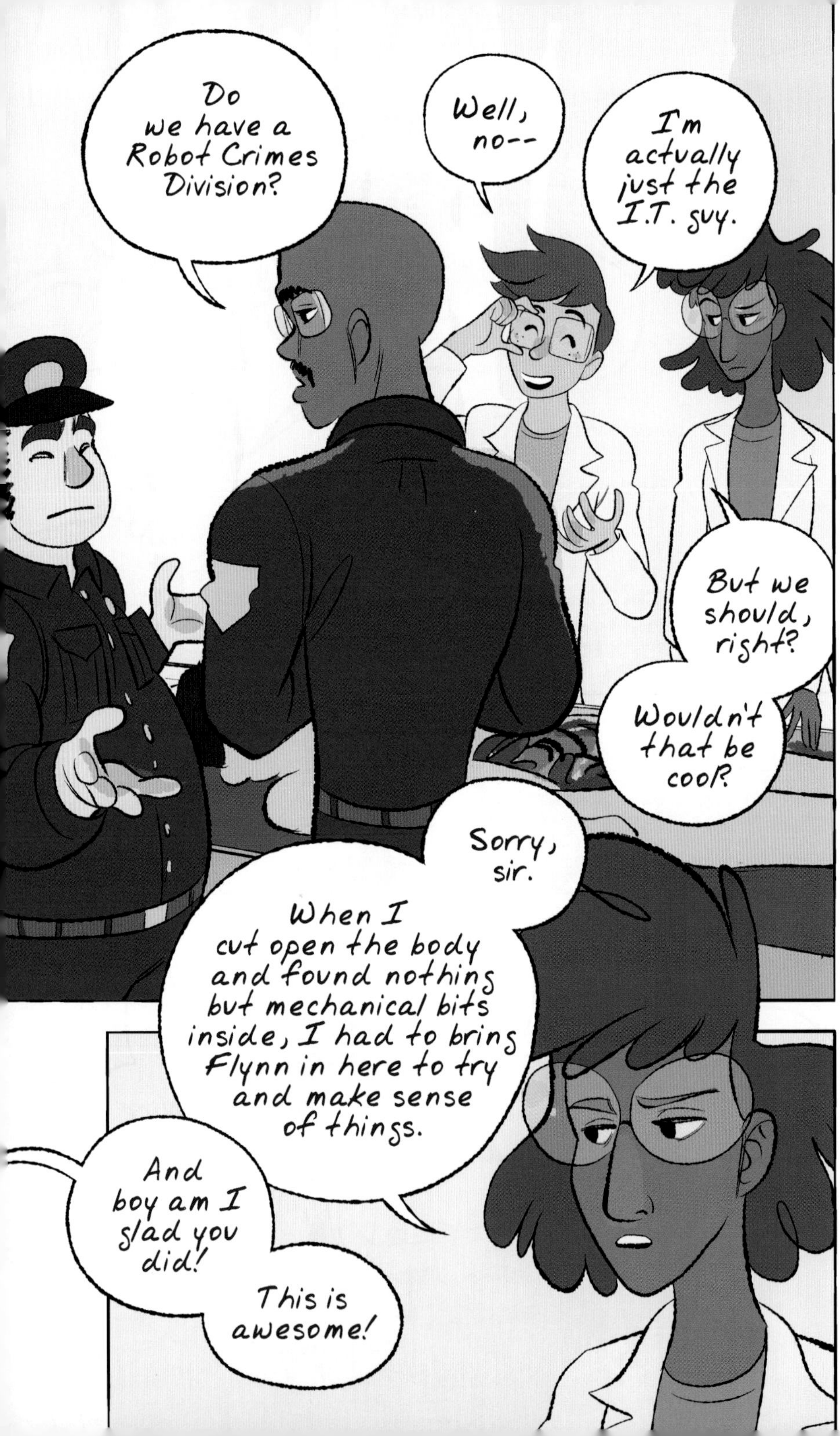
Do we have a Robot Crimes Division?
Well, no--
I'm actually just the I.T. guy.
But we should, right?
Wouldn't that be cool?
Sorry, sir.
When I cut open the body and found nothing but mechanical bits inside, I had to bring Flynn in here to try and make sense of things.
And boy am I glad you did!
This is awesome!

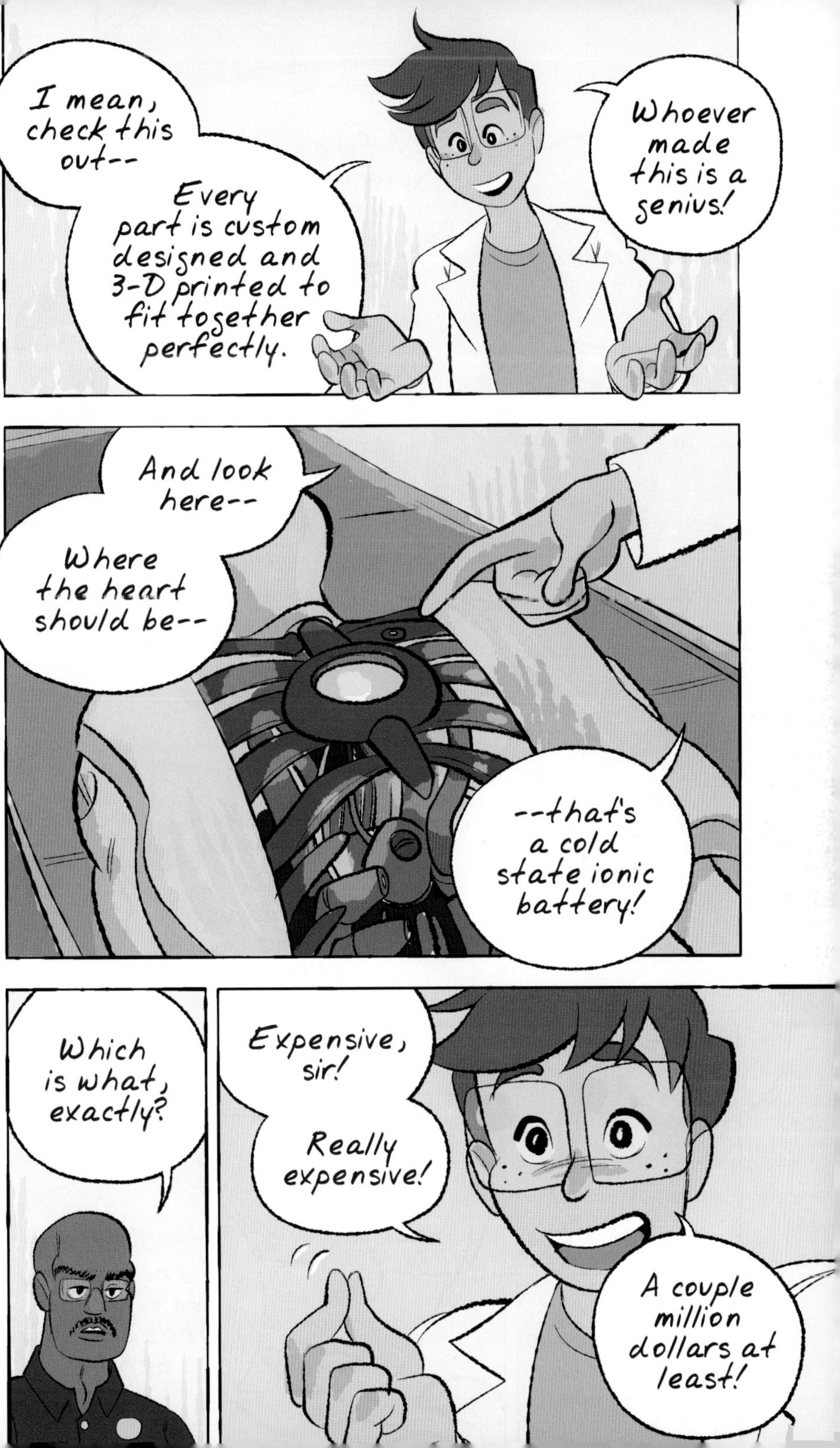
I mean, check this out--
Every part is custom designed and 3-D printed to fit together perfectly.
Whoever made this is a genius!
And look here--
Where the heart should be--
--that's a cold state ionic battery!
Which is what, exactly?
Expensive, sir!
Really expensive!
A couple million dollars at least!

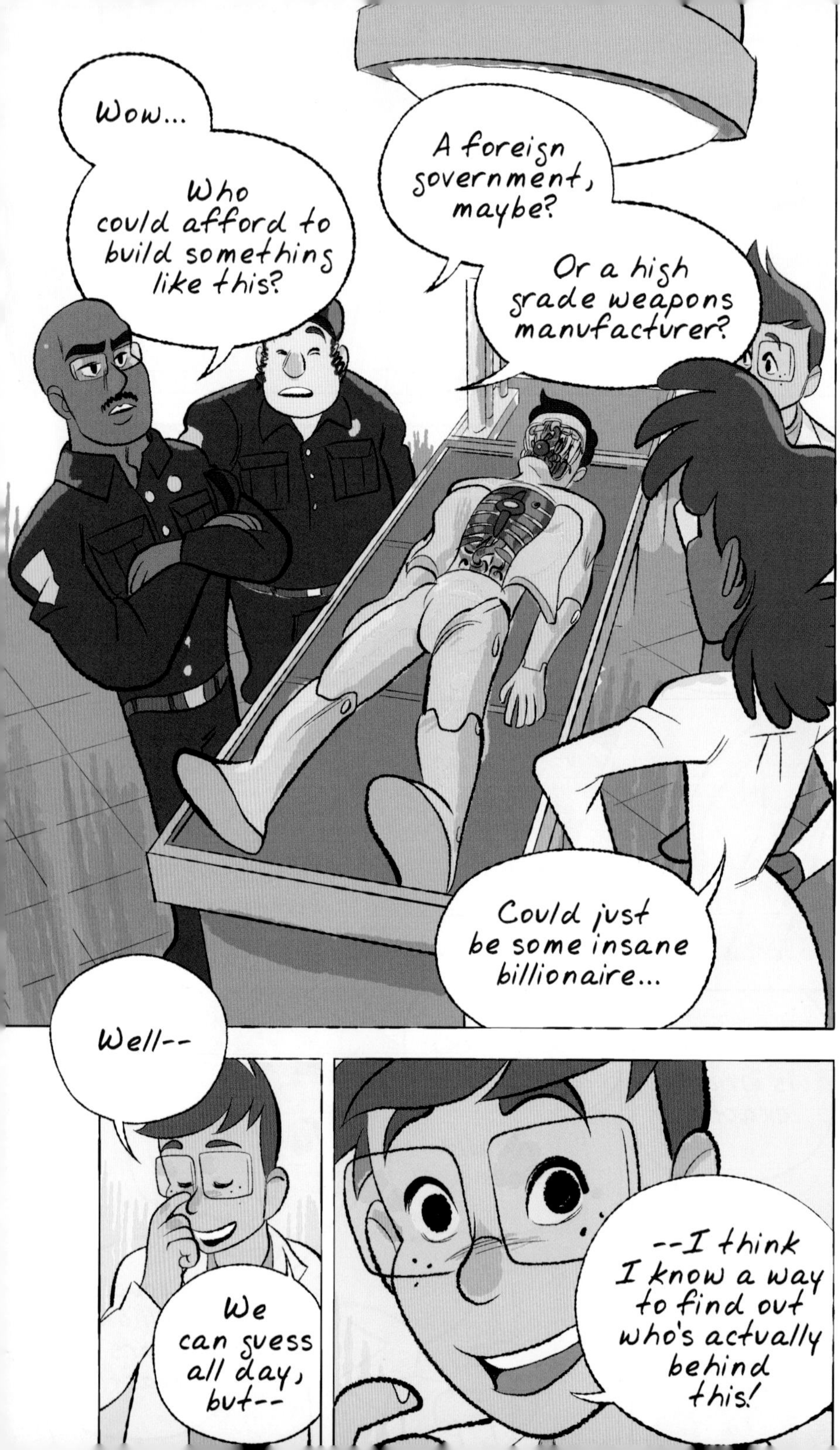
Wow...
Who could afford to build something like this?
A foreign government, maybe?
Or a high grade weapons manufacturer?
Could just be some insane billionaire...
Well--
We can guess all day, but--
--I think I know a way to find out who's actually behind this!

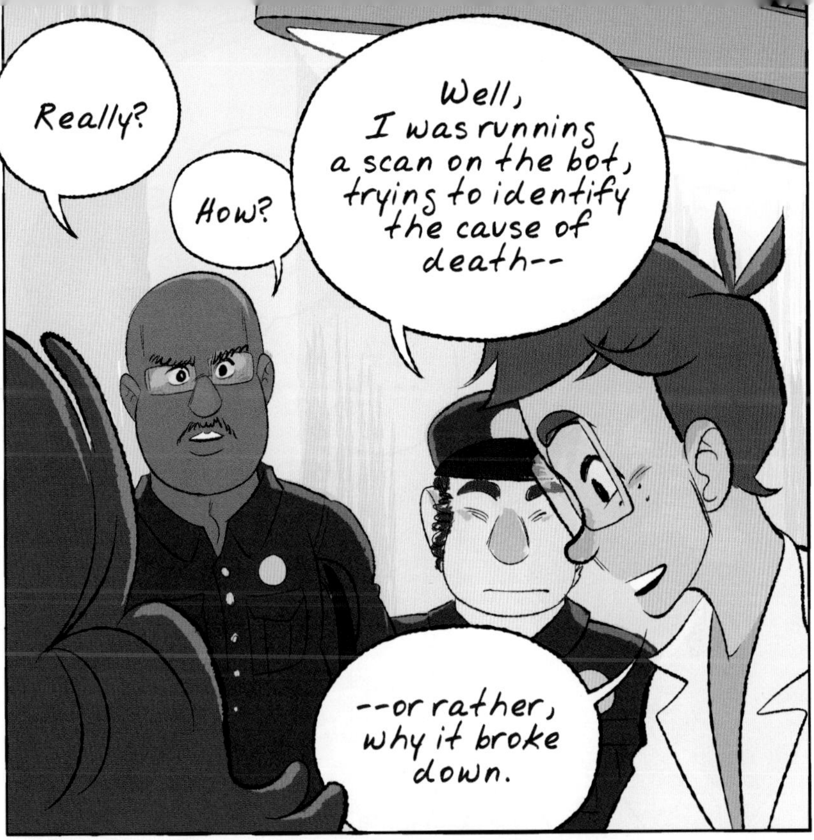
Really?
How?
Well, I was running a scan on the bot, trying to identify the cause of death--
--or rather, why it broke down.

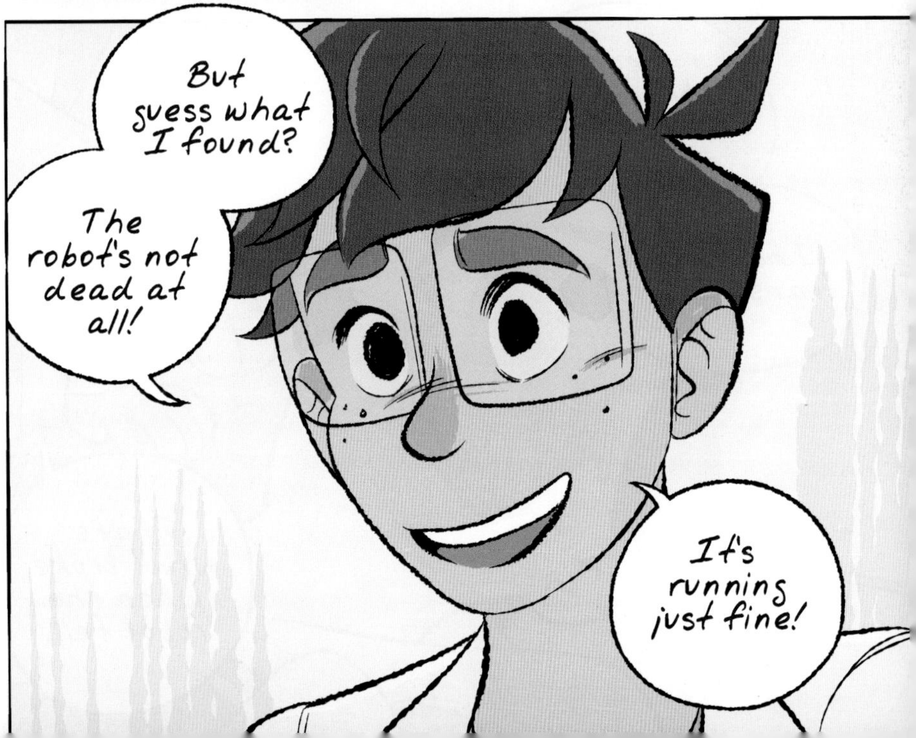
But guess what I found?
The robot's not dead at all!
It's running just fine!

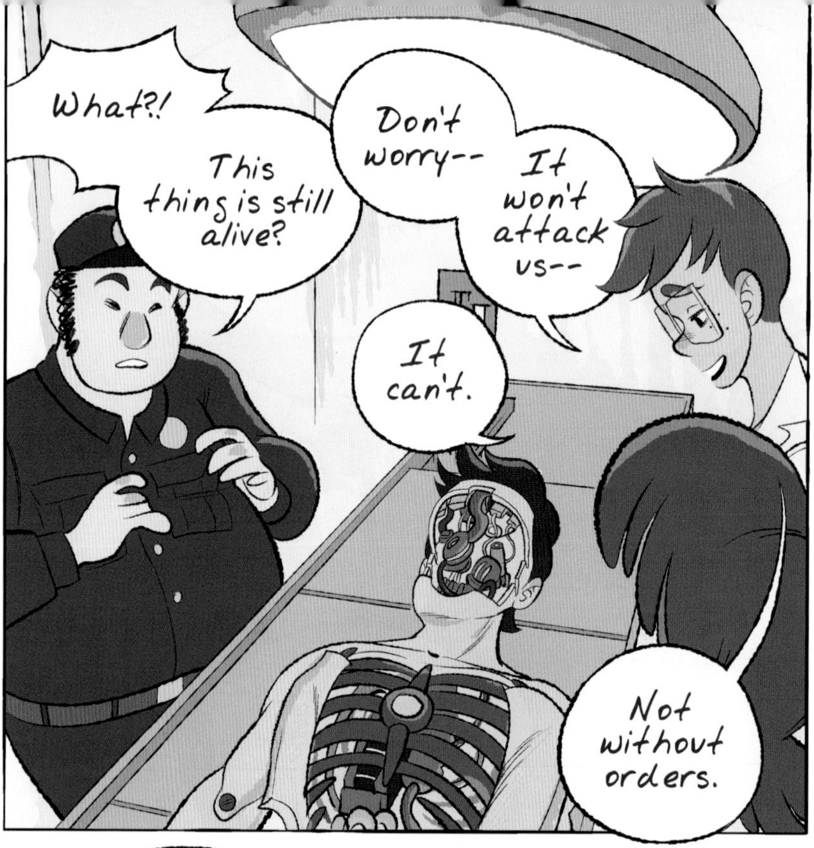
What?!
This thing is still alive?
Don't worry--
It won't attack us--
It can't.
Not without orders.

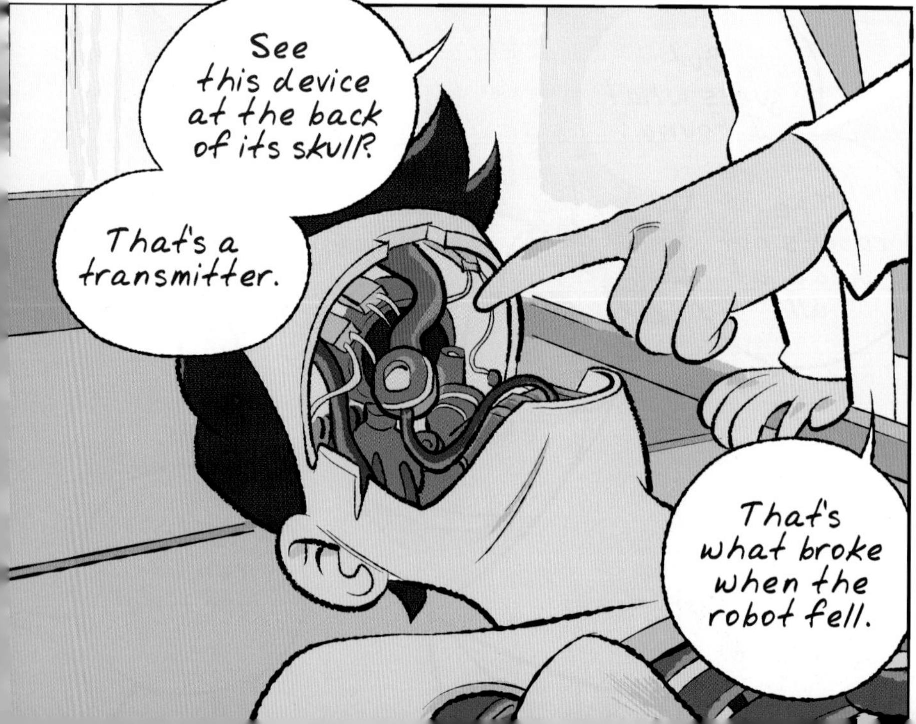
See this device at the back of its skull?
That's a transmitter.
That's what broke when the robot fell.

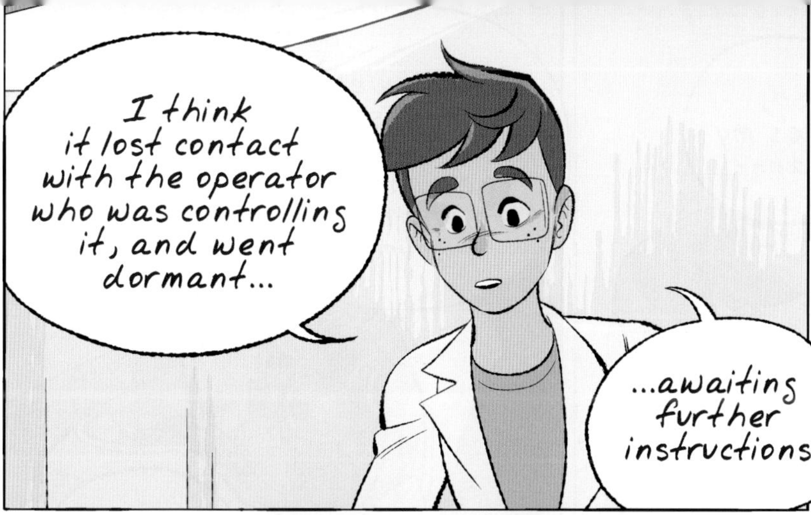
I think it lost contact with the operator who was controlling it, and went dormant...
...awaiting further instructions.

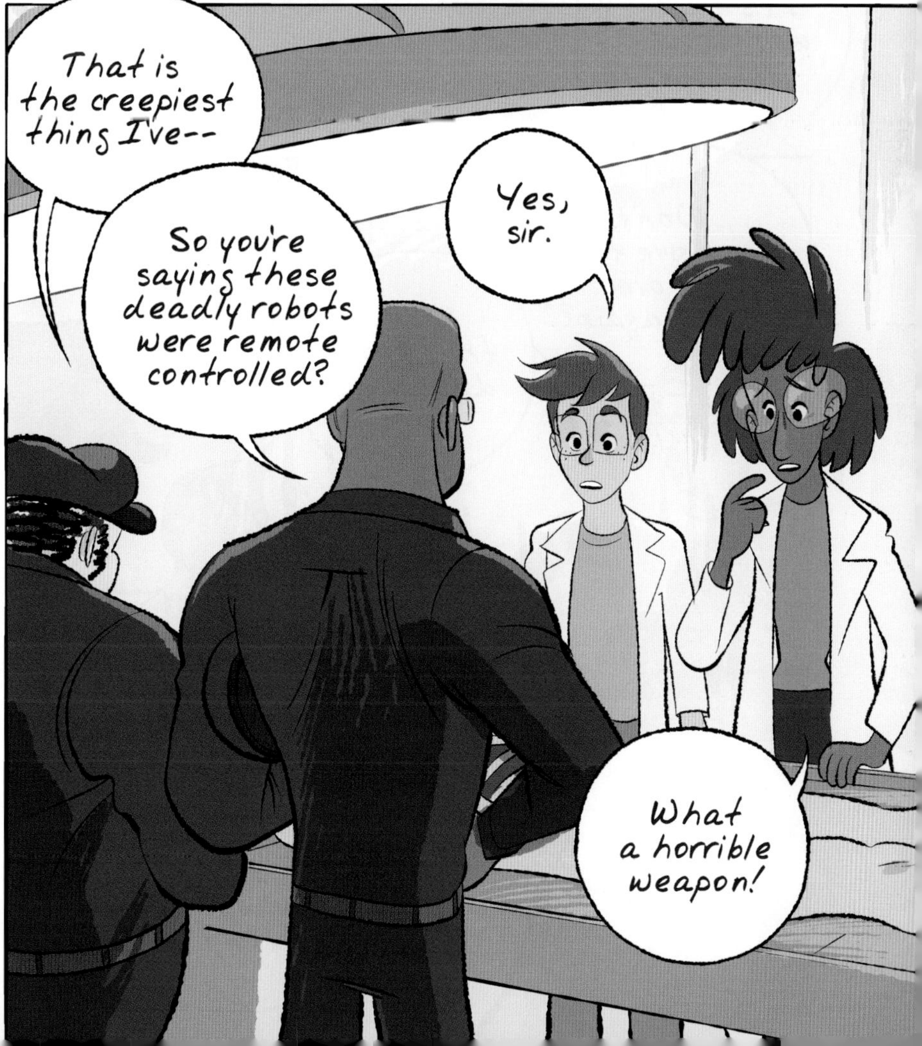
That is the creepiest thing I've--
So you're saying these deadly robots were remote controlled?
Yes, sir.
What a horrible weapon!

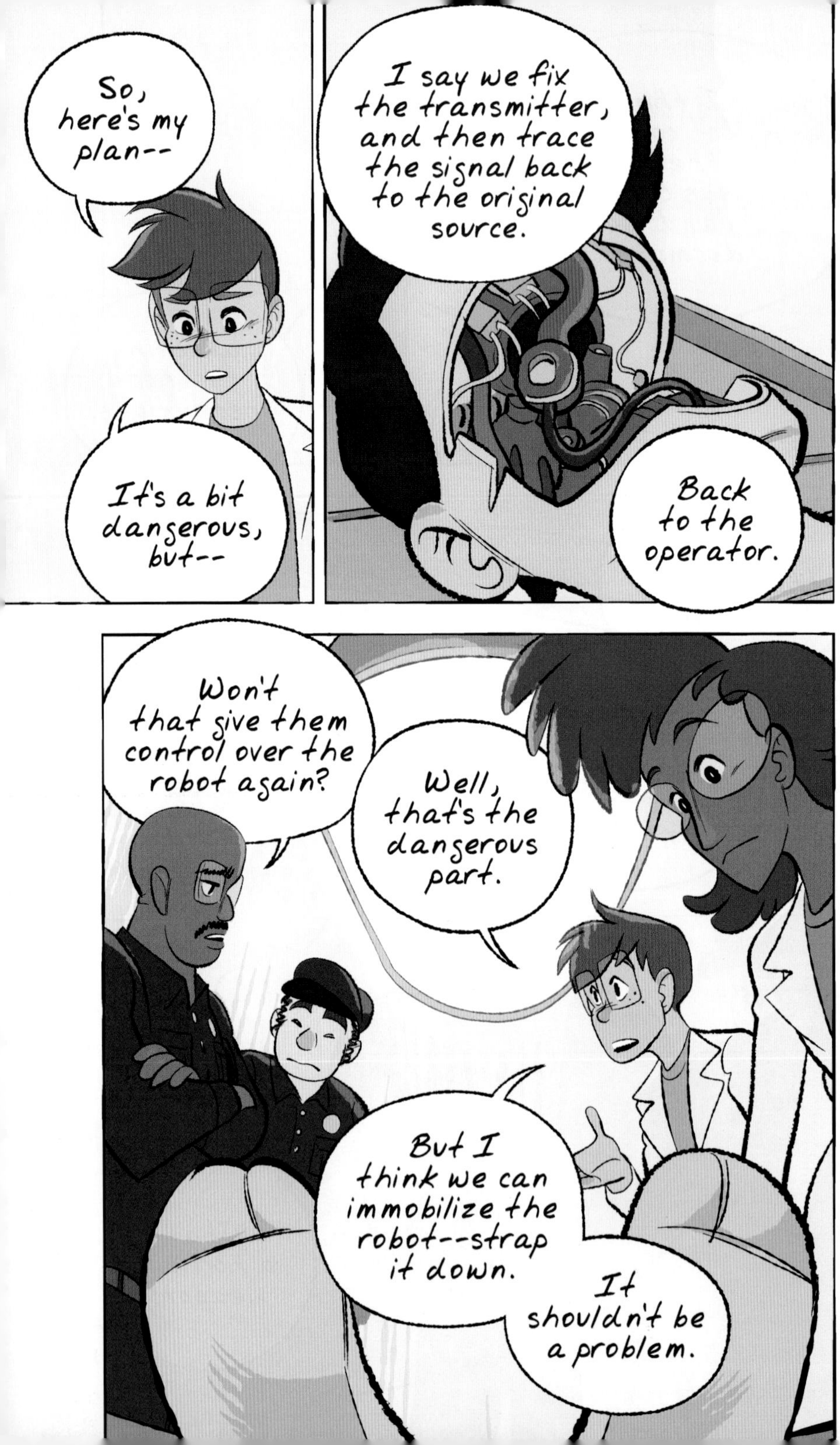
So, here's my plan--
It's a bit dangerous, but--
I say we fix the transmitter, and then trace the signal back to the original source.
Back to the operator.
Won't that give them control over the robot again?
Well, that's the dangerous part.
But I think we can immobilize the robot--strap it down.
It shouldn't be a problem.

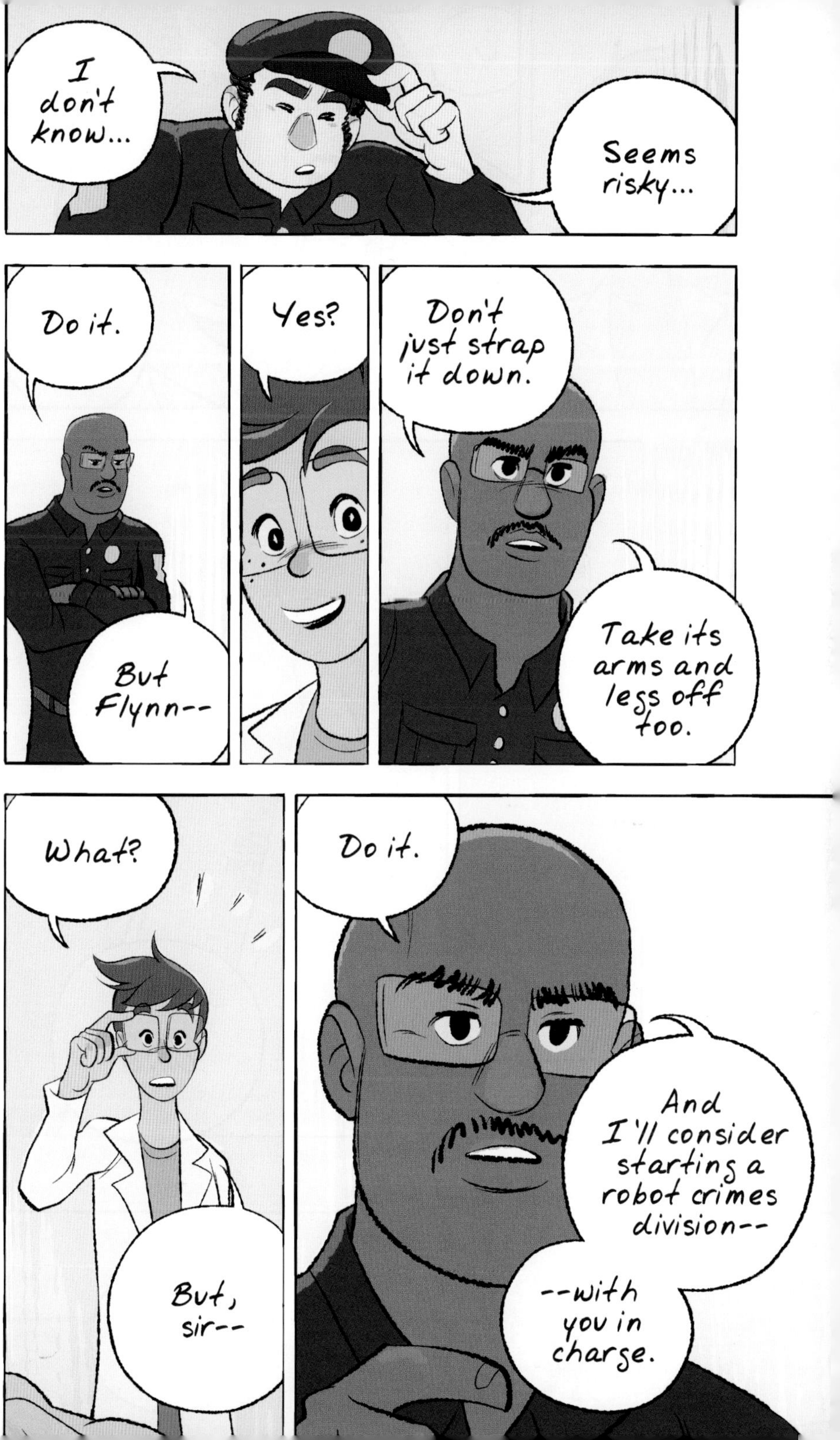

I don't know...
Seems risky...
Do it.
But Flynn--
Yes?
Don't just strap it down.
Take its arms and legs off too.
What?
But, sir--
Do it.
And I'll consider starting a robot crimes division--
--with you in charge.

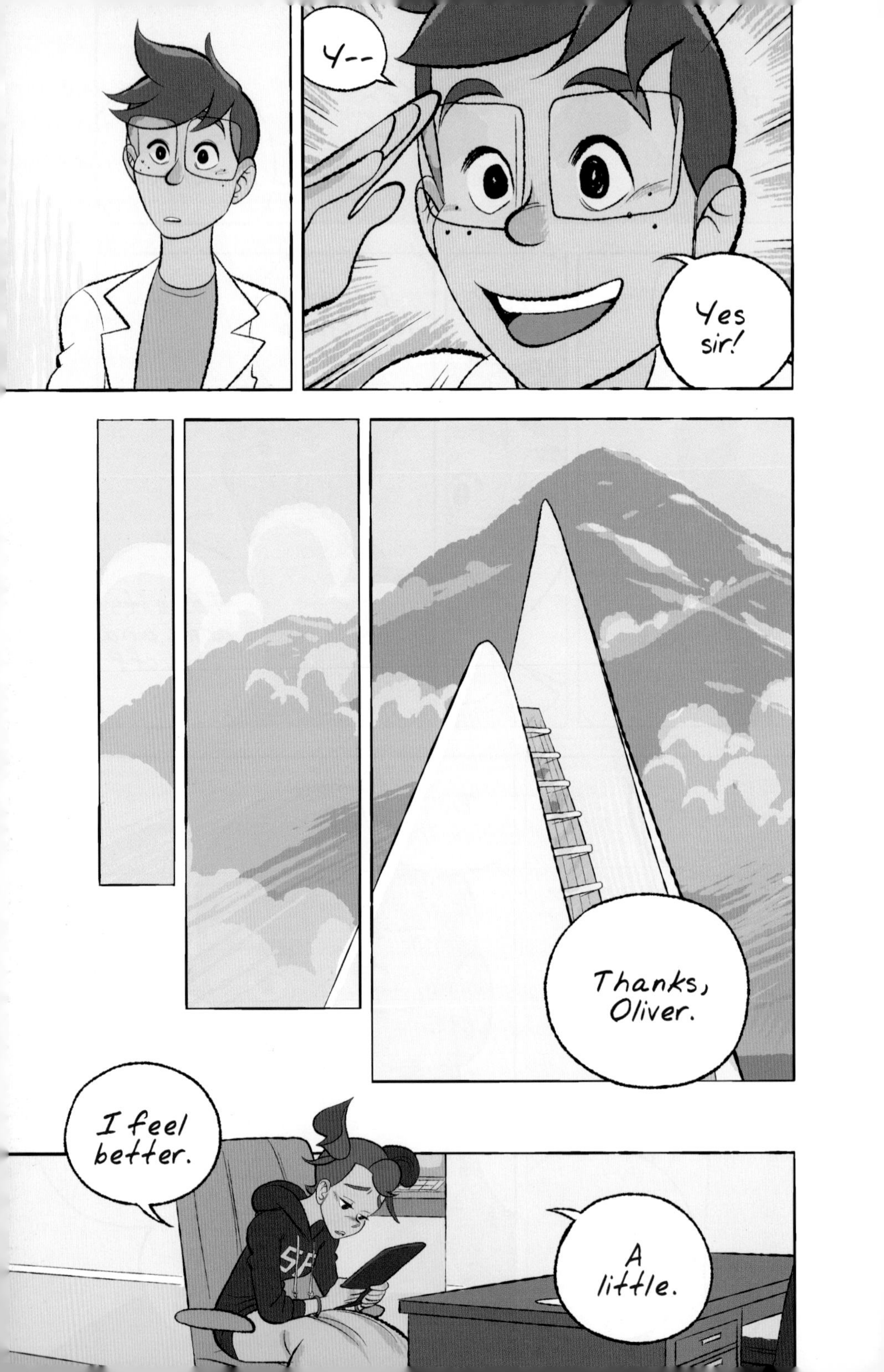
Y--
Yes sir!
Thanks, Oliver.
I feel better.
A little.

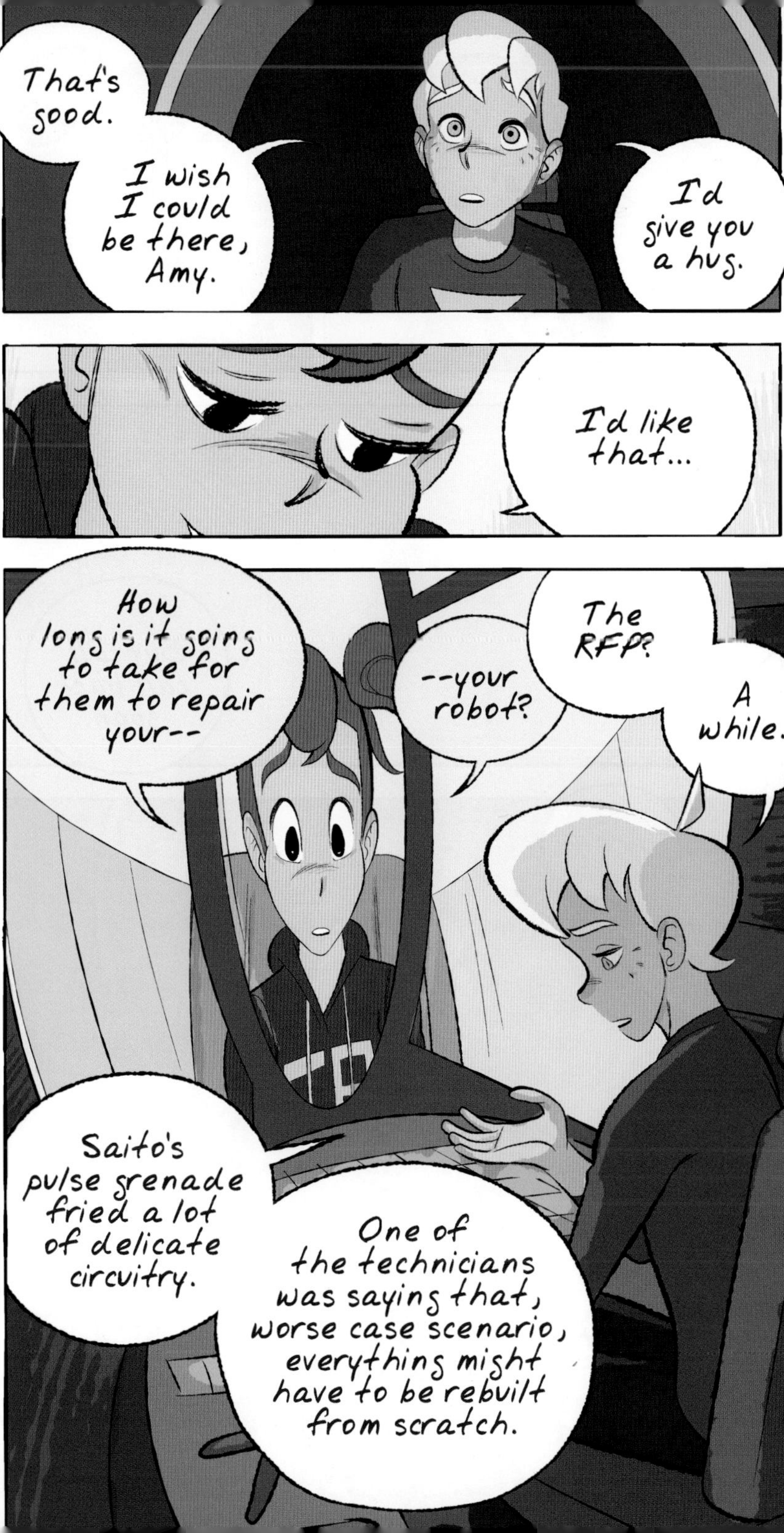
That's good.
I wish I could be there, Amy.
I'd give you a hug.
I'd like that...
How long is it going to take for them to repair your--
--your robot?
The RFP?
A while.
Saito's pulse grenade fried a lot of delicate circuitry.
One of the technicians was saying that, worse case scenario, everything might have to be rebuilt from scratch.

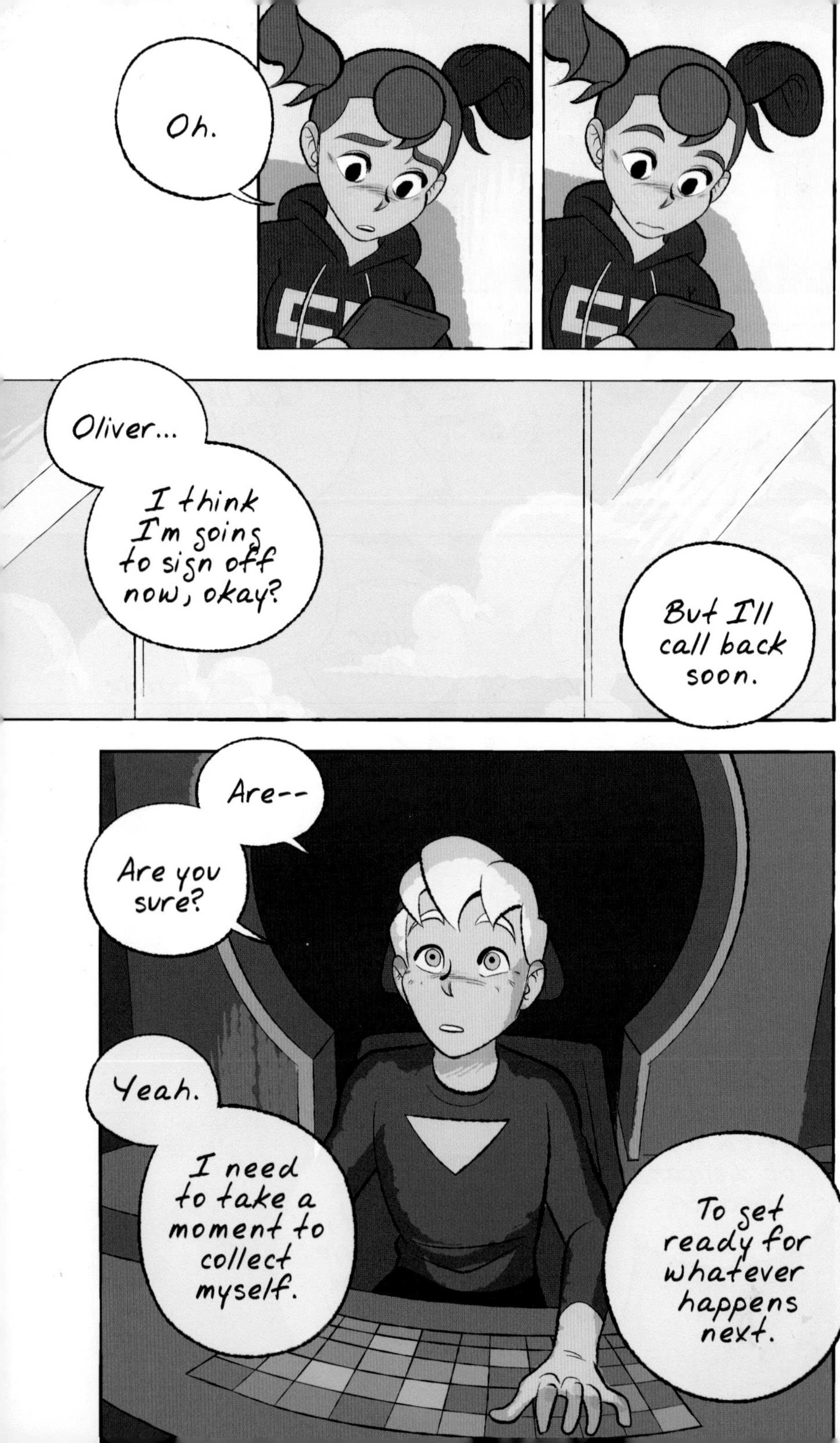

Oh.
Oliver...
I think I'm going to sign off now, okay?
But I'll call back soon.
Are--
Are you sure?
Yeah.
I need to take a moment to collect myself.
To get ready for whatever happens next.

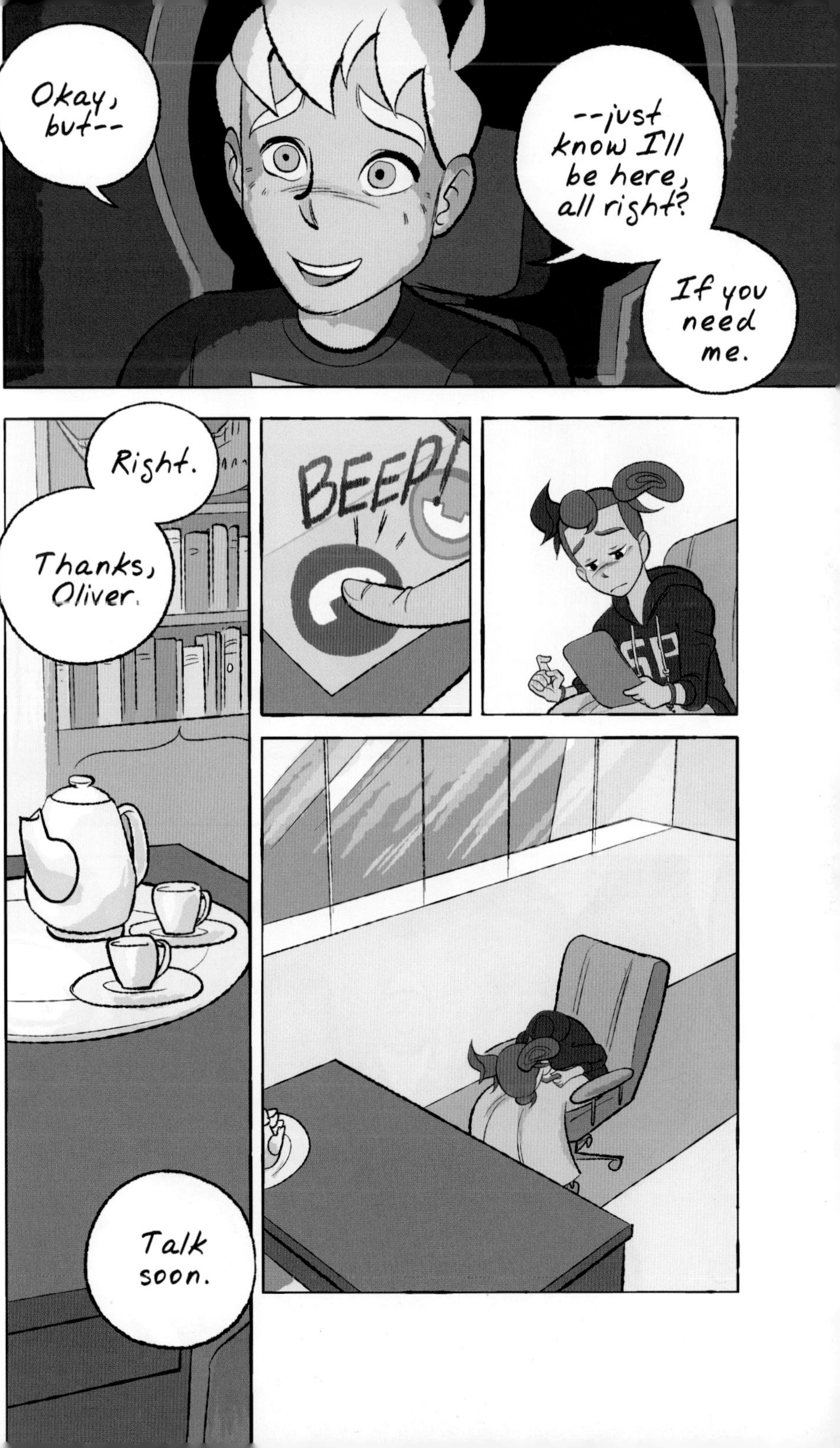
Okay, but--
--just know I'll be here, all right?
If you need me.
Right.
Thanks, Oliver.
BEEP!
Talk soon.

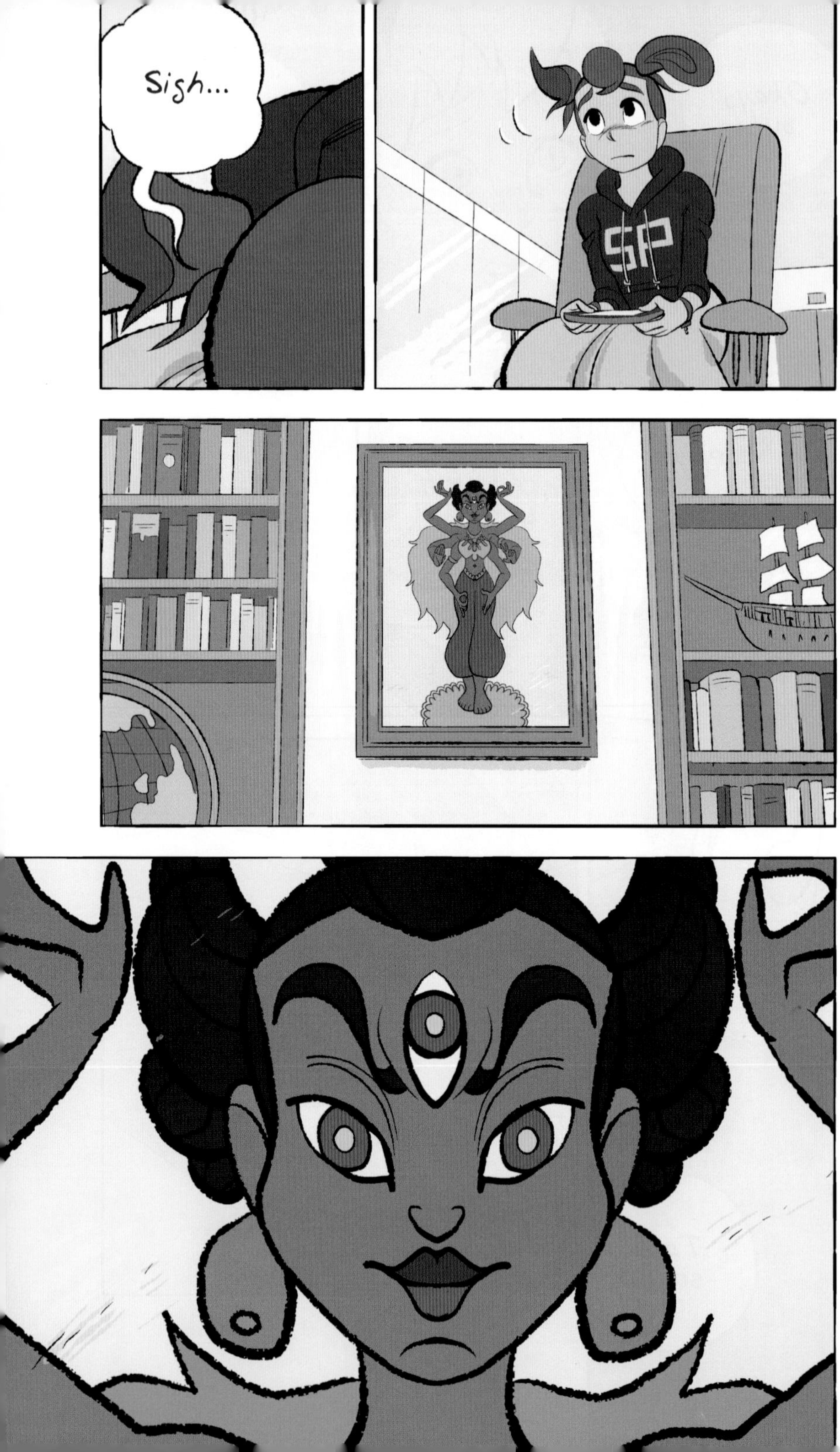
Sigh...

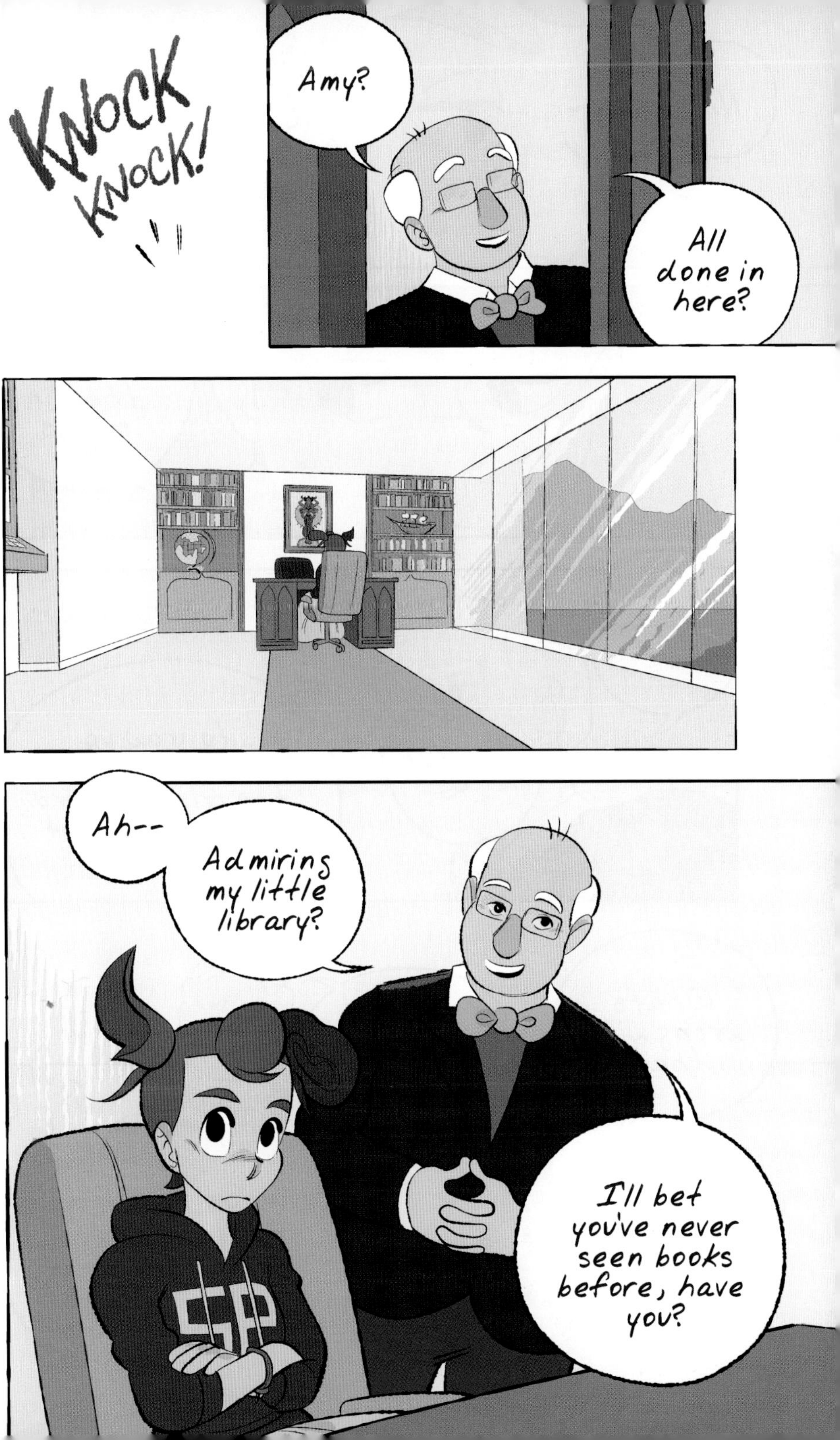
KNOCK KNOCK!
Amy?
All done in here?
Ah--
Admiring my little library?
I'll bet you've never seen books before, have you?

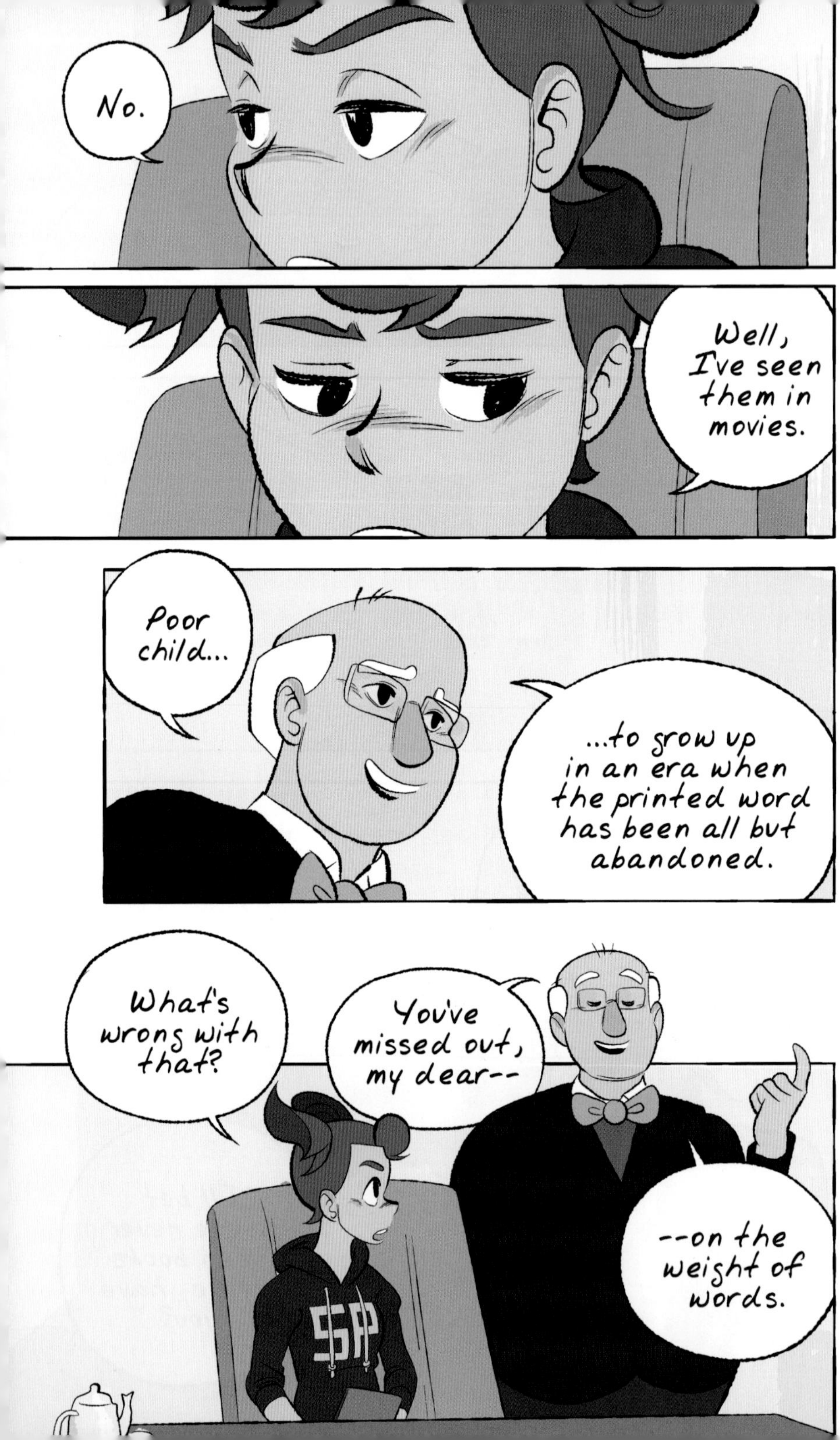
No.
Well, I've seen them in movies.
Poor child...
...to grow up in an era when the printed word has been all but abandoned.
What's wrong with that?
You've missed out, my dear--
--on the weight of words.

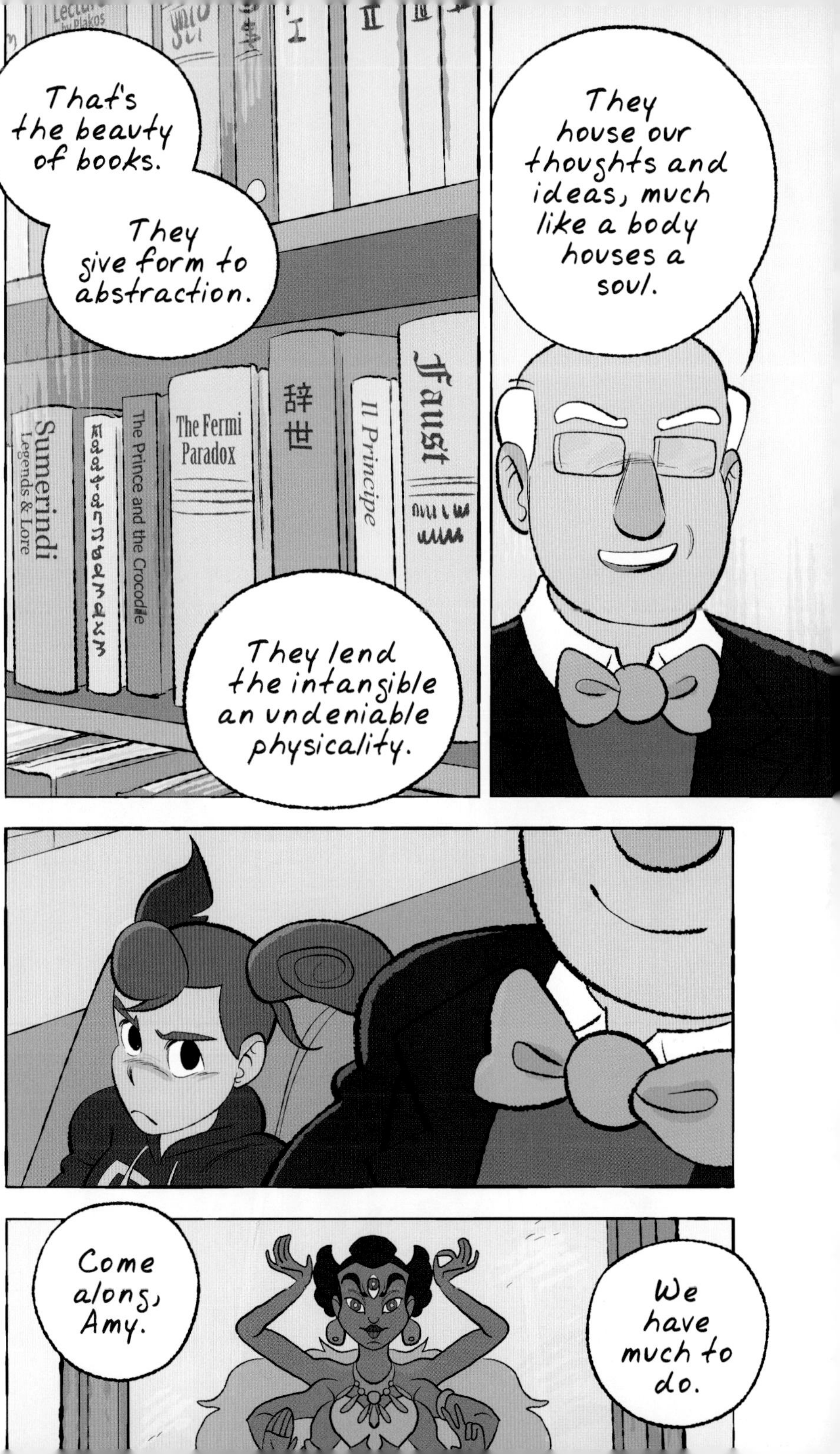

That's the beauty of books.
They give form to abstraction.
Sumerindi Legends & Lore
The Prince and the Crocodile
The Fermi Paradox
辞世
Il Principe
Faust
They lend the intangible an undeniable physicality.
They house our thoughts and ideas, much like a body houses a soul.
Come along, Amy.
We have much to do.

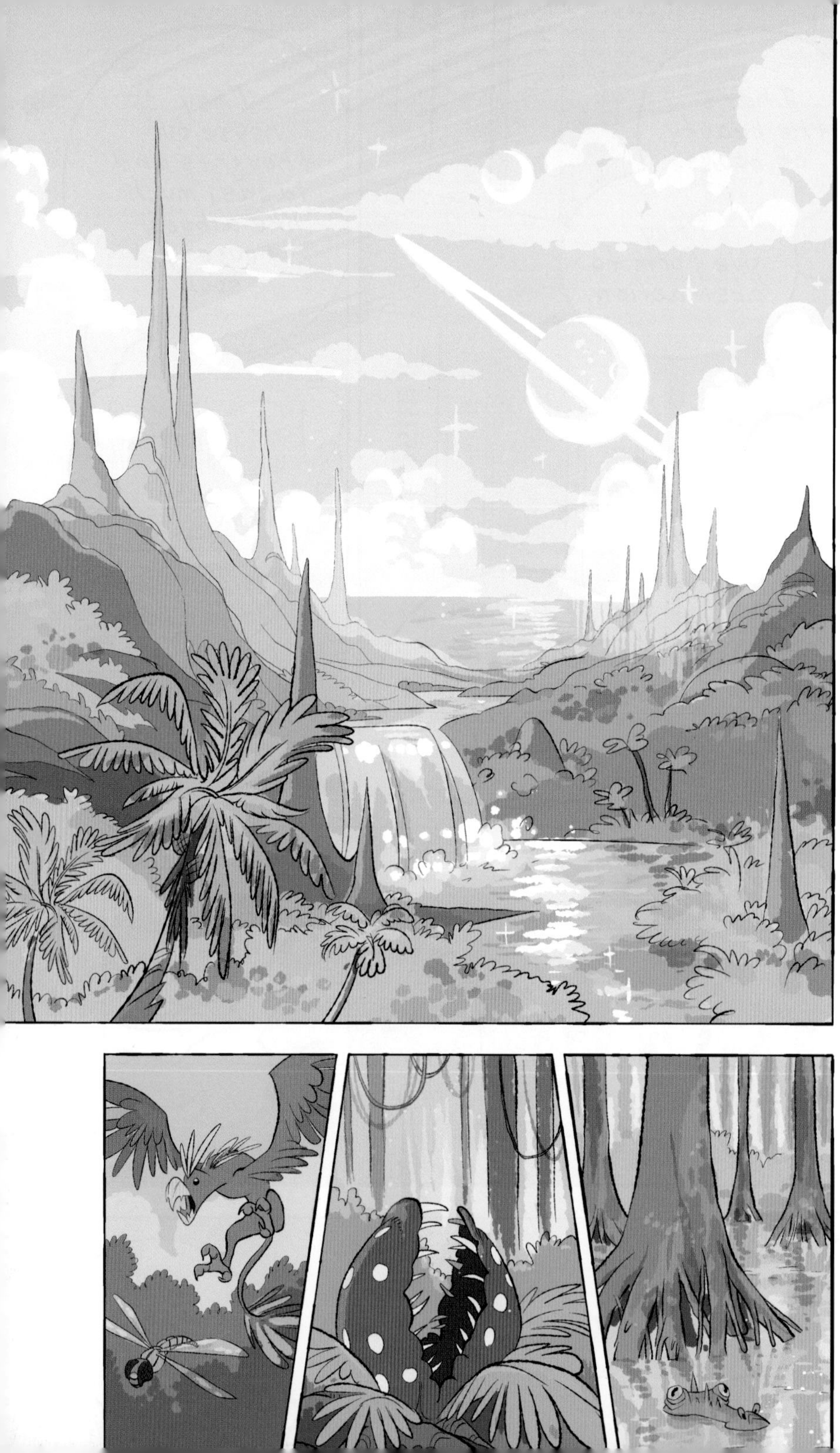

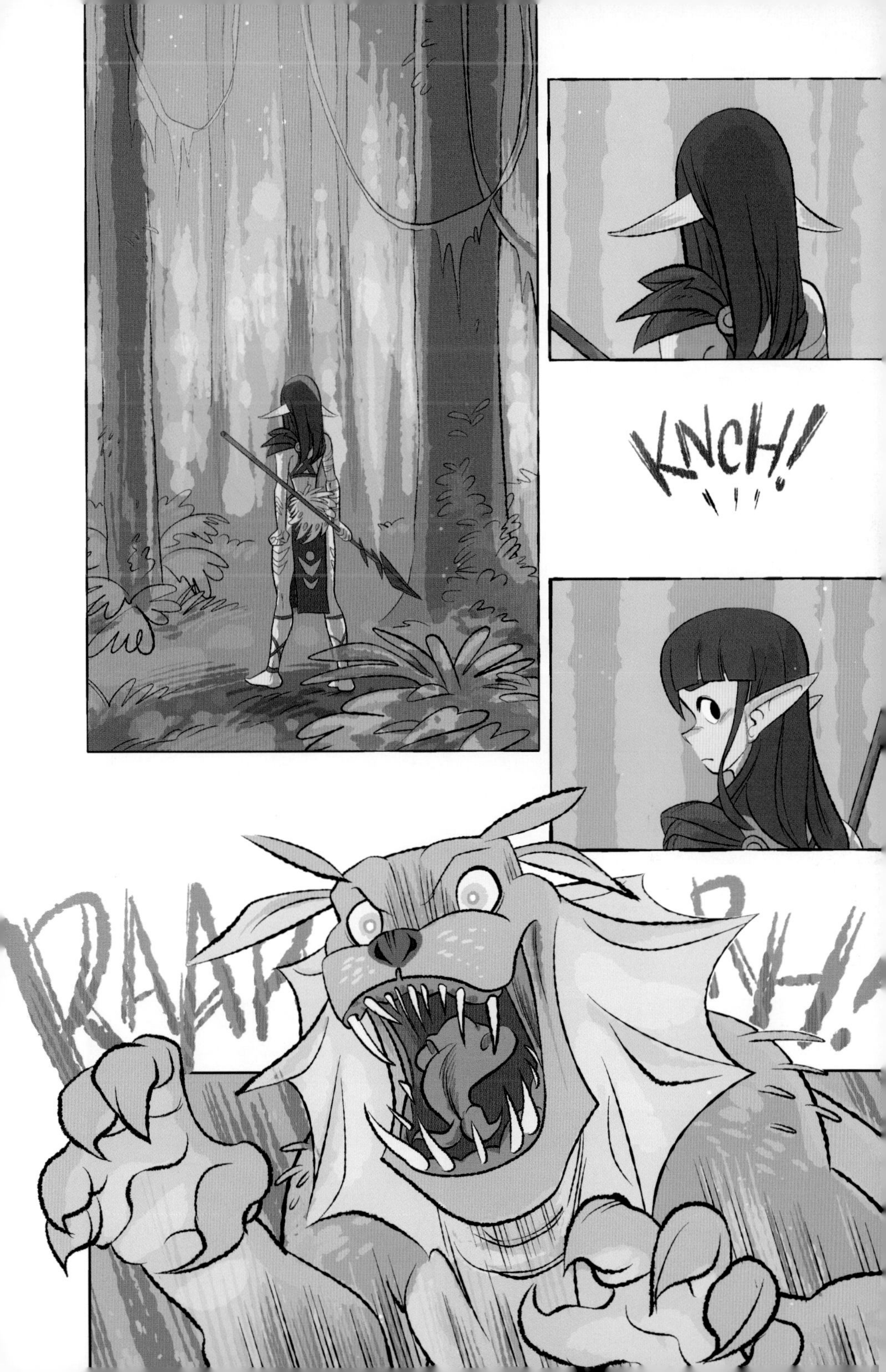
KNCH!
RAAARRH!

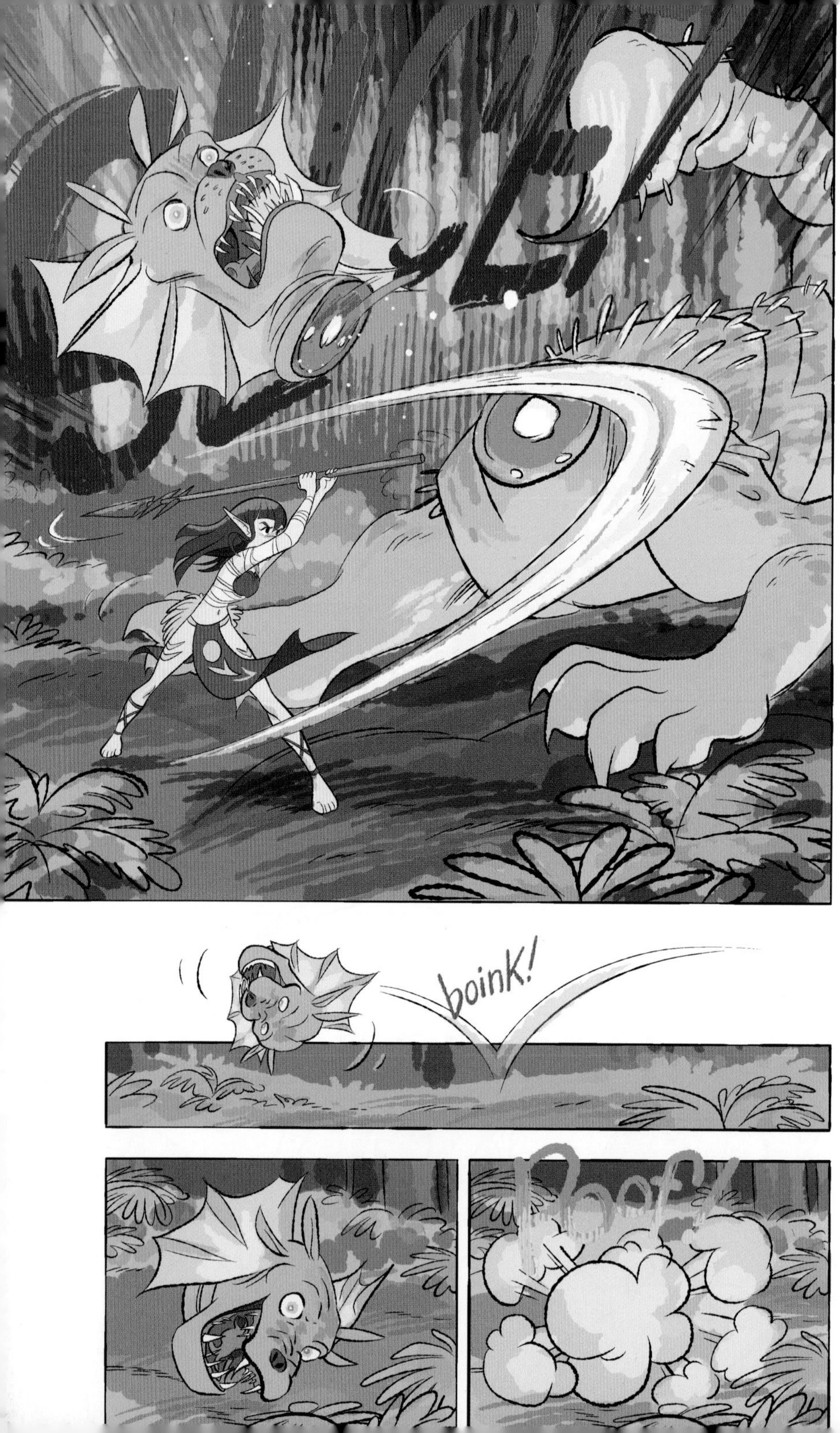
boink!
Poof!

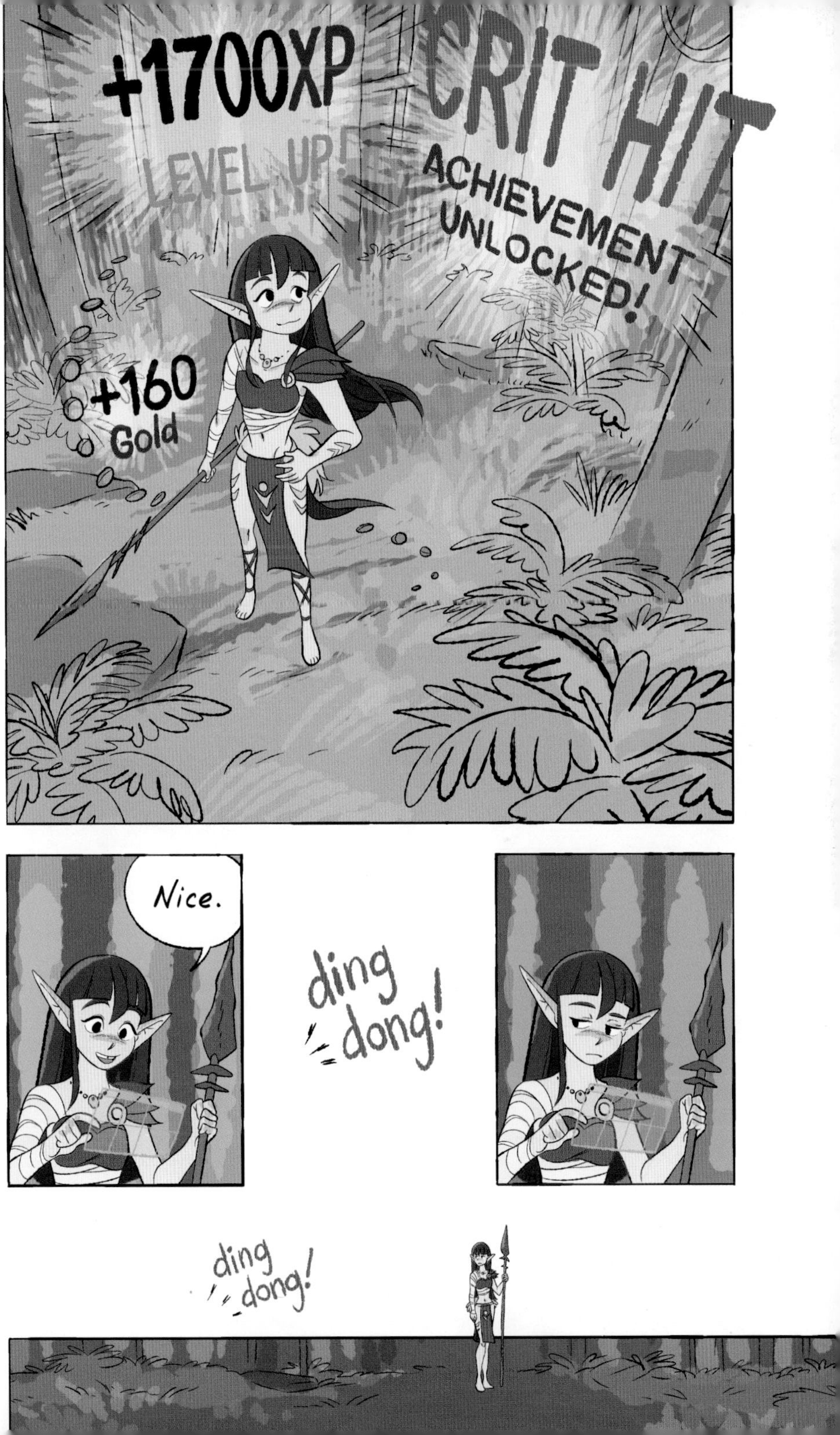
+1700XP
CRIT HIT
LEVEL UP!
ACHIEVEMENT UNLOCKED!
+160 Gold
Nice.
ding dong!
ding dong!

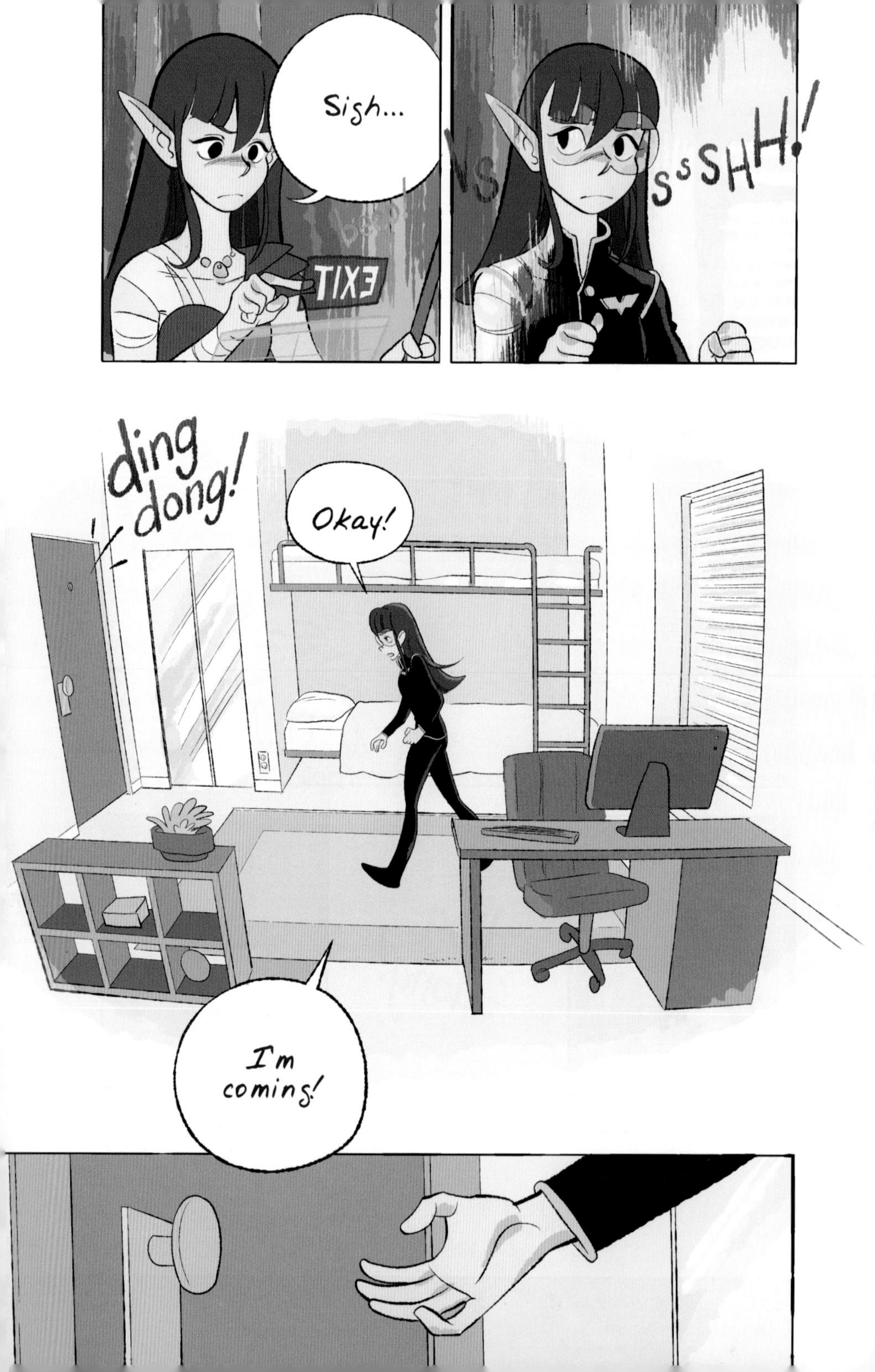

Sigh...
SsSHH!
ding dong!
Okay!
I'm coming!

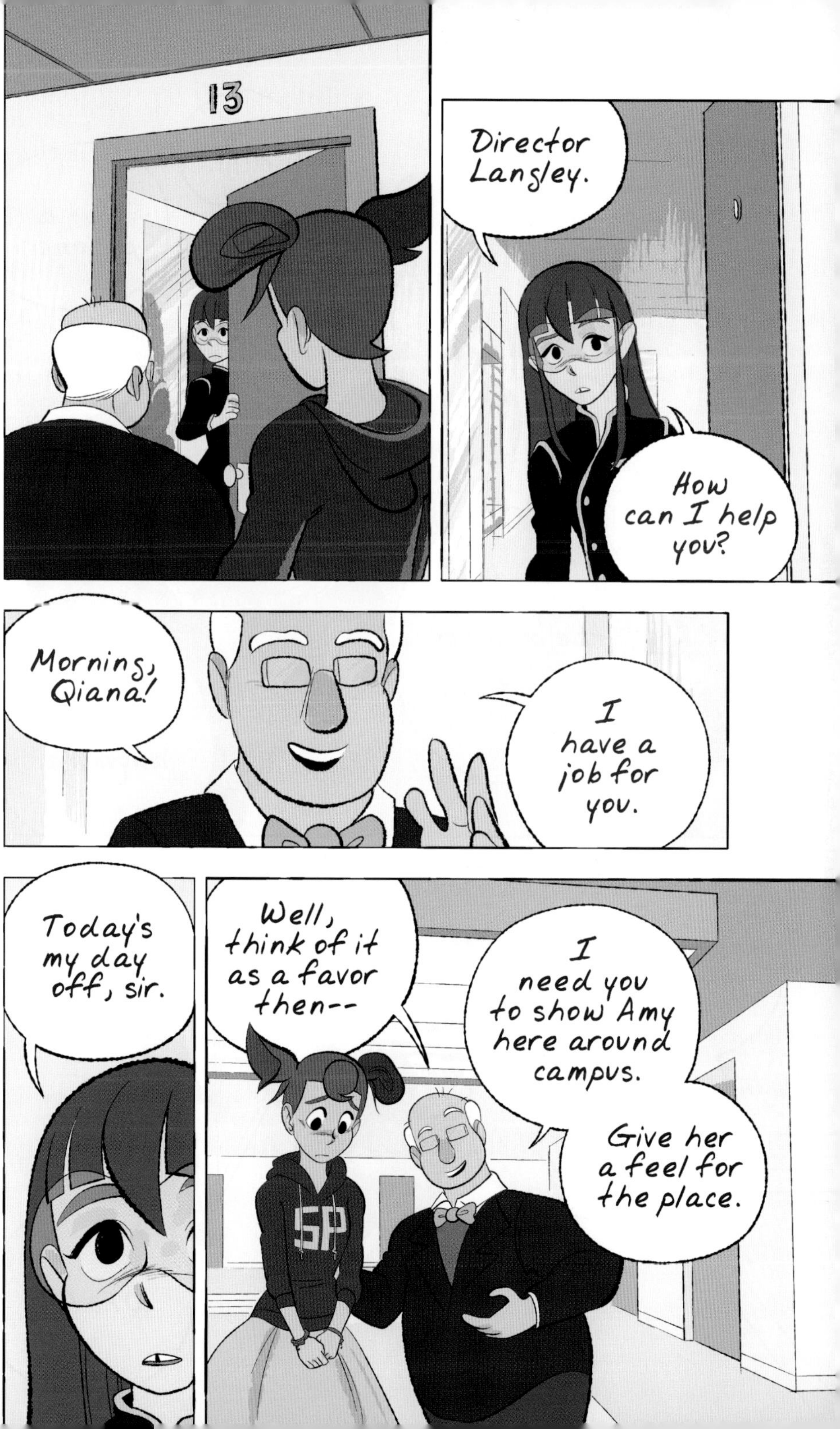

13
Director Langley.
How can I help you?
Morning, Qiana!
I have a job for you.
Today's my day off, sir.
Well, think of it as a favor then--
I need you to show Amy here around campus.
Give her a feel for the place.
SP

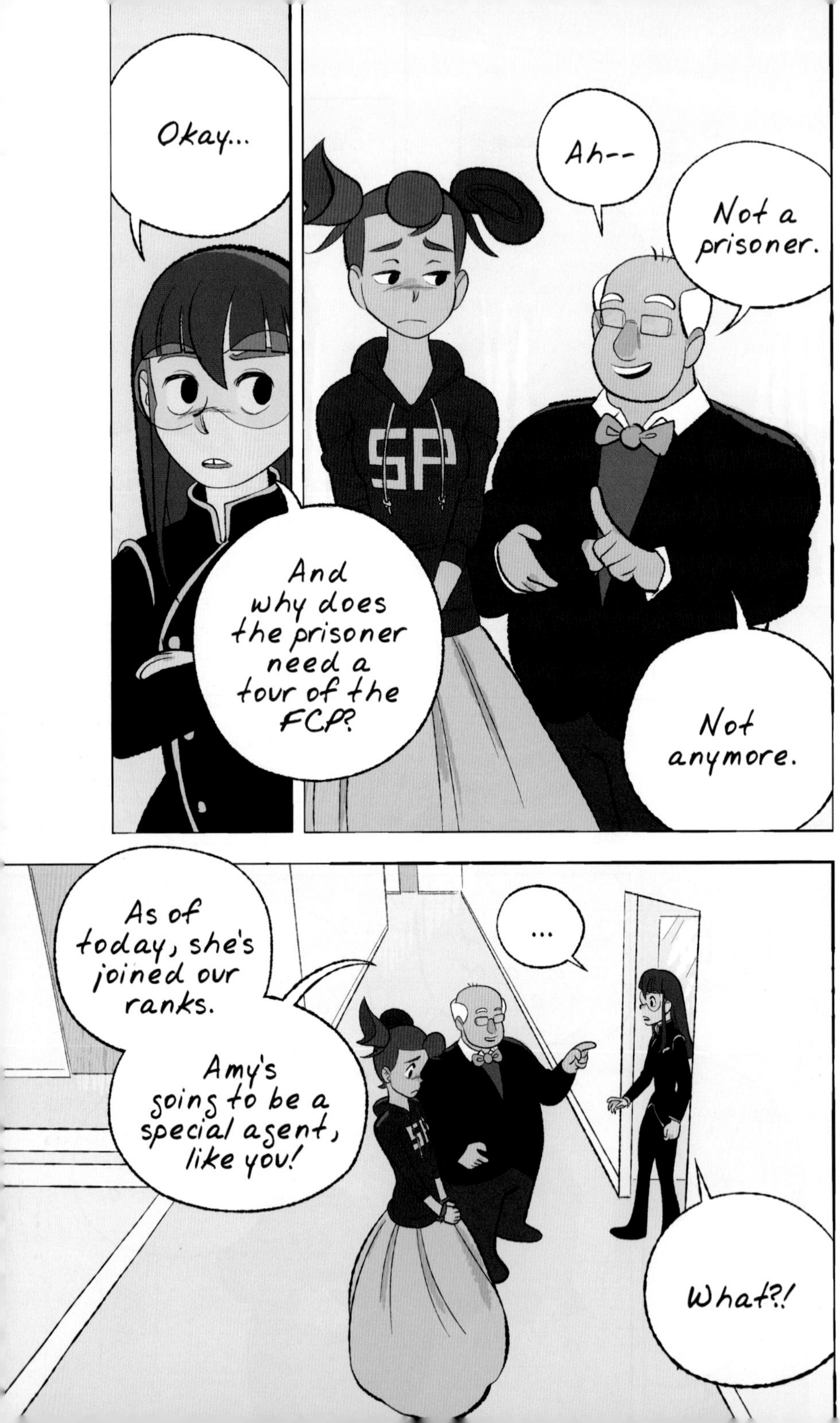
Okay...
Ah--
Not a prisoner.
And why does the prisoner need a tour of the FCP?
Not anymore.
As of today, she's joined our ranks.
...
Amy's going to be a special agent, like you!
What?!

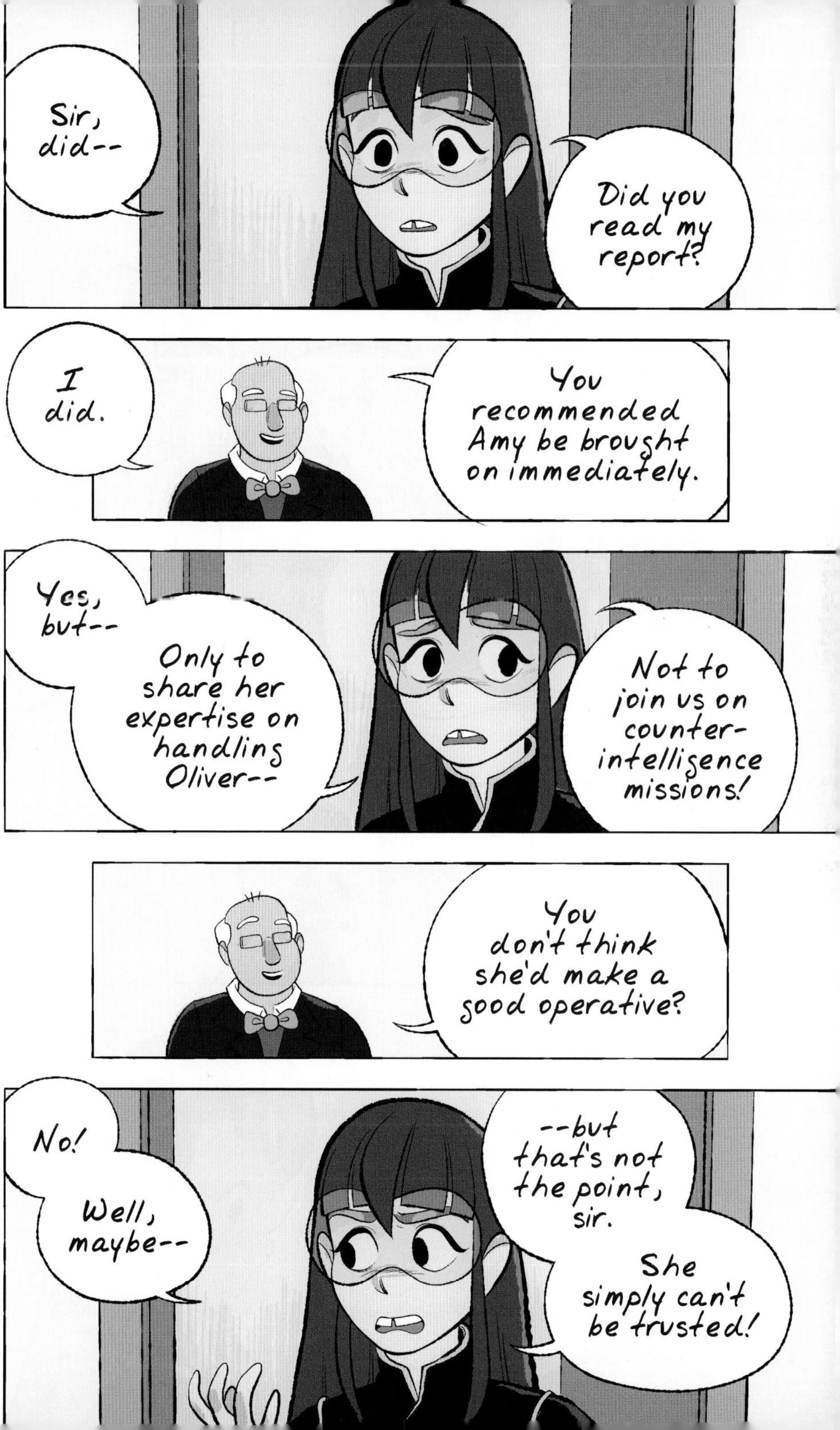
Sir, did--
Did you read my report?
I did.
You recommended Amy be brought on immediately.
Yes, but--
Only to share her expertise on handling Oliver--
Not to join us on counter-intelligence missions!
You don't think she'd make a good operative?
No!
Well, maybe--
--but that's not the point, sir.
She simply can't be trusted!

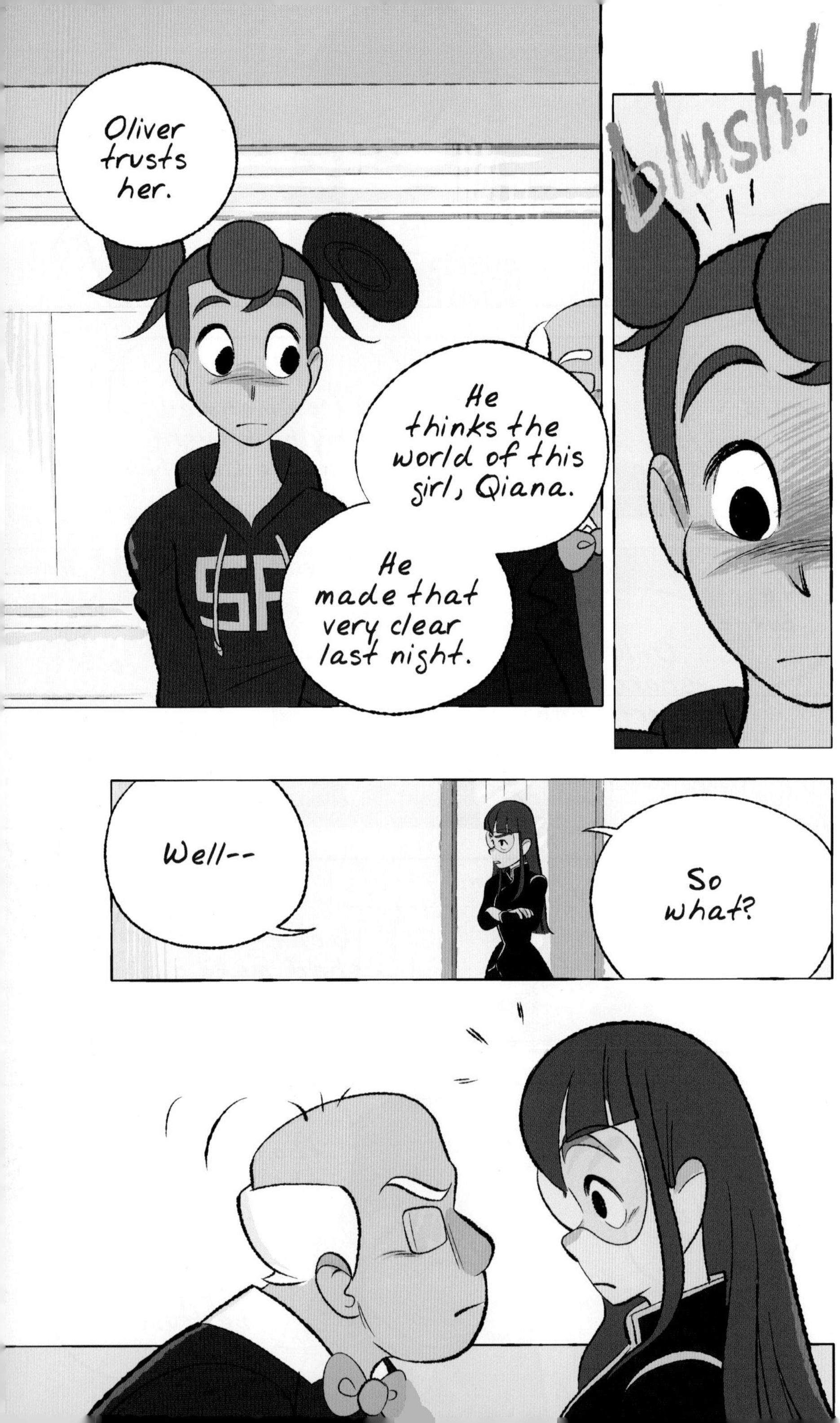
Oliver trusts her.
He thinks the world of this girl, Qiana.
He made that very clear last night.
blush!
Well--
So what?

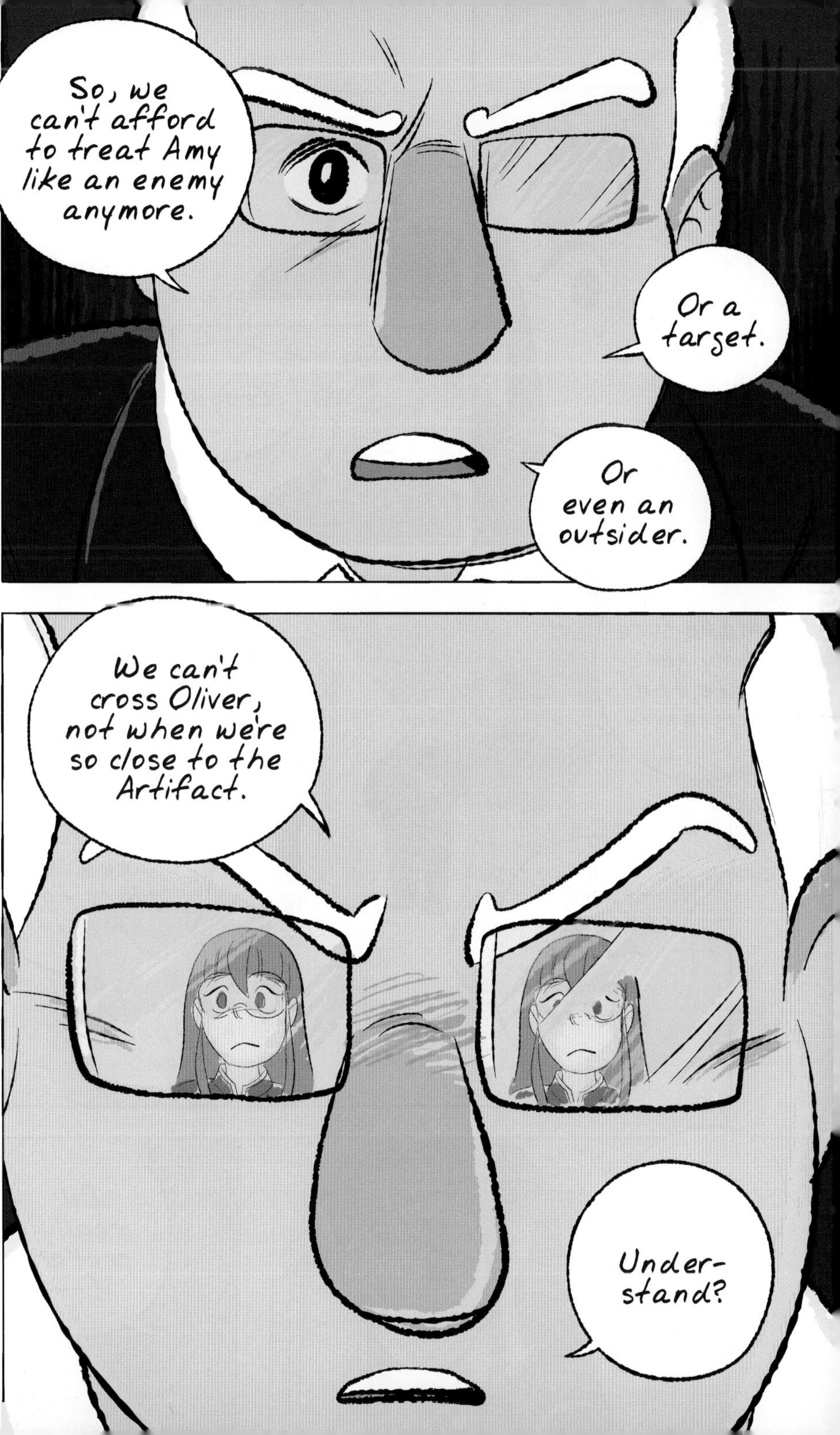
So, we can't afford to treat Amy like an enemy anymore.
Or a target.
Or even an outsider.
We can't cross Oliver, not when we're so close to the Artifact.
Under-stand?

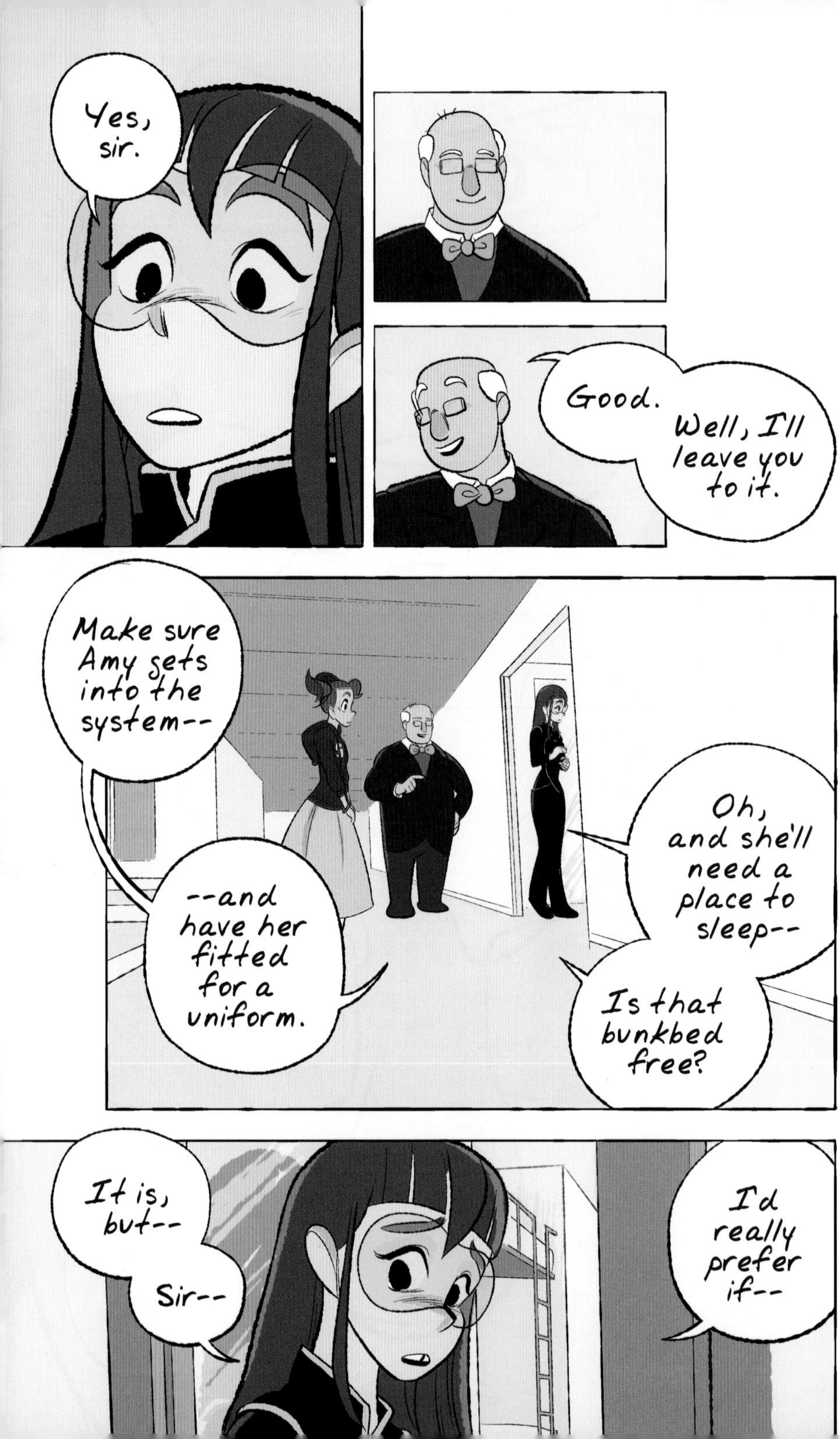
Yes, sir.
Good.
Well, I'll leave you to it.
Make sure Amy gets into the system--
--and have her fitted for a uniform.
Oh, and she'll need a place to sleep--
Is that bunkbed free?
It is, but--
Sir--
I'd really prefer if--

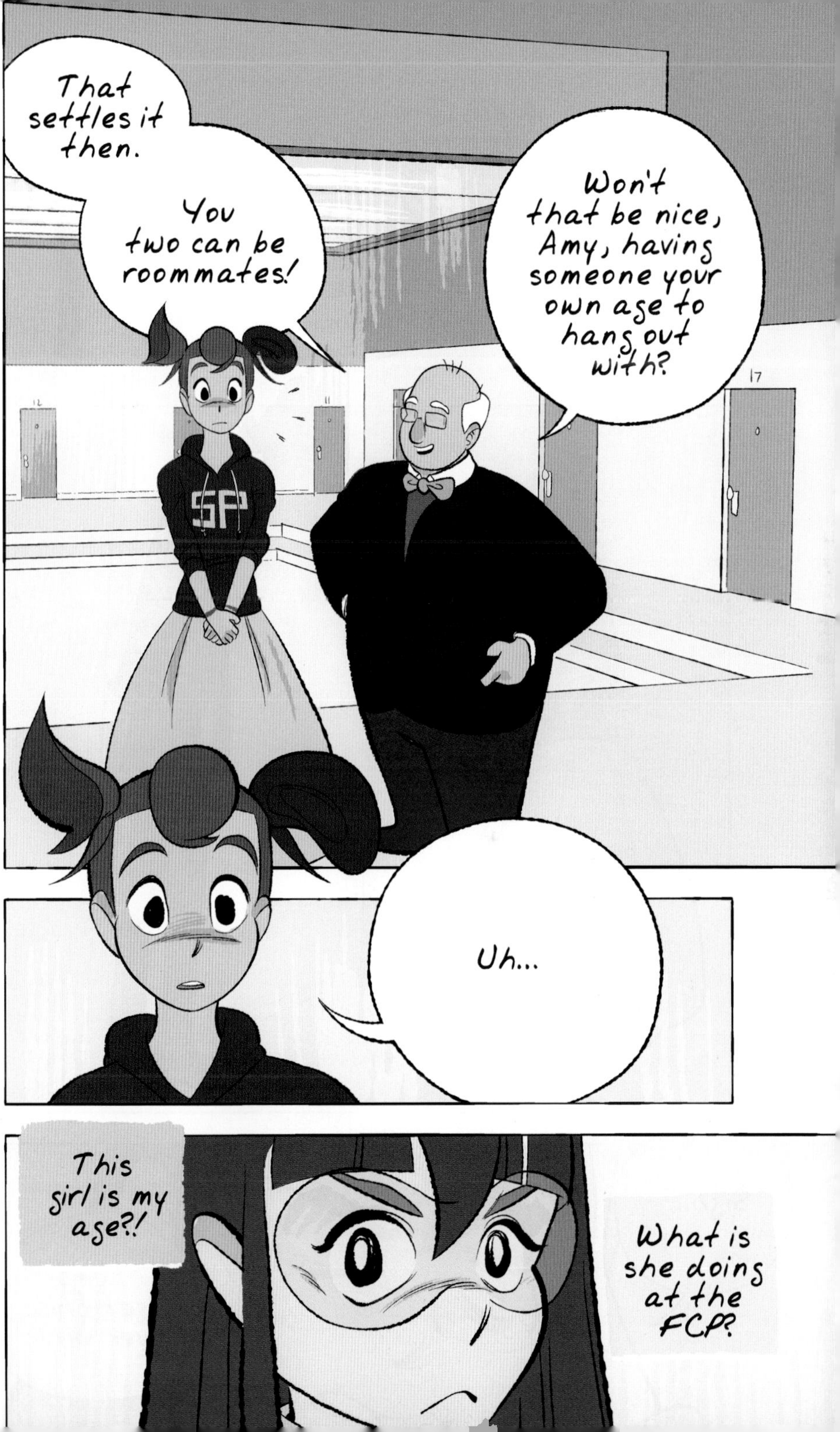
That settles it then.
You two can be roommates!
Won't that be nice, Amy, having someone your own age to hang out with?
Uh...
This girl is my age?!
What is she doing at the FCP?

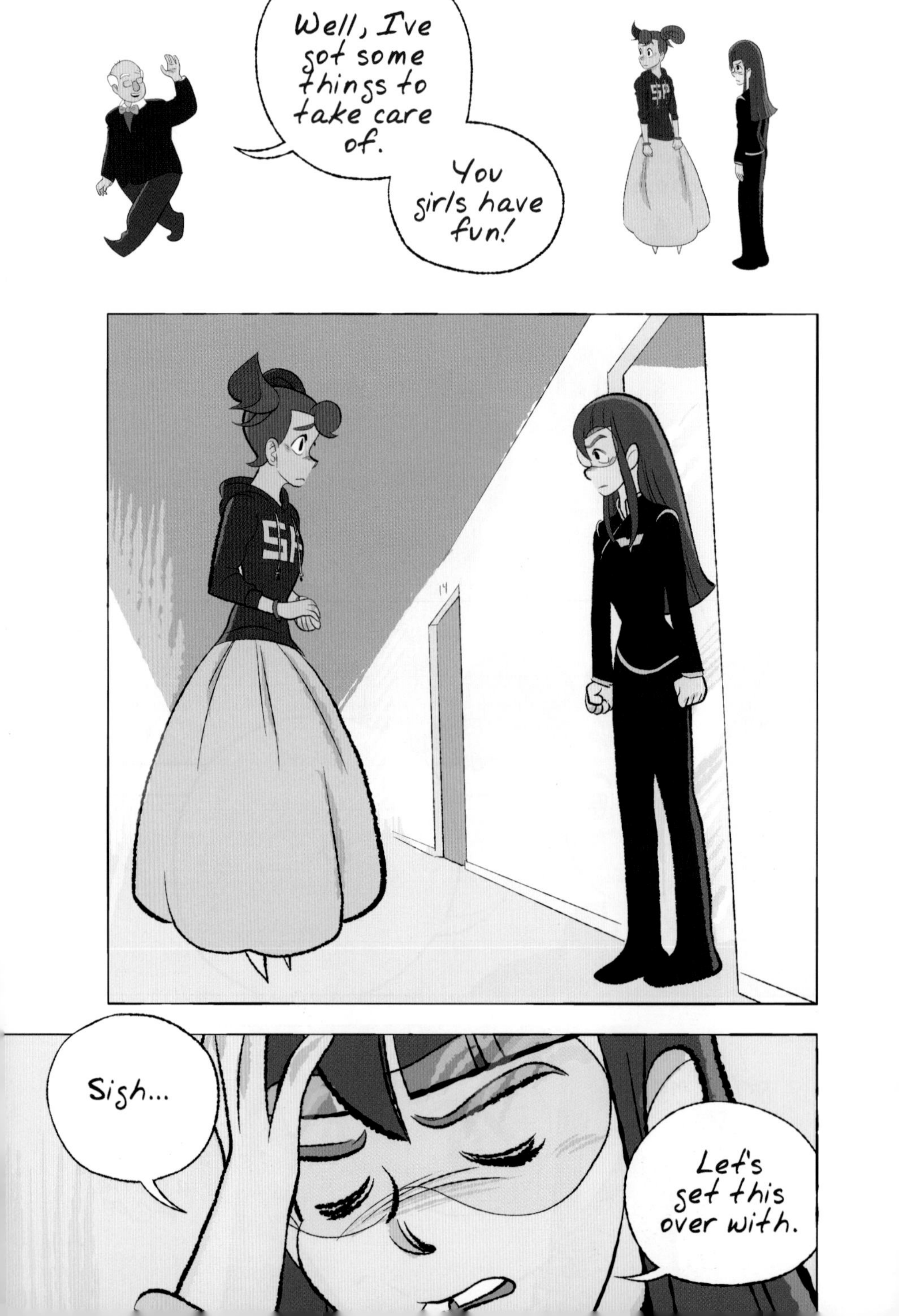
Well, I've got some things to take care of.
You girls have fun!
14
Sigh...
Let's get this over with.

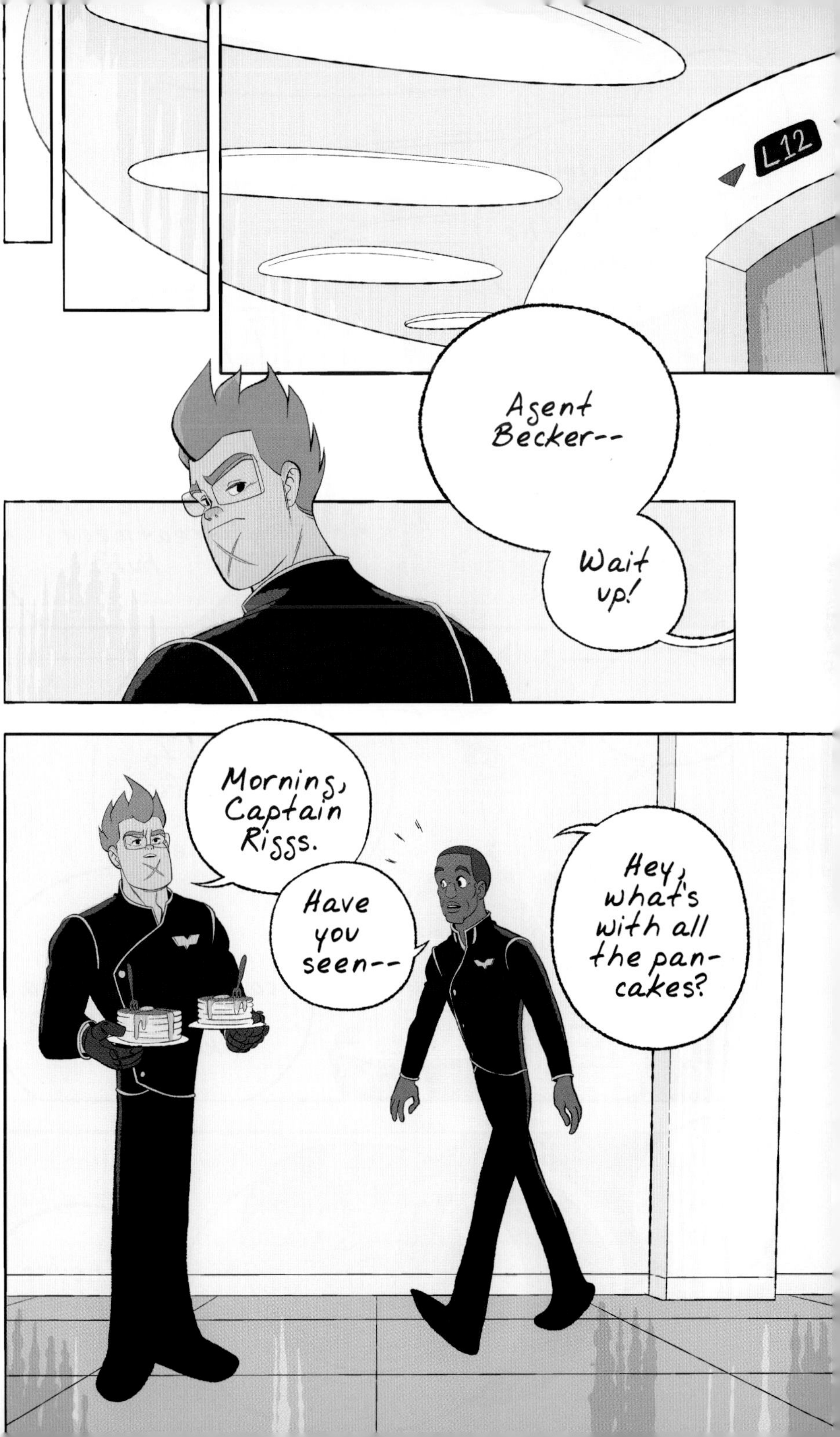
L12
Agent Becker--
Wait up!
Morning, Captain Riggs.
Have you seen--
Hey, what's with all the pan-cakes?

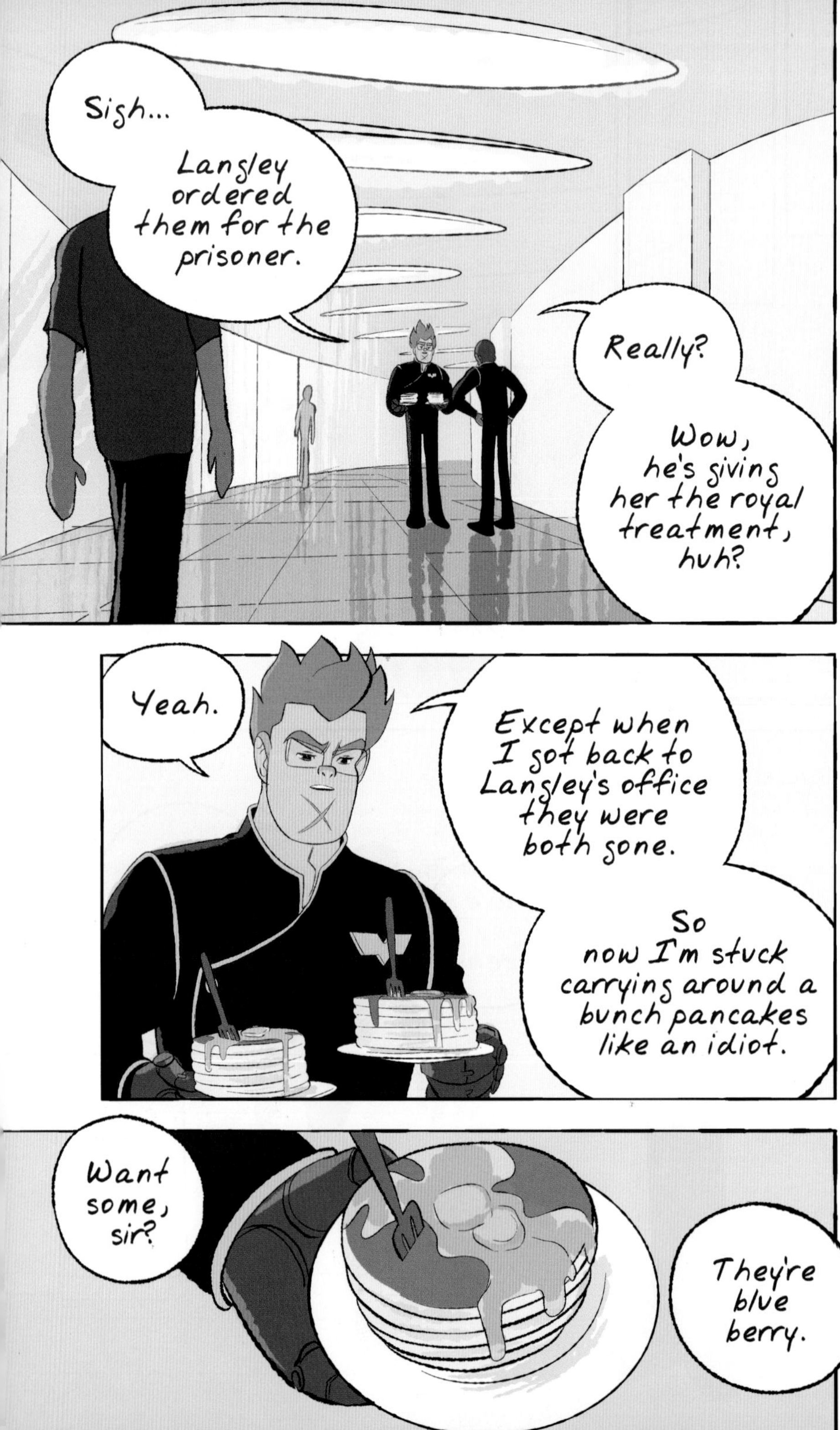
Sigh...
Langley ordered them for the prisoner.
Really?
Wow, he's giving her the royal treatment, huh?
Yeah.
Except when I got back to Langley's office they were both gone.
So now I'm stuck carrying around a bunch pancakes like an idiot.
Want some, sir?
They're blue berry.

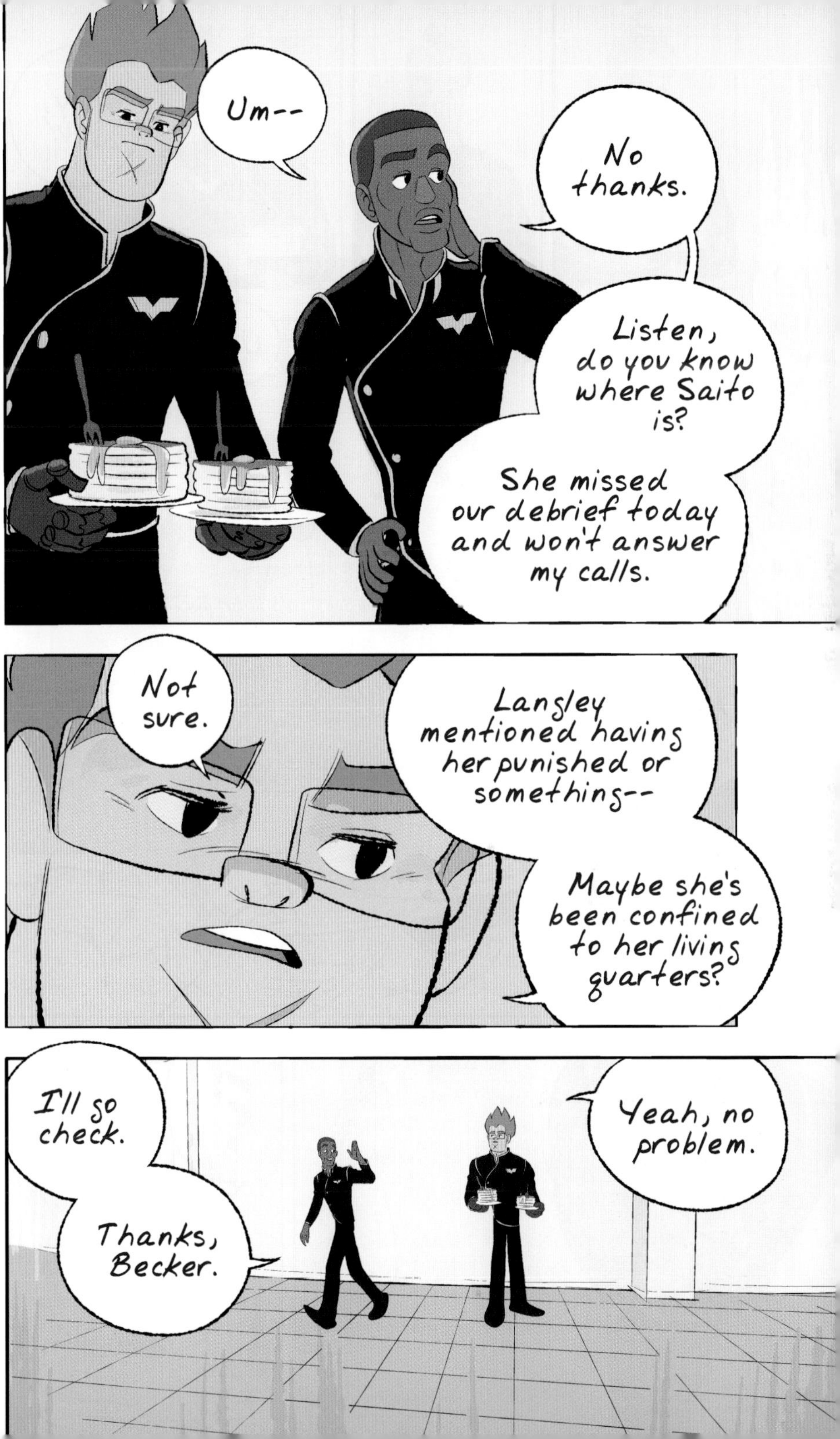
Um--
No thanks.
Listen, do you know where Saito is?
She missed our debrief today and won't answer my calls.
Not sure.
Langley mentioned having her punished or something--
Maybe she's been confined to her living quarters?
I'll go check.
Thanks, Becker.
Yeah, no problem.

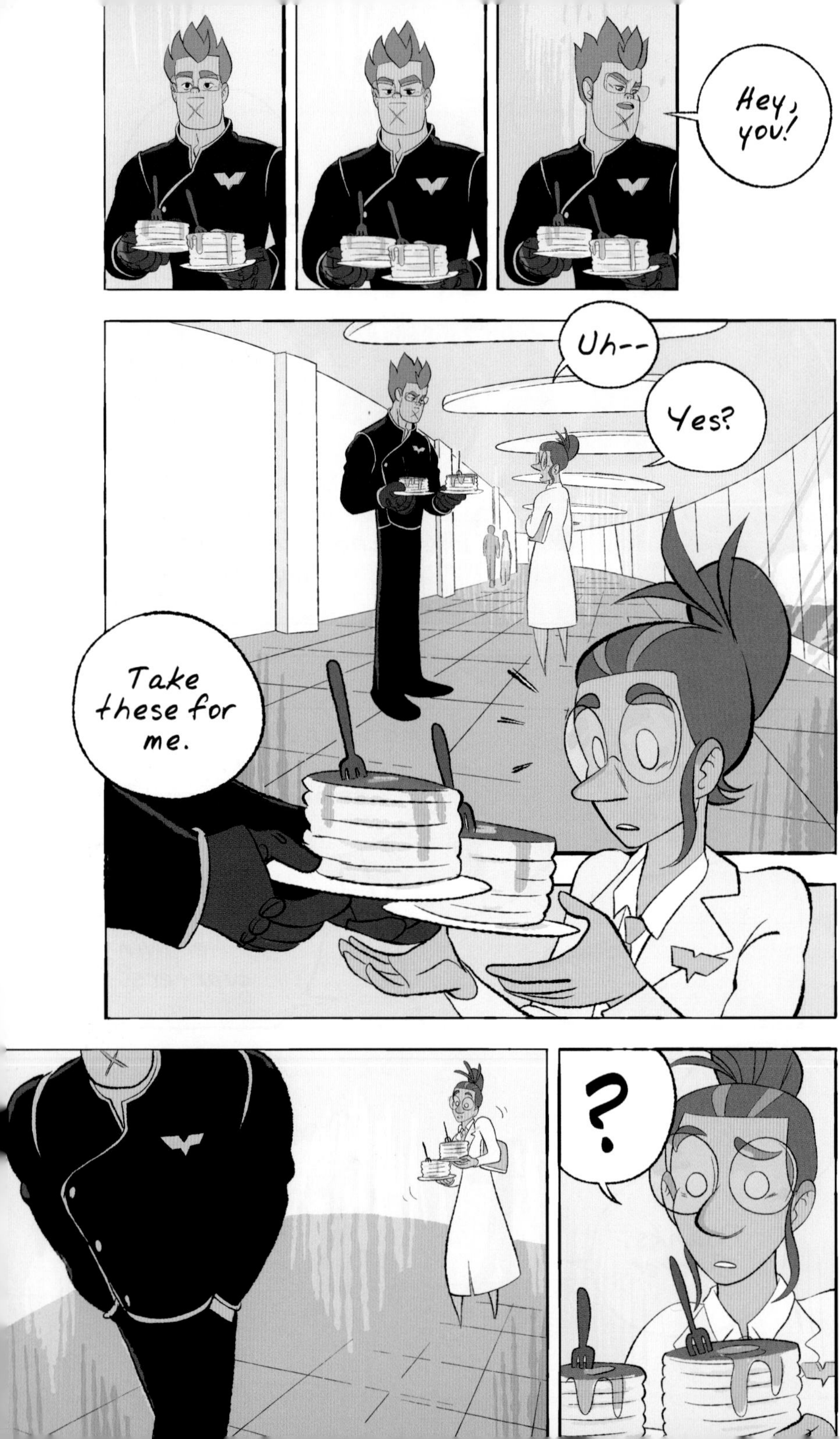
Hey, you!
Uh--
Yes?
Take these for me.
?

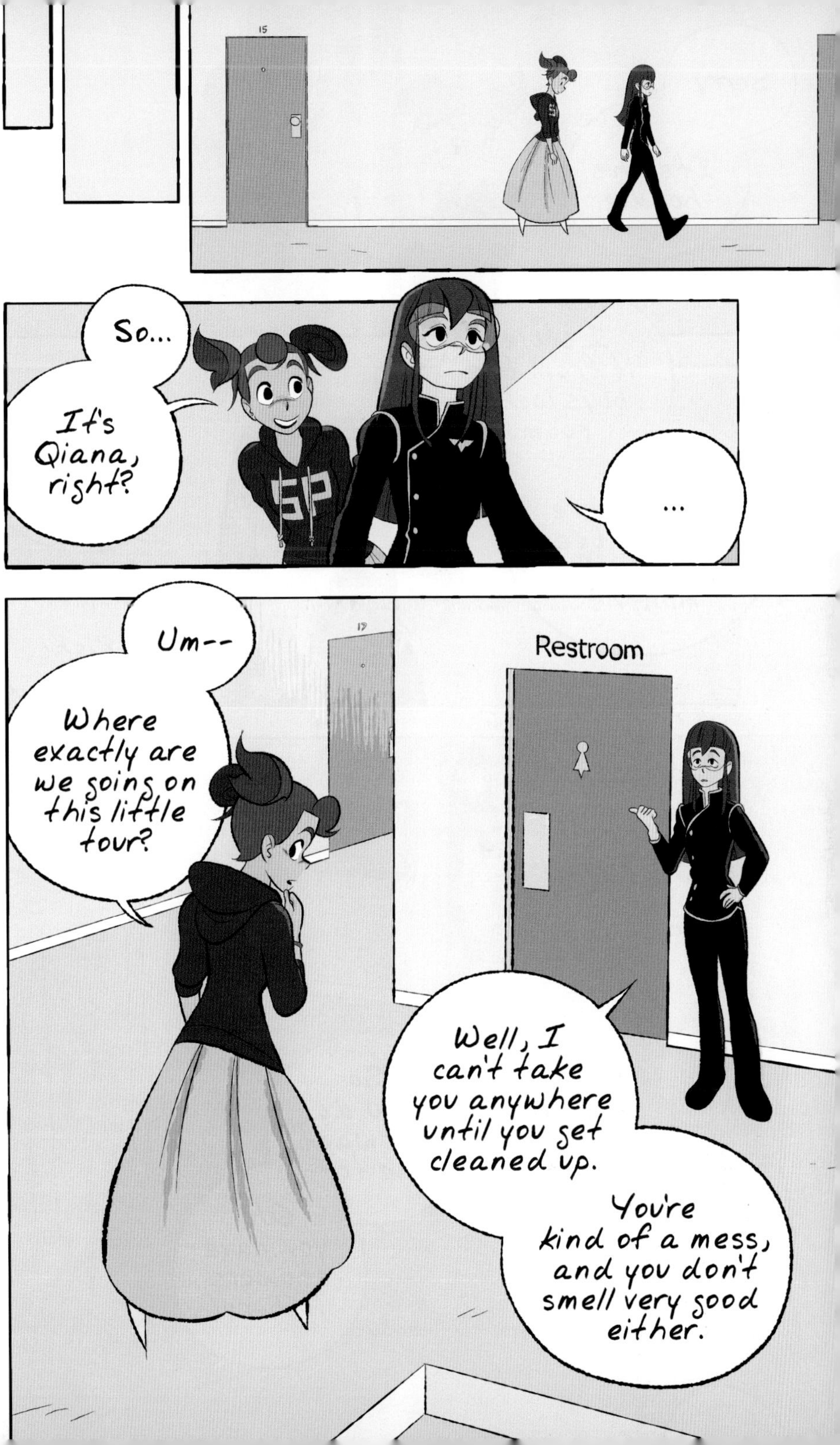

15
So...
It's Qiana, right?
...
17
Um--
Where exactly are we going on this little tour?
Restroom
Well, I can't take you anywhere until you get cleaned up.
You're kind of a mess, and you don't smell very good either.

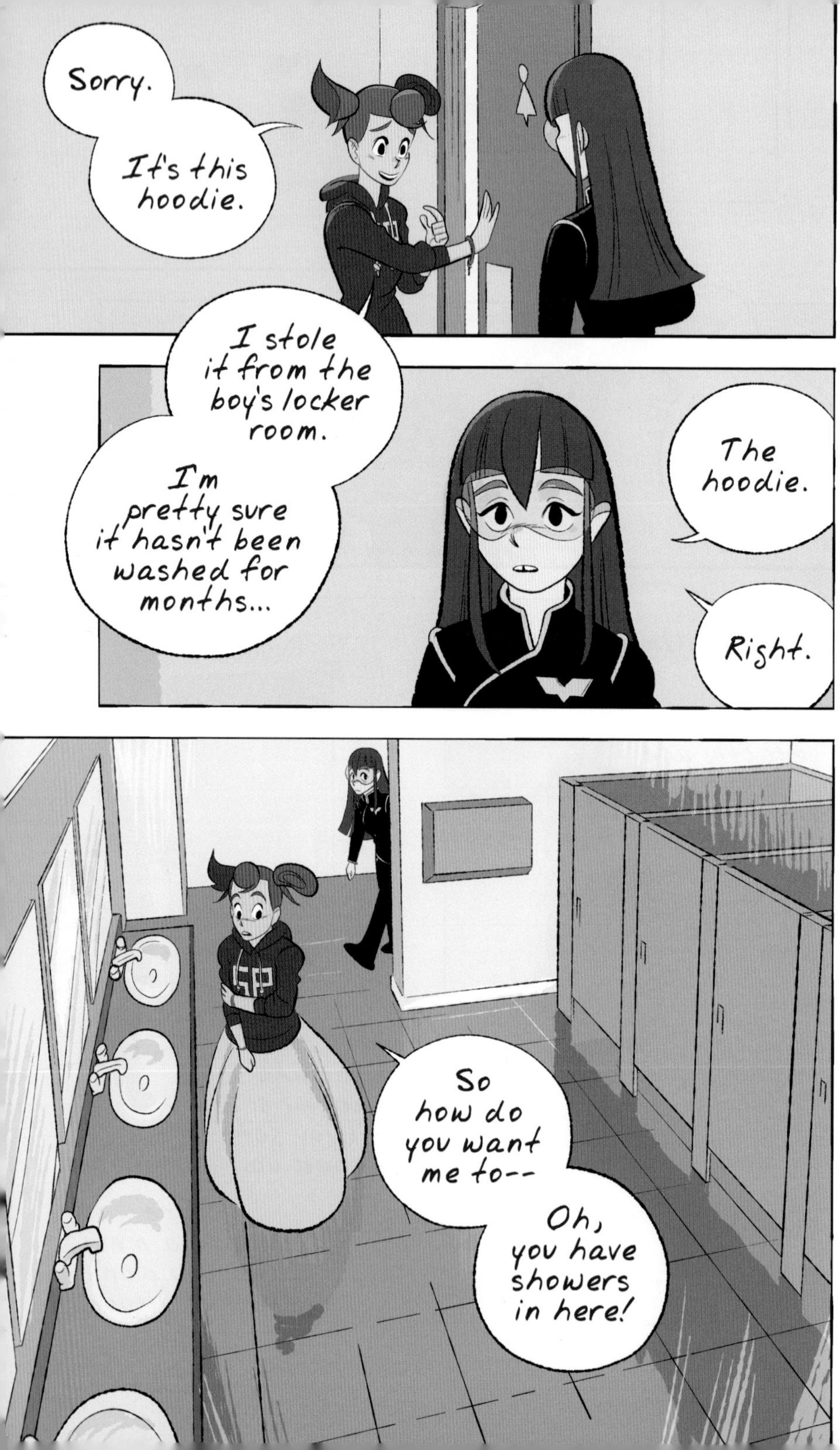
Sorry.
It's this hoodie.
I stole it from the boy's locker room.
I'm pretty sure it hasn't been washed for months...
The hoodie.
Right.
So how do you want me to--
Oh, you have showers in here!

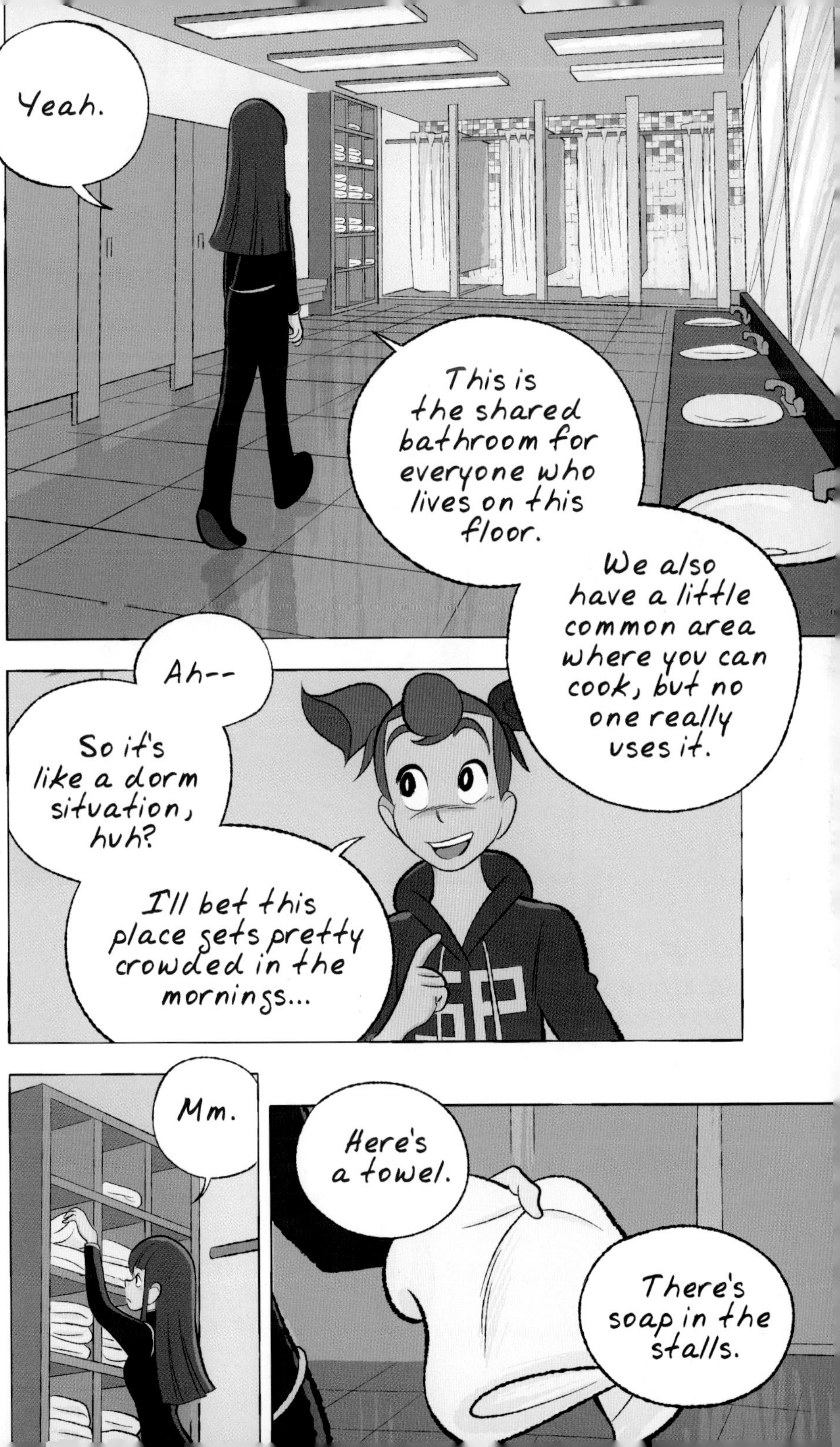
Yeah.
This is the shared bathroom for everyone who lives on this floor.
We also have a little common area where you can cook, but no one really uses it.
Ah--
So it's like a dorm situation, huh?
I'll bet this place gets pretty crowded in the mornings...
Mm.
Here's a towel.
There's soap in the stalls.

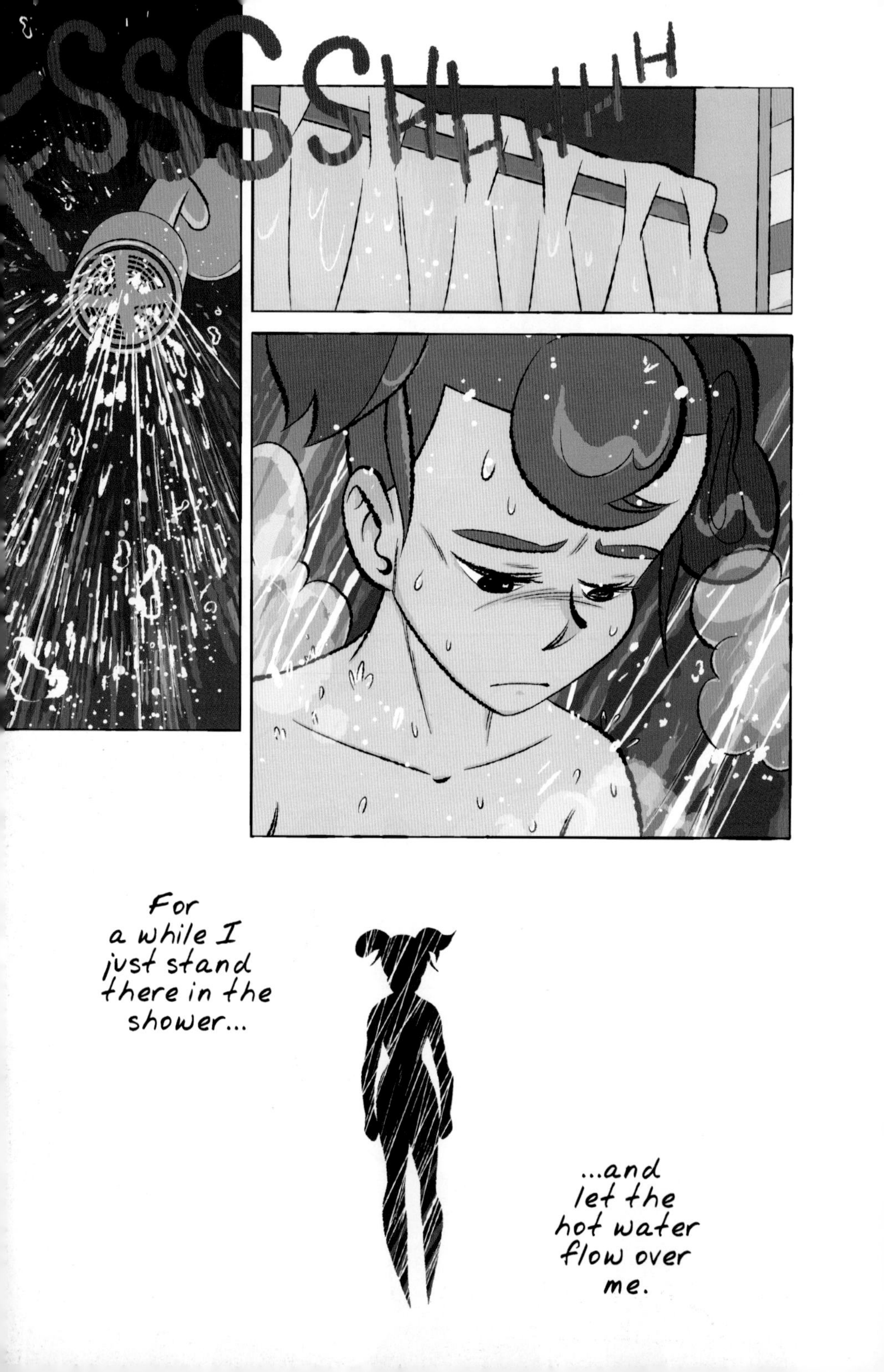
SSSSHHHHHH
For a while I just stand there in the shower...
...and let the hot water flow over me.

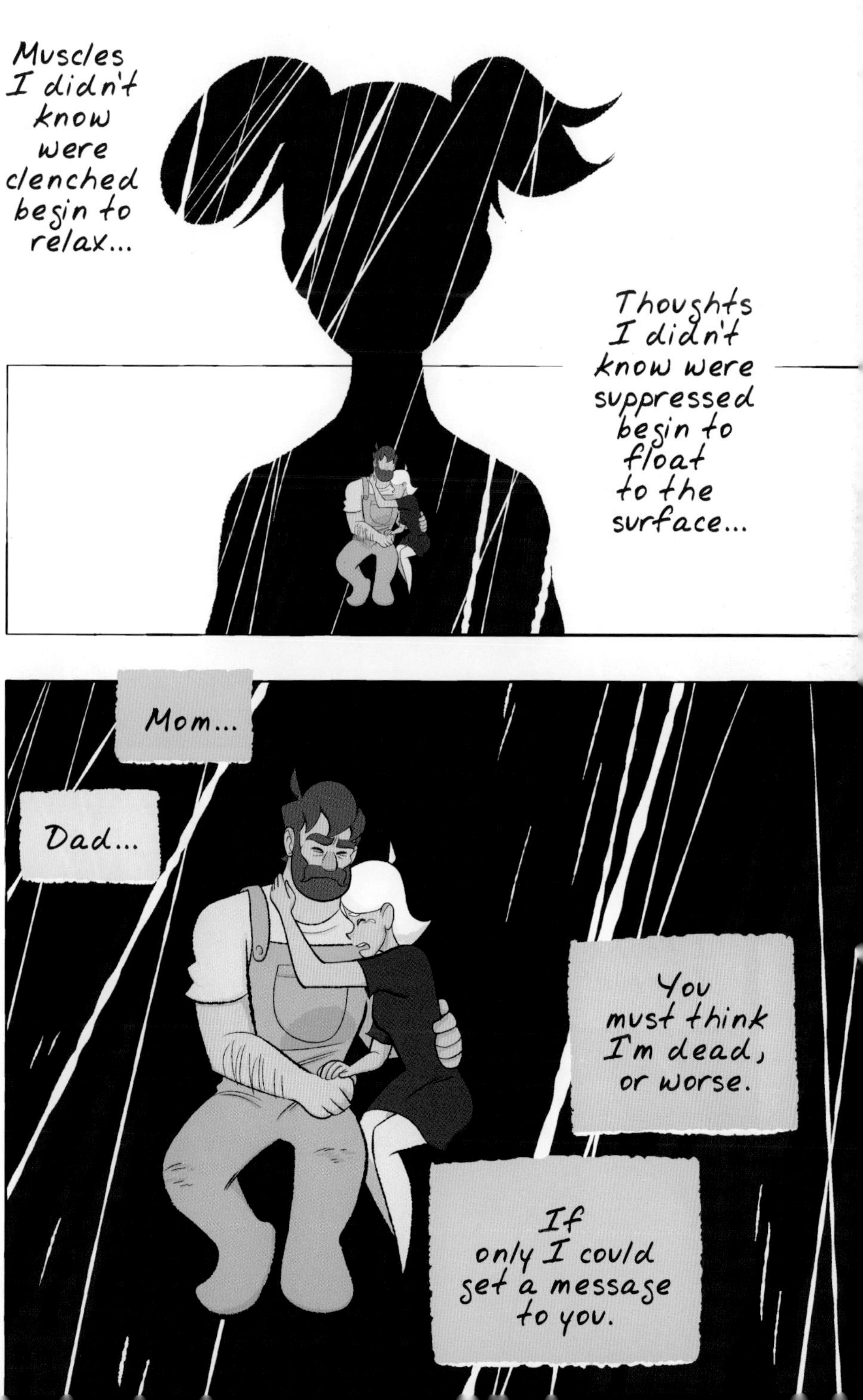
Muscles I didn't know were clenched begin to relax...
Thoughts I didn't know were suppressed begin to float to the surface...
Mom...
Dad...
You must think I'm dead, or worse.
If only I could get a message to you.

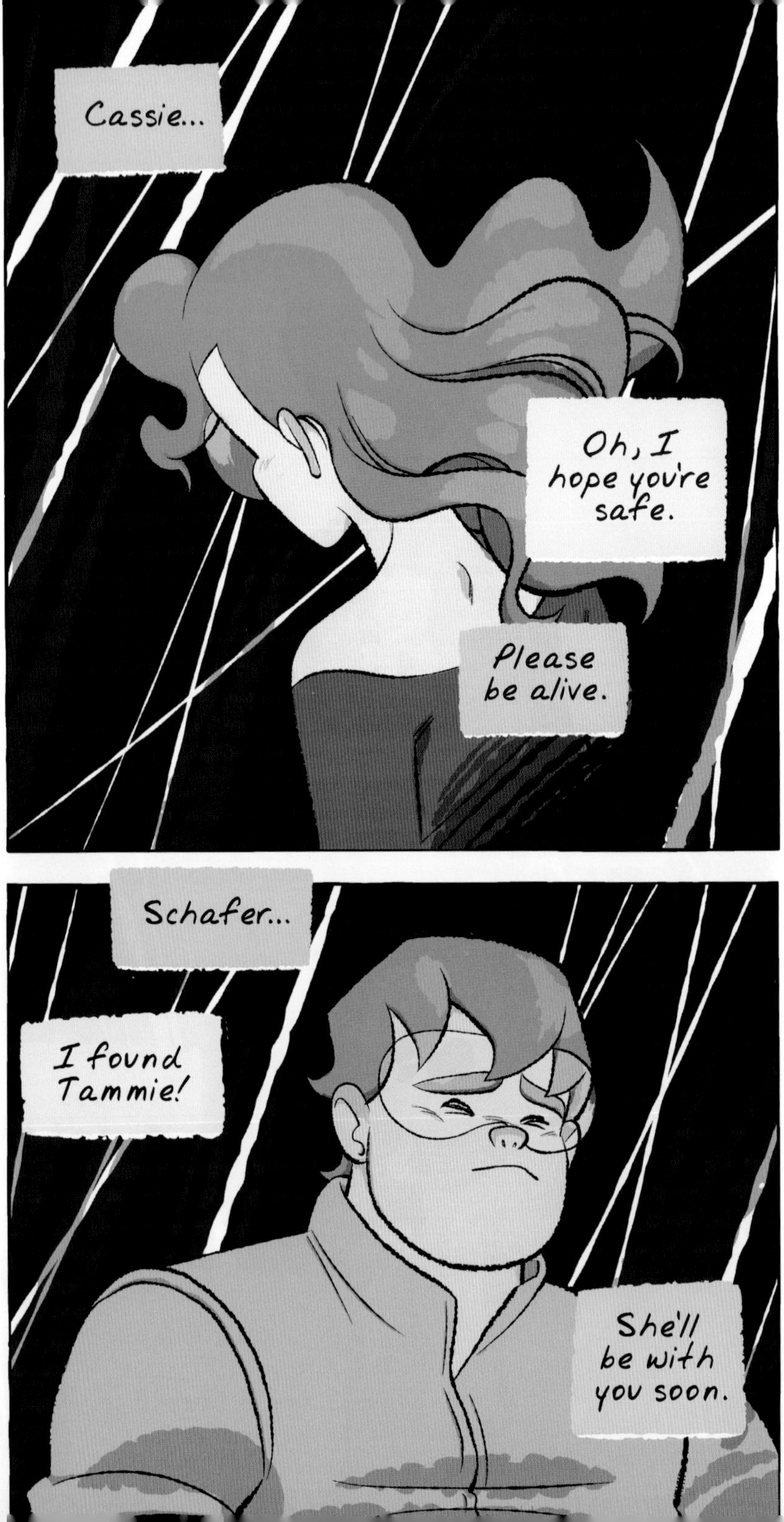
Cassie...
Oh, I hope you're safe.
Please be alive.
Schafer...
I found Tammie!
She'll be with you soon.

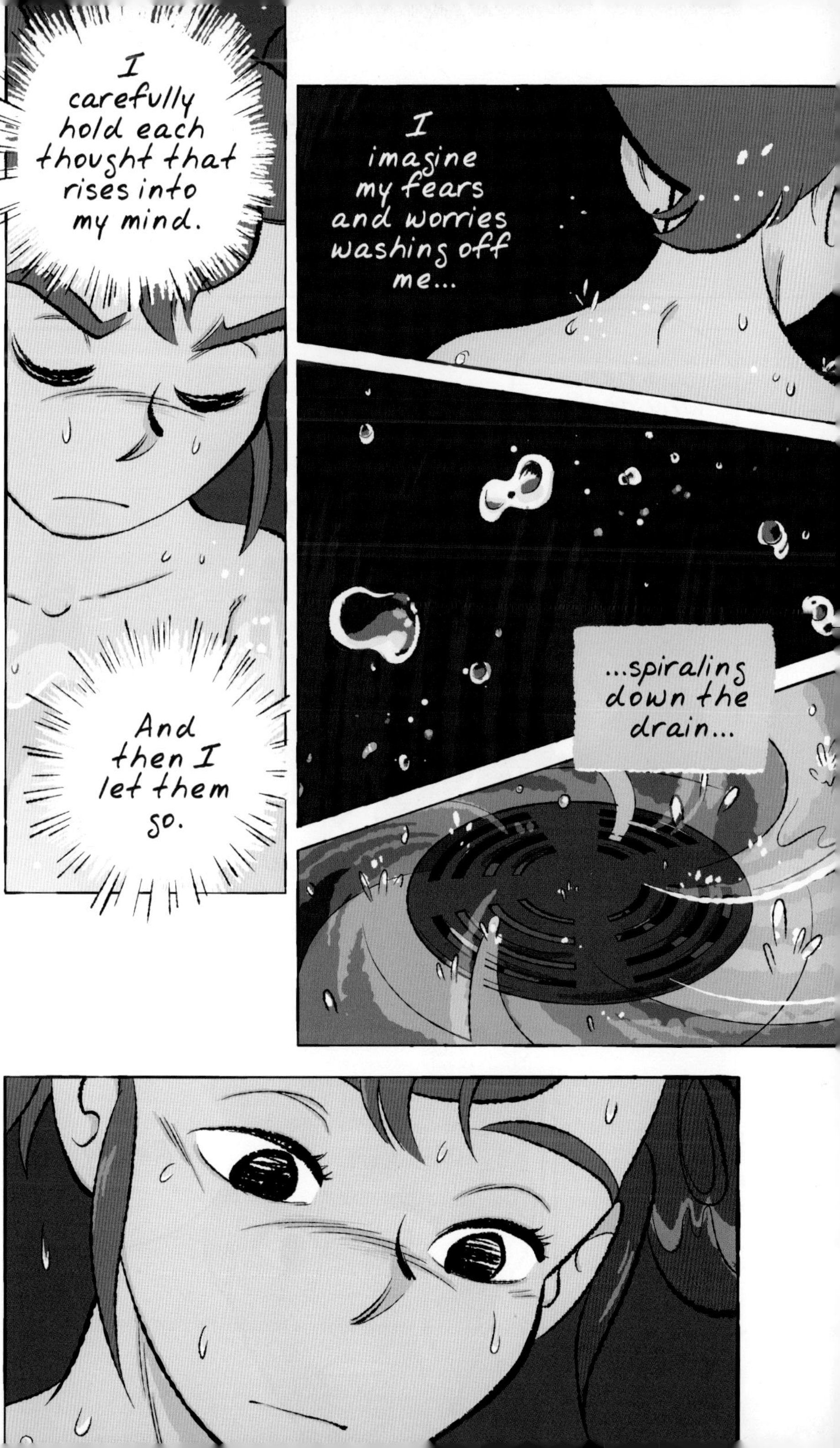
I carefully hold each thought that rises into my mind.
I imagine my fears and worries washing off me...
...spiraling down the drain...
And then I let them go.

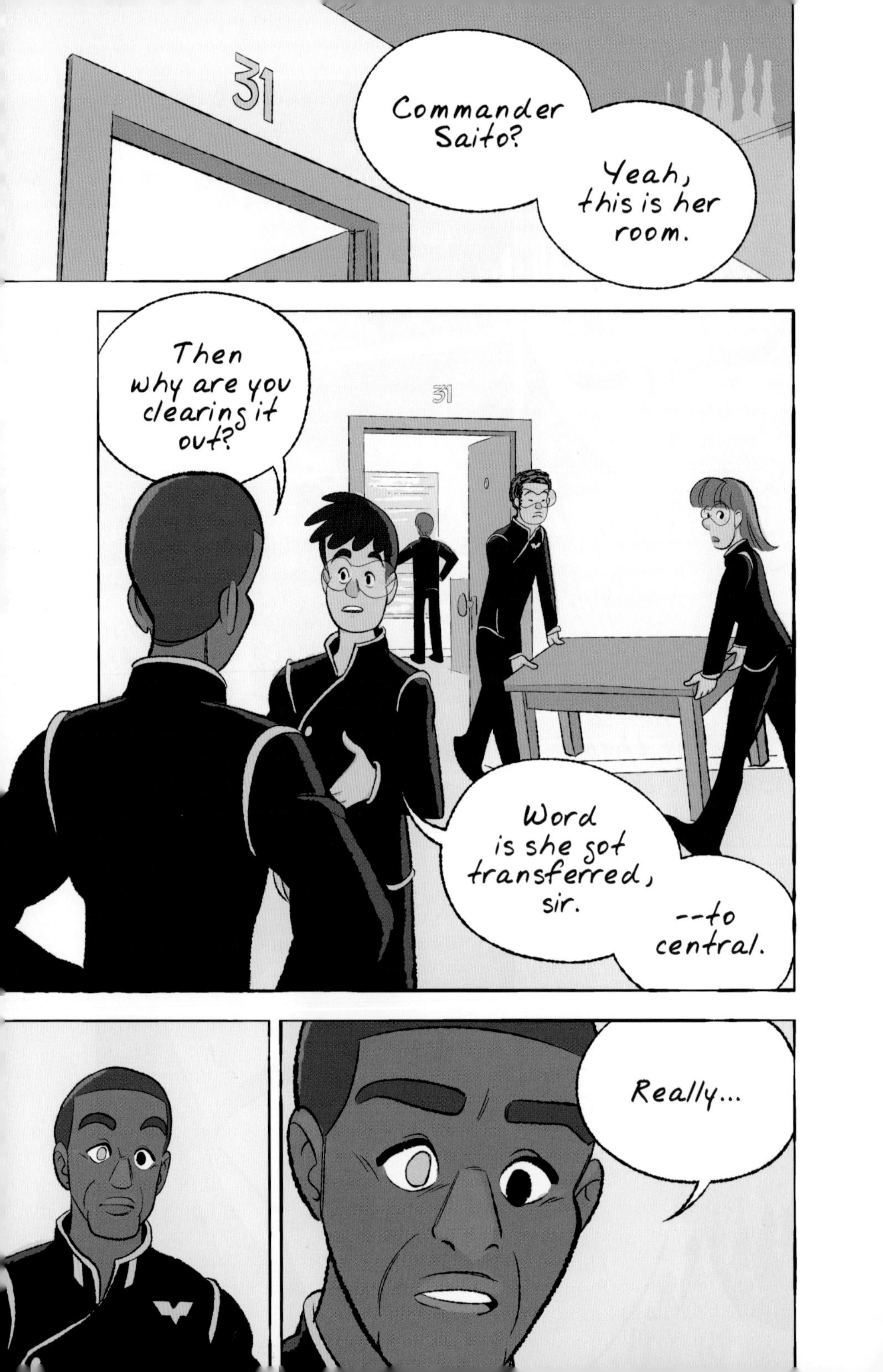
Commander Saito?
Yeah, this is her room.
Then why are you clearing it out?
Word is she got transferred, sir.
--to central.
Really...

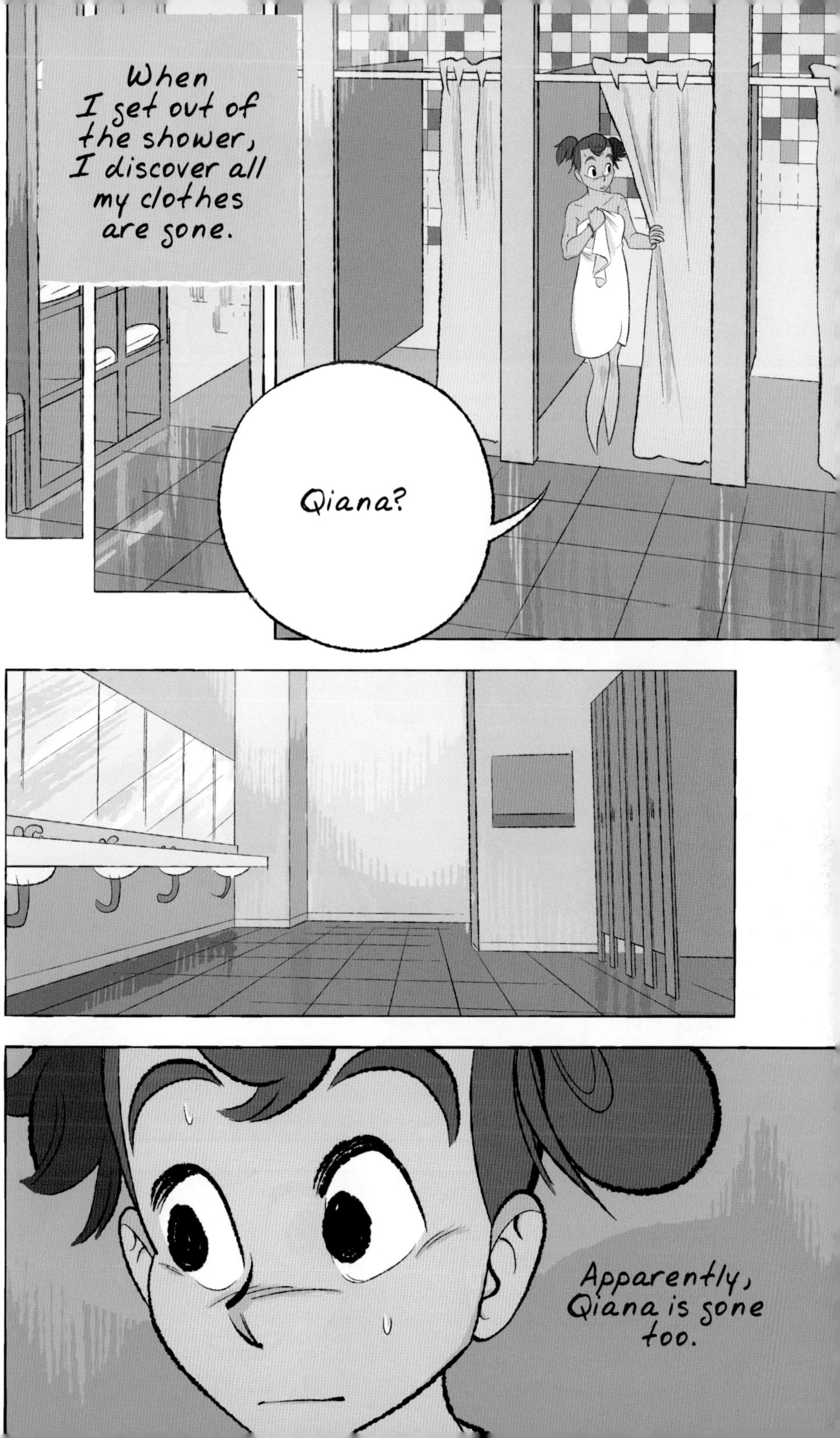
When I get out of the shower, I discover all my clothes are gone.
Qiana?
Apparently, Qiana is gone too.

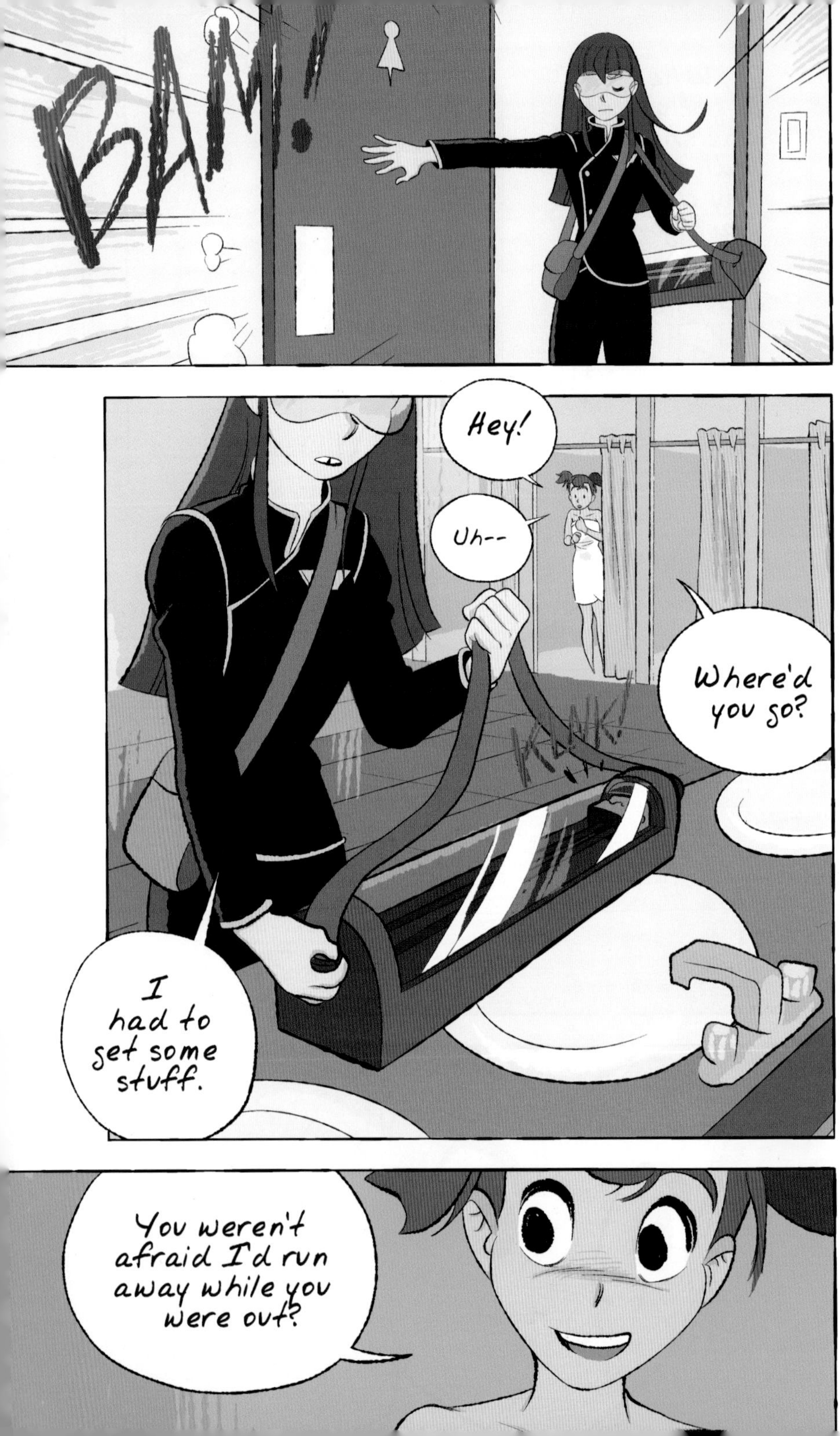
BAM!!
Hey!
Uh--
Where'd you go?
KLUNK!
I had to get some stuff.
You weren't afraid I'd run away while you were out?

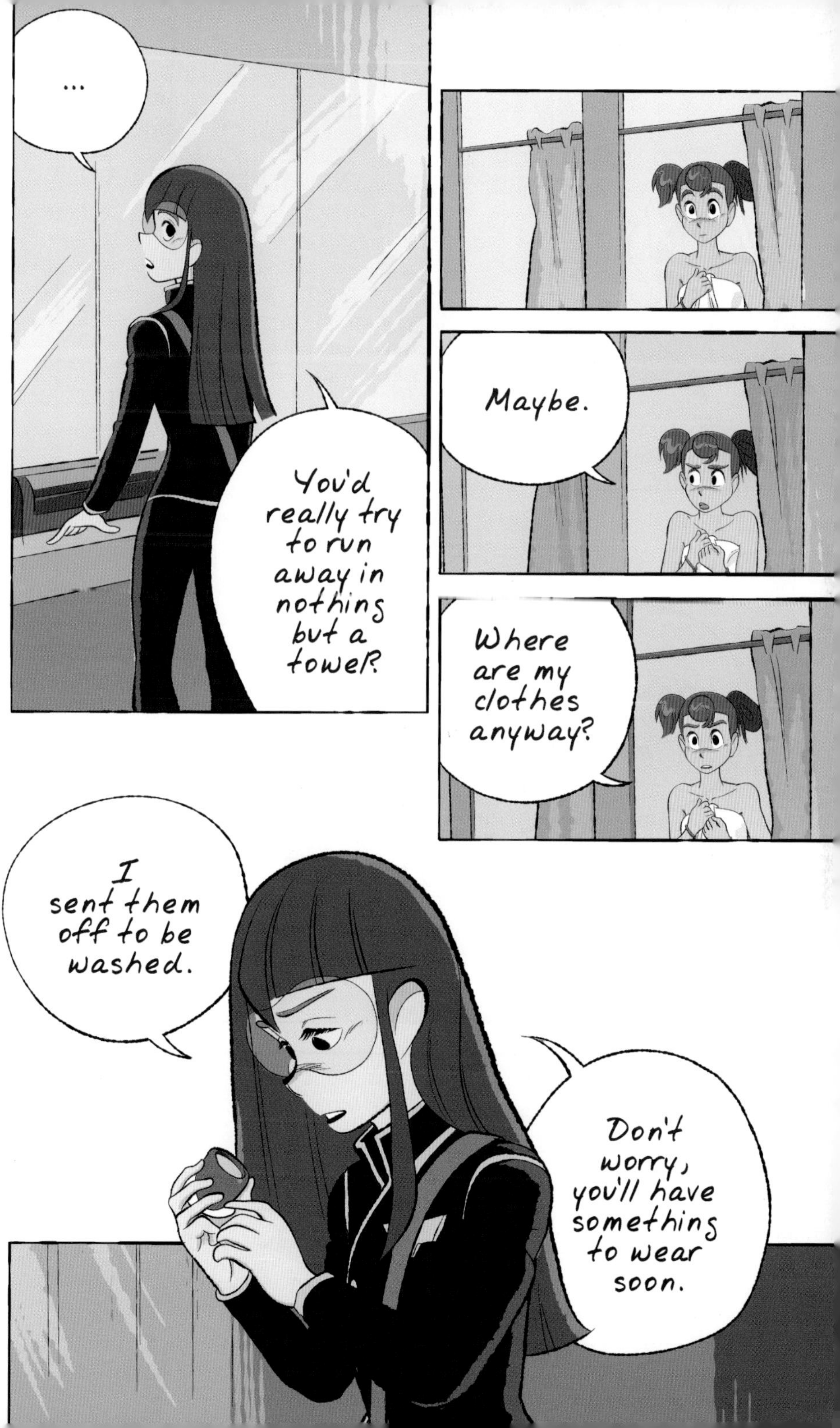
...
You'd really try to run away in nothing but a towel?
Maybe.
Where are my clothes anyway?
I sent them off to be washed.
Don't worry, you'll have something to wear soon.

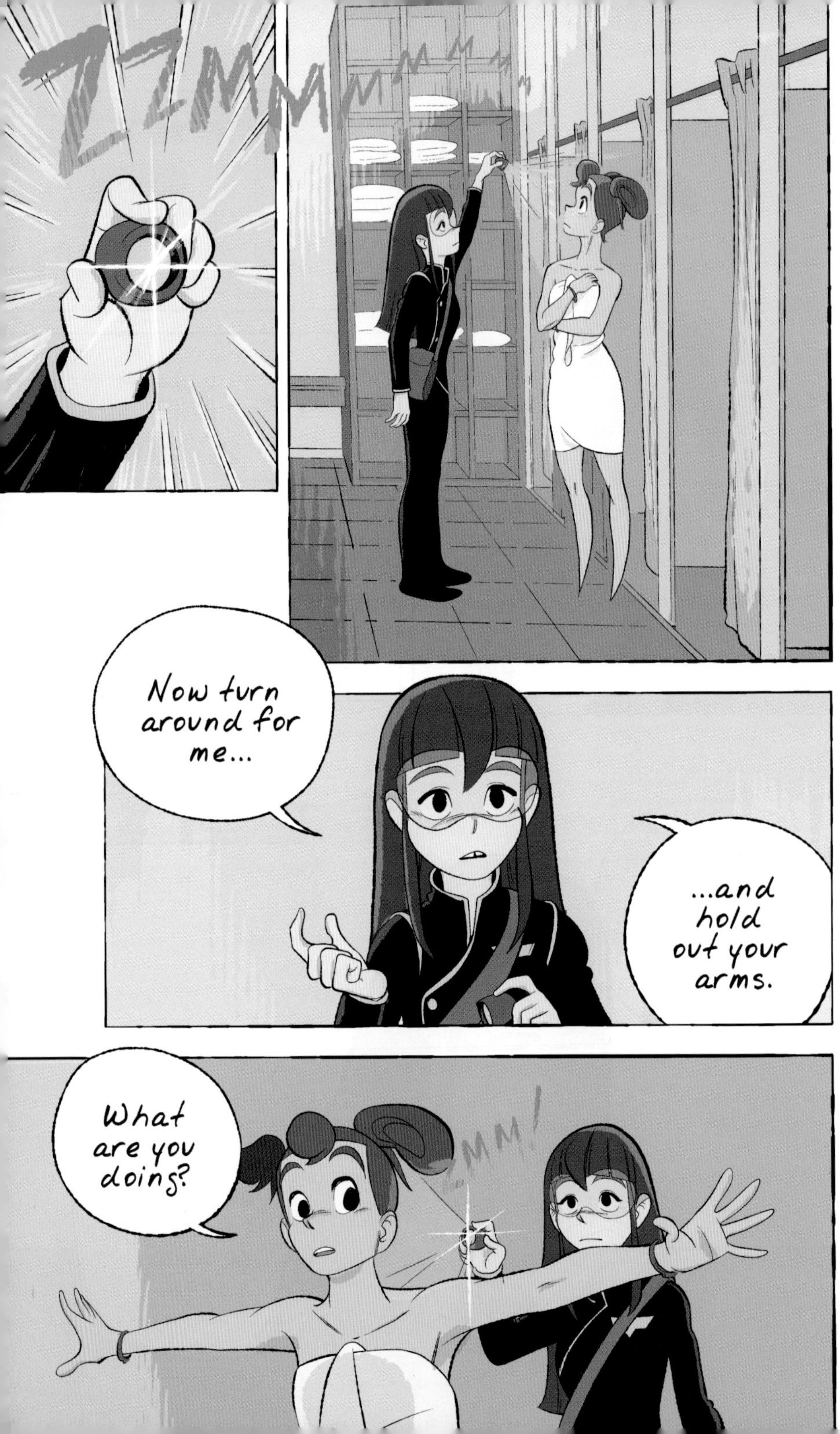
ZZMMMMMMM
Now turn around for me...
...and hold out your arms.
What are you doing?
ZMM!

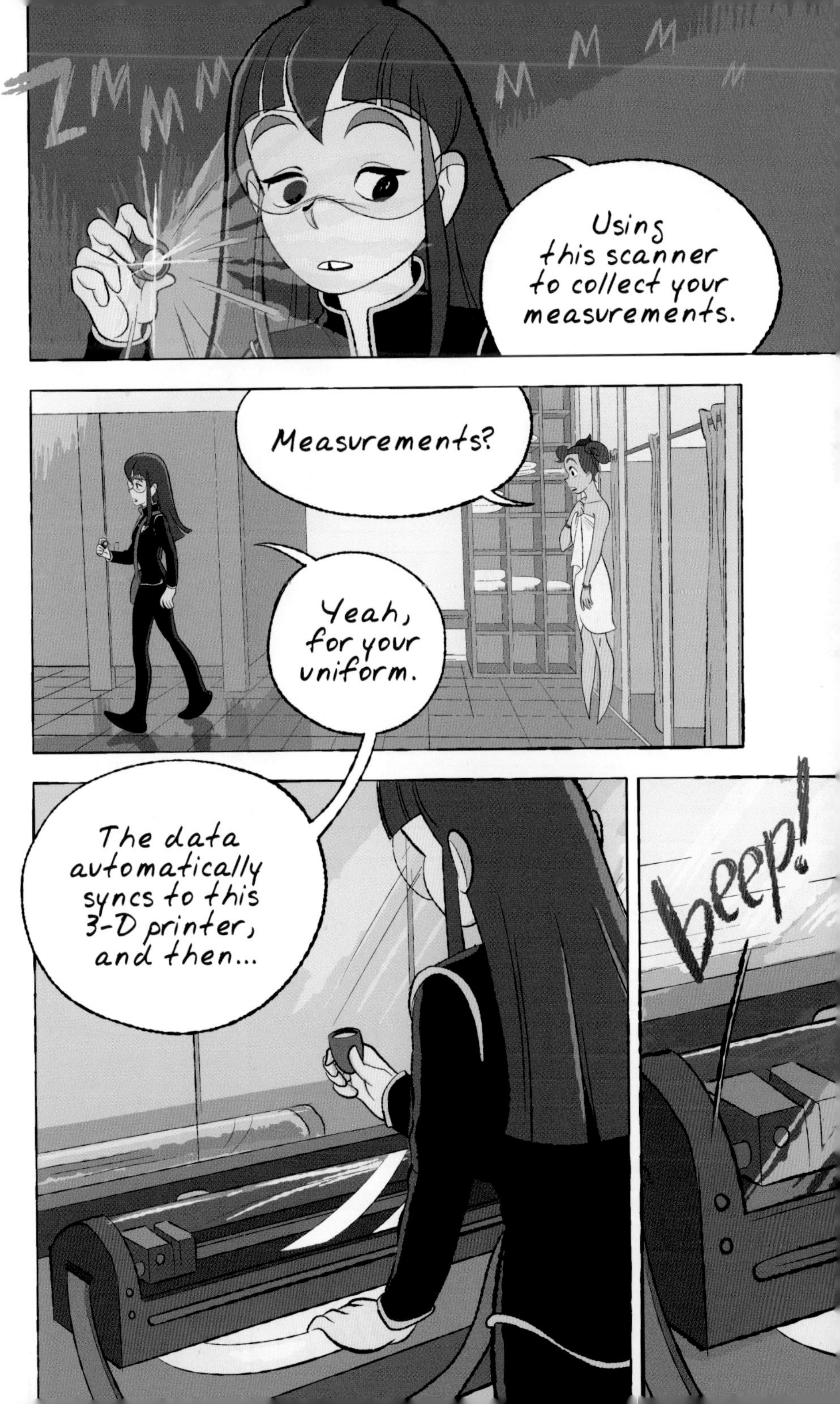
ZMMMMMMMM
Using this scanner to collect your measurements.
Measurements?
Yeah, for your uniform.
The data automatically syncs to this 3-D printer, and then...
beep!

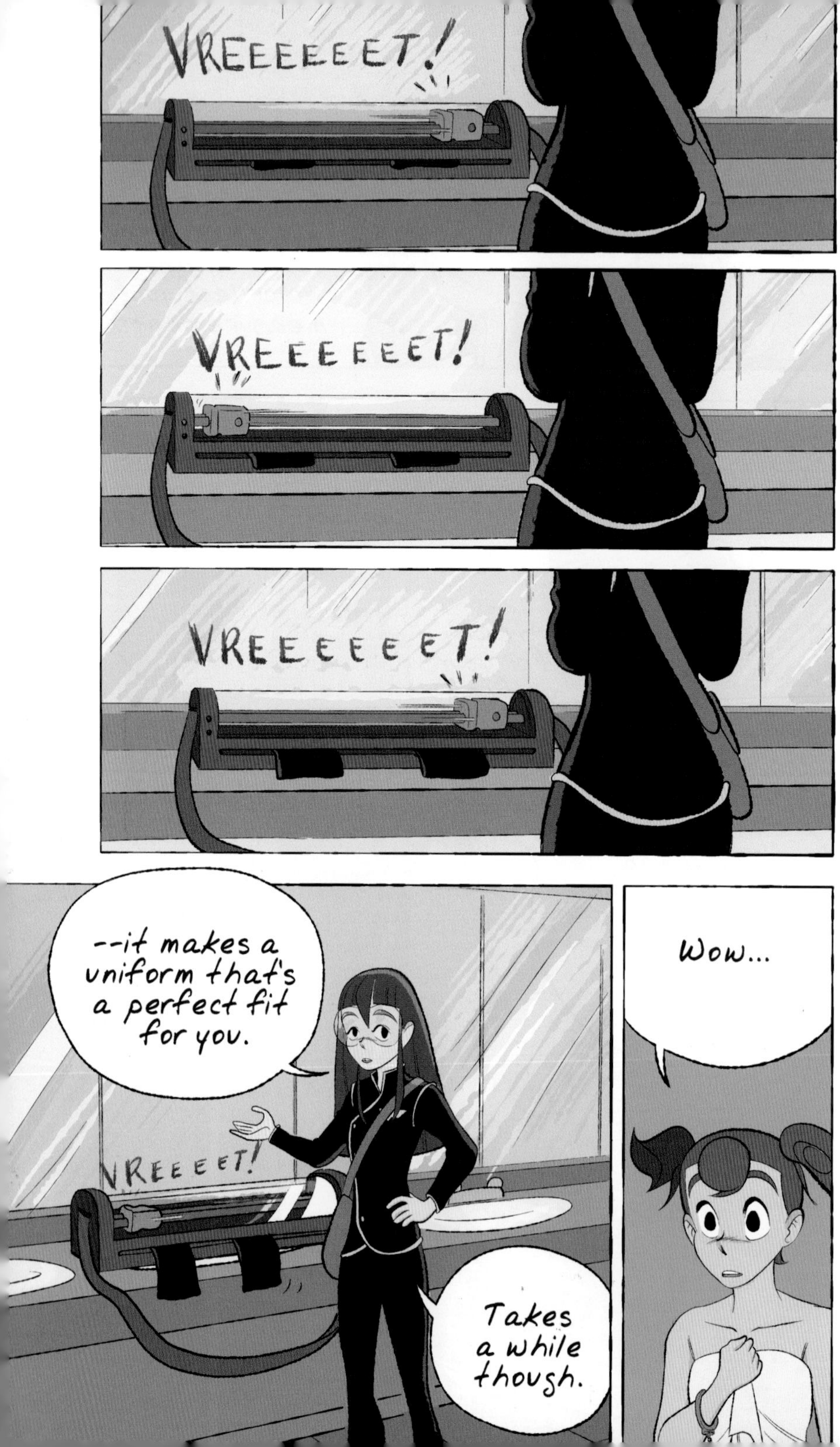
VREEEEEET!
VREEEEEEET!
VREEEEEEET!
--it makes a uniform that's a perfect fit for you.
VREEEET!
Takes a while though.
Wow...

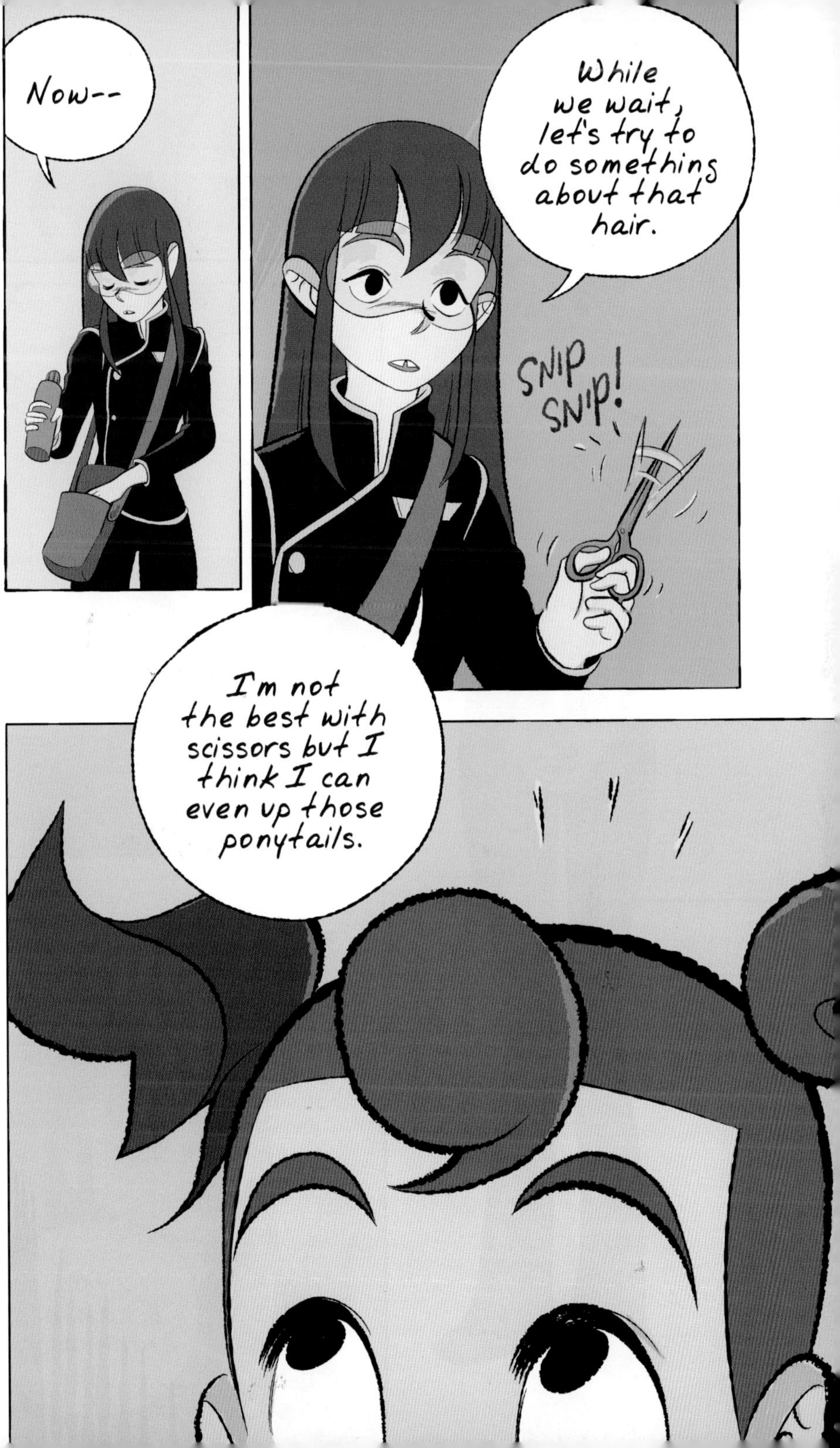
Now--
While we wait, let's try to do something about that hair.
SNIP SNIP!
I'm not the best with scissors but I think I can even up those ponytails.

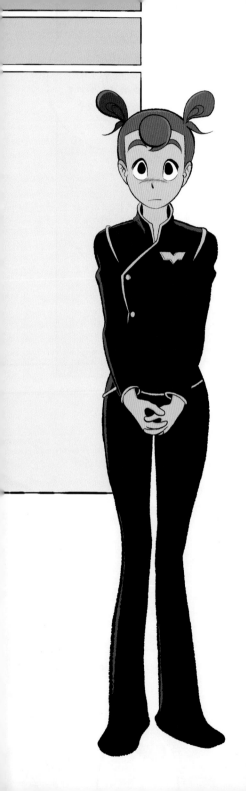

How's the uniform feel?

Hmm...

It's a bit stiff...

3-D printed garments are like that at first--

It'll break in eventually.

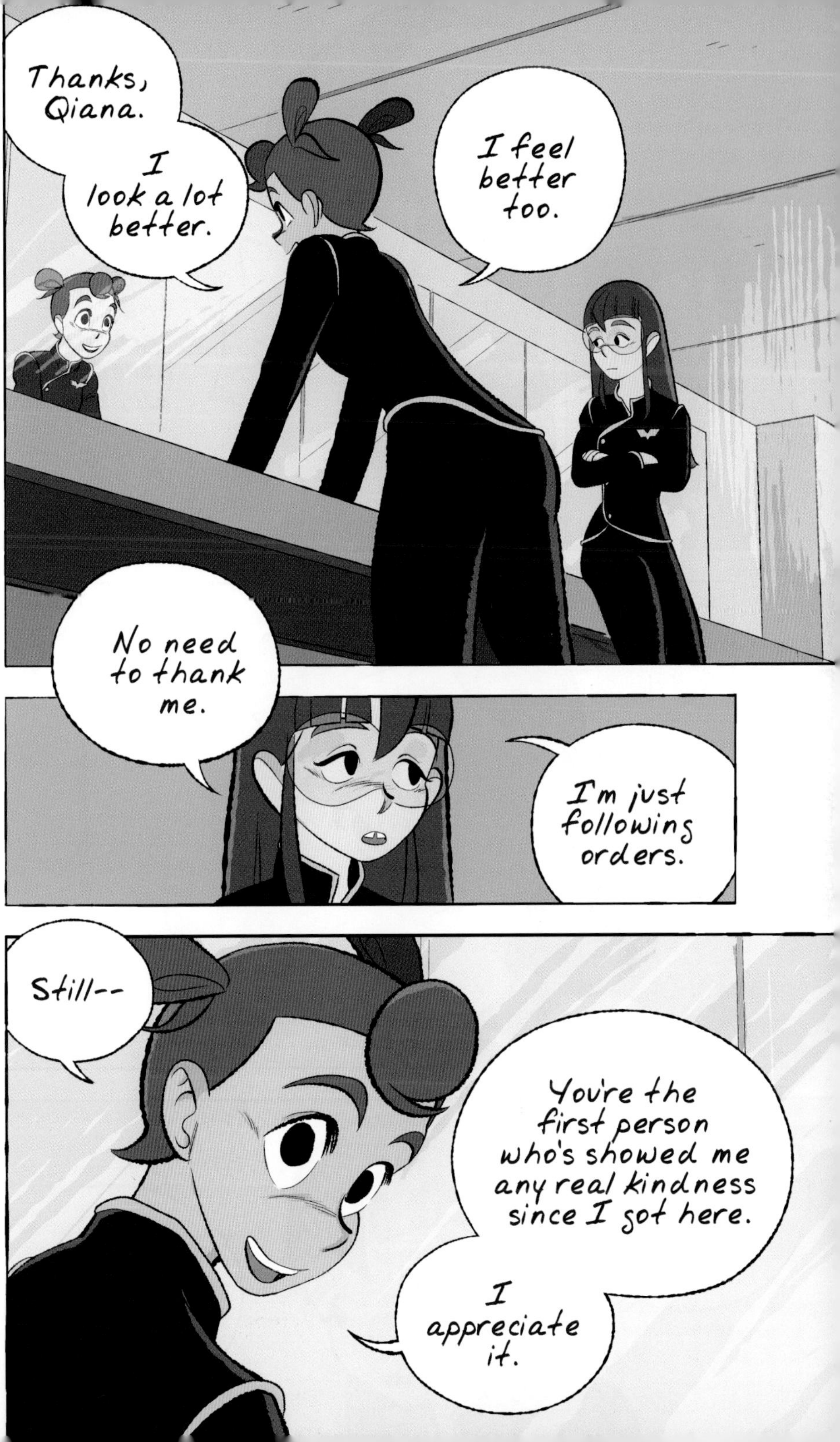
Thanks, Qiana.
I look a lot better.
I feel better too.
No need to thank me.
I'm just following orders.
Still--
You're the first person who's showed me any real kindness since I got here.
I appreciate it.

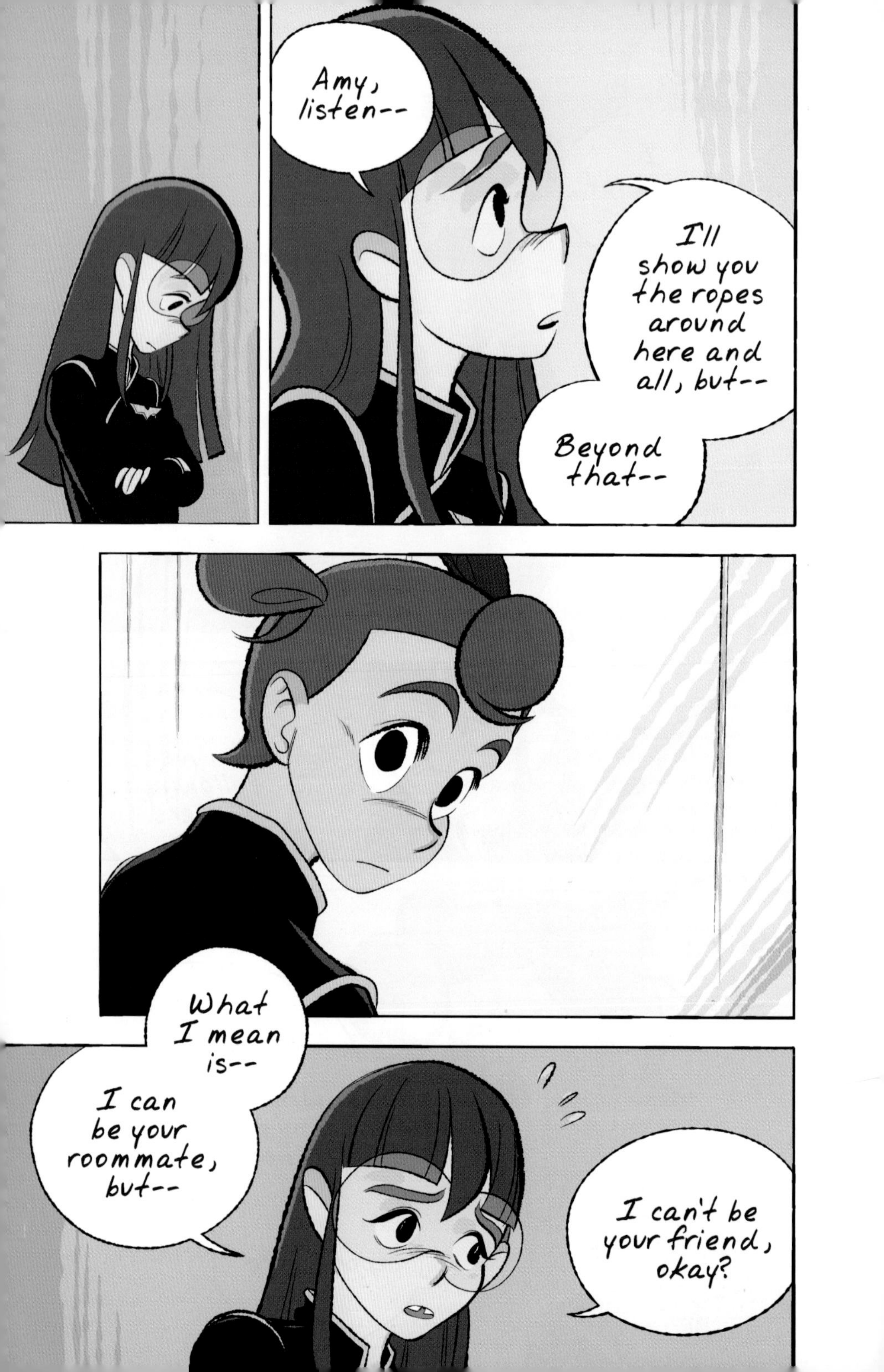
Amy, listen--
I'll show you the ropes around here and all, but--
Beyond that--
What I mean is--
I can be your roommate, but--
I can't be your friend, okay?

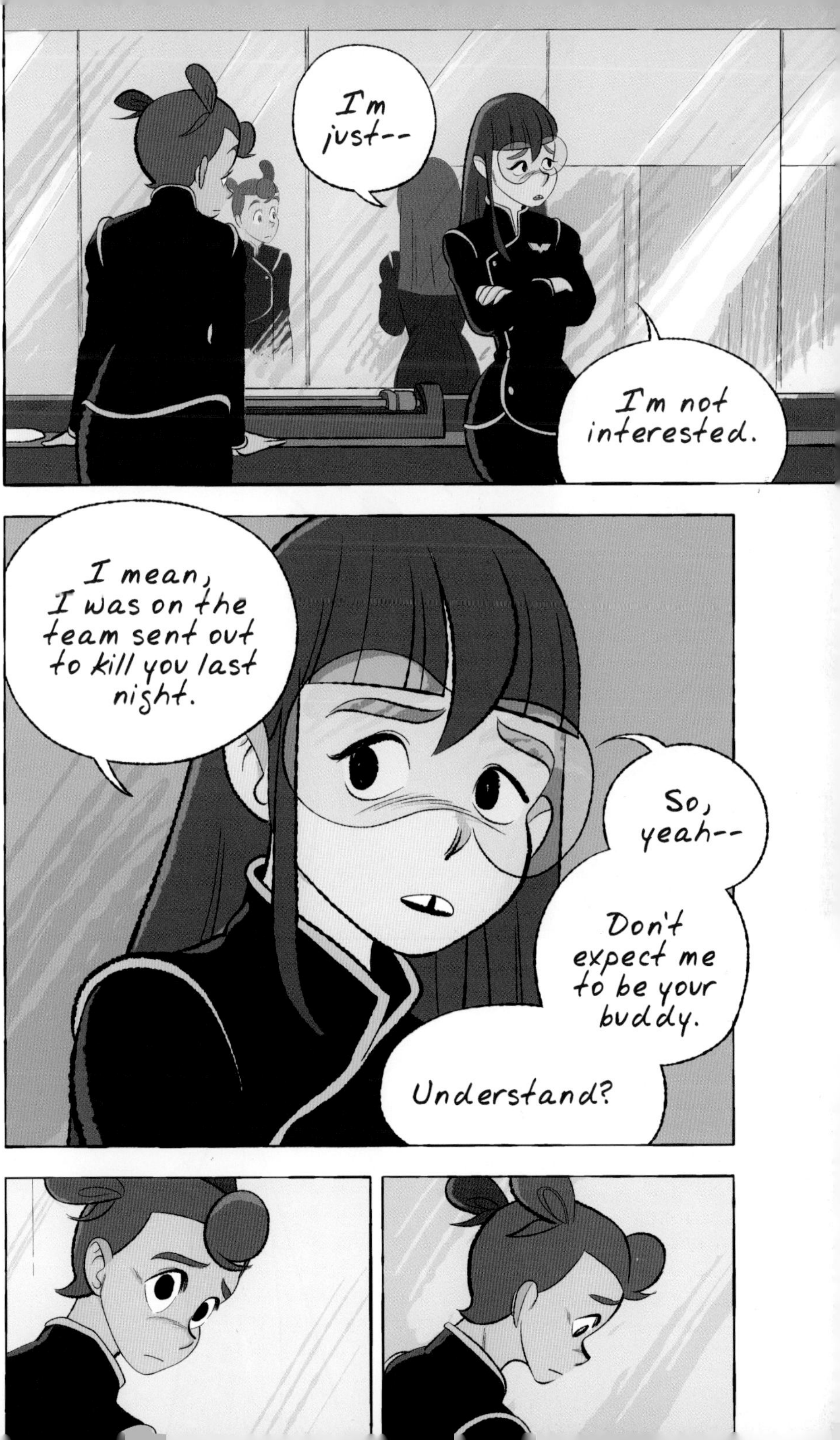
I'm just--
I'm not interested.
I mean, I was on the team sent out to kill you last night.
So, yeah--
Don't expect me to be your buddy.
Understand?

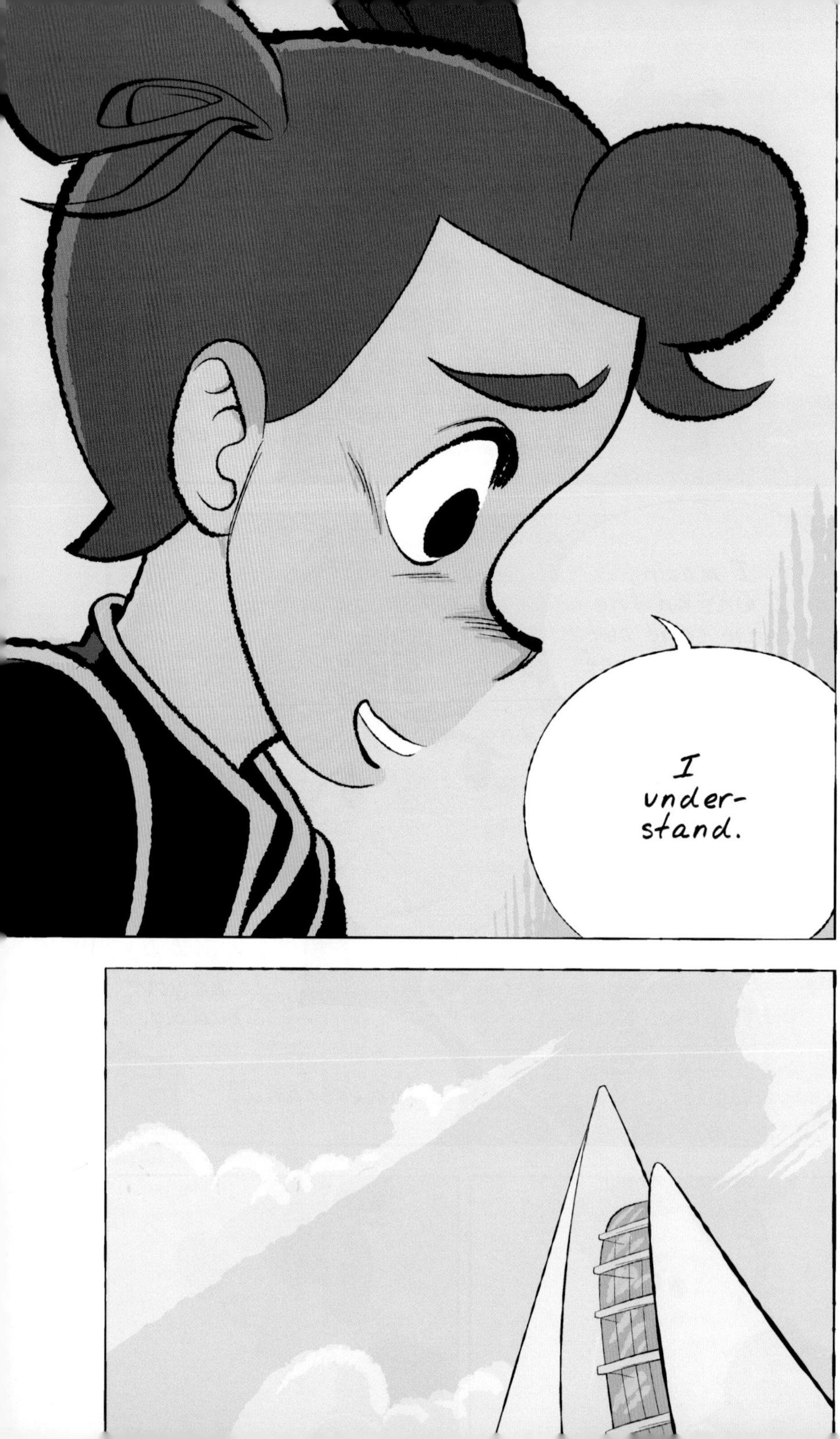
I under-stand.

Li'l Amy

by
Stephen
McCranie

You got your lunch, Amy?
Yep!
You got your hard hat?
Your overalls?
Your pickaxe?
YEP!
TAKE YOUR KID TO WORK DAY!

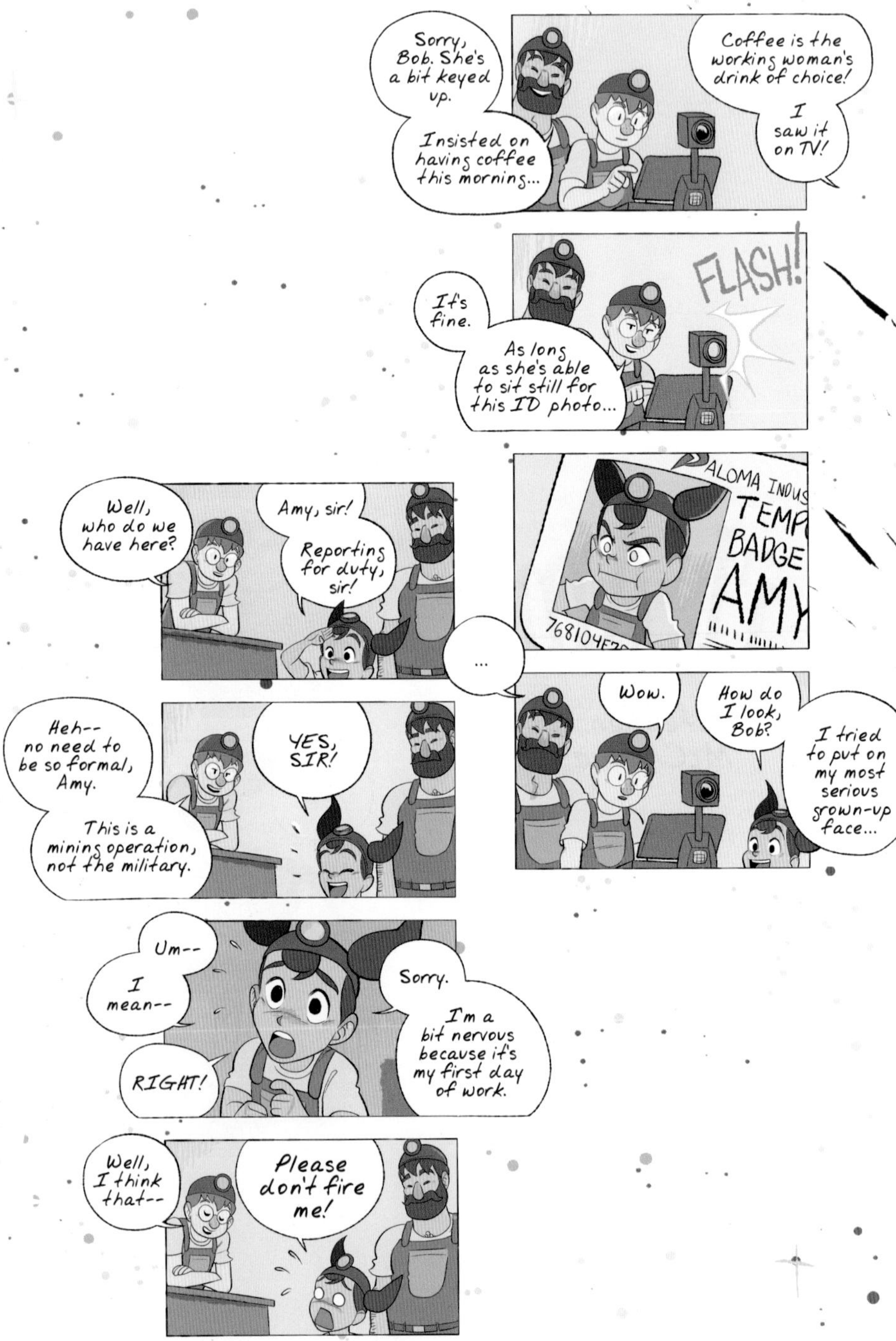

Sorry, Bob. She's a bit keyed up.
Insisted on having coffee this morning...
Coffee is the working woman's drink of choice!
I saw it on TV!
FLASH!
It's fine.
As long as she's able to sit still for this ID photo...
ALOMA INDUS
TEMP
BADGE
AMY
768104E7
...
Wow.
How do I look, Bob?
I tried to put on my most serious grown-up face...
Well, who do we have here?
Amy, sir!
Reporting for duty, sir!
Heh-- no need to be so formal, Amy.
This is a mining operation, not the military.
YES, SIR!
Um--
I mean--
RIGHT!
Sorry.
I'm a bit nervous because it's my first day of work.
Well, I think that--
Please don't fire me!

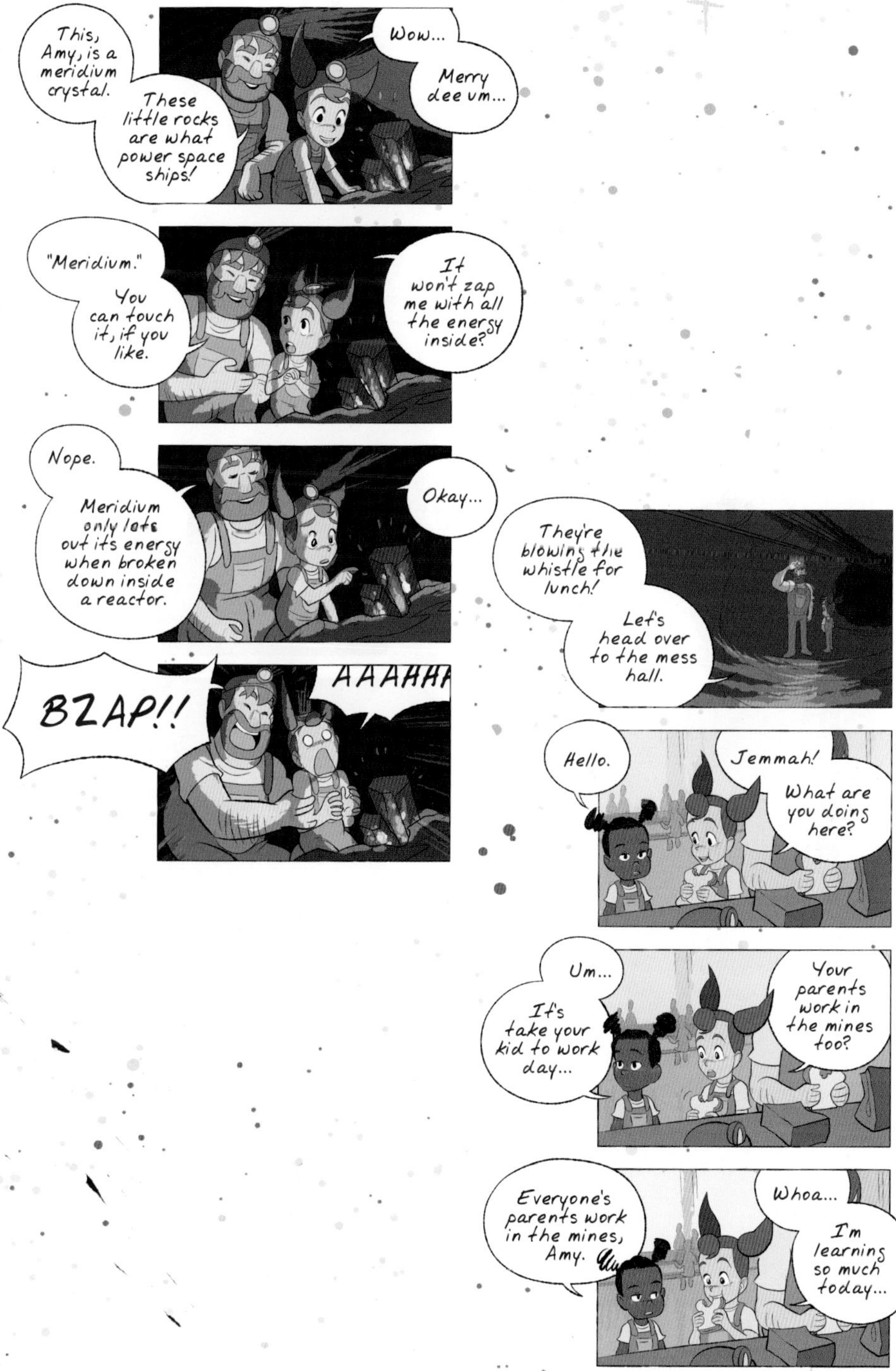
This, Amy, is a meridium crystal.
These little rocks are what power space ships!
Wow...
Merry dee um...
"Meridium."
You can touch it, if you like.
It won't zap me with all the energy inside?
Nope.
Meridium only lets out its energy when broken down inside a reactor.
Okay...
BZAP!!
AAAAHH
They're blowing the whistle for lunch!
Let's head over to the mess hall.
Hello.
Jemmah!
What are you doing here?
Um...
It's take your kid to work day...
Your parents work in the mines too?
Everyone's parents work in the mines, Amy.
Whoa...
I'm learning so much today...

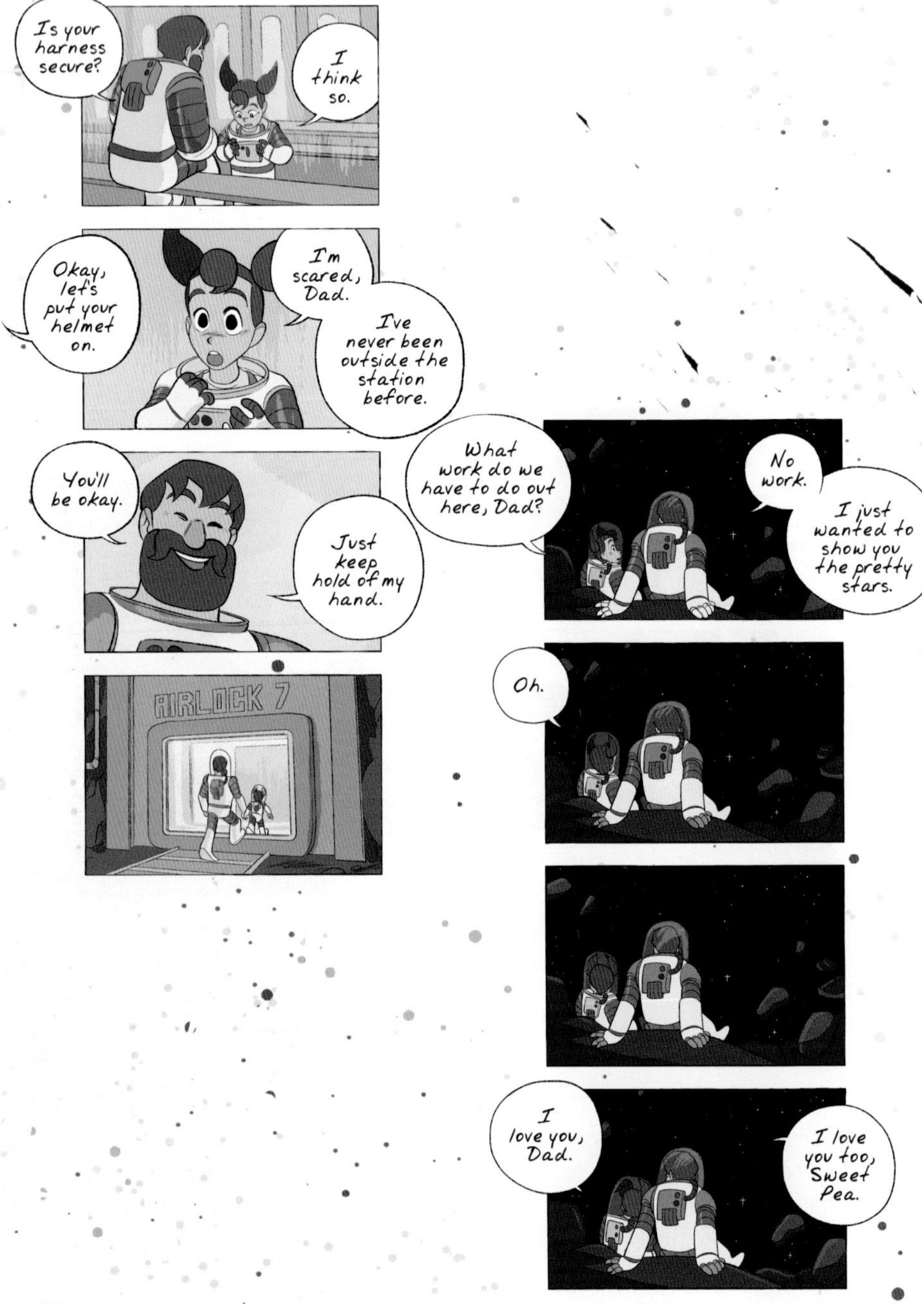
Is your harness secure?
I think so.
Okay, let's put your helmet on.
I'm scared, Dad.
I've never been outside the station before.
You'll be okay.
Just keep hold of my hand.
AIRLOCK 7
What work do we have to do out here, Dad?
No work.
I just wanted to show you the pretty stars.
Oh.
I love you, Dad.
I love you too, Sweet Pea.

COMING SOON . . .

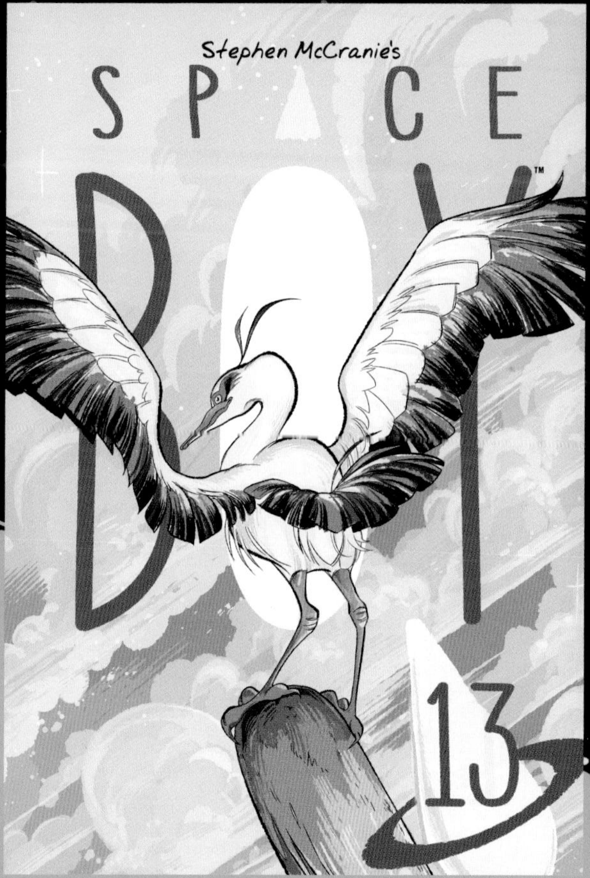
Stephen McCranie's
SPACE
BOY™
13

The investigation into the Homecoming Incident turns deadly in the latest explosive volume of Stephen McCranie's *Space Boy*!

Amy struggles to adjust to her new life at the FCP, making new friends and reuniting with old ones, all the while haunted by the specters of the night before. Meanwhile, Cassie and Schafer begin to turn up new leads in the case, unaware of the manipulations of a mysterious National Security agent, James Silbur. And finally, the truth of Tammie's abduction is revealed to the world!

Available July 2022!

YOU CAN ALSO READ MORE *SPACE BOY* COMICS ON WEBTOONS.COM!

HAVE YOU READ THEM ALL?

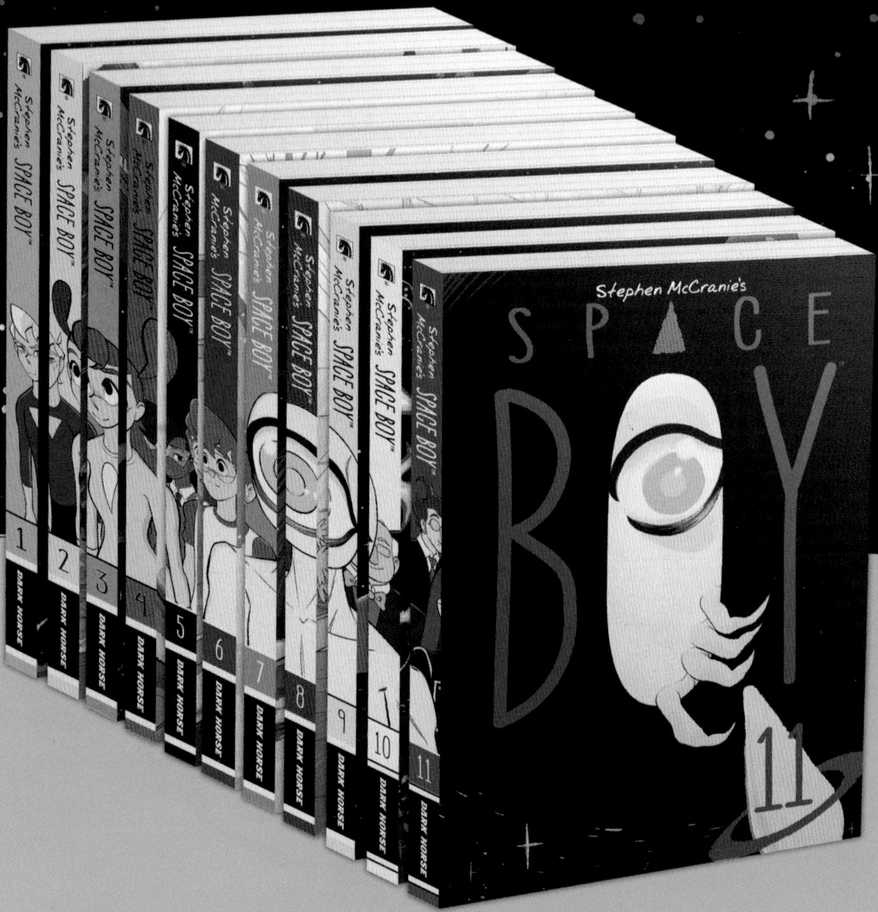
Stephen McCranie's
SPACE BOY
11
DARK HORSE

VOLUME 1
$10.99
ISBN 978-1-50670-648-1

VOLUME 2
$10.99
ISBN 978-1-50670-680-1

VOLUME 3
$10.99
ISBN 978-1-50670-842-3

VOLUME 4
$10.99
ISBN 978-1-50670-843-0

VOLUME 5
$10.99
ISBN 978-1-50671-399-1

VOLUME 6
$10.99
ISBN 978-1-50671-400-4

VOLUME 7
$10.99
ISBN 978-1-50671-401-1

VOLUME 8
$10.99
ISBN 978-1-50671-402-8

VOLUME 9
$10.99
ISBN 978-1-50671-883-5

VOLUME 10
$10.99
ISBN 978-1-50671-884-2

VOLUME 11
$10.99
ISBN 978-1-50671-885-9

AVAILABLE AT YOUR LOCAL COMICS SHOP OR BOOKSTORE. TO FIND A COMICS SHOP IN YOUR AREA, VISIT COMICSHOPLOCATOR.COM. FOR MORE INFORMATION OR TO ORDER DIRECT, VISIT DARKHORSE.COM.

MINECRAFT™

AVAILABLE NOW...

MINECRAFT

MINECRAFT
VOLUME 2

MINECRAFT
STORIES FROM THE OVERWORLD

MINECRAFT
WITHER WITHOUT YOU
1
KRISTEN GUDSNUK

MINECRAFT
WITHER WITHOUT YOU
2
KRISTEN GUDSNUK

MINECRAFT

SFÉ R. MONSTER, SARAH GRALEY, JOHN J. HILL

Tyler is your everyday kid whose life is changed when his family has to move from the town he's always known. Thankfully, Tyler has a strong group of friends forever linked in the world of Minecraft! Tyler, along with his friends Evan, Candace, Tobi, and Grace have been going on countless adventures together across the expanses of the Overworld and are in need of a new challenge. They decide to go on the Ultimate Quest—to travel to the End and face off against the ender dragon!

Volume 1 · ISBN 978-1-50670-834-8 $10.99
Volume 2 · ISBN 978-1-50670-836-2 $10.99

MINECRAFT: STORIES FROM THE OVERWORLD

From blocks to panels, Minecraft explorations are crafted into comics in this anthology collection!

With tales of witch and pillager rivals finding common ground, a heartless griefer who bit off more than they could chew, and valiant heroes new (or not!) to the Overworld, this anthology tells tales that span the world of Minecraft. Featuring stories from star writers and exciting artists, this collection brings together stories from all realms, leaving no block unturned!

ISBN 978-1-50670-833-1 $14.99

MINECRAFT: WITHER WITHOUT YOU

KRISTEN GUDSNUK

Jump into the Overworld with the first adventure of a three-part series from the world's best-selling videogame Minecraft!

Cahira and Orion are twin monster hunters under the tutelage of Senan the Thorough. After an intense battle with an enchanted wither, their mentor is eaten and the twins are now alone! The two hunters go on a mission to get their mentor back, and meet an unlikely ally along the way!

Volume 1 · ISBN 978-1-50670-835-5 $10.99
Volume 2 · ISBN 978-1-50671-886-6 $10.99

AVAILABLE AT YOUR LOCAL COMICS SHOP OR BOOKSTORE!

To find a comics shop in your area, visit comicshoplocator.com.
For more information or to order direct visit DarkHorse.com

MOJANG STUDIOS

DARK HORSE BOOKS

DARK HORSE BRINGS YOU THE BEST IN WEBCOMICS!

These wildly popular cartoon gems were once only available online, but now can be found through Dark Horse Books with loads of awesome extras!

BANDETTE
By Paul Tobin, Colleen Coover, Steve Lieber, Alberto J. Albuquerque, and others

- Volume 1: Presto!
  ISBN 978-1-50671-923-8 | $14.99

- Volume 2: Stealers, Keepers!
  ISBN 978-1-50671-924-5 | $14.99

- Volume 3: The House of the Green Mask
  ISBN 978-1-50671-925-2 | $14.99

- Volume 4: The Six-Finger Secret
  ISBN 978-1-50671-925-2 | $14.99

MIKE NORTON'S BATTLEPUG
By Mike Norton

- The Devil's Biscuit
  ISBN 978-1-61655-864-2 | $14.99

- The Paws of War
  ISBN 978-1-50670-114-1 | $14.99

THE ADVENTURES OF SUPERHERO GIRL - EXPANDED EDITION HC
By Faith Erin Hicks
ISBN 978-1-50670-336-7 | $16.99

PLANTS VS. ZOMBIES
By Paul Tobin, Ron Chan, Andie Tong, and others

- LAWNMAGEDDON
  ISBN 978-1-61655-192-6 | $10.99

- BULLY FOR YOU
  ISBN 978-1-61655-889-5 | $10.99

- GROWN SWEET HOME
  ISBN 978-1-61655-971-7 | $10.99

- RUMBLE AT LAKE GUMBO
  ISBN 978-1-50670-497-5 | $10.99

THE PERRY BIBLE FELLOWSHIP 10TH ANNIVERSARY EDITION
By Nicholas Gurewitch
ISBN 978-1-50671-588-9 | $24.99

AVAILABLE AT YOUR LOCAL COMICS SHOP OR BOOKSTORE | To find a comics shop in your area, visit comicshoplocator.com. For more information or to order direct, visit DarkHorse.com

DARK HORSE BOOKS